Guernsey

Rachel's Story

By

Peter Lihou

Dedication

To my Grandparents and family, those who left, those who stayed, and all those who suffered during the occupation.

Acknowledgements

To my editors, Gill and Maureen, and all those at Acclaimed Books.

Copyright

First published as two volumes, 'Rachel's Shoe' in 2008 and 'The
Causeway' in 2010

This volume first published in January 2012. Revised April 2014

ISBN: 978-1468089332

Cover by Sam

Published by Acclaimed Books

www.acclaimedbooks.com

The Author

Peter Lihou was born in 1950 on the South Coast of England. His parents had both de-mobbed from the Air Force and his father, a wartime pilot, was trying to build a career on mainland England as opportunities in his island home of Guernsey were limited. A family of four, the Lihous lived in the south and north-east of England before returning to the ancestral homeland of Guernsey in the 1960s. Peter was awarded a BSc (Hons) from the Open University, an institution he still greatly admires. He also became a Fellow of the Institute of Directors in 1986 in recognition of his years directing UK businesses, and has since held a number of senior business management roles. Like his father, Peter left the island to further his career and lived for many years in the Cotswolds with his wife and four children. In 2005 he returned again to Guernsey for a further five years before moving again to the mainland. He now lives in Cornwall where he now indulges his passion for sailing and writing.

www.peterlihou.com

www.rachelsshoe.com

Guernsey

Part 1: Rachel's Shoe

Part 2: Liberation

Part 3: The Causeway

Part 1: Rachel's Shoe

CHAPTER ONE

Waves lapped sedately against the hull of the small wooden sailing craft. Painted ornately on its transom was the name *Flying Fish* - not a half-considered name, but one that Tom's father and grandfather used on all their boats to remind them of the faraway places they had visited on board vessels that sailed from the island of Guernsey. At fourteen years old, he was one of the few teenage boys not to be evacuated before the Germans occupied Guernsey in the summer of 1940. Now almost a year on, the absence of most of his friends left him time to indulge his passion for fishing, all the more interesting as it was strictly forbidden to use a boat so far out without permission or an escorting soldier.

Although almost dark, the rocks and sea around *Fish* still radiated the warmth of another Indian summer's night. Two lobster pots and an old bucket seething with mackerel scented the sea air as Tom tweaked the tan sail on *Fish* to gain an extra knot through the glassy water. His mackerel line jerked again. This really was a good shoal and, if he could just stay with it for a while, the family would have lots to trade for bread and milk. He knew he shouldn't push his luck with German patrol boats in the area, but couldn't resist following this shoal as it weaved its way north of Guernsey towards the Casquets rock.

Tom had refused point-blank to leave his family once his father had enlisted and, knowing how well he handled a boat, they believed him when he said he would risk sailing back across the Channel if they sent him away with the other evacuees. In truth, they welcomed his help and tried to turn a blind eye to his nocturnal activities. There was little else to occupy a lively fifteenyear-old. But now it was getting late and his mother would be fretting. She had no doubts about his seamanship and conditions out there were not rough, but the Germans scared her. She knew they might shoot first and ask questions later, especially if he tried to escape their clutches. The Germans seemed paranoid about English spies and a lone figure in a small boat at night represented a real prize for enthusiastic young officers.

Sensitive to her concerns, Tom was about to tack *Fish* and head for home when he heard the dreaded low-pitched rumble. This was not thunder, but the powerful Mercedes engines on a German patrol boat. He looked around his horizon. Had he been spotted? Where were they? The nearest cover was the Casquets rock, and the wind as well as tide would take him there in a few minutes. As he hauled on the mainsheet, *Fish* glided more swiftly through the water. Her bow waves now rushing down each side were clearly visible from his elevated position as the angle of heel increased.

The rumble grew louder and a bloom of light appeared over Tom's right shoulder. They were sweeping the approach channel north of Guernsey that led into the waters known locally as the Little Russel. Any ships attempting to make the harbours of St Sampson or St Peter Port would do so via the Little Russel. Probably just routine observations, but their track would take them closer and closer to *Fish*.

As the patrol boat ploughed through the water, the noise of its engines was no longer a distant rumble, but grew louder and louder just as the silhouette of the boat itself expanded on the night horizon.

Tom raised the topsail of his gaff-rigged boat and moved forward to hitch on a foresail. His movement forward altered the balance of *Fish* and she suddenly fell off the wind and slowed. This was the last thing he needed; without the extra sail he would surely be too slow to reach the Casquets before being spotted. The trouble was that the extra sail, although tan like the rest, would make him a bigger target for the powerful searchlight of the Germans.

As soon as the foresail was raised, Tom moved back to the tiller and hauled in each sheet even further. Too tight and the sails would stall, but he needed the maximum performance before that happened. The shadowy mass of the Casquets grew ever larger.

This was a huge rock that had boasted one of the first lighthouses built in the early 1700s. Fortunately for Tom, it was turned off by the Germans. They now used it as a radio station to listen to British shipping, and Tom was hoping it was currently either unmanned, or the occupant's attention was elsewhere. It was also fortunate that his small shallow-draft craft could approach the rock with little fear of grounding, whereas a German patrol boat would use extreme caution on such a hazardous obstacle, especially in the dark.

Tom glanced around to see the light beam drawing closer to him. It was just seconds away as *Fish* slid between the outlying rocks. He yanked the sails down and let the momentum carry *Fish* close to the main mass of rock. All around him the black of night switched to daylight when the powerful searchlight fell upon the Casquets. Every detail of the limpets on the rocks and swirling waters were slammed into stark relief. He reached out and grabbed the nearest outcrop to bring *Fish* to a stop with nothing more than a bump. The light should have passed by now, but it had ceased sweeping and was fixed on the Casquets. Behind the rocks, he was no longer visible to the patrol boat, but its engine noise had diminished only slightly, in fact rather than speeding past the Casquets it sounded as if it was actually slowing to approach and possibly moor. This was bad: they must have seen him. They were stopping to search for him.

The engine roar all but died as the patrol boat made its closing approach to the rock. Tom could now hear instructions being shouted. Were they orders to shoot to kill? Or could they simply be making ready the fenders, mooring ropes and calling out the final distances to the helmsman? He didn't want to wait around to find out, but casting off now would be insane. They would surely see and capture him or worse, blow him out of the water. Either way it would be curtains. Tom suddenly thought of the catch on board and what a waste it would be if it went to a bunch of German officers.

A black cloak dropped on Tom as all around him the bright light was again replaced with the darkness of night, made even blacker now that his eyes had adjusted to the light. He blinked and almost lost his grip before tying *Fish* securely to a conveniently placed but old and almost completely eroded mooring ring. From his position on the west of the rock, he could no longer see what the Germans were doing. Figuring it would be better to see them approaching, and maybe even give himself up, he edged his way closer until they were in view. Then closer still, until he was within earshot.

Pretty much at water level and crouched beneath an overhanging outcrop of rock, Tom listened to the voices above. They made no sense to him as he understood not a word of German, but he sensed there was no urgency in their tone. On the contrary, they were relaxed and jovial. They were not searching at all. Tom could hear the pop of bottles opening and he peered around the rock again. They had stopped to drink beer!

***

Between the rocks of a tiny headland on the north shore of Guernsey, Daisy Le Breton located the spot where her son Tom kept *Fish*. She was relieved to see it was still missing; somehow it helped to know he was still at sea on such a calm night. But where was he? She searched the horizon for a glimpse, but knew it was pointless. Tom had mastered the art of invisibility at sea by navigating *Fish* from rock to rock until she was far enough out not to be seen from the shore at night. Daisy considered the huge constructions she had just passed. Tom wouldn't be able to do this when the new German bunkers on the common were complete.

Part of Tom's deception relied upon the state of tide being low enough for exposed rocks on the reef to provide cover. With the tide now rising, not only would the current be against him, but his cover would gradually be reduced until he was forced to rely largely on the cover of darkness. Clear summer skies and a crescent moon meant that this was by no means going to be complete. Fortunately a steady breeze would allow him to make progress against most of the tidal current. But where was he? There was definitely no sign of anything in his usual approach from the south-west. She looked north and her heart stopped. There was the bright light of a German patrol boat heading purposefully towards the Casquets. She had told him time and time again not to sail that far from Guernsey, no matter how tempting the catch. That was it. He would be arrested and given hard labour. The Germans would make little or no concession for his youth. They would set an example. That, of course, assumed he was sensible enough not to try to escape the powerful boat, in which case the consequences would be far, far worse.

**

After a few more bottles, the Germans' voices grew louder until one broke into song. He had a terrible voice, but before long the jeering of his fellows gave way to a semi-drunken choir. As frustrated as Tom was to be pinned down on this rock, he could not help smiling at his situation. Relaxed and clearly dodging their duties, this bunch seemed a good deal more human than when they goose-stepped along the quay in Town.

Eventually, the singing came to an untidy halt and a voice muttered unconvincing authority as the group slipped and grappled their way back to their boat. A few moments later, the engines roared to life and it was on its way back towards Guernsey, on a somewhat less straight track than when it arrived!

It was only now that Tom realised the warm sea water had crept up around his legs and was rushing past him rapidly. He straightened up and staggered back to where *Fish* had been left.

To his horror she had gone. The frail mooring ring had given way to the load of *Fish*, levered by the rising tide. Tom had not expected to be so long. But all was not lost. A few yards across the water, *Fish* was wedged against an outlying rock by the racing tide. She was starting to shift. Without thinking, Tom dived into the current and swam towards her. He too became caught up in the rapid stream. His young body strained every muscle to recapture his precious boat. *Fish* shifted and as she started to drift away, Tom launched himself forward, gaining no more than a finger-hold on her transom. They were now washing away from the Casquets at an alarming rate as Tom strengthened his grip until he was able to heave himself aboard. When he finally slumped into the bottom of *Fish*'s cockpit, he could just see the retreating outline of the patrol boat disappearing in the opposite direction.

Now in clear water, Tom reached into a locker and found his brass compass. The island of Alderney was to the north-east and this tidal stream would pass it offshore, carrying him with it unless he did something. The trouble was that a fourteen-footer like *Fish* could only manage a boat speed of five knots top, and this tide was closer to six. Worse still, if he stayed with it, there was a channel to the west of Alderney called *The Swinge*, notorious for even faster tidal flows, and *The Race* of Alderney to the east was not much better if he misjudged his navigation. He raised all available sails and gripped hard on the tiller.

The eight-mile passage to Alderney was fraught with danger. Not only was it almost dark with the distinction between rocks and gloomy patches of water increasingly blurring, but Tom knew there were unseen eyes everywhere, as the German guards would be on binocular watch both on the coast and in patrol boats. The tidal stream was rapid, but without reference to land he felt stationary, as the body of water under him was all that carried him on his way. His conspicuous sail might be seen when he got close to the island, so he would only have oars to release *Fish* from the stream and position his land fall. He was no mathematical genius, but Tom could work out in a flash the likely speed and direction of the stream, his distance over the ground and the exact point at which he would place an oar over the transom and skull *Fish* towards land.

That point was fast approaching; the dark mass of the Casquets rock had to remain on an imaginary transit line with the southern shore of the island. He was now starting to drift to the north as the stream was diverted from the island. He dropped the sails and with his oar in place, Tom oscillated his hands back and forth to propel *Fish* onto her new course. At first she hardly responded: the stream was just too fast. He worked his hands harder, there was no way he could come ashore on the northern side of the island, and Germans would be everywhere. They would also be concentrating most of their observation on the sea area to the north and west, the direction of England, of freedom. *Fish* started to move more quickly through the water; he was leaving the worst of the stream. Not long now. Mercifully, there was no sign of life on the shore.

The timber hull crunched onto a gravel beach and each successive wave bounced it a little further into the secluded cove. Tom looked around and with relief realized he was surrounded by high rocks that would certainly hide him and *Fish*'s mast in the darkness.

Tom knew he couldn't rest for long; soon the tidal stream would reverse and it would be at its strongest to carry him back to Guernsey at low tide. This meant shifting *Fish* constantly or having to drag her down the beach – a noisy option on this quiet night. He decided a better idea would be to move *Fish* now, further out beyond the low-water mark, and secure her until the stream reversed. It was whilst he was gently feeling his way back out of the cove that he heard the sobbing.

His ears must be deceiving him. It was surely a gull or maybe even a puffin. This was after all puffin territory and many seabirds occasionally emitted almost human sounds. There it was again. This is crazy, he thought, it sounds like a child, but everyone knows there are no kids on Alderney, just Germans and slave labourers.

With *Fish* securely moored out of sight from land and the sail stowed, Tom gingerly investigated the source of the sobbing. The rocks were wet and in the blackness of night he struggled to distinguish between the hard pimples of the brown granite and the local seaweed known as wrack; the latter sometimes formed part of his diet but was also perilously slippery when still attached to rocks. He moved up to the higher outcrops that were seldom covered by the sea and devoid of wrack. Here, the granite was topped with smoother boulders that had fallen from the cliffs beyond and eroded over the eons into a variety of rounded shapes silhouetted against the night sky.

As he rounded one large boulder, he found the source of the sobbing. Below him, the diminutive figure of a young girl in a ragged dress was sitting by the water's edge with tears running down her face. Tom looked around. What was she doing here? Surely there must be an adult with her?

Tentatively, he scrambled towards her, announcing his presence in the only way he thought appropriate.

'Hello.'

The girl shot up and almost slipped from her perch. Her instinct, like Tom's, was to scan around instantly and assess the scale of the threat. Her pretty brown eyes were wide with fear. But it was just a skinny fifteen-year-old boy with badly cut fluffy light brown hair flopping on his tanned face, and he didn't appear too menacing. The girl spoke in almost perfect English tinged with a German accent.

'Hello, who are you?' A pause. Then, 'Are you a prisoner?'

She flicked her long dark curly hair aside and wiped her tears on a small piece of cloth that appeared from the sleeve of her dress.

Tom replied, 'My name is Tom and no, I'm not a prisoner; at least not yet. But surely you can't be. You are too young to be in a labour camp.'

The girl looked a little less panicky now; this boy seemed friendly enough and for a moment it would be nice to forget the burden that weighed on her young heart so heavily.

'I am Jewish. I work in the kitchen. What do you mean too young? I am thirteen years old, a teenager, quite grown-up and certainly old enough to be a prisoner. But I work in the kitchen and because Mama taught me to speak English and a little French, I sometimes translate for the Germans with some of their prisoners. If you are not a prisoner, what are you? I thought all the locals had left.'

He smiled at the girl, and thought it seemed that every young girl is determined to be a few years older than they are until they reach a certain age as a woman, when they want to be thought of as younger than they are. Tom explained his presence on the island, including how his mother and grandparents were likely to be reacting to his absence. But it was the girl's dilemma that concerned him.

'How on earth did you get to be in a labour camp? And why are you so upset? ... And what's your name?'

She seemed relieved to open up. 'My name is Rachel and I am upset because I am in this horrible place and my family have been taken away or killed by the Nazis. I lived near Munich in Germany until last year when soldiers raided our house and killed Papa when he argued with them. They forced Mama and me out of the house with hardly any of our things and for two days we stayed with the local cobbler who agreed to shelter us. Then the soldiers came back and took us away.'

Tom asked in a sympathetic tone, 'Is that because you are Jewish?'

'Yes, we hadn't done anything wrong; the soldiers just hated us and took us away. Mama pleaded with them to let us go, but they wouldn't. In the end she said she had something valuable and needed to tell the officer in charge. So they took us to an office and I sat outside with an angry-looking guard whilst Mama spoke with a soldier in an office. Then they came out and Mama spoke to me. She said she had to go with them to one place and I had to go to another. She loved me very, very much and would try to come and get me soon but it might be a little while and I should be a brave girl. Oh yes, and she said I must look after my shoes, especially my right shoe. I don't know why, but I must always keep it safe; it seemed important for some reason. Then they took her away. Mama was crying. That made me cry. I just knew something very bad was happening. Mama always told the truth but I didn't think I would see her again soon, especially after what happened to poor Papa. I miss them both so much.' Her brown eyes glassed over.

'The next thing that happened was the soldier who had spoken with Mama shouted up some stairs and gave some papers to a man. They made me stay in that dingy office for three days, sleeping on the floor in the corner of the room. Then Hans came. He was the son of the officer and he told me his father had agreed with my mother that I would go with him to a small island called Alderney to work in the kitchen. He had been stationed in Alderney and would keep an eye on me. Hans is nice; he has stuck up for me when some of the horrible Germans have made nasty comments. It's like they don't see a little girl, they just see a slave, and from what I have seen, the slaves are treated worse than animals.'

Tom tried to cheer her up. 'You are lucky to have Hans looking after you.'

Sobbing again, Rachel looked up at Tom and took a deep breath. 'That is just the trouble. As if I haven't been through enough, now they are sending Hans away and I will be left to fend for myself. They have already started jeering at me and saying things will be different when my friend goes. It's hardly a party now.' She just got this out before breaking down into a flood of uncontrollable tears.

He placed his arm around her and tried to calm her, but he could see that her situation was desperate. News had reached Guernsey of the treatment of Jews in Germany and the camp on Alderney was only ever referred to in hushed voices. Looking around, he noticed that the tide had almost gone out; he must make his move soon. He watched a piece of driftwood as it was carried out into the channel. The answer was obvious. He couldn't leave Rachel here; she must come with him. They would make it look like she had fallen into the sea and drowned.

'Rachel, who knows you are out here? And have you brought anything with you?'

She looked puzzled. 'No one knows except Hans that I come here sometimes. They don't lock me up because Hans says it would not be right to put me with the men prisoners and they know I can't get away from the island anyway. The only thing I have is what I am wearing - oh yes, and an old cloth I use as a shawl. It's just up there where the path comes down to the beach. Why are you asking?'

'Rachel, you must escape with me. We will get you back to Guernsey and you can hide out with my family. But we must make it look like you fell into the sea and drowned. We must go now or the tide will be wrong. Take off your shoes.'

As if a light had been switched on inside, she beamed at him.

'Really, you can rescue me? Oh thank you, Tom, thank you I... I... I...'

She flung her arms around his neck and knocked them both off the rock into the now shallow water below them. Then the questions started.

'Where is Guernsey? Won't your parents mind? Won't you all be in danger? Will the sea be rough? I get a bit scared of the sea.'

'We'll talk on the way. First, slip your shoes off and place them up there where the rock is dry. They will look for you and hopefully, finding your shawl, they should come down here and see your shoes and think you have fallen in.'

Rachel started to slip her shoes off but remembered, 'Tom, I can't leave my shoes. It's what Mama said. I don't know why, but can we just rely on them finding my shawl?'

'This is more important. We must make it look convincing. What did your Mama say again?'

She explained again that her mother had told her to look after the shoes, especially the right one. It seemed bizarre in the circumstances why one shoe would be more important than the other. Rachel must have got it wrong, but the parting words of her mother meant a great deal to her and Tom did not wish to press the point.

'Okay, we will just leave the left shoe on the rock and take your right one. There is no time to figure it out now. Give it to me.'

He wedged the shoe above the waterline in a crevice between the rocks. It would look as though she had caught her foot and fallen.

Soon Tom had helped a very wobbly Rachel into the bows of *Fish* and cast off smoothly into the night.

Rachel clung to the sides of *Fish* with all her strength as the small boat bounced around, propelled only by Tom's sculling. Before long they would catch the southbound tidal stream and be carried back to Guernsey. A mile from the coast of Alderney, Tom raised his sails and *Fish* was no longer drifting but again sprang to life.

***

Daisy returned to her isolated cottage on the edge of L'Ancresse Common. Her parents-in-law, Tom's grandparents, were waiting in the kitchen. The family always congregated in the kitchen and although they owned their own fisherman's cottage at Rocquaine in the south-west of the island, her in-laws regularly stayed over now that their son John was away fighting somewhere on the North Atlantic. John, Tom's father, was an expert mariner and had raised his son from an early age to know and respect the sea. However, as they now gathered in front of the kitchen stove, it was not the sea that worried them, rather it was the patrol boat that Daisy had seen off the Casquets. Grandfather John (senior) was neither tall nor stocky; he had more of a wiry physique. Yet despite this he carried a calm toughness that exuded authority as he tried to reassure the women. He never said a lot; perhaps because Molly and Daisy left little opportunity when they were on a roll, but when he did, it was always profoundly sensible.

'It doesn't mean a thing. He could be anywhere. The chances are he hid from the Germans and is sitting out the tide.'

Grandmother Molly drew the red gingham curtains to obscure the mirroring blackness from the windowpanes. Just a fraction shorter than her husband, with a grey bun perched on the back of her head, she looked every inch the warm and loving grandmother. Wiping her hands upon her apron (for no particular reason) she sighed and looked knowingly at her daughter-in-law, acknowledging that once again her husband was probably right.

'Don't worry, dear. If the Germans had him they would have been here by now, searching the place. Those fast patrol boats don't hang about. We just have to be patient, and if he has gone into hiding, we may have to accept it could be a long wait.'

Daisy remembered why she doted so much on her inlaws. Who else could turn a situation like this into an almost routine occurrence? She placed the kettle onto the stove and took a deep breath. Of course they were right, she must be patient. A cup of tea would help pass the time.

Both of Daisy's own parents had passed away sometime ago and, apart from a sister living in Weymouth, her only family now, apart from Tom, was on John's side. Grandpa John and Molly had never tried to fill her parents' place, but their presence was a great comfort to Daisy. Tom was also very close to his grandparents and before the occupation, loved to go fishing with Grandpa when his dad was at work as the master of a pilot boat. With working hours governed completely by the tide, any sizeable shipping required a local pilot to ease them alongside the quay in St Peter Port. John would be ferried out to the ships in a tug and he would take over as temporary master to instruct the helmsmen on the delicate manoeuvre, or take the helm himself to ensure the ship came to rest without damage to it or the quayside. On the bridge of English warships, John would now put these skills to good use whenever they rendezvoused at sea with a submarine or another ship, although the latter rarely came alongside. He would also often be the first choice of helmsman when they reached port or the busy waters approaching a major dock. Perhaps it was his confidence in knowing exactly what he was doing, but John had the ability to make light of almost any situation. He put things in perspective; usually with a throwaway remark that left everyone in stitches.

Daisy missed her husband, as did his parents, especially on a night like this when his sense of humour would have helped them all to cope.

Since John joined up, at the outbreak of war, Daisy had worked hard to fulfill the rôle of both parents. Although like most parents she worried about Tom whenever he was out of sight, she forced herself not to smother him. She knew that if John had been around, he would have encouraged the boy to take to the water at every opportunity. Whilst Daisy drew the line at encouragement, she nevertheless tolerated Tom's passion for fishing, sometimes a few miles offshore, without any hint of her true concern.

Had Tom known, he would almost certainly have reined back a little, but oblivious of his mother's feelings on the matter, he stayed out as long as the fish were biting.

Secluded on the edge of the common, with only the modest illumination from a crescent moon, the cottage would have looked like just another murky hill shape, were it not for the square of yellowy light escaping the window. This weak show of light emitted by the kitchen oil lamp and diffused by the curtains should already have been extinguished by thick blackout curtains. The family inside regularly risked the wrath of the Germans to give Tom a guiding light across the common to the sea on his way home.

CHAPTER TWO

The epicentre of the Bavarian Nazi party, Munich in the early 1940s was not the place for an affluent Jewish family to be. Since being forced to wear the Star of David on their sleeves, Jewish residents were singled out for abuse and humiliation wherever they were seen. Their homes were often daubed with JUDE painted in large letters as if this were some sort of insult; arrests and disappearances were common. Hitler had convinced the majority of Germans that their great empire's economic failure was principally the fault of the Jewish community. The only answer was to purge their nation of all non-Aryans and confiscate their possessions.

The Levi family had lived in what was originally a suburban district and had now been absorbed into the city. Their town house on a wide boulevard was spread over five floors including the basement, and they even boasted their own private garden. They had done well, by anybody's standards. Joshua was a chemist, and when he joined his father in the family firm, he was immediately impressed with the potential of some of the opportunities to be exploited by the latest scientific advances. Although somewhat a traditionalist, before he died Joshua's father had allowed him his head and the firm had flourished. In particular, and somewhat ironically, it was in the field of synthetic material dyes that the largest contributions to the family fortunes were to be made. Ironically, because the massive upscaling of Germany's military had created the biggest demand, to ensure a consistency of colour required for uniforms by the Reich hierarchy. But times had changed. The factory, although technically still owned by Joshua and Freda Levi, was now managed by the military. Joshua was not only a businessman, however. As the most experienced chemist, he led the research into new products. It was this that had shielded the family from the worst extremes of the Nazi party and its supporters throughout the 1930s. The military knew that the work Joshua was leading on stabilizing dyes could have great benefits for them, not just with uniforms, but with a range of applications from camouflage to flags. It would be possible to produce new vibrant colours that would stay in the material for longer without losing any of their original tone. At a time when the age and use of materials resulted in SS officers sometimes being confused with desert troops, this was seen as highly desirable. The uniforms would last longer and look better, and Hitler was obsessional about appearances.

The small team of Aryan chemists that Joshua led knew that he was deliberately eking out the research project. He knew that as soon as he announced the formula, he would become dispensable. So he worked on, reporting regularly on the blind alleys but occasionally producing enough progress to satisfy everyone that the end would eventually be achieved.

It grieved him deeply that his fellow Jews were suffering so much under the Nazi regime, but he could not change that and he could provide some hint of normality for his family by continuing his work. So, each day he would cycle from his grand home to the factory and work away all day on a combination of real experiments into the use of polymers, and bogus experiments that were destined to fail.

It was in the spring that their world finally collapsed. A group of thugs from the Hitler Youth movement had taken up a position outside the Levi residence. The family inside were terrified as first abuse, then bricks, were hurled through their windows. Joshua and Freda huddled around their young daughter, Rachel, in the centre of their second floor sitting room.

Joshua said that with any luck they would get bored soon and go. They had no reference to draw upon for how bad things could get. In their lifetime, Germany had been a law-abiding, respectable society and in their circle of friends it was the arts that dominated any non-business discussions, rarely politics. However, now they were forced to consider the deeper scars that beset their country. Joshua could no longer stand back and allow his family to be threatened in this way.

'I will go and reason with them. They must know that our firm has kept most of their families in work for years. We have been good to them; we have paid much more than other firms and been kind when they have needed time off or had domestic problems.'

Freda never questioned her husband, but fear riveted her. These were no longer rational people - they were a mob, and reason was not something they would respond to. She broke her silence and pleaded with him not to go.

She might have succeeded, but a shattering of glass announced that bricks could and would now reach this floor. Rachel screamed.

Joshua ran from the room and as he hopped down several steps at a time to emerge in the hall where their wide central staircase split majestically, he realized they were pushing the front door open. He charged at the door and shouted at them to stop. He pleaded, 'This is the Levi family house! Everyone knows we are good to the local people!'

The door sprang open, sending him flying backwards across the hall. As he lay on his back, a tall blonde youth walked casually up to him. 'You are a filthy Jew and you have sucked your wealth from our people too long. Now you can get out and take your vermin family with you.' He raised his arm brandishing a large club; it crashed against Joshua's skull.

When he came around, Joshua was in the street. To his horror he saw Freda and Rachel emerging from the doorway to run to his aid.

What happened next would be imprinted in slow motion on the young Rachel's mind forever. One of the youths began to scream abuse at Freda and the stunned Joshua rose to his feet. As the youth began to push Freda backwards, Joshua rushed forwards and grabbed his collar. Freda grabbed Rachel and pulled her screaming towards the house as the youths turned upon her father. As if from nowhere, a group of soldiers appeared just as Joshua hit out to free himself from the youths.

25

His fist landed squarely on the jaw of the tall blonde youth, who fell backwards and lay inertly on the pavement. The group stood motionless for an instant and looked down at their friend; their eyes then turned upon Joshua with hate and he knew what would happen next.

As Joshua raised his fist again to clear a path for his home, a single shot rang out. Then silence fell.

Muttering about filthy Jews and there being one less to worry about, the youths dispersed without a word of reprimand from the soldiers. As Joshua lay bleeding in the street with the last pulse of life draining from him, Freda ran to his side. Rachel froze on the doorstep for a whole ten seconds before her wail filled the air and the tears flooded down her young cheeks.

It was only a few days later that the soldiers came again.

This time it was to tell Freda her home had been commandeered for the Reich. She was given thirty minutes to collect her possessions and leave. That Freda was in mourning for her husband, that she had a young daughter, that she had no place to go, counted for nothing.

There was no point in carrying possessions. Freda carried her memories inside and there was little else that would be of use in the years ahead. She decided to collect some important papers that confirmed the family heritage: deeds to their house, insurance policies and share certificates. She dressed Rachel and then herself in layers of clothes, too much for the approaching summer, but Freda reckoned that what you could wear would serve better than what you could carry.

A few minutes' walk from their home was the office of the legal company that had looked after the Levi family and its business affairs for three generations. Freda and Rachel were taken to a small office at the back of the building with a window overlooking a pleasant courtyard. One entire wall was taken up with a bookcase full of legal books that were also scattered over the desk in front of the window. An old man sitting behind this looked up at them, smiled at Rachel, and addressed Freda.

'I have been expecting you, my dear. I heard all about Joshua.

I am very sorry. I fear you may be about to ask me for help I cannot give, but please tell me why you have come.'

Freda had known Hr Rosenberg all her life. He had been a guest of Joshua's parents many times and had often been seen in a huddle with Joshua after synagogue. But this was no time for emotion.

'Hr Rosenberg, Rachel and I have nowhere to go and I must ensure her safety. Can you please put us up for a while and tell me what I should do with these valuable papers?'

His eyes watered over as he looked into Freda's face and began, 'You know, I would do anything to help you, but I no longer have a home to offer. The SS visited us a few days ago and threw us out. I have been told to attend a marshalling point tomorrow to be shipped to a so-called holding camp in another part of the country. As for your papers, let me see.' He took the bundle from Freda as she whispered to him about her sadness at his fate.

'Your husband's share certificates, like most of your family assets, are now the subject of probate and cannot be traded until that is resolved. As for the rest, they would have a value in normal times, but not now. Much would in any case be confiscated by the Reich. But your own share certificates could be traded, if you are not forced to relinquish them by the authorities.' He paused, rummaged through a drawer full of papers and resumed. 'Ah, as I thought, we have a client bank account set up. There may be one last thing I can do to help you. It's not much, but at least we can put your documents in a safe place. There is still safe passage across the border to Switzerland for German bank officials and if one of my clerks takes the deposit box to the Munich office today, it will be safely installed in a Swiss vault by the end of the week. Who knows if this nightmare will ever end and if...' He realized that Rachel was also listening intently and quickly changed the subject. '... and if in the future you want to get access to your papers, it will be easy.'

Looking directly at Freda, he whispered, 'This client account will not be traceable to someone of our religion; it is a numbered account for a Swiss bank. All you need to do is tell me a password and I will set it up with your belongings safely installed this afternoon. Oh, and you need this key for the safety deposit box. Shall I put all the documents in?' He handed her a small key and a paper with the number of the account on it.

Freda was thinking about a password when Rachel tugged at her sleeve. She asked politely if they would be long. As Freda looked at her, she thought about how well behaved her daughter was. In spite of all they were going through, Rachel's eyes still lit up and she still found a smile for her mother. There was something in Rachel's expression that brought back the memory of another time, light years ago and yet just a few months earlier. It was a happy memory: Joshua and Freda had been woken by Rachel jumping onto their bed. They wished her a very, very happy birthday as Rachel clambered between the clean white sheets of their sumptuously comfortable bed. Along with the kisses and cuddles, Rachel received a very special birthday present wrapped in colourful red and yellow paper with a huge golden ribbon. Inside was another layer of wrapping paper, this time blue and green, and once that had been discarded a further layer appeared, now of orange paper and so on, through no less than six layers of colorful paper, each with a ribbon tied carefully around it. The manner in which this present was wrapped was itself a preview of the gift and as Rachel worked her way through, her smile grew wider and wider and she went faster and faster until the final layer was torn unceremoniously from the remaining box at the centre. The image on the lid confirmed what Rachel had suspected was coming: a *matryoshka* Russian nesting doll was inside. Rachel had seen this in the window of a department store in town and desperately wanted it. So much so that Rachel had already named her, and for weeks afterwards little hints had been dropped into conversations about Anoushka, to the delight of Rachel who giggled excitedly.

Anoushka was the name given to a queen in a story her father had made up about a medieval royal family that lived in a castle high in the Bavarian Alps. Her largest doll was finely dressed, just like the Queen, but each smaller one inside was less elegant until the final fifth doll was the model of a tiny peasant girl. Anoushka's story was of rags to riches, a pretty young peasant girl marrying a wealthy young prince, eventually becoming the Queen and living happily ever after with her King in a beautiful castle.

The irony was not lost on Freda, who despite experiencing much the opposite of Anoushka's fate, dared to believe that Rachel might one day be as happy as that princess.

She wrote the name Anoushka on a slip of paper and handed it to Hr Rosenberg. She said nothing of the memory that was still too poignant to say out loud.

Freda told Hr Rosenberg she would keep her own share certificates, as they were the only thing she could freely trade, but the rest of the papers including Rachel's identity card were handed over to go into the bank deposit box. She left Hr Rosenberg, thanking him for his help and wishing, although not believing, his fate would improve.

Now destitute, mother and daughter took to the streets. Their old friends and neighbours soon proved either unable or unwilling to assist them. So they slept rough and wandered, hiding in alleyways at the first sign of the Hitler Youth or any gangs of young people or soldiers. Freda was at her wits' end; she no longer cared what became of her, but she cared desperately about her young daughter. How could their wealthy and intellectual friends ignore their plight? Just as Freda's faith in humanity was at its lowest, an old man restored her belief. Hr Weinstock, the nearby Jewish cobbler, took pity upon the two of them and offered sanctuary in his modest shoe shop. This was a man who hardly knew them, who in their previous existence had every right to resent their overt wealth and privilege. But it was he who extended the charity to them, knowing that his own quiet existence would now be more exposed. People would talk and the Nazis would visit soon.

In his tiny sitting room with Rachel tucked up and asleep on a mattress in the corner, Freda discussed their plight with this kind stranger. Hr Weinstock knew nothing of wealth, but he knew about politics and what he told Freda confirmed her worst fears.

'The disappearance of Jews is no coincidence, no more than the so-called holding camps exist to distribute us to faraway places. Freda, you must face it, they will destroy us. If there is anything you can do to save yourself or little Rachel, do it now before it is too late. They will come for us all very soon.'

Freda contemplated what he had told her; several minutes later, she spoke. Her words were strong and unemotional.

'Hr Weinstock, you have been good to us, but I want to ask you one more favour. There is almost nothing that will protect my daughter and me from the fate you describe. Our enemies are obsessed with hatred. The only possible glimmer of hope will be to appeal to another obsession, and pray that it will save at least one of us. Rachel's future is all that matters now. Despite all that has happened I still possess the share certificates for the Levi business. Not much else is worth anything now. I don't even know if we will ever regain our house or the money in our bank accounts, but there may come a time when the business is again in private control and when that happens it may be worth a great deal. My husband's shares and our few remaining valuables are now in a Swiss bank and in any case couldn't be transferred yet, but perhaps I can use mine to barter for Rachel's life. If she survives...'

Freda's pragmatism faded as she looked across to her sleeping child. With a deep breath, she continued.

'If she survives, I want her to inherit her father's shares. Who knows? They may one day be worth something again. Anyway, it is all I can give her. She is too young to understand and will surely forget the password or lose the key to our deposit box, or someone will steal them. I was thinking, could you make a safe hiding place in her shoe? One of us might survive to tell her. I have always taught her to take care of her clothes, and in good

Jewish fashion, not to be wasteful; I will make sure she understands that she must look after her shoes. Maybe one day she will realize the significance.'

The two of them looked into each other's eyes. Had it really come to this? Freda's plan was full of flaws.

Rachel was just twelve years old. Of course, she would lose her shoes, grow out of them or they would be taken from her, and could Freda really trust any German to keep his word on Rachel's safe conduct?

Also, Rachel was not a streetwise child. Well educated and impeccably mannered yes, but she had never had to fend for herself and knew absolutely nothing about managing money. So the idea that this little girl would understand the importance of share certificates and bank accounts, when her whole world was being turned upside down, was bizarre. Freda too had limited experience, having always left money matters to her husband. She only knew that Joshua had often quietly impressed upon her the success of the business and how it was becoming very, very valuable. Surely this could be used to make a deal for Rachel's safety? She was under no illusions that the Nazis would take pity on a child; they saw only a Jewess. She also knew that they were well disciplined and that what she was proposing was dangerous. But there were no other options; she must appeal to their greed.

It seemed hopeless, but hope was all they had left, and for Freda it was hugely important if she was to have any chance of keeping her sanity. She must save Rachel. If she could do this, she could face whatever the Germans threw at her.

Hr Weinstock agreed to help and that night mustered all his skill and the best leather he could find to create a secret compartment inside the heel of Rachel's right shoe. He was a skilful cobbler, and by morning the shoe with its secret cargo looked identical to the left one. Folded carefully and wrapped in waxed paper in the heel were a small key and a metal plate with two numbers stamped on it. First the number of the bank account 2011856 and then, 2021940, the date of Rachel's twelfth birthday. Not wanting to risk the account number, key and password together, this would be a clue to guide Rachel to her memories of that happy day.

Amongst the various documents to be interned in the bank deposit box deep in a vault across the border in Switzerland was a single share certificate for five thousand deutschmark shares in Levi Industries. One share more than Freda's own certificate, this was a controlling interest in the family firm. In 1940, this was more valuable than their house, even at face value. The true value was a great deal more.

When Freda and Rachel awoke, they found the old man sleeping in his workshop with the shoe resting on the apron across his lap. Freda sat her daughter down on a stool and slipped her shoes onto her small feet. They fitted well and still had some room for growth. She clipped on the buckles and stood back to admire the shining black leather and smart heels. Especially the heels. Thinking that Hr Weinstock would soon wake, Freda began to search for a tea caddy. But even this relative normality was not to be allowed. A sudden crash, and old Hr Weinstock's front door caved in. The jackboot responsible heralded three German soldiers who immediately demanded papers.

The noise woke the old man from his short slumbers and the three were pushed out into the street.

'You are all under arrest under the restrictions of non-Aryans laws. You will be transported to a muster point with the others of your kind. Your papers, hurry... The child has no papers, why not?'

Freda forced herself not to panic; she knew that she must not be seen as desperately trying any ploy. 'My daughter's papers were in our house when it was commandeered by the Reich. If we can go to her room, I will search for them. But your commander is in the town, is he not? I am sure he would be glad of some information I can give before we reach the muster point. Perhaps he can decide?'

The soldiers looked at one another; this one had some

arrogance. But she had that wealthy air to her so, rather than strike her, they played along a little.

'What information? You can tell us and we will make sure he gets it.'

Freda had expected this.

'I am Freda Levi of the factory; there is a fault with one of the dye machines that will spoil many uniforms if I do not get someone in authority to deal with it. I can explain it to him in just a few minutes.'

Again they looked at each other. Two of them appeared not to care if all the uniforms were ruined but the other a meticulous young man - took command.

'Okay, you will come with us. It is in any case on the way to the station. The old man can go on. Bring your brat.'

Rachel clung to her mother's side. The young German leaned forward and pushed his face close to Freda's. 'If you are wasting our time, you will see we have excellent pest control in our city now.'

One of the soldiers frogmarched Hr Weinstock ahead of them, repeatedly shoving his rifle butt into the old man's back. Freda had no time to thank him, as they too were pushed forward in the direction of a group of soldiers further down the sidewalk, Freda carrying a small bundle wrapped in a cloth. When they reached the group, they saw they were congregating outside an office set up in a neo-classical town house. Freda knew this to have been the home of another Jewish family.

The groomed soldier instructed them to wait on the sidewalk as he disappeared inside, leaving the other soldier to watch them. By contrast, this one appeared scruffy and undisciplined. Freda was an attractive woman, and his leers were unrestrained. One of the other soldiers called out to him, 'You want us to babysit, Manfred, whilst you take her in the alley?'

Rachel looked up at her mother fearfully, but as Manfred considered this offer, the first soldier emerged from the doorway and instructed them to go inside.

In what had once been an elegant drawing room off the main

hall, a German officer sat behind a desk with files and papers all over the floor around him. He was reading some papers on his desk as he spoke. Freda was told to enter and when Rachel started to follow, a large hand grabbed her shoulder and pushed her onto a chair outside the door.

'This had better be good, Jew. You know well that she should always carry her papers on her.'

Freda pulled out her own papers from the bundle and showed him that Rachel was mentioned on them. Then with fear almost paralyzing her throat, she whispered, 'I can make you rich. I am Freda Levi.' She paused to check his reaction. Would he be greedy, would he be disciplined? She had no way of knowing.

Without moving his head, his eyes moved up to look at her.

He barked a command to the soldier still waiting by the door. Freda was struck cold.

'Close that thing and wait outside.' Then to Freda, 'Go on.'

Freda gathered her wits and began slowly. 'You know of my family, I think. We own the factory that makes all the dye for the uniforms of the Reich. You must also know that we can no longer access our bank accounts because of the laws that were introduced, but we have money in Switzerland which after the war…'

'Is that it?' he interrupted. 'You waste my time by telling me you will pay me later? You must think I am a fool. All Jewish money will go to the Reich, and if you can't access your account, how do you think I will?' He was on the verge of shouting an order through the closed door when Freda tried again.

'No, wait. That is not all. I have something I can give you now. Look.' She pulled a share certificate from the bundle she had been carrying in her cloth. But before giving it she steeled herself to say, 'If I give you this, can you get my daughter to safety?'

The officer looked at her and reached out for the paper. 'Hmm, this is perhaps a little more interesting. But where are your husband's shares?'

Freda explained that Joshua had been killed and his personal assets would be subject to a lengthy delay in probate. They were probably still at their house, but the shares that she owned were nearly half of the firm.

'Okay, so why should I not just take this and kill you both?'

Her stomach turned, but Freda remained calm and smiling at him, she forced her reply. 'Hr Generalleutnant,' (she noted his rank from a sign on his desk) 'I am sure you know that a signed transfer document will make the certificates beyond question yours, whereas in future years others may question how you came about them.'

He looked down at the certificate again and considered. Four thousand, nine hundred and ninety-nine deutschmarks. This was worth more than he earned in a year, perhaps even five years, and after the war this would make him rich. Of course if he got caught he would be shot, but if he laid low until the fighting was over, things would be very different under a civilian regime. In any case, who would know? This woman would never survive and the child was too young to understand what was happening. If it became too risky, he could just decide to do nothing with the shares. In the meantime, the military were doing a fine job running the business.

He looked up at Freda and thought about her comment that the shares may be worthless if there was suspicion about how they had been obtained. He needed her signature, and there was little point in risking a forgery when she was sitting in front of him. This whole deal was potentially worth too much.

Freda watched his eyes grow greedier by the minute; it was going her way. She tentatively offered the last paper from her bundle.

To whom it may concern

This is to confirm a transaction for the transfer of 4,999 ordinary shares in Levi Industries to the holder of the share certificate name: ... ...

In return for the above shares, ... guarantees the protection and safe passage of Rachel Levi to a place of safe keeping until the end of the war. She will not be interned as the inmate of a concentration or other camp and every effort will be made to transfer her to an authority outside of those who are anti-Semitic during or after the war.

This agreement is entered into freely and without coercion of any kind.

Signed

....
Freda Levi
Date............... 1940

He read the paper and looked up at her. If she had not been a Jew, this woman would have been quite something. She had planned this meeting carefully; the note in her own hand would make the validity of the transfer beyond question. If she signed this and he entered his name, he would need to ensure the girl was safe and whilst he knew that would be difficult, he had an idea of how he might do this. What the hell, if she didn't make it who would know whether she died during the war or after it?

Freda recalled how Hr Weinstock had guided her on exactly what to say. He was no legal expert, but he knew about the concentration camps and he knew that Rachel's best chance of surviving would be to ensure she never went to one.

'My name is Helmut Stein; you write it in the spaces. I will send the child to a labour camp in the Channel Islands but not as an inmate; she will work in the kitchen. My son Hans has been posted there and he will take her. Beyond that I can make no promises. Your own fate is out of my hands.'

Freda gasped as she reached out to take back the paper. She added his name in the spaces and signed it, then offered it to him again.

'Thank you. Oh, thank you, Hr Stein,' she burst out. 'You cannot imagine what this means to me.'

With a callous look, he simply grunted and took the paper. An order was barked at the door and the soldier outside entered.

'Take her away and bring in the child.'

As Freda walked out of the office, she looked down at her daughter sitting outside the door. She crouched down to speak to her, but the soldier pushed her forwards. Freda stared back into the office, beseeching the officer to give her a few moments to say goodbye. Confused and now crying, Rachel also turned to look in around the door. Hr Stein simply nodded to the soldier and put up one finger to indicate how long they had.

The tears tumbled from Freda's cheeks as she whispered her goodbyes to Rachel. Nothing had ever hurt so much; the pain was unbearable. Rachel was still crying too. She didn't really understand what was happening, but if her Mama was crying, and Mama never cried except with joy, she knew this was bad. Freda tried to pretend she would see Rachel again soon, she told her to be brave and to go with the man who would take her somewhere safe. Freda tried to convey the importance of keeping her shoes, especially the right one, but even this now seemed unimportant compared to the prospect of never seeing her again. As the soldier's hand finally grabbed her shoulder again after what had seemed like just a few precious seconds, she steeled herself with the thought that at least Rachel might now be safe.

CHAPTER THREE

Fish glided through the water with only the sound of waves lapping at her sides. This was why Tom loved sailing so much. No noisy engine or smell of diesel, just man's ability to harness nature's power, as silent and clean as nature herself. The breeze against her cheeks, Rachel too was exhilarated by their silent progress through the night. She perched in the bows and realized this was only the second time she had ever been in a boat. How different from the first time. This time there was no thunder of engines, no overcrowding of German soldiers, and her fear about an uncertain destination was replaced by the excitement of discovering a new land. Rachel understood what made all the difference – freedom.

Her thoughts were interrupted by the voice of her rescuer, this boy who had changed her world in minutes from the bleak prison camp to an adventure under the dimly lit moon.

'Rachel, as we approach Guernsey there may be things in the water I can't see in this light. Could you please keep a lookout? We will certainly be passing crab pots and there are some large storage pots just under the surface I don't want to hit.'

Rachel agreed, and was commenting on how irresponsible it was to leave these hazards hiding below the surface when Tom pointed out that several were his, and they kept the catch fresh until he had time to collect it. She felt a little embarrassed until he reassured her by saying she wasn't to know. Filled with a sense of purpose, Rachel searched into the night for anything that might have been a lurking danger as *Fish* continued on her journey.

They were just an hour from Guernsey's north coast and making good time, when Tom's heart sank. Straight ahead and coming towards them, the patrol boat was once again doing its rounds. He surveyed the situation. If he maintained this course, they would be on him in less than ten minutes. If he made for land, they would almost certainly cross his course - assuming they were again travelling to the northern approach of The Russel. Going back was not an option. Even if the wind had been in the right direction (which it wasn't), there was no way he would risk them finding Rachel on board a small boat off the coast of Alderney.

Tom decided to head for a small island to the east of Guernsey called Herm. It was a long shot, because the searchlight would easily pick them out if it fell upon them, but it was the only course to possible safety downwind and with the tidal stream now racing south at full speed.

'Rachel, we must make a detour. You see that shadow with a light straight ahead? It is a German patrol boat and it is heading our way. I am going to make for another island, but they may catch us. If they do, we must pretend you are staying with us on Guernsey. It's our only hope. Don't say you are Jewish, say you were on holiday from England when the Germans arrived in the island and have been too scared to come forward. Do you understand?'

Rachel was stunned; how had she missed seeing the boat? Was this the end of her freedom? She meekly confirmed that she understood, but was still taking it in when Tom called out to her that he was altering course and she should keep her head down. As she emerged again on the new tack, she noticed that in a few short minutes the dim shape of the patrol boat had already grown significantly. Out of the corner of her eye, she saw another shape, this time much closer, in the water.

'Tom, look! I think there is a crab pot or even a storage pot!' She pointed to a large round object floating menacingly just beneath the surface a few yards from their starboard bow.

Tom ensured they were far enough way not to hit it but close enough to see what it was. As he gazed over the side, he studied the unfamiliar shape. It wasn't a crab pot or a storage pot. The large round object had spikes protruding like a giant conker. He took a deep breath; it was a mine!

Fortunately the tide was carrying the mine further south and they were now headed south-east so they were unlikely to get close to it again. He pulled harder on the mainsheet and *Fish* sped away into the darkness. Some cloud obscured the moon and it was suddenly even blacker as they raced through the night. Even the patrol boat was no longer visible. Tom and Rachel both sighed with relief.

Tom calculated that they would soon be reaching the reefs off the northern coast of Herm. He asked Rachel to look out for rocks. Now was the time to decrease sail a little and feel his way through the rocks towards Herm. He lashed the tiller of *Fish* and stood up to release the halyard of her topsail. Whilst standing at full stretch in the darkness with Rachel peering over the bows, his plan was destroyed.

The bright beam of a searchlight suddenly appeared out of nowhere and within seconds it fell upon them. Dazzled by the light, Tom clung to the mast and the two of them hardly dared to speak. All around them the sea was illuminated like daylight and the rocks Rachel had been seeking were standing in all their glory calling to her, 'Here we are!'

Behind them the island of Herm was also visible; they had nearly made it. Another half, maybe even just quarter, of an hour and they would have reached safety. Tom's heart sank. He spoke quietly to Rachel.

'Remember what we said, Rachel. You were on holiday from England, okay? Have you ever been to England? Is there anywhere you know?'

The hopelessness of their situation sunk in as they realized that Rachel had no idea about England. She had never been there and, if questioned, it would soon become obvious she was not English. Tom knew the Alderney Regiment may by now have realized that Rachel was missing and they would very quickly put two and two together.

A loudhailer crackled. A voice in broken English called, 'You there on the boat! Do not move. We will come alongside. Move and we will shoot to kill.'

The voice on the hailer would have been deafening on a quiet night like this had they been close to them, but they must still be some way off, and her engines were almost quiet. Tom realized this was why they hadn't heard her coming. She could have been drifting, a spot of late-night fishing, perhaps? These searchlights were so powerful, they could be half a mile away. Could they run for it?

Tom's mind was racing; there was still plenty of wind and he could now see the course between the rocks clearly. Or they could jump in and swim for it, but could Rachel swim? Had they spotted her in the bows? Maybe she could slip over the side and swim for Herm?

The brightest circle of light remained fixed upon them as the sound of the patrol boat's engines grew louder. Still dazzled, they now heard a distant voice. Someone on the boat was shouting in German; he must have been on the bows away from the wheelhouse. The voice sounded familiar; it was the singer who had led their choir hours earlier on the Casquets.

'Rachel, did you hear what he said?'

'He told them to radio the harbour and say they were going to investigate something near Herm.'

There was a slight delay before the sound of the explosion reached them. Light flooded the entire skyline and it seemed as though the earlier searchlight had been just a torch beam around their boat. This was an order of magnitude greater. The air was filled with flying debris, the sea became wild, as though a tidal wave had hit them. The noise soon followed - an enormous roar, accompanied by a blast of air rushing across them, enveloping them completely. Then an instant later, a second explosion as the patrol boat's fuel ignited, making sure there could be no survivors. As the fireball burst upwards into the sky, the entire east coast of Guernsey became visible, nearly three miles away.

Fish span in the water. As Rachel wedged herself into the bows, Tom was hurled through the air into the foaming sea.

Some more cracks and bangs for just a few seconds, and the silence again fell. The scene was eerie as what was left of the patrol boat continued to burn. Tom surfaced to find the water calmed and *Fish* drifting downwind towards the rocks. But her drift was impeded by the topsail and the gaff to which it was attached, now blown off the mast and trailing in the water by the halyard that Tom had been releasing. A strong swimmer, he made for this floating lifeline and as he hauled himself towards *Fish*, a head peered over the bows.

Rachel's face was ashen and her eyes were like dinner plates.

'Tom, are you all right? I was terrified when you were thrown off. What on earth happened?'

When he finally heaved himself over *Fish*'s gunwales, Tom explained that the patrol boat had hit the mine they passed earlier. They were both shaking and his voice wavered as he recalled to Rachel how the young German soldiers had been drinking beer and singing at the Casquets. They were no longer soldiers but somebody's sons, perhaps husbands or brothers. That night was a tragedy for their families somewhere far away in Germany.

But there was no time to linger. Tom checked that everything was again as it should be on *Fish* and set sail for Herm. In the distance he could already hear air-raid alarms going off and the roar of engines starting up in St Peter Port harbour. Powerful beams of light began to search the sky and then sweep the Little Russel for British warships. It was clearly pandemonium over there. Skirting around the north coast of Herm, *Fish* was now on the far side of the island and out of sight from Guernsey. From the background noise, it was clear they soon found the wreckage of the patrol boat. The din of engines and shouting told the story of their frantic search for survivors. *Fish* was gliding along past the Shell Beach as the sky above cleared completely of cloud. The warm evening was soon lit by the effervescence of moonlight reflecting off the millions of tiny broken shells that formed the beach.

Rachel was fascinated; this beach appeared to be pure white dusty sand. How could it be made of shells? Tom explained that an ocean current carried the shells and deposited them there over countless years. This seemed a parallel universe to events on the other side of the island.

As they passed the southern end of Shell Beach and rounded a rocky outcrop, Tom again lashed his tiller and this time took down the main and topsails. *Fish* slowed as he whispered to Rachel, 'We are very close now, and I have no idea if there will be soldiers here. When I signal to you with my hand, take this rope and jump out of the boat into the water. Don't worry; it will only go up to your knees. Keep hold of the rope until I join you. I will take down the foresail.'

Tom navigated *Fish* down a narrow channel between two high outcrops of rocks. The rocks formed a secluded cove with sand at the shore. As *Fish* grated onto the beach, Tom signalled and Rachel jumped off the bows, clutching the rope. Her expression was serious now; she had a most important task to perform. Tom smiled inwardly as he released the foresail halyard and pulled the sail down, bunching it as it came. He stowed it in a small locker and bounced over the side to join Rachel. 'Well done,' he said encouragingly. The beach only offered a few feet of sand (to Rachel's disappointment, not shells) before reaching a cliff in which the dim shape of a cave could just be seen.

Tom hauled on the bows of *Fish*, dragging her up the beach until she was hidden in the cave.

'I doubt anyone will see her here unless they are searching very hard. Let's rest until the commotion has died down on the other side and in the morning we will see how the land lies.'

The two of them climbed back into *Fish* and lay down in the cockpit sole, facing head to foot. Tom was looking down the boat and out of the cove, Rachel towards the cove and Tom's reassuring face. Bunched up main and topsails for cushions, some shuffling about, and the two were soon overwhelmed by tiredness. Rachel thought about her own family and how much she missed them. Since leaving Alderney she had not thought of them once and this made her feel guilty, as if they were watching somewhere and hurting because she had forgotten them. She apologized to her mama and papa and vowed to keep them in at least a corner of her mind all the time, then yawned and through half-closed eyes took a last look at Tom before yielding to the night.

Tom watched as the young girl fell asleep. How on earth had he ended up in a cave at the back of Herm with a refugee child, having escaped the clutches of the Germans and narrowly missed being blown to bits by a sea mine? He wondered what his mother and grandparents must be thinking and, as he played back the events of the night, he too surrendered and allowed the exhaustion to overcome him.

CHAPTER FOUR

Tom awoke first as the sun shone directly onto his face. Still drowsy, he sat up and looked out down their secret cove. At the entrance, a group of puffins drifted on the breeze, occasionally diving into the warm sea to emerge later, breakfast between beaks. Tom realized he hadn't eaten since yesterday afternoon and was very, very hungry. He rummaged around in one of the lockers, grabbed the bucket that was still wedged in a corner of *Fish*, and as quietly as he could, he stepped out onto adjacent rocks.

Rachel emerged from a deep sleep to the smell of cooking mackerel. Rubbing her eyes, all she saw in front of her was the inside of the cave and smoke rising from somewhere near *Fish*'s bows. At first, her mind did not engage. Then she remembered where she was and turned to see the bright sunshine lighting up the sea, the puffins and... no Tom. She tried to force her mind to determine if this was a serious problem and thought again about the smoke. Was *Fish* on fire? Had Tom been captured? As the first stirrings of panic arose from within, a head popped up over the bows.

'I see her ladyship has awoken!' Tom mused.

Rachel beamed at him. Scurrying to the bows, she looked over at the fire and makeshift spit that Tom had created. A fat mackerel was cooking on it, and she was ravenous.

Tom poured some water from a small jerry can into the lid which doubled as a beaker, and handed it to Rachel. A few minutes later they were each tucking into half a mackerel, with another on the spit. Although there was nothing to eat it with except their fingers, and it was piping hot to hold, it was absolutely delicious. The tender, moist and just slightly salty fish fell apart in her mouth. Rachel could not remember when a breakfast had been that good before. True, the whole package added to it: she was refreshed from her deep sleep, safe in their secret hideout, and Tom's company was about as good as it could get after the mostly horrible soldiers she had been tolerating. Added to all this was the beauty of Herm. It felt like a tropical paradise as the early morning sun beat down upon them through the clear blue sky. After breakfast, she ventured down the beach to wash in a rock pool, and was almost dry by the time she reentered the cave.

Tom was busying himself covering the embers of their fire with sand before sorting out the sails in *Fish* when Rachel returned.

'Tom, do you think the soldiers will be looking for us?'

Tom considered for a moment before answering.

'Nobody on board the patrol boat could have survived that explosion and the last report we heard them make by radio said they were about to investigate something near Herm. The watch on shore would have certainly assumed that whatever that was, it was to do with the explosion. They probably realized it was a mine. I think their choice of words saved us. Of course, in Alderney they will be looking for you by now, but if our plan worked, they should assume you drowned. In any case, they will not imagine you were connected to the patrol boat or explosion. Try not to worry; I think things are finally going our way. But we must see where we go from here. In Herm, before the occupation, there used to be a few residents, a farm, a chapel and even a small school. We must take a look and see if anyone is still here. Let's find out. Come on.'

Rachel was about to join him when she noticed her single shoe still in the cockpit sole of *Fish*. She reached over and grabbed it before catching Tom up a few paces ahead of her.

Tom laughed when he saw the shoe.

'You are not still carting that around, are you?'

Her look confirmed that she was.

Just a small distance from the cave was another beach, this one called Belvoir or 'beautiful view'. Quite appropriate, Rachel thought as her toes sunk into the warm sand. They left the beach and headed uphill on a small path. Rachel put on her one shoe and picked her way carefully; the path was a bit rough on her bare foot. On the left was a house that looked deserted. Tom said they should crouch down and pass it silently, just in case, and they walked on further up the hill. By now Rachel's foot was starting to hurt and the hot sun was getting to her.

When she let out a particularly troubled 'ouch', Tom decided it would take forever at this rate. He turned his back and said, 'Come on, I'll give you a piggyback.'

Rachel was not at all sure what he meant and she knew that 'piggies' were probably frowned upon in a good Jewish family, but she trusted Tom, and when she finally worked out what he was offering she was delighted to be carried. Especially with her arms around Tom's neck.

At first, Rachel's tiny weight hardly registered with Tom but as they climbed further up the hill and the sun grew hotter, he began to feel it. At the top of the hill the path crossed another that led off at right angles in both directions. Tom eased Rachel off his back and climbed onto the bank bordering a field. From this elevated position, he could see all the way down to the west and northern coasts of the island and all the way across to Guernsey. He could also see Alderney clearly to the north.

His eyes retuned to where the patrol boat had been lost the night before. A flotilla was searching the sea. Just inland, some small boats had been left on a beach and soldiers were spread out, searching the undergrowth.

When Rachel joined him she immediately focused upon the soldiers.

'They are searching for us, aren't they?'

Before Tom could speak, a man's voice cut in. 'Now why would they be doing that, little girl?'

They both nearly fell from the bank with the shock. But before shock could transform into blind fear, the voice again cut in. 'Don't worry, I won't turn you in. But I think you might tell me what you are doing here, and perhaps we should get you somewhere a little less visible. If you can see them, they can see you, you know.'

The man had been standing on the other side of the bank,

surveying the scene himself. He was quite old and dressed rather scruffily, Rachel thought.

'My name is Harold and I look after the cows here on Herm's farm. Let's get you back to the farmhouse and Olive will get you cleaned up.'

Rachel looked down at her dress, now dirty and torn, although her face was clean from her early morning wash. Tom still looked (and smelt) like he had spent the night with his fish. He whispered to Rachel, 'It's all right, he's local. We can go with him.'

Harold led the way a short distance down the path to a farmhouse, with the evidence of cows all around the yard. Again Rachel relied upon Tom to save her feet, this time from cow muck. He carried her to the door. Inside, a traditional farmhouse kitchen spread before them, a wood burning stove gave off unnecessary additional heat and a neat-looking middle-aged lady in a floral apron pounded dough on a large table in the centre. But the most immediate sensation was the smell of bread baking in the stove. The aroma filled their senses and, despite their recent breakfast, managed to arouse their taste buds again.

Although Olive heard them say (unconvincingly) that they had eaten, she went right on and prepared scrambled eggs on toast with a mug of tea (which Rachel detested) for them both. As they filled to overflowing, Tom asked about the soldiers.

'What were they looking for? You must have heard the explosion, and nobody would have survived that.'

'Heard it …!' Harold replied, '… It damn near gave me a heart attack. But the soldiers won't be looking for survivors anymore. They want to find out what caused it. If it was sabotage, there will be hell to pay. Which brings us neatly back to you two urchins; you seemed mighty suspicious up there on the hill, and apart from the obvious question of what you are doing here, why would they be looking for you?'

Rachel and Tom looked at each other. Should they tell them their story? Could they trust them?

Olive had stopped pounding her dough again and was now

looking at the two of them. It was when she said it didn't matter if they wanted to keep their secret and asked if everything was all right that Tom became convinced he could trust them. He smiled at Rachel and said quietly, 'It will be fine. We need help.'

When Olive and Harold had heard their story, Olive threw down the towel she had started to clutch and rushed over to Rachel. Before Rachel could move, Olive had both of her arms around her; she lifted her from her seat and, squeezing her until she almost burst, cried out, 'You poor dear little thing, what has the world come to? How could anyone take a child away from their mother? You've been through so much, you poor child.' Tears were welling up in her eyes as she hung on to Rachel before finally depositing her back in the chair.

Harold looked knowingly at Tom who was taking the scene in quietly. 'You have a lot more years than your age, young man. Your parents will be proud of you.'

Tom felt embarrassed but said politely that his dad was away at sea and his mum and grandparents must be worried about why he hadn't returned last night, especially with all the commotion. Before long, it emerged that Harold knew Tom's dad, as did most people who were in any way connected with boats in the islands. Harold had helped his brother Monte many times with his ferry between Herm and Guernsey, and Monte came into frequent contact with all the harbour staff, including the pilot skipper.

In fact, Monte had called in earlier and left a large wooden box with them for safe keeping. Olive was curious about the contents, especially as water seemed to be dripping out of it onto her floor, but Monte had just fobbed her off, saying it contained spare parts for his ferry boat. He was due to pick it up later and she would be pleased when he did, as he had asked them to keep it tucked away, which was his code for out of sight from the German soldiers.

Eventually Harold, looking first at his wife then at the two young people, spoke about the way forward out of their dilemma. It was clear they had got this far with a great deal of courage and a degree of luck, but there was no plan for what to do next.

'Rachel, we must find a safe hiding place for you until we can get you away. The population in Guernsey is so low now that it would be too risky for you to attempt to integrate like a local - and in Herm it is even worse. Someone talking carelessly could jeopardize your freedom. For the time being you must stay with us in our attic bedroom, but you must be very careful, as the soldiers come here all the time to collect milk and eggs. Tom, you must get back home. Your mother will be beside herself with worry.'

They spoke for a while about how Tom could get away, but soon realized it could not be during daylight and as he had not arrived on the ferry, he could not return on it without raising questions. The soldiers monitored all passenger movements between the islands. So it was decided he would leave that night in *Fish*. In the meantime Harold would ask Monte to get a message to Tom's mother, simply letting her know that he was safe and would return that night.

Tom helped Rachel settle into the attic which she loved. It was a large room with the sloping walls of the roof decorated in flowery wallpaper. At one end was a gable window from which Rachel could look out over the entire north of the island. From here she could see the soldiers searching the area of the explosion and the expanse of sea across to the north of Guernsey. Also in the room was a skylight window that let the sunlight in, but this was too high up for her to see out of without standing on the bed directly below it. Once Olive had brought up and put on the bed linen, it was a wonderfully inviting bed, and even though Rachel had slept like a log on *Fish*, she was quite looking forward to tucking up under the clean white sheets. It was another world from the dirty mattress in the storeroom where she had slept in the Alderney camp. Harold had brought up a table and chair and Olive had even found some children's books left in a cupboard by their grandchildren, who had often stayed in this room. Having Rachel there reminded the couple of those happy times when the whole family was together at the farm.

When Monte called in for his regular cup of tea in the morning, Tom and Rachel were introduced. He was the double of Harold, although a few stone heavier and with permanent laugh lines etched into his face. In his bumbling way Monte tried to make jokes about their plight and, when he suggested that it might be fun to pretend to his mum that Tom had somehow sabotaged the patrol boat, Olive quickly became very agitated and insisted that he took this seriously. He was given precise instructions on what to say and what not to say, as Harold felt it was best if Tom told his family about Rachel when he was safely back at home. It was also decided that once he had done that, Harold would come over to speak to Daisy about Rachel.

After their talk, Monte left the farmhouse and disappeared into the cowshed. Olive and Harold looked furtively at each other and Olive muttered that Monte would end up in trouble if the Germans found out. Tom was keen to know what Monte was up to, but thought it was not his place to ask, so when Rachel said she was again going to look through the books and now also some clothes that Olive had found her, he slipped outside and made his way to the cowshed.

Carefully stepping between the cowpats that populated the yard, Tom entered the large shed and waited for a moment while his eyes adjusted to the light. He looked around, but there was no sign of Monte. One by one, Tom walked past each empty cow stall - the cows were still in the field - until he reached the far end. Still no sign of Monte.

Tom was puzzled. From the kitchen window he had definitely seen Monte enter the shed. Just then he heard a clunk followed by 'Damn it!' It was Monte's voice and it sounded like he had just dropped something, but where was he? Slowly walking towards the area which he thought was the source of the sound, Tom felt something fall upon his face. He looked up as a beam of sunlight shining through a crack in the door illuminated hundreds of dust particles and tiny pieces of straw that were slowly floating down towards him. Above was a mezzanine floor with a ladder that had been pulled up, clearly by Monte. Tom could now see his shape moving around, but still could not make out what he was doing. He didn't have to wait long to find out. Another clunk came from above, followed by the sound of something rolling. The rolling sound stopped and Tom saw a shape falling through the air towards him.

'Catch it!' Monte yelled as his face now peered over the edge. 'Go on, Tom, you can do it!'

Tom moved slightly backwards so he could get a better idea of what this thing was on its way down to him. It looked like a glass electrical valve. Cupping his hands together, Tom braced himself for the catch that every schoolboy cricketer dreamt of.

'How's that!' he shouted in triumph as his hands closed around the valve.

Monte congratulated him before sending down the ladder so that Tom could join him on the mezzanine. When his head emerged over the top, Tom could see a wooden box with all sorts of electrical components: wire, valves, a battery and a number of Bakelite switches.

'Wow! Is this what I think it is?' He smiled at Monte.

With a look of pride on his face, Monte smiled back and confirmed that he had collected all of the parts needed to build a radio transmitter, especially now that he had retrieved the vital crystal and some other parts still wet - from the wreckage of the patrol boat. Monte was on the scene instantly and had got away just a few short minutes before the Germans had arrived last night. He had even seen the shadow of *Fish* escaping, and was not totally surprised when he was introduced to the two young adventurers earlier that morning. But he now put on his most serious expression and spoke solemnly to Tom.

'You know of course that this is strictly forbidden by the Germans? You must keep this to yourself, Tom. Don't tell anyone, not even your friends.'

Tom agreed and asked if Monte knew how to put it all together. Pointing at a well-worn book lying next to the battery, Monte whispered in reverence, 'This little gem is all I need. *The Boy Electrician* is packed with information about radio. With its help, I will get it working in no time.' He patted the old book lovingly and was in full flow describing its fascinating contents when a voice came from below.

'Tom? Are you up there?' Harold called. 'Time is getting on and we will get some unwelcome visitors soon.'

Tom left Monte to it and, for the rest of the day, he and Rachel stayed out of sight in the attic. They talked at length about their likes, dislikes and lives. As they chatted, they became more aware of each other. Rachel had of course noticed that this older boy was nice-looking. He wore green corduroy trousers that had been cropped into shorts at the knee, a red woollen checked shirt and a pair of white plimsolls. He was thin, quite tall for his age, and to Rachel seemed very grown-up. Most importantly, he looked kind, and kindness was exactly what she needed right then. Tom had one of those faces that were wise before their years. His green eyes looked knowing as he listened to Rachel describing her family and her life in Germany. For his part, Rachel was of course much too young to be considered anything other than a little girl. But she was pretty, and he liked her company. He found her surprisingly easy to be with, as she would chat away about almost anything.

She did not linger long on the part of her story just before she left Germany: it was too upsetting. And as she changed the subject, her large deep brown eyes fixed upon his face. Now searching for the slightest clue to his reaction, she was describing the clothes that Olive had found for her. This was about the last thing in the world that interested Tom, but he was patient and felt relieved that she was relaxed and that, despite all she had been through, she actually sounded happy. He even managed to voice an opinion about whether the red frock or the blue one suited Rachel's hair colour the best. Needless to say, no opinion would be completely safe, but all Rachel really wanted was to talk with him, and if possible detect anything that could loosely be construed as a compliment.

They were again sitting around the kitchen table when the time came for Tom to go. They both sighed, and Rachel felt just a little flutter of panic. Would he make it home? Would he be able to come back to see her? And how long would she have to wait there?

Herm was beautiful and a sanctuary after the labour camp, but it was still unknown to her, and scary with the soldiers around. Besides, so much had been transient in her life recently, she feared this sudden good fortune might end and she would not see him again. As he walked away, tears began to form in her eyes.

Tom looked back and realized she was upset; he tried to reassure her but explained that although he would visit whenever he could, he didn't know how easy this would be: it all depended on the soldiers. He smiled at Rachel and left the farmhouse to walk back to *Fish*, accompanied by Harold.

'Monte was telling me the Germans are still active in the Russel. Apparently they found a piece of metal from the mine, so they have been sweeping the area in case there are any more. But, as darkness is starting to fall, they will be unlikely to continue, just in case. So you need to keep your eyes peeled as you leave the cover of the rocks on the northern shore of Herm. Your mum knows you will be on your way and chances are she will meet you when you tie up. Here, take this.'

Harold handed Tom one of Olive's old shopping bags and he peered inside to find thickly-cut cheese sandwiches, an apple and a small container with milk in it. As they left the path and made their way across the sand of Belvoir Bay, Tom thanked him and said he hoped they could all get together soon to discuss Rachel's fate.

Fish was secure in the cave where she had been left earlier that day. Just a day! It seemed as though a week had passed since he saw her. They dragged her down the cove and Tom jumped aboard as Harold gave a final push and waved him on his way.

A few minutes later Tom had raised the sails and darkness was falling all around him. The diminishing crescent moon still allowed the hint of a glow as opposed to a light, but this was all Tom needed as he navigated between the rocks off Herm's coast. As he left the cover of the last potential hiding place, and made his way out into the open channel of the Russel, he could see that all the Germans boats had returned to port.

Settling down to a perfect night-time sail and his excellent sandwiches, Tom felt a mixture of pleasure to be returning home, and sadness that he was leaving Rachel without knowing when he would get back. He felt a brotherly responsibility towards her and his young chest was still full of pride about the way he had rescued her from the German labour camp. He knew his dad would be proud of him and surely his mum and grandparents would be too, when they got over the initial shock and concern about the danger he was in.

North of Guernsey now, Tom began his navigation between the rocks towards a secret mooring where *Fish* was hidden from view. First, skirting around the north of Platte Fougère rock and through the rocks known locally as the Brayes, then a smaller separate group, before coming to an outcrop reaching offshore from the eastern side of L'Ancresse bay.

His final approach to Guernsey was shielded by a high walled sixteenth century fort that stood prominently on the headland. Fort Le Marchant was now in disrepair and so even the Germans were cautious about using its commanding position as a lookout point. This created an essential blind spot for Tom, blinkering anyone looking out to sea.

Beneath the fort, a large rock shaped like a smiling face further masked the outcrop that Tom followed into the gully where he moored *Fish*. Inland on the common was Bunker Hill, one of the few high spots on an otherwise low-level landscape, with a small row of cottages perched on the top. Set apart from the other cottages and to the east was the isolated home of Daisy and John Le Breton.

There was some uncertainty in Tom's mind about what the

enemy soldiers had declared he was and was not allowed to do. Since the occupation began, the Germans had first banned the use of small boats for fishing, and then they allowed it, but only within a mile of the shore. Then they insisted that fishermen were accompanied by one of their soldiers. Refusing to be restricted, Tom ignored these rules, just as his family ignored the strict blackout by leaving on a muted kitchen light to give him a leading mark for home.

Tom now steered for this light and following the outcrop towards the shore, entered a narrow channel leading into a secluded gully. The entrance to the gully was only visible once inside the narrow channel.

A crude iron spike rammed between the rocks had been sufficient to hold many small fishing boats safe in the gully over the years. Tom lashed his mooring lines to this, wedging *Fish* securely between the pink granite rocks. The locals were familiar with these iron spikes and knew their value to fishermen, but to non-seafaring German troops they were more like relics of some previous construction that had long since lost its significance.

With *Fish* secured and sails stowed, Tom gathered what remained of his catch in the bucket and set off across the rocks towards the common. He had not travelled far before he came across his anxious mother waiting on the headland.

'Tom dear, thank goodness. You must be exhausted. I got the message. Are you all right?'

Tom reassured his mother that all was well, and that his enforced expedition was simply his way of putting safety first and keeping out of the way of the soldiers. Of course his mother knew this was an understatement, but she was in no mood to chastise her son and wanted only to hold him close and celebrate his safe return. The two of them strolled across the common towards the yellow guiding light of 'Houmet Cottage' and the warm welcome of home.

Tom did not mention Rachel at first. He waited until his mother and grandparents had fussed enough and had accepted that there appeared to be no immediate danger. The dilated pupils of the women's eyes were beginning to diminish and grandfather was no longer attempting to relight his empty pipe, so Tom thought it safe to expand upon his adventure.

At first he tried to play it down, until he realized that his exploits were never going to sound mundane. So he went for it, with all the details and emotions he felt necessary to convey the experience he and this little girl had endured.

In an occupied community, there would inevitably be those who would attempt to create normality with their invaders or even exploit the opportunities that might arise. If this was so in Guernsey, these people were not in the circles known to Daisy and her kin. For them, like the majority of islanders, the occupation was to be endured and however pleasant individual Germans might be, they were still the occupying force. The Le Breton family did not fall into panic when they learned of Tom's dangerous expedition; on the contrary, they were immediately proud of him and praised his courage. Daisy wanted to know all about the young Rachel, about her background, her experience in the labour camp, and most of all, about her current situation with Harold and Olive. Like any mother, she was concerned that there was a connection back to Tom in the event of her capture, but she forced herself to ignore this fear and focus unselfishly upon Rachel's plight. Tom was sensitive enough to appreciate this and was equally proud of his mother.

Now safely at home, Tom yawned with the release of concentration that had been so necessary over the past twenty-four hours. Knowing his family were now around him and he was out of danger back at home, his body suddenly reclaimed its right to sleep and he could barely keep his eyes open as Mum, Grandma and Grandpa studied him intently – just to double check there was no permanent damage.

They all agreed that the morning would be a better time to discuss the situation, and the tiny kitchen emptied as they found their bedrooms.

Outside on the common, a pair of eyes watched, as the yellow square of light in the Le Breton windows was extinguished.

CHAPTER FIVE

Rachel awoke to the sound of cows demanding attention as they meandered into the milking stalls of the cowshed. She rubbed her eyes and stood up on her bed to peer out of the skylight window. It was a beautiful day with clear blue skies; the sun beamed high over the horizon. She could see down to the beach, which was now deserted, and across to Guernsey. Somewhere over there, she thought, Tom will now be with his family. She wondered when he would return and what they would be saying about her. Would his family resent her for the risk that Tom had taken in rescuing her?

Then, as her attention moved further north to the faraway island of Alderney, Rachel felt a chill come over her. She remembered how the soldiers had taunted her and was experiencing a mixture of relief to be away and fear they might come after her, when the sound of footsteps outside her door announced the arrival of Olive.

The door inched open as Olive's smiling face appeared around it. 'Oh, you are awake, dear. Are you ready for some breakfast?'

Twelve-year-old girls are often in between two stages of maturity and Rachel was no exception. Sometimes her mood was that of a teenager wanting to be taken seriously, sometimes a little girl just needing a cuddle. When Rachel was tired, early or late in the day, the 'grown-up' teenager was not quite robust enough to subdue the more open child. Rachel bounced off the bed and darted across the room to Olive who, now waiting with open arms, needed no persuasion to accommodate a much needed loving cuddle.

When asked if she was feeling all right, Rachel explained that she had felt a little frightened at the thought of the soldiers on Alderney. Olive listened attentively and reassured her that there were no signs whatsoever that the soldiers were looking for anyone, no unusual activity in the Russel, no extra troops searching Herm and from what she had heard, Guernsey seemed relatively quiet, despite the recent loss of the patrol boat.

Downstairs, Harold, Olive and Rachel sat around the kitchen table and set about another of Olive's hearty breakfasts. Despite the rations, there was always plenty on the farmhouse table. At least, plenty of eggs and milk and home-made bread. Fortunately, Harold possessed a unique early warning system; she was called Myrtle. Myrtle was a vociferous Guernsey cow that was convinced every human was capable of milking her. All Harold needed to do was to leave Myrtle in the yard outside the farmhouse door and she would announce any visitors loudly.

The three of them could therefore start each day with relaxed conversation before the delicate task of deciding how to occupy Rachel without endangering her.

Rachel loved Herm and quickly adopted Harold and Olive as substitute parents, although she forced herself to feel guilty if too many hours passed without thinking of her real mama and papa.

Within the first week Monte had set up a meeting between the grown-ups, comprising Harold and Monte, Daisy and Grandpa John. The topic of conversation was of course Rachel. The meeting had been on the White Rock, St Peter Port's main quay and an easy place for the subterfuge of loading Monte's ferry boat. When the provisions were aboard, the group leaned upon the sea wall looking out into the Russel and deliberated upon the safest strategy.

Clearly the best place for the time being was on Herm, but they all recognized that a young girl would soon get bored on such a tiny island without any friends of her own age to keep her company. They asked each other if anyone knew people who could make contact with England. Nobody did, and with a few disappointed 'ums', they fell silent. Harold, Daisy and John were lost in thought as Monte began to study Daisy and John's faces. He was clearly struggling with something when Harold looked up and caught him by surprise.

'What is it?'

They all now looked at Monte and he returned a significant,

questioning expression to Harold, who simply repeated, 'What?'

Monte was now acutely embarrassed and decided he had no option but to tell them what was on his mind.

'Well, this is of course top secret, but I have all the parts to make a radio. We could use that to contact England. Young Tom knows about it, but I asked him not to mention it to anyone.'

Still absorbing what had been said, Daisy and John turned to Harold as he replied, 'Brother, I know you are a dab hand at this electrical stuff, but can you really get that box of bits going? And if you did, we can't just broadcast to England, the Germans will be monitoring. They would find out about her and track her down. They can pinpoint exactly where transmitters are located, can't they?'

Monte confirmed that they could do something called 'triangulation', but it took time to set up, so messages needed to be short and you had to move around to different locations to transmit. This, of course, presented its own dangers, as the paraphernalia of radio equipment and batteries was not compact enough to be easily concealed. Especially the somewhat 'Heath Robinson' set up that Monte would put together.

But assuming they could find a way to do this, who would they call and what message could they give, bearing in mind the whole world could be listening?

At this point a group of German soldiers further along the quay began to take an interest in the group and walked towards them purposefully.

A hasty agreement was reached that the conversation would stop and they would all give some thought to the problems and meet again as soon as they could without raising suspicion.

The soldiers seemed satisfied as the group dispersed with Daisy and John taking to their bicycles and pedalling off down the White Rock, whilst Monte and Harold descended the thick wooden ladder to Monte's ferry boat *Capwood*. As *Capwood* was cast off and pulled away from the quayside, Monte opened the cavernous locker where he stored his mooring warps.

Gazing in, the answer to one of their dilemmas dawned upon him.

***

As Daisy and John freewheeled the last yards downhill across the common for home, Tom opened the cottage front door and stepped out to meet them, followed closely by Molly.

Wheeling their bicycles into a lean-to attached to the cottage, Daisy addressed them first. 'It all went very well and Rachel is fine. Olive and Harold are happy to keep her with them for now. You were right, Tom; they are very nice people and it is brave of them to risk taking her in. We don't think it is safe to move her to Guernsey, at least not yet, and although we all agreed it would be best to get her away to the mainland, we don't know how we can safely make contact. That's about it, isn't it, Dad?'

John added just one comment. 'Monte mentioned the radio, Tom, but we can't use it without knowing what we are doing, so for now, it's no use to us.'

Tom and Molly considered what had been said. It was an anti-climax but they understood that Rachel's, and everyone's, safety must come first.

'Can I go and see her?' Tom ventured.

Molly took a deep intake of breath and was about to speak, shaking her head as she did so, when John cut in. 'Let's see if we can get the Germans to agree to you working on Harold's farm. The school is out next week for summer and we could argue it will help the Jerries with their supplies if you do a bit for Harold, and maybe even help Monte occasionally. Otherwise, it will be too dangerous during daylight hours.'

Tom knew that Grandpa was giving him the unofficial okay to go at night, but he would need to be careful, and it would all be much safer if the Germans agreed to him working there.

Daisy looked at her son and then at John, who smiled

reassuringly at her and reached out to squeeze her arm before disappearing inside. All this subterfuge went over Molly's head as she followed her husband indoors, believing they had agreed that Tom would wait for the Germans to give permission.

That evening, under the auspices of another fishing trip, Tom set out across the common towards *Fish*'s secret mooring, unaware that his every movement was being monitored.

*****

Harold and Monte arrived back at the tiny harbour of Herm and once *Capwood* was tied up, unloaded the various supplies they had collected onto the quayside. Monte found the old wooden handcart next to two German soldiers who were leaning lazily against a wall. They loaded the cart and pushed it off the quay and towards German headquarters at the White House Hotel. Most of the provisions were unloaded here, but the remainder were for use at the farm, and the two were soon on their way up the hill with the privacy to talk more openly on the quiet and deserted track home.

Monte had mentioned his idea that the locker on *Capwood* would be perfect to conceal a radio on the way over to Herm. Discussing it now in more detail, they both recognized that this was the answer, as *Capwood* could move around to different locations and they wouldn't need to manhandle the radio from place to place. Monte suggested he could construct a false bottom for the locker to make it shallower, with the radio underneath. The mooring ropes could still fit in a shallower locker and if anything they would be easier to reach.

'We can even use the flagstaff mast on the wheelhouse roof for the aerial,' Monte enthused. 'When we have dropped this lot off, I will have a go at finishing putting the radio together.'

When they reached the farm and unloaded the animal feed into a small barn, Harold took some kitchen supplies into Olive, whilst Monte disappeared into the cowshed and up onto the mezzanine. With the supplies put away in the larder, Harold sat at the kitchen table and spoke as Rachel and Olive listened attentively to every detail of the White Rock meeting. When he had explained carefully that they would need some time to consider the safest way forward, he turned to Rachel and smiled sympathetically.

'And so you see, my dear, we have to make sure you are completely safe before we do anything, and that might mean you will have to stay here with us for a while. It may be a little boring I'm afraid, but apart from the farmhouse, you should stay in the small kitchen garden unless you speak first with us. We will do what we can to keep you from getting bored, but you must be patient.'

Rachel thanked them for looking after her and assured them that her situation was infinitely better than it had been when she was at the camp. She would be patient and try not to get under their feet.

Olive was amazed at how mature this little girl could be sometimes. Perhaps it was her upbringing or the experiences she had been forced to endure, but most children would have complained bitterly about having their movements so restricted.

The day passed without much happening, apart from the occasional curse and even a loud bang coming from the mezzanine. It was early evening when Monte returned with a large grin on his face. He beckoned all of them to come with him, but Olive insisted that Harold alone should go.

Up on the mezzanine, Monte had laid out the contraption across a makeshift table.

'This won't be the final layout...' he hastened to report. '...When we get it onto *Capwood*, it will fit easily into the locker.' He switched on a black toggle switch and went on to explain what all the parts did, as the loose collection of parts joined up by various wires warmed up. After a few minutes the valves were glowing brightly. 'Now listen to this.'

He turned a large Bakelite knob and noises emerged from a

five-inch speaker that was hanging by a piece of string from the table. At first a whistling noise, then as Harold inspected the wire aerial reaching for the roof beams, a voice rang out as clearly as a bell. 'This is London calling. London calling. Here is the seven o'clock news from the BBC and this is Alvar Lidell reading it....'

Harold was very impressed with his brother. He smiled a proud smile and patted Monte on his back as Monte turned down the volume control. 'Well done, old chap, you've excelled yourself this time.'

Even at this age Monte was deeply moved by his older brother's praise and his chest filled as Harold went on. 'This is the microphone?' he asked, pointing at a large metal stork covered in a mesh with a switch at its base. 'If I were to press this, would it transmit?'

'Oh, yes,' replied Monte. 'If you were to press that switch we could transmit from here to the south coast of England. The trouble is, we would also be heard very loud and clear in Guernsey and all over Normandy if anyone tuned in to our frequency. We must be very cautious about pressing that switch, and when we use the radio at all we should wear these.' Monte picked up a pair of headphones next to the microphone. He untwisted one of the wires leading to the speaker and gestured to Harold to put the headphones on.

The BBC was now confined to the insides of the headphones and Monte's ears noticed the quiet night again as Harold was engrossed with the news from England and the long list of 'messages' that followed. Although excited about the success of his electrical construction, Monte was also very aware of the risk that the Germans might discover it. His senses were subconsciously as tuned in as the radio, scanning the quiet outside, to distinguish between the usual night sounds of wildlife scurrying and cattle shuffling from the voices of German soldiers or the footsteps of their jackboots.

The noise from below in the cowshed was therefore disproportionately loud when it came. First a thud, as if someone had walked into a beam, then the unmistakable sound of a milking bucket kicked over. He froze and instinctively looked at his brother still immersed in the news from London. Should he try to warn him? Perhaps he should simply switch off the radio, but then Harold would surely break the silence and speak, revealing their position to whoever was below.

As his heart began to race, a whispering voice floated up from below. 'Hello up there. Is that you, Monte?' Monte peered over the edge to confirm that the voice was indeed that of Tom and not a trap laid by the Germans. 'It's Tom. Are you up there? How is it going?'

Monte exhaled for the first time since he heard the noises below. A strained and worried look gave way to his usual jocular expression as he welcomed Tom.

Tom was invited up onto the mezzanine to witness the progress Monte had made with his radio. Having been impressed that it would receive, Tom could only take it on trust that the transmit mode also functioned; it was far too risky to transmit without a clear purpose. So a test was out of the question.

The remaining light of a summer's evening softened the outline of the farmhouse when he made his way across the yard to visit Rachel. She was delighted to see him and insisted on telling him absolutely everything that had happened to her since their last meeting, in the minutest of detail.

Tom explained that he would try to get a job on the farm so he could visit her more often, but the Germans would have to agree.

***

The Germans did agree, as John had predicted. They saw only the benefits of a helper on the farm. A helping hand on *Capwood* was also acceptable; of course, the soldiers had no reason to be suspicious of his motives.

The remaining summer of 1941 was idyllic for Rachel. Tom visited daily, and as there were so few soldiers on Herm, it was easy to keep track of them. There were major defensive constructions on Guernsey that stretched most of the available occupying forces, supervising slave labour or supplies. A certain complacency set in and the two youngsters were given permission to go down to the beach at Belvoir Bay, as long as Monte or Harold could spare the time to keep watch.

Rachel loved to sit in the surf and giggle uncontrollably as the waves rolled in over her. Tom liked it best when the tide was far in, as the beach sloped steeply and he could dive into the waves from the shore. The two talked incessantly and their friendship grew.

Olive always ensured there was a picnic lunch for them to take with them, so their dream world was hardly interrupted by the adult population at all. Hardly but sadly not completely. It was on Monte's watch one warm Thursday morning - when the soldiers should all have been accounted for - that the incident happened.

A young German corporal nicknamed Spike - in reference to his particularly severe haircut - was on duty near Herm harbour when a group of senior officers arrived by ferry. As they passed Spike, one of them asked what was on the menu for lunch. Spike explained that although the White House was normally a hotel, as it had now been commandeered to be military HQ on Herm, the menu was no longer much different from that in the barracks.

This answer did not go down well with the top brass, who had been led to believe that bass was an almost daily item on the Herm menu.

Spike was duly dispatched with rod in hand to catch lunch from the Shell Beach, known to be a fruitful spot for bass. Being a resourceful type, he decided the walk to Shell Beach was unnecessary energy expenditure, and instead opted for a small sailing dinghy beached in the harbour. Once his bag was full with sand eels for bait, courtesy of his fellow soldiers, he pushed off and headed away from the harbour towards the south of the island. Of course, Monte saw all of this from his vantage point above, but being out of earshot, could not have figured that Spike would follow the channel round the south coast cliffs and head up the other side of Herm towards Shell Beach, Belvoir being directly en route.

The soldier was enjoying a stunning summer's day as he crept up the east coast of Herm. Puffins were diving in and out of the water as he passed Selle Rocque and the sea was so transparent, he was already anticipating a fine catch to justify this excursion. The east coast of Herm has a number of tiny islands just offshore and Spike decided to cut inside these close to the shore, as the tide was high and the wind directly behind him.

As he passed between Herm and an interestingly named island called Caquorobert, Belvoir beach opened before him. Expecting a solitary journey to Shell Beach, Spike was surprised to find two children engrossed in a mixture of conversation and splashing, oblivious of his presence.

Recognising Tom from his ferry duties, he called out to them and steered the dinghy closer to be within earshot. 'So this is what you do when you are supposed to be working, Tom!'

Tom and Rachel span around in unison and froze when they saw the small boat approaching with a German soldier on board. Rachel let out a small cry and asked Tom what they should do. Should they run?

Tom had spoken with Spike before and he certainly did not look threatening, sailing along in a dinghy. In fact he was smiling at them. Before they could decide how to react, he spoke again. 'Don't worry; your secret is safe with me.'

Rachel's sense of panic increased.

'I tell you what, you point me towards the best spot for some bass, and I won't say anything about your girlfriend to Monte!'

Their faces flushed with embarrassment as Tom muttered, 'Surely he doesn't think we are like that? He must see you are too young for boyfriends.'

The atmosphere on that beach was a cauldron of emotions. Fear of discovery, relief that he hadn't seemed to work out the significance of Rachel, feelings between the two of them unspoken but never far from the surface, indecision about what to do next. As they worked through this chemistry, Spike's expression seemed to be changing. He was thinking about them. His gaze fell upon Rachel. Tom looked at her too. Her features were not typical of the other children in the islands, and there was something about her dark hair and eyes. He looked back at Spike and decided the situation needed to be defused as quickly as possible.

'Well, okay, Spike, but please don't say anything to anyone. It will only get back to Monte and you know how he will tease me. You need to go to the north end of the beach at Alderney Point, but be careful as there will be quite a stream at high water. Oh, and fish into the wind. What bait have you got?'

Spike was easily diverted from his growing curiosity and was pleased to get the local knowledge for his expedition. His mind was now focused upon catching lunch for the officers and when his reply to Tom that he had sand eels for bait was greeted with approval, he simply thanked him and waved an offhand goodbye before setting the tiller for Shell Beach.

As the small craft sped away, Rachel considered how she should respond to Tom's comment about her being too young for boyfriends. She deeply wanted to correct him, but given the gravity of what they had just been through, decided to choose a better moment.

'That was close.' She tried to open a less emotional dialogue. 'Do you think he will tell anybody?'

Tom replied with slight concern that he didn't know. He thought probably not, because for Spike there was really nothing to report - they were just two young people messing around on a beach. Why would he suspect anything?

Conversation was not exactly stilted, but there was now something in the air between them. Something unresolved, that they knew they could not discuss, and it wasn't about the fact they had been seen.

CHAPTER SIX

'I understand what you are saying, Hans, but your concern for the child has clouded your judgement. This issue is not her loss, although that is of course sad.' Helmut added this last comment so as not to appear completely heartless to his son. 'The issue that we must face is, have we done enough to secure our shares in the business?'

Helmut's younger son Freddy listened attentively to his father, and then spoke deliberately. 'If my understanding is correct, Father, the Jewess got you to sign a paper that transferred her shares to you, but stated that a condition of the transfer was that the girl would be looked after.'

'Yes, that's right, Freddy, but it also stated she must not go to a camp. If at some time in the future there is a dispute over the legality of our shares, I don't want some lawyer taking our business away from us. We sent her there for her own safety, but taking a simple view, they might say we broke the agreement as the girl was sent to a camp and died.'

Freddy thought for a moment before he spoke again.

'But you say there is only one copy of this transfer form, so who will ever know? And if it is such a problem, why don't we just forge a new transfer slip without her stupid conditions on it? We have a good copy of her signature to work with.'

Hans looked disbelievingly at his younger brother. Had he really been so indoctrinated that he had lost all of his compassion for these poor people? He felt as if he was not just from a different family but from a different species.

Helmut explained that, whilst forgery was always an option, it was a last resort because it might just be discovered. The question was bound to be asked why this woman had transferred her most valuable possession to a German officer. In any case, it might not come to that, if they could establish that the girl had simply had an accident. As for her presence in the camp, it could be seen as a matter of record that she was not technically listed as an inmate, merely a kitchen worker. They must simply ensure that the death was listed as accidental.

'Hans, you are no longer posted to Alderney and you must go wherever the Reich needs you, but Freddy, whilst you remain in the youth movement, I can pull some strings to get you a temporary assignment out there. I will say you may be joining SS military intelligence and the experience will be good for you and the Reich. When you get there, you must find out as much as you can and speak with the officials. I don't know if it will be a local coroner's inquest or if the military will pronounce the cause of death, but you must find out and ensure the right verdict is given. Presumably we know she is dead. She couldn't have survived, could she?'

This question was directed at Hans, who shrugged his shoulders and replied, 'Father, I was sent off the island the next day, so I don't even know if a body was found. There was an uproar going on because one of our patrol boats hit a mine the night before, so nobody was interested in what had happened to her. All I know is that I got a report that she was missing that morning and presumed drowned as her shoe was found in a rock at the water's edge.'

And so Freddy's long journey across France by train was organized. As he passed through this large and varied country, he began to realize the might of the empire to which he owed his allegiance. The Reich was truly immense; in his mind only the Roman Empire came close to comparison by size or sheer splendour of organization. This was by far the longest journey he had undertaken and he felt privileged to be doing it in the uniform of a loyal German, an Aryan.

As the succession of trains rhythmically pulsed along their tracks, emitting a wonderful smell of steam from their coal-fired engines, Freddy felt cocooned in the dream world of the carriage. Sometimes he slept with his head slipping from the seat cushion to the cool window; sometimes he just dozed, viewing the passing world through half-closed eyes. The variety of passengers either intrigued him - if they were German soldiers - or irritated him, if they were French.

He used the hours that slowly passed to consider his strategy on arrival. His father had given him papers and orders to explain his presence in the islands. He was to make enquiries about the disappearance of the Jewish girl and report back. He should be assisted, but was not required to give further information. This would be sufficient to convince the locally based military that he was just on another SS witch hunt for Jews, and they would not be suspicious. Freddy decided he should try to keep a low profile and request that his mission should be kept from the local population, just in case she had survived and was in hiding somewhere. He hoped this wasn't the case, as he could return more quickly if there was a body to prove accidental death, but he knew he would not be popular if he got it wrong.

The final leg of the train journey rumbled to a close in the early hours of a wet Cherbourg morning. One of only a handful of passengers, he disembarked with his small suitcase carrying the civilian clothes that might sometimes allow him to mingle amongst the locals, plus a spare Hitler Youth uniform. Fortunately he could both speak and understand English, but his accent was a giveaway. He rubbed his eyes and started for the station exit, showing his ticket to the disinterested official as he left.

The harbour was not difficult to find and there was no shortage of German craft moored there. Even at this early hour it was a hive of activity. Gunboats were being loaded with munitions, cranes swung bulging cargo nets over the holds of supply vessels, and weary troops lined up patiently on the quayside. Freddy approached the nearest supply ship and was about to look over into the hold when an irate officer barked at him, 'What are you doing? Don't you know that this area is off-limits?'

Somewhat intimidated by the rugged looks and high-ranking uniform of this naval commander, Freddy offered his papers and explained that his orders were to get to Alderney. Taking the papers and reading them, he looked at Freddy and his tone altered.

'We do not run a ferry service for the SS. You people spend so much of your time on these fool's errands it's a wonder we are winning this war at all. Go down the forward gangway and present yourself to the captain. Tell him I sent you and keep out of the way.'

Once on the bridge and with explanations over, the captain advised him that they would leave within the hour at high tide, and Freddy was welcome to join them on the bridge for the short journey to Braye Harbour in Alderney.

Short the journey may have been - in fact just a few hours – but, for Freddy, it was one of the worst experiences he had endured.

Not long after establishing himself in a corner of the bridge, he had decided to relax by reading one of the Führer's latest 'insight' publications. Oblivious to the raised eyebrows and grinning faces of the crew, Freddy was studying the text intently when the ship left its berth. He also hadn't noticed that the earlier light rain had turned into a downpour.

Out at sea they found themselves ploughing into fifteen-foot waves against a southwesterly headwind. The crew smiled at each other as Freddy looked up in panic when a particularly large wave hit them. This stretch of water was notorious in these conditions, and they knew that his attention to Hitler's propaganda would soon result in seasickness.

'It's best to keep your eyes on the horizon,' they gibed, knowing it was already too late. And when he eventually stumbled out onto the deck to empty what little contents were in his stomach, their true feelings about the SS became apparent. Although Freddy was still too young to be part of it, it was common knowledge that the youth movement was the ideal training ground for potential SS recruits. Many soldiers, especially in the Navy and Luftwaffe, were uncomfortable with the tactics of Hitler's so-called 'elite'.

When the ship finally came alongside the quay at Braye Harbour, Freddy was as white as a sheet and angry at the lack of sympathy from his compatriots. He left with a grunt of thanks and walked towards the hotel where he was to be billeted whilst on Alderney. By now the sky had cleared and the morning sun was beaming down on the picturesque island. Picturesque, that is, apart from the dozens of soldiers and vehicles that were scurrying around the harbour and the hill that led up to the town of St Anne's.

His hotel room was small but comfortable and the window overlooked the bustling High Street. Once unpacked, Freddy pulled off his shoes and lay on his back on the single bed in the centre of the room. There was enough room to walk around the bed, and a seat by the window would serve well if he needed to relax in the evenings. Freddy did not think of himself as a mean-spirited person, but he was convinced that the rest of the world should bow to German dominance and recognize the superiority of the Aryan race. As he lay on his back, he reflected on Hitler's book and contemplated how the Jews were responsible for all of the social evils that had beset his country, and how right it was that they should be kicked out along with gypsies and other spongers.

When he eventually visited the slave labour camp, he was therefore unmoved by the plight of the inmates or by their emaciation. His visit took place in the afternoon of the day he arrived. Having rested for a while and recovered from his journey, he washed and changed into a fresh Hitler Youth uniform. Downstairs he was in time for lunch, and welcomed the potato omelette he was served. He left the hotel and found the office of the German administration on the island, a short walk further up the High Street.

His papers scrutinized and his orders understood, he was assigned a young corporal with a motorcycle and sidecar. Pieter was not much older than him and was curious as to why the Hitler Youth would be involved with an SS assignment. But he knew better than to question the hierarchy and kept conversation to a polite and friendly minimum. He was to take Freddy to the camp and wait outside for him to return.

75

Pieter enjoyed speeding along the unkempt Alderney roads, especially once they were out of St Anne's. He opened up the noisy machine as Freddy's knuckles tightened their grip on the sidecar. Approaching the perimeter fence of the camp, Freddy could have noticed the gaunt faces looking out at him or the cloud of dust surrounding and choking the quarry workers labouring to extract granite for the construction of coastal defences. He didn't; he only noticed the tidy-looking barracks where the soldiers hurried in and out, preoccupied with the papers they carried, or deep in conversation about the organization of their slaves.

Pieter handed the guard at the gatehouse a note, and the two of them were admitted. Another guard was summoned and they were led to one of the prefabricated offices they had been watching. This office was raised slightly and steps led up to a wooden terrace adorned by plant pots. Totally incongruous in the surroundings, the hut could have been at home in a holiday camp. Inside, Freddy was led to a room where the officer in charge of security sat at a desk. Pieter waited outside.

The conversation was stilted. The officer was clearly unhappy about the interference in 'his' camp and did not care for the implied suggestion that security might be lax. Freddy was not fazed; he hadn't come all this way to be stonewalled, and his father had told him the investigation might be resented. But it was not sensible to alienate this man. After all, the true purpose of this investigation was nothing to do with security; they just needed to know if the girl was dead or alive.

'So your guard first realized she was missing around midnight when she would usually have been asleep in the store room?'

'That's right, but you need to understand that night was very busy; a patrol boat hit a mine off Herm and we were instructed to check the coast for enemy minelayers or further mines. The guard reported she was not there when he went to the kitchen storeroom, but we didn't know where she was and frankly, we had more important things on our minds. She had a watcher, you know; your namesake, actually. He had brought her here and was soft, so he made sure she had an easy time. But you can't speak to him; he has been transferred now.'

Stein was a common name, and fortunately Freddy did not look like his older brother Hans, and his attitude was so different the officer did not even consider there may be any family connection.

'So those of us not guarding the workers were all out on watch, and it was only in the morning we realized she still hadn't turned up. But why the interest? Jewish kids are not exactly our top priority and accidents happen, don't they?'

'So you are sure it was an accident?' Freddy sidestepped the question.

'Look, when we got around to looking for her, we found a rag the kid had used for a scarf near the beach. So we looked on the beach and rocks and found one of her shoes stuck in a rock near the high-water mark. It looked like she had got it stuck and gone in. I don't know, but maybe she hit her head and was washed out to sea, drowned in any case. I don't see what else it could have been; a kid like that couldn't have escaped and if she went in, that would be it.'

'But no body has been washed up. If she had fallen in, which way would the tide have taken her?'

'That's easy; Alderney has one of the strongest tidal streams in the world. We talked about this with the local and Guernsey police afterwards. It depends when she went in, but most likely she would have gone south, if she went in that night before midnight. They thought that this was likely as otherwise she would have been back by then. So that would be towards Guernsey, Herm or possibly Sark; otherwise if it was much later, north and out into the Channel.'

Freddy thanked him for his help; he could see no advantage in taking this further. Before leaving, he asked for the name of the local policeman who had investigated and, when outside again, he asked Pieter to take him there next.

***

Alfred had been the sole policeman on Alderney for many years and found these times most distressing. There were hardly any locals living on the island since the occupation and whatever was happening at the camp, it very much upset him to see the state of the labourers. Nevertheless, he tried to conduct the few minor official tasks that weren't taken over by the military as efficiently and professionally as possible.

When the young man from the Hitler Youth movement entered his tiny office and showed his credentials, the hairs on Alfred's neck bristled. What on earth was a young man like this doing on SS business? Freddy asked his questions and Alfred answered those he could, but nothing new was emerging and it was clear that Alfred was of the same opinion as the officer: she must have drowned. Asking if that would be on the official report, Freddy was reassured to hear that both the local coroner and the German military would be likely to conclude 'Accidental Death'. However, in these cases they would often wait for a few weeks, just in case the body was washed up and it could be confirmed. After that, the time in the water would finish with the evidence.

That night Freddy was feeling good; his first day had seemed to accomplish all that he had hoped for. He enjoyed a seafood meal in the hotel restaurant and went to his room for a quiet read in the armchair. Looking out of his window, the street below was filling with German soldiers and off-duty guards from the camp frequenting the two pubs either side of his hotel.

He slept well and in the morning decided to risk another boat trip. This time to Guernsey, Herm and Sark. He was sure his father would not be satisfied unless every stone had been turned. He also felt it would look bad to go back after just half a day.

He wore civilian clothes, but they did nothing to hide his obviously Aryan features. Freddy was quite tall and blonde. He had never really done any physical work and carried a hint of

78

puppy fat around his face and his waist. This, along with a sprinkling of embarrassing freckles, ensured he would not be mistaken for someone older.

Much to his surprise the sea was kind to him, and the patrol boat that dropped Freddy in Guernsey sped across the twenty-three miles without seeming to hit any waves.

Guernsey's St Peter Port harbour was glorious. He had been told it was a stunning harbour but was still not prepared for the sight as his boat slowed in its final approach between the White Rock and Castle Cornet. The backdrop to the harbour was a myriad of colourful houses perched upon the hill that rose behind St Peter Port and the lush cliffs slightly to the south that added a large splash of greenery. With the sun on his back and an altogether more pleasant crew for company than his last trip, things were looking up for Freddy.

All that was needed now was some routine enquiries and he could be on his way back to German soil, mission accomplished.

Spike was indulging in his second mug of tea when the curious young German entered the White Rock Café. There were few seats available and as Spike's friends had settled for one mug, the seat opposite him was vacant. Freddy sat down and scrutinized the menu.

'The English and their breakfasts!' he remarked to Spike. 'Bacon and eggs with sausages - it's like a main meal.'

Spike was uneasy about this young man; something told him to be wary. There was a certain arrogance about him; with just a few words between them he sensed this was someone who thought he had authority. He was also young, young and not in uniform. Something a little odd here in occupied Guernsey.

'Try ordering it. All they have is eggs. You just arrived?' The arrogance was soon confirmed.

'I am here on an important mission to find out about a missing person. Perhaps you can help me. I will just get some food.'

As Freddy ordered his breakfast, Spike decided to forego the second mug and left the café.

During the course of the day, Freddy visited the local police station and military headquarters. There was some surprise about why this young person had travelled all the way across Europe to ask questions about a Jewish girl who seemingly had simply had an unfortunate accident, but they cooperated and answered his questions. No body had been found, and the tide that night would have brought the child past the rest of the Channel Islands. The local police even arranged for Freddy to meet with the harbour master. His knowledge of the waters around Guernsey was second to none.

As Freddy walked along the quayside towards the harbour master's office, he noticed a launch being loaded with cargo by a local man, assisted by a boy. In the bows of the launch he spotted Spike, and was about to walk on past when Spike saw him and called up, 'Did you find your missing person, then?'

Unsure of the sincerity of the question, he replied, 'No. It looks as though the little girl was drowned.'

Monte momentarily froze; he stared straight into Tom's wide eyes as the conversation continued. Spike had taken more of an interest now that he learned it was a child.

'That is too bad; I have a child of my own. I didn't realize earlier that you were looking for a child. I'm sorry I sloped off, is... was the child family?'

'Good heavens, no. It was only a Jewish girl from the camp in Alderney, but we need to be sure what happened.'

Spike looked up at Freddy, not quite sure how to react. He knew there were elements of the Reich whose morality seemed to have been totally removed, but he was not prepared for such callous words to come from one so young.

'Anyway, I must go and speak with the harbour master to find out about the tides. It is just possible the kid was washed up here or on the other islands, one way or another.' There was a smile on his face as he spoke the last words. Spike could feel his blood rising but thought better of a confrontation; instead, he returned his attention to the two loading the launch as Freddy walked on.

Watching Tom now, an image came to Spike's mind. Tom on the beach at Belvoir in Herm with a young girl. Now that he thought about it, the girl had not looked like a local, and why hadn't he seen her before?

Tom looked at Spike and as their eyes connected, something passed unsaid between them. Tom was willing Spike not to remember that day, the intent in his eyes flashed a momentary and unintentional signal across the boat. Spike's eyes widened with the recognition and Tom looked away guiltily. He looked up at Monte who had resumed pulling down boxes from the quayside and placing them on the deck. Monte glanced around at Tom and not knowing about the incident on the beach, still crouched from lowering a box, he whispered, 'Tom, we need to talk about this. We must keep Rachel out of sight.'

Now he too saw the guilt on Tom's face.

'What is it? Why are you looking like that?'

Spike left his perch in the bows and was heading directly for Tom. Monte slowly straightened up to his full height as Spike confronted him.

'So, this secret liaison, Tom... I don't suppose the girl had anything to do with what we just heard?'

Monte was now in the horns of a terrible dilemma; something had happened, how did Spike know about a girl, about Rachel? He focused on Spike's words and realized it was only at this moment that Spike had connected Rachel with the boy's enquiry. If Monte struck him now, they could get *Capwood* away from the side and be at sea in minutes. Maybe they could get to her before the alarm was raised. He panicked. Looking around, he could see there were German soldiers everywhere. Even the obnoxious German boy had hardly progressed much further along the quayside. What should he do?

'I...I thought we agreed you wouldn't mention my girlfriend, Spike?' Tom lied, unconvincingly.

'This does put a slightly different perspective on it.' Spike paused and, looking into Monte's frightened eyes, went on, 'Look, not all Germans approve of this thing with the Jews. I am a soldier; I don't fight kids, whatever their race. I have a daughter too.'

Monte and Tom looked at each other for a clue about what they should do next. Spike was the enemy, but if he really was sympathetic...? They could only ponder for a moment before the realization hit them that they had no choice. Spike had already worked it out. If he wanted to turn them all in, he would - and there was little they could do to stop him. But he hadn't called out to the boy.

Tom spoke first. 'Spike, she hasn't done anything wrong, she hasn't harmed anyone, she is just a child.'

He would have continued but Monte cut in. 'Nobody else knows. If you could just see your way to not speaking about this, well...'

Spike interrupted. 'I told you, I don't fight kids. You are lucky, Tom, I am a man of my word, and I didn't mention seeing you with her. Besides, your tip got me a couple of fine bass for top brass. Some of us hate the SS as much as you do and we don't have much time for the Hitler Youth, either. He seems to think she is dead, so as far as I am concerned, let him think that. But you had better be more careful in future; somebody else with a different view might not keep your little secret. If this upstart keeps looking long enough ... well, I think you know what will happen.'

Monte extended his hand to Spike who, looking quickly around to check no one was watching, reciprocated the firm handshake. Their eyes were full of mutual respect.

As *Capwood* headed away from the quay, the three of them watched Freddy leave the harbour master's office.

CHAPTER SEVEN

'It's no good, we must get her away. Spike may be trustworthy, but it is only a matter of time before something else goes wrong - and what sort of life would she have locked up in the farm like a prisoner?'

Harold was speaking with Olive and Monte across the kitchen table. Several days had passed since Spike had informed them that Freddy had left Alderney and returned to Germany. Spike had asked one of his comrades in Alderney to find out what Freddy was up to. It seemed that he was leaving, but that no official cause of death would be given for a few more weeks in case a body turned up. This had angered Freddy, who just wanted the 'accidental death' verdict given. His investigations and the wait for the final verdict had raised Rachel's profile with the Germans locally. There was even a notice put up to look out for her body on the beaches. Far too many people now knew about her disappearance.

'I have got the radio set up and working on *Capwood...*' Monte began, 'but I don't know how to make contact. I listen quite often when there aren't any Jerries on board. There's lots of coded messages for people, you know the sort of thing: *The doves will fly south this weekend* - but how do we start the conversation?'

They decided to enlist the help of John Le Breton. He might not know, but he had many contacts on Guernsey. When Olive had finished preparing lunch, they called Tom and Rachel in from the garden and Monte took Tom to one side.

'Listen, old chap, we need to arrange a powwow with your grandfather. When you go home later can you let him know I will be coming round tomorrow morning?'

Tom was curious about what they were intending to discuss, but he realised that such conversations should not take place in Rachel's earshot in case she became worried.

The next day Monte and John met in the Le Breton cottage at

L'Ancresse. Tom had been out fishing the night before and so Molly and Daisy had been able to prepare a mackerel lunch. The two men then left the cottage and walked outside on the common: what they needed to discuss should only ever involve the fewest people.

'We need help, John. We don't know how to make contact with the mainland and somehow we have got to get her away from here.'

As John began to reply, a figure wheeling a bicycle appeared over one of the small grassy mounds. Ignoring him but still cautious, John spoke quietly. 'There are people who might help. I can try to find someone, but it is dangerous - very dangerous - for everyone involved.' The lone figure came closer now and they could see his face - not one that they recognized. He nodded; they passed.

'He looked a bit rough,' John commented. They turned to watch the stranger, who now seemed to be staggering slightly.

'A bit early for that, isn't it?' Monte commented.

'He didn't look drunk; if anything, he just looked exhausted.' As they were about to resume their conversation, the man suddenly dropped in a heap on the common, with the bicycle on top of him. He started to try and get up, but clearly couldn't muster enough strength, so just lay back down again. The two ran towards him and disentangling him from the bicycle, John noticed the 'dog tag' around his neck.

'Okay, my friend, we had better get you away from here.'

With each taking an arm they unceremoniously dragged the stranger back towards the cottage, leaving the bicycle where it lay.

As they burst in through the door, John called out to a surprised Daisy, 'Daisy, be a love and rustle up something to eat, will you? I think this poor chap is starving.' Molly rushed in and grabbed a chair for him, and the two men gently deposited him onto it.

'Okay, you are safe here, my friend. How long since you have eaten?'

The man appeared to be in his mid-twenties. He was unshaven, with dark hair and stubble. He looked very thin and had sunken features through the obvious lack of food.

His eyes wandered as he tried to speak; he didn't hear or didn't register the question. 'I must tell Gus. We can do it but the tides... radio station...' With that, he collapsed on the floor.

Monte and John carried him upstairs where he was placed in a comfortable bed and left to sleep.

Daisy and Molly looked in on the stranger whilst he slept. Every now and then he spoke in his sleep. A picture was emerging, and it was clear that this British soldier was on some sort of reconnaissance mission to do with the Casquets lighthouse.

Whilst he slept on upstairs, Monte and the Le Bretons took stock of the situation. John spoke first as they met around the kitchen table.

'If we thought we had problems over Rachel, they just doubled. We don't know if the Germans have any idea this man is here, nor how he intended to get away, but we must now make contact urgently with the mainland. Monte, I was about to say outside that we can get messages through the Red Cross, but they need to be coded and seemingly innocent. It is hard to think how we can word a message to convey this situation without giving the game away. You all know of course that we could be shot for aiding him, let alone what they might do to us over Rachel.'

Tom had been keeping out of the way whilst all this went on, but now he was called upon to help. 'Tom, you had better get some distance between us and that bicycle. We don't know where it came from, but it won't have been England. It has almost certainly been stolen and the victim will have reported it, so don't go on the main road. Ride across the common to Chouet and leave it in the bushes near Les Amarreurs.'

At this point, Daisy chipped in, telling Tom to be careful and not to get too close to anyone in case the cycle was recognized. As he left the kitchen, she told the others what the man upstairs had been saying in his sleep. They were all puzzled. Why would the British be interested in the Casquets? They had been picking through his ramblings and speculating for an hour when the kitchen door slowly opened.

'You seem to know more than is good for you.' The soldier spoke, apparently restored somewhat by his sleep. 'I must learn to keep my mouth shut. Thanks for taking me in; I was exhausted. I have had very little sleep, and it's now very difficult for me not to lower my guard. I am also very, very hungry.'

Molly leapt into action, making soup and sandwiches and overruling the young man when he apologized for his abrupt demand.

'Don't be silly. You must be starving. What have you been living off?' She realized they had no idea what to call him, so got straight to the point. 'If your name is a secret, by all means give us a false one, but we need to call you something.'

'My name is John, but most of my friends call me Apple. It's just a nickname I had better not go into now. I don't know how much I blabbed, but you seem to know quite a lot about why I am here. Probably best I don't fill in the details.'

As Apple attacked the cheese sandwiches and vegetable soup, he became more relaxed and told them how he had been living off seaweed and limpets for most of the time. He had managed to snare a couple of rabbits weeks ago but recently had had no luck. Over the last few days he had lost too much energy to hunt and although tempted, stealing food was too big a risk. He had watched their house from the common, and realized that Tom often went fishing. He had also picked up something about the way they sometimes greeted each other and spoke in hushed voices. Was something going on?

Tom came back, sweating from his bike ride and sprint back across the common. He had not wanted to leave the cottage with so much happening.

As he opened the kitchen door, Apple jumped up in a reflex action and was about to throw himself into attack when Daisy yelled at him to stop, explaining it was just Tom returning. He returned to his seat as a startled Tom edged his way past and found the sink, a jug of water and another of Molly's sandwiches.

John explained what had happened and how Rachel was now at great risk.

Apple reinforced this. 'You have been very brave, especially you, Tom. Orders from the SS are taken very seriously, and although the Jerry foot soldiers would probably have resented them, they would certainly have turned you all over to the SS. So where is the child now? ...No, don't tell me; I don't need to know right now.'

Apple explained that although he had arrived alone, there was a contact on the island who would help him get away. That was where he was going when they came across him. He had a pre-arranged meeting date and had no option but to steal the bicycle to get there. He asked about the bicycle and was concerned when they told him it had been got rid of. How would he make his rendezvous? Could he borrow one of their cycles?

It was agreed that Apple would take the cycle Monte had arrived on, but that John would accompany him to ensure he knew the way. Apple had to find a fisherman's hut near Bordeaux harbour. He had to be there between 16:00 and 18:00 or wait for a further week.

The two men left the cottage as Monte bid his farewells to return to Herm; any later and he would miss the tide. Tom walked with him to the edge of the common where a horse-drawn bus operated a service to town.

'What's going to happen now, Monte? It's getting pretty risky.'

'Don't worry, Tom, finding Apple will help us. To be honest, your grandfather and I were struggling a bit to work out how we could get Rachel away. The problem might now be solved for us.'

Tom waved a farewell to Monte and walked back to the cottage. It was a relief to have the tiny kitchen to just himself, his mother and grandmother. But the air was full of tension. Molly was worried about John going with Apple to the rendezvous. What would happen if the Germans knew? It could be a trap.

**

On the way John explained about Monte's makeshift radio. If he needed to use it, he only had to ask. Apple reflected on the help this man and his family were giving. They were risking their necks, but were only concerned with getting him and the girl back to safety.

'It may well be useful, John, and if I might ask, that little boat Tom has tucked away - do you think we might borrow it at some point?'

'We will do everything we can. The only problem will be convincing Tom that I should take you and not him.' They grinned at each other briefly and freewheeled down the hill.

As the men rode towards the small harbour at Bordeaux, there were a number of locals tending their boats and some sitting on the low sea wall chatting. John tried to keep well clear, as most of them knew him and he did not want to be forced to introduce Apple. He waved - an offhand wave - as they pushed on down a track on the northern edge of the harbour. Here, a few cottage gardens formed one border and a pebbly beach the other. As they progressed past the last garden, the track ended and the pebbles of the beach took over. Ahead was an old granite-built hut with a rusty corrugated iron roof. Outside, a bicycle leaned against the wall.

'I had better do this bit alone,' Apple commented as they dismounted and he leaned his cycle down onto the beach. John simply nodded.

As Apple approached the hut, every nerve in his body was alert. His eyes scanned the brush behind the hut and quickly checked the beach as well as the sea beyond for anyone approaching. John, too, looked around. Nobody seemed interested in them.

Although the door was open, there was little light inside, just a square by the entrance, enough only to give the figure inside a silhouetted profile. A quiet, dignified voice broke the silence. Silence - apart from a gentle lapping of waves on the shore pebbles, and an occasional gull squawking its presence.

'Are we expecting the weather to turn?'

The reply came, 'Not while the high pressure lingers over the Bay of Biscay.'

'It is good to see you are all right, Apple. I have been worried about how you must have coped all these weeks.'

'Well, survival training is fine, but the last week has been tough. Sleep deprivation has set in, as Jerry has been up and down the coast of Guernsey since they lost that patrol boat. Was that a local job?'

'I wish we could claim it, but it seems they hit a mine one of yours, or should I say ours, I believe. My position in the States of Guernsey gives me access to most of the senior military sources. Now we need to get you away. Are you all set? I presume your "recce" is all complete now?'

'Yes, that's all done, but we do have a complication. There will be two passengers, not just one. Can you let them know?'

'I don't see why not. Presumably you'll need transporting out to the pick up?'

'Possibly not. I have some support now and should be able to organise a boat. I can also monitor the airwaves, so if you can confirm the message, we can probably avoid another meeting.'

'Okay. I'll continue to come here each week until the week after the pick up, just in case anything changes or goes wrong. Your message will be *Birthday greetings to Lucy, who will be seven this week on the 13th.* Lucy's age will be the time and the birthday, the date. Have you still got the coordinates?'

'Yes, I memorized that latitude and longitude, so with the help of a chart, a compass and some dead reckoning, we should be spot on. Thanks, my friend. I hope I don't see you again until we have got Jerry out of your beautiful island.'

With that, Apple turned quickly and left the hut. A few minutes elapsed before the Guernsey States Deputy also left.

Apple and John cycled back to the cottage and that night Apple slept all through the night for the first time in a month.

***

Monte and John met several times over the next few weeks and Tom managed to see Rachel nearly every day. Monte moved *Capwood* from the normal harbour mooring - one which dried out at low tide - to one just offshore, making the excuse that he needed to work on the boat before it could take to the bottom again. What he really wanted was to be further away when he listened to the BBC's evening broadcast.

Each night Monte patiently listened to the multitude of birthday greetings and cryptic messages, hoping that Lucy would soon have her big day. Finally one September evening it came. He was in the process of bleeding the air out of his diesel engine when the birthday greeting was announced. A polished BBC voice gave, and then repeated, the message, 'And we now have a message for little Lucy from her grandparents. It reads, *Birthday greetings to Lucy, who will be five this week on the 28th*. I repeat, *Birthday greetings to Lucy, who will be five this week on the 28th*. And now, a greeting for Anthony from Mum and Dad serving overseas…'

Monte almost dropped his screwdriver as he scrambled to place his ear as close to the set as he could. Five a.m. on the 28th then. A slight disappointment that his radio would not be used to transmit and acknowledge the message was overcome by the sheer excitement that at last they would get Rachel and of course Apple to safety. The 28th, he thought, that is just three days away.

Monte scrambled over the side into his dinghy and rowed ashore. His mind raced as he thought through their plan. There was a lot to do.

The next day Rachel must be moved. She would need to be prepared; nobody had told her what was happening. At least the weather looked good. It shouldn't be too rough for her. But the moonlight, what about the moonlight? It would be tricky.

When the news reached Tom's family back in Guernsey, hurried preparations were made. A chart was soon spread onto the kitchen table, and Apple drew two intersecting pencil lines from the latitude and longitude coordinates. The point of intersection was five miles from the north-west coast of Guernsey. With favourable wind and tides, they would need to set off no later than 3:00 a.m. to be on the safe side. They drew another pencil line to represent the compass course they would follow from where *Fish* was moored to the intersecting lines. 315 degrees was the course to steer. Tom confirmed his compass was on board, as well as a device to measure speed.

But first they had to pick up Rachel.

This part of the plan troubled them all. The young girl must be placed in a barrel and taken to the harbour on the old handcart. Monte had practised this routine daily for two weeks now, to familiarize the Germans with the sight of him taking a barrel down to the dock and loading it onto *Capwood*. The first time they were curious until he explained that he was collecting home-brewed Guernsey beer for the Germans at the White House Hotel. Of course, for this to succeed he had to actually transport beer most days and take back the empty barrel but, so that Rachel would not have to endure the smell of the beer, he kept a clean empty barrel at the farm.

The next morning Harold, Olive and Monte explained to Rachel what was about to happen. She was distraught. She could see no reason for leaving and wanted to stay at the farm with her daily visits from Tom. It took all of them an hour to calm her down and get her to accept that this was best for her safety and that she would see them again as soon as the war was over. She must leave that night. Her final day was spent as close to Olive's apron as she could manage. They were both quiet, too emotional to speak. But Olive fought hard to be positive about the future. Harold tried to make light of it, but it was only now that she was leaving that he realized how attached he had become to her. The time raced by, just when they all wanted it to be slow. Their last remaining hours came to a close.

Olive was crying copiously as she looked down at the tearful little girl cramped into the barrel. Monte tried to reassure her that he would be as gentle as he could, but she must be as quiet as a mouse.

As the lid closed Olive had to turn away, and the men loaded the barrel onto the handcart. They disappeared down the track and Olive returned to the house. With tears still running down her face, she looked around the room that had been home to Rachel. All her clothes were still neatly folded on the shelf, and under the bed was her little shoe. This was the single shoe Rachel had carried all the way from Alderney and before that, her home in Germany. Olive placed the shoe on a shelf over the bed and otherwise left the room as she found it.

As the cart approached the docks, Monte and Harold avoided anything that looked like a pothole in the track. A few soldiers stood on the pier, looking out at the sunset over Guernsey.

'That's it, Monte - get some more beer in!'

Spike was among them, and he saw the tension in their faces. He watched as the two men slowly manipulated the empty barrel off the cart and onto *Capwood*, waiting at the dockside. He was about to joke about the fact that Harold's help had been enlisted, and they seemed very careful all of a sudden. He stopped himself and a chill came over him. So this was it, this was the escape plan. Spike looked around at his fellow soldiers, then at the barrel now on board *Capwood*. The girl was in there. The others didn't suspect a thing as Harold let go of the bow line and *Capwood* slipped away from the quayside, towing the dinghy behind it.

Monte said something to Harold, who shot a startled glance

directly at Spike. But they kept going; they were gambling that Spike would keep his mouth shut and let them get her away. *Capwood* was now motoring off in the direction of Guernsey. The setting sun reduced all detail to that of a shadow theatre, and moonlight took over the job of faint illumination across the water.

Spike smiled to himself at their audacity. He was not about to risk sharing their secret even with his friends, and he was pleased Monte and Harold trusted his discretion. It was hard to keep track of *Capwood*'s progress from his position, but she seemed to have stopped about a mile out, with her beam towards Herm. She was close to the Brehon Tower, a disused Napoleonic naval fortification currently unoccupied by the Germans. What were they up to?

As *Capwood* rolled with the swell, Harold opened the top of the barrel and reached in to lend Rachel a helping hand. She was upright in no time and not much the worse for her experience. The barrel was resealed and Harold helped her over the side of *Capwood*, hidden from Herm, into the dinghy. He rowed for the tower still out of sight behind *Capwood*'s beam, with Rachel perched on a tiny bow seat behind him. When the two of them were safely inside, along with the dinghy, *Capwood* resumed its journey to Guernsey where it would stay for the night before returning on its way back in the morning.

It was not what anyone would call a pleasant experience. Brehon was infested with rats and stank of bird droppings. But it was safe, and Harold quickly constructed a platform out of fallen lumps of granite onto which he securely placed the dinghy. To most little girls, a night in a place like this would have seemed a nightmare, but Rachel had endured much worse in her young life, and with Harold's company and a few surprises he had brought from Olive, the evening was not too bad. In fact, it brightened considerably when he told her that they had an early start as Tom would be collecting her, so she should try to sleep.

It was still dark when *Fish* bumped alongside the Tower. Tom called in to them as he secured *Fish* to a mooring ring. Harold appeared first and then a very sleepy Rachel, rubbing her eyes and yawning as she walked. They exchanged a few pleasantries before Tom guided Rachel onto *Fish* and cast off, leaving Harold alone and waiting for Monte to collect him.

As *Fish* glided serenely across the waves, Tom persuaded Rachel to close her eyes and get some more sleep. She was still curled up amongst the sail bags when Tom made his final approach under the cover of Fort Le Marchant.

Waiting on the rocks were Daisy and John. John put one foot down into *Fish* and reached down to pick up the sleeping Rachel. Sure-footed, he carried her across the rocks, despite the half-light and slippery seaweed scattered around.

The 27th was a day none of them would forget. Daisy and Molly spent most of it fussing over Rachel and nervously preparing food, as if in preparation for some kind of approaching famine. The men were preoccupied with their plans for the coming rendezvous. At 5:00 a.m. the next day, a British submarine would surface in the Channel just five miles away from Guernsey.

'Grandfather, I know I'm supposed to be just a kid, but I can handle *Fish* and there will be less weight on board if I go.'

Apple had tried to persuade them that they should sacrifice *Fish* altogether and not risk either of them going. He would take Rachel on his own. Fortunately this idea was squashed early on, when it was pointed out that there was a local boat register that linked *Fish* to the family. If the sub was spotted and *Fish* was discovered nearby, they would be in trouble. Even if she was scuttled, a patrol boat might get to her before she went down in the event that a quick getaway was called for. No, it made sense for one of the men to go. Of course, Apple realized that the subtext for all of this was that they wanted to be with Rachel until she was safely on board the submarine. They were also reluctant to lose their boat unless absolutely necessary. Apple deferred to this and let the two of them debate who would be best to helm *Fish*.

'Tom, I know you are more than capable, but think of your mother. I am old and if anything goes wrong we need you to look after her and Grandma.'

Tom could see that he was not likely to win this argument; adults always took control in situations like this.

The conversation moved on to the detail of the trip. Apple took them over it again and again. They both knew every eddy and current that would flow, and they could predict the weather from the pattern over the last few days and the present wispy high clouds in the sky. They also knew exactly how *Fish* would handle in these conditions and could predict the time they would reach the rendezvous to within minutes. The rendezvous time coincided with high tide, a decision probably calculated by the Navy to give the sub the maximum amount of water, as it would be relatively close to the reefs around the island. Tom and John had revised their departure time to 3:30 a.m., almost exactly an hour and a half before high tide. This would ensure a growing northerly tidal stream to help carry them to their destination, although *Fish* would then struggle against this stream for the return journey. The wind was light from the south-west, giving them ideal conditions to carry full sail and achieve a boat speed of around five knots through the water or with the tide, perhaps seven or eight knots over the ground. They should reach the rendezvous area half an hour before the sub, but they must keep away from the precise location until it surfaced; the wash would certainly capsize *Fish*.

All day there was nervousness in the air. Daisy noticed the affection between her son and Rachel, and could not help herself quietly mentioning to him how pretty Rachel was. For her part, Rachel responded to the warmth of the family, but not far from her consciousness was the thought that she would soon be leaving all of them.

The debate over who would helm *Fish* was settled soon after lunch. John decided it would be worthwhile to repoint the brickwork around the chimney. He found it hard to cope with the anticipation without keeping busy, and convinced himself that this would both give an air of normality to the cottage and give him an excellent view of any unusual troop movements around the common.

Unfortunately, whilst craning to see further east, he nearly lost his grip and fell. Reaching out for the ridge tiles, he prevented his fall, but he twisted and pulled a muscle in his back. This confined him to a chair for the rest of the afternoon and his repeated attempts to prove he was all right only made him worse.

The family ate a light supper and turned in early that night. Nobody slept. Tom was on a camp bed in the kitchen so that Rachel could sleep in his room. It was hot, and all the windows were left open to catch the slight breeze. In their separate rooms they lay there, sometimes staring at the ceiling, sometimes turning over and fluffing up their pillows. John was agitated; he had not wanted Tom to go, but the pain in his back gave a constant reminder that he must keep still. In the front room, Apple was calm. He was fully prepared, but as the only military person, his antennae were scanning for the slightest sound that might indicate their plan had been compromised.

Daisy and Molly worried about everything that could possibly go wrong and across the water in Herm, Harold, Olive and Monte felt impotent now that their part was over.

At 3:00 a.m. Daisy rose first and put the kettle on. Nobody needed to be woken, and as they wandered one by one into the kitchen, hardly a word was spoken. John reached painfully to close the kitchen windows so that the tranquility of the common would not be disturbed by any noise that was made. This also allowed them to light a small oil lamp now that the blackout curtains could be closed and would not flap open in the breeze.

The tea was welcome, but nobody wanted to eat that early and so a quick wash was all that was needed before they set off. In almost total silence, Daisy, then Molly, hugged Rachel and whispered to her as the little girl tried to smile back through tear-filled eyes. John cringed again as he attempted to give Rachel a bear hug, bringing a sympathetic smile to everyone's faces.

Apple stood quietly by the door once he had thanked them all for helping him, but could not help emitting an air of impatience; he was keen to get going. Finally, Tom looked to his mother and reassured her he would be all right. John's last-ditch attempt to convince everyone he could do it was kindly, but resolutely, ignored by everyone.

The lamp was dowsed and Tom, Rachel and Apple set off into the shadows outside. Apple carried a small parcel containing the chart.

The grass of the common was damp with dew and it was light enough under the moon to see where they were going, or to be seen. So they crouched, and ran for cover from each mound on the common to the next. Then finally, they left the grass for the rocks that skirted around the imposing silhouette of Fort Le Marchant and down to where *Fish* was waiting.

With Rachel squatting in the bows and Tom at the tiller, Apple pushed off and scrambled on board, positioning himself amidships to balance the boat. First, the foresail went up to pull them out of their cove and once clear, the gaff-rigged mainsail was hoisted to its full height. *Fish* responded by throwing up a bow wave and cutting through the water with ease. As they left Guernsey behind them it became just a murky shape in the background. Occasionally they passed rocks that also appeared as vaguely contrasting dim shapes around them until there was just the dark of the sea and a blurred distinction with the shades of the sky.

Apple was careful to ensure that *Fish* cast off at exactly 3:30 a.m. and as soon as they were under way, a small device was dropped over the transom which trailed behind *Fish* on a length of cord. The cord was connected to a small indicator mounted on the transom and as the device spun in the wake behind them, it twisted the cord, which told them how fast they were going through the water. This log, the compass and the chart were all they needed to navigate to the rendezvous. Tom did his best to maintain a boat speed of five knots on the trailing speed log and a course of 315 degrees. Every fifteen minutes, Apple checked and noted the speed and course with Tom and marked their position on the chart.

Other than this, very little was said as *Fish* sped on its way. They were all tired and the two youngsters quite emotional. But when they had been at sea for just over an hour, Rachel and Tom realised how little time remained and the two started to talk. At first, they were even a little formal. Neither was sure how they should behave, and there was hardly a reference for this kind of situation. So they began tentatively. Had Rachel enjoyed being on Herm? Wasn't it fortunate they had come across Harold? The conversation moved on to her room and how generously Olive had supplied all her children's possessions, especially as Rachel had none. Then Rachel sat upright.

'I did have one thing - my shoe!'

She suddenly remembered the shoe that her mother had told her to look after. How could she forget it? It was back there.

Apple had been distracted by the conversation, but hardly listening until this point. What was she saying? Surely she didn't expect them to go back and get a shoe?

Tom tried to calm her down, but the shoe was not really the issue any more. It was like a safety valve that had just blown on her emotions, and Rachel sobbed inconsolably. Tom looked to Apple for guidance on how to help her; he couldn't stand seeing her cry. But Apple just shook his head and his expression told him to just let her get it out of her system.

Rachel was rambling now, and had moved quickly from the shoe to how she would never see it or any of them again. They would soon forget about her when she was away and no longer a burden for them.

Tom could leave it no longer; he asked Apple to take the tiller for a little while and they changed places. He leaned forward to Rachel and said, 'Rachel, of course we won't forget you. I ... er, I mean we ... care far too much about you for that. Listen, when the occupation is over you can come back. Your shoe will still be there. I'll make sure Olive keeps it. Not that she is likely to lose it anyway - she keeps everything.'

Rachel laughed at the thought of all those cupboards full of their children's books and toys.

'That's better. Anyway, you must come back, because I want to know how you get on. We can even try to write to each other. The Red Cross will get some letters in and out of the island.'

Rachel stopped sobbing. She had heard him say it: *he*... cared far too much about her.

They returned to their original seats as the rendezvous drew closer. Rachel looked down the boat to Tom, who was no longer trying to avoid her searching gaze. He smiled at her and they both blushed profusely.

'Apple,' Tom began, 'Apple, what will happen to Rachel when she gets to England?'

Apple explained that this was not exactly his territory, but he would ask the War Office if she could stay with his relatives in Yorkshire. Lots of youngsters had been evacuated there to escape the bombing raids over London and the south-east. Whatever happened, he would make sure he knew where she was, and he or his family would look after her.

'Can I come back to Guernsey when the soldiers go?' 'Rachel, you are a free person now. England is not like Germany. Jewish people are our friends. You will be free to go wherever you want. But we have to be patient; we have a war to win first.'

With that, the boat fell silent again. They were lost in the thought of the war being over. No more being ordered around, no more scrimping to survive.

Apple had been checking his watch repeatedly over the past twenty minutes.

'Okay, Tom. We are here now. Let's heave to.'

Tom brought *Fish* around into the wind and lashed the tiller to point her towards the wind, whilst Apple backed the foresail so that it opposed this direction. The net result was no forward movement, and only a very slight drift downwind. This practice had been used by sailors over the years to ride out a storm or make a boat safe to work on at sea.

At exactly 4:55, about one hundred yards away from them, the water became disturbed. They watched in awe as first the conning tower pierced the waves, then the huge grey shape of the hull broke the surface. Waves pushed out away from the sub and rolled towards *Fish*, sitting beam on in their path. Tom moved swiftly forwards and reached out to grab Rachel, before the first wave set *Fish* see-sawing where she waited. Nothing was lost from the sudden eruption and whilst Apple was commenting that it was a bit close for comfort, Rachel looked up at Tom and their eyes met. He took longer than needed to release his hold on her arms, but she didn't mind, and when he did eventually release her, they both realized that Apple was watching with a large grin on his face.

A figure appeared on the conning tower.

'Okay, Apple. Is that you?'

'I jolly well hope so, for your sake. We can't go on meeting like this.'

Corny, but some customs needed to be observed.

Fish was released from her dilemma and now Tom was steering for the sub. As they came alongside the mainly submerged deck, Apple leapt off and handed a mooring line to a waiting submariner.

The next few minutes were over almost instantly for Tom. As he sat there alone in the blackness, with nothing at all to be seen except the dark sea and sky, he had never felt so alone in his life.

He reflected on those last few minutes together. Rachel had been helped off, they had smiled at each other and she seemed to turn to say something, but Apple was hurrying her away towards the conning tower. Then the submariner cast off *Fish*'s lines and pushed her vigorously away. Apple called down to him, 'Don't worry; I'll take care of her. You get straight back safely. Well done, Tom, this won't be forgotten.'

As Rachel descended into the tower, Apple unceremoniously launched her up to the rail so she could see over it. There was just time to wave and shout their goodbyes when a voice came from below, a muted siren called out, and the figures disappeared from view.

Moments later the sub began to move slowly and graciously through the water. Her nose began to dip and as she blended into the background, the diminishing shape of the hull was enveloped by the dark sea.

CHAPTER EIGHT

When the sub descended and Tom returned through the darkness to Guernsey, the tide and wind had been against him. It was a difficult feat of navigation and took him several hours of tacking back and forth, but eventually he made it home in the early hours of the morning.

Although he had seen the sub safely away, it was still a relief when sitting in *Capwood* off Herm harbour a few days later, he and Monte heard the BBC announcement,

'...And the next message is from Lucy. Lucy wishes to thank everyone for the lovely party and she has now gone to live with the family at the house with the orchard. I repeat ...'

In classic BBC voice the announcement was repeated and Tom smiled at Monte.

'That's good. I was hoping they would let her live with Apple's family in Yorkshire. He will look out for her.'

Monte agreed and they went on with their business of cleaning *Capwood*. Soon she would be beached so they could repaint her. Monte liked to do this each autumn so that she had better protection through the winter.

Over the following weeks something like a routine returned to the lives of Tom, his family and new found friends on Herm. He continued his late-night fishing and carried on working with Harold and Monte during the day. He wasn't sure when he would hear from Rachel, but it wasn't long before the first letter arrived, courtesy of the Red Cross.

It was an autumn evening when he returned home, brandishing driftwood for the stove. There on the mantelpiece - the traditional place for letters - was an envelope addressed to Tom. His heart lifted when he saw it. Daisy and Molly looked at each other knowingly.

Whole sentences had been inked out by the censor, but this did not spoil his enjoyment.

Dear Tom

I arrived safely after our journey and a short stop off in •••• to be interviewed by the •••• spoke to them about me staying with his family and they said I could. So now I am in •••• at their lovely home. His mum and dad are really nice and spoiling me completely. He has a sister too who is lovely and very sophisticated. My room overlooks the village square so I can see when the other children go out and meet there. There are lots of evacuees staying on farms and houses nearby.

•••• said I should say I don't know how often or how many letters will get through to you but I will try to write and I hope you can too sometimes if you are not too busy. I miss you.

*Please give my love to your mum and grandparents and of course ••••
and •••• in ••••*
Your friend
Rachel

Tom read and reread the letter several times. She seemed fine, she was safe, she missed him!

Tom did not want to acknowledge that the improvement in his mood was connected to the letter, but the smile on his face that evening was noticed by all his family.

Over the weeks and months ahead this became a familiar story. In fact, he started to become slightly moody if Rachel's letters were delayed, only to be even happier when they eventually appeared on the mantelpiece.

He replied each time within a few days, but was unadventurous in expressing his feelings. He told Rachel about the quantity, type and size of the fish he had caught and went into great detail about the weather and sea state around the island. Rachel was less inhibited and was soon finishing her letters with 'Love from Rachel,' rather than 'Your friend'.

Around a year later, one particular letter interested the Le

Breton family greatly. It included a note from Apple and a press cutting.

Dearest Tom

I really enjoyed your last letter - it was so good to hear from you. You must have been very proud catching that Conger eel on your own, it must have been huge! Please be careful though because •••• told me they have very sharp teeth and can even bite you when their heads have been cut off. I was pleased to hear that your gran is feeling better - please give her my love.

•••• wanted to include a little note to you and your family so here it is.

Hello everyone! I just thought you might like to see the enclosed cutting from the newspaper. I hope you are all well. All my best wishes, your friend,

....

Rachel went on to describe the latest outfit that Apple's sister had bought in London (deleted) and the walks that she went on with his mother in the country around .....(also deleted). She finished with growing familiarity,

With all my love
Rachel

Tom turned to the press cutting. After reading it quickly and expressing his surprise that it had got through the censors, he exclaimed, 'Wow! Look at this!' and showed it to the family.

DARING COMMANDO RAID IN THE CHANNEL ISLANDS

On September 3, 1942 British commandos carried out a daring raid on a German-held lighthouse in the Channel

Islands.

The Casquets Lighthouse off Alderney was being used as a radio station by the enemy, who were taken by surprise by our commandos.

The war office has confirmed that German prisoners were taken and there were no casualties, in what they described as a text book operation. German military sources are reported to be furious about the audacity of the raid which took place under their noses on Hitler's so-called 'Atlantic Wall'.

The lighthouse is situated in the midst of treacherous rocks and currents and our commandos exhibited great skill in executing this raid.

It is thought that an earlier reconnaissance mission contributed to their success.

Another poke in the eye for Jerry!

The laughter exploded in the Le Breton cottage and they congratulated themselves on their part in aiding Apple.

When news of the raid got out in Guernsey, the family had to bite their lips at the comments being made. They did not want the Germans to know of their involvement.

Friends and neighbours speculated about the operation. Who had been involved? What about this earlier reconnaissance mission? Whilst they all agreed the news was brilliant, some were concerned about the reaction of the Germans. Relations were tense for weeks afterwards. Even Spike, who was by now almost a welcome visitor at the farm on Herm, was not happy. This was a military disaster for them in the islands; it made their troops look hopeless. 'Not even a shot fired,' he muttered to his fellow soldiers on the dockside. 'What were they thinking of?'

Further commando raids were carried out during the occupation and each time Tom suspected that Apple may have been involved. If relations with the Germans had become frosty over the Casquets raid, they positively froze over when another saw four German soldiers killed as they tried to escape from commandos raiding Sark. Then, to utterly humiliate them, a further raid was carried out on the Casquets in 1943. This was rumoured to include amongst the commandos the movie star Douglas Fairbanks Junior, adding even more to the bravado of the raid.

Apple was too sensible to make any further references to these activities; he knew that might draw attention to the family as the Germans would be reading their mail. So Rachel and Tom continued to correspond, with less contentious subjects like fishing or fashion being their main focus.

So from 1941 to 1945 the two shared their thoughts by letter. They also grew and, increasingly over that period, shared their feelings, especially about each other. When they parted, Rachel had just turned thirteen years old; now, she was seventeen. Tom had been fourteen and was now eighteen - nearly nineteen - years of age.

Tom now felt happy for their relationship to move on; she was no longer a little girl. But he struggled to know how to do this by letter. So Rachel led and he followed. As her letters became more familiar, so did his, although always a few paces behind hers. As the years passed there was no sign of their affection diminishing - the opposite seemed to be happening.

Rachel had been overwhelmed by Tom from the moment they met. He was her knight in shining armour and although his feelings had grown more slowly, by the time she boarded the submarine they were already deep. The dreamlike existence on Herm had cemented their affections and given them the opportunity to explore each other's personalities. This foundation made possible the growing intimacy that developed through their letters. Whilst the censors inhibited their freedom of expression, they also injected a sense of 'forbidden fruit' that fuelled their desire to be together.

By the time Tom read the last letter before reuniting with her, the relationship was on another plane.

Darling Tom

I know I must be cautious about what is said in our letters but our friend tells me that soon we may be together again. I can't wait to see you. They say absence makes the heart grow fonder but Tom what I feel for you is so much more than I can put in words.

I know I was just a skinny child but Tom I have grown up now and my feelings for you have grown with me.

As soon as it is possible I want to be by your side again and I know it is forward of me to say this but I hope that we never have to part again. You are the most important thing in my life and you cannot imagine how I have felt to read that you feel the same way about me.

Let us hope it is not long now.

Your everloving

Rachel xxx

It was not long. Rachel stood in his arms just three weeks after that letter and the two felt as though they had never been apart.

Part 2: Liberation

CHAPTER NINE

Old Maurice found it hard to sleep; the hunger took a grip most nights and reached a climax of discomfort early in the mornings. The morning of May 9th, 1945 was no different – except, as he unwound from his curled up position to go and find a drink of water, for some bizarre reason the haze outside his cottage window intrigued him, persuading him to go outside onto the exposed northern headland that bordered his home.

He stared through the half-light, although his mind was still tormenting him to scavenge for something to subdue the pangs of hunger that gnawed at his empty stomach. Eyes still tired from a sleepless night, the shape emerging nearly passed unnoticed as he began to respond to the call from his body and go down to the rocky outcrop to fish, or find wrack. But the shape did not escape him; the grey mist contained a dark form, in fact a number of dark shadowy forms. There was something there, out at sea.

The early morning sun was already burning the hazy veil away and as it did so, some of the shadowy forms transformed into shapes. Maurice was riveted as the shapes metamorphosed into ships, and the ships into a fleet. The Liberation had come at last.

Out of the mist, British warships cruised into the Little Russel, defying any occupying forces to confront them. Their might was awesome, but resistance was not expected, as intelligence had already reached the fleet that few Germans soldiers were now left on the island.

Maurice fell to his knees and wept with joy, his hunger now forgotten. Then just a few seconds later he reclaimed his wits, jumped up with more vigour than his age should have allowed, and ran, shouting, back towards the line of cottages that included his home.

Before long the whole neighbourhood, the whole parish, the whole island was up and cheering and waving, ecstatic with joy.

On the bows of the leading destroyer, fragile amongst the anchors and beneath the guns, a lone young woman gazed towards Guernsey, her long dark hair flowing like the figurehead of an ancient ship. Rachel was returning to find the most valuable thing left in her life - Tom.

The ships dropped anchor off St Peter Port, and smaller boats and landing craft reclaimed the precious islands that were the only British soil to fall to the Germans. The crowd was huge; makeshift and previously hidden flags were waving; there was cheering; horns were blown, even gramophones were played through open windows. And as the first British soldiers stepped ashore, the cacophony of sound erupted into a climax. Everyone who could literally jumped with joy. Everyone, that is, except the group of German soldiers waiting patiently and long-faced on the quay.

Tom had been asleep when his mother burst in, shouting hysterically. He had been dreaming about the book he was reading at the time, and in the precise moment his mother had chosen to intervene in this dream, Tom was on the deck of a square rigger, fighting the battle of the Nile. Daisy therefore needed to compete with the cannon fire, explosions and shouting in Tom's head. She was stunned at how long it was taking to reach him, and beside herself with excitement.

Over on Herm, Harold had been first to see their arrival as he rounded up his cows for milking. He, Olive and Monte now joined the rest of the small crowd on Herm's tiny breakwater to wave at the ships.

Of course, town was the place to be, and everyone who could, cycled or walked towards it. Soon *Capwood* was full of people from Herm, and boats from Sark could also be seen heading towards the centre of the Bailiwick of Guernsey.

Tom's family were no exception, and by ten in the morning, they were leaning their bicycles against the sea wall, to continue on foot to the White Rock pier. As they found one of the few remaining viewing points not deep with people, Tom cast his eyes over the scene. The magnificent ships were at anchor off St Peter Port and a flotilla of small boats was encircling them, sounding horns and waving. Naval launches were also busy taking the troops from the ships to shore. When Tom saw Monte in *Capwood*, he called out. At first, Monte didn't see him, but when he did, he seemed to go even more hysterical than the others. Tom was thinking what a card he was when he realised Monte was trying to tell him something. He was pointing frantically at the nearest naval launch heading for the port. Tom tried to see what all the fuss was about, and then he saw her. Surely it couldn't be? There, wedged between a group of soldiers and also looking in Monte's direction, was Rachel. Monte was now frantically pointing and shouting to her to look up at the quay. She turned her head in Tom's direction and all around him the noise subsided. They didn't wave, they hardly moved; they just looked at each other. Tom was mesmerised. Rachel was no longer a girl, she had grown into a beautiful, curvaceous young woman. Her pretty face was surrounded by dark flowing hair and her eyes sparkled as she gazed back at him. As he looked at her, the rest of the world was completely shut out of his mind.

In front of his face, Tom became conscious of a vague moving outline. It was another face - his mother's face. Her mouth was open but he couldn't hear anything.

'Tom, Tom! Look, it's Rachel! Look, near Monte. It's Rachel!' Suddenly the silence was burst and first Daisy, then John were grabbing him and forcing his arm up to wave. Hadn't he seen her? What was the matter with him?

As the launch approached harbour, Tom walked slowly along the wall towards the seaward end, his gaze not faltering, his arms slightly stretched in front of him, and a single-minded look on his face. The crowd parted in his path. He would have thanked them if he had seen them. His pace matched that of the launch closing on the pier head, and as it rounded it, Rachel was in full view. She wore a knee-length coat with a headscarf tied around her neck, gracing one of her shoulders. The coat hugged her slim waist and full bosom. They smiled, she blushed, and he carried on to the steps at the quayside.

The soldiers on her launch were very aware of this stunning

woman in their midst, and were somewhat disappointed to see
the look on her face as Tom came into view. Some teased
Rachel a little, but they were all good-humoured, and helped her
to the side so that she could disembark early.

'Make way for the lady...' one of them yelled, shoving his
colleagues out of the way. 'Can't you see she is meeting
someone?'

When the launch touched, she jumped off, and they all yelled
approvingly. A large patchwork bag was handed up to her, and
Rachel climbed the steps towards Tom, who was descending in
the opposite direction. Rachel's heart was pounding as she saw
that the boy she had dreamt of was now an even more handsome
man. He was simply dressed in a traditional blue 'Guernsey'
and canvas shorts. His face was now more masculine but he still
sported a flock of unwieldy fair hair. His clear blue eyes were
wide with excitement as they took in her beauty. They met
halfway on the landing and stopped in their tracks.

As they embraced, they were now both unaware of the rest of
the world and the rowdy noise around them. They had both
grown, but she was still at least a foot or so shorter than him.
Still entwined, they parted just slightly and looked into each
other's eyes, he bowed his head and their lips met.

At first their moist lips barely touched - this moment was to be
savoured. She closed her eyes, feeling weak, her knees
buckling. Tom hugged her more tightly. Every cell in their
bodies pulsated with the passion that had been denied for so
long.

As they kissed, Daisy appeared at the top of the stairs. She was
about to call down when she realised that even the soldiers had
now stopped their cheering. They were looking up at Daisy and
one gestured with his hands as if to say, I don't think so, Mum. I
think you need to give them a minute!

Out in the harbour a queue of launches was starting to form as
the lovers' embrace captivated the troops. They were no doubt
thinking of their loved ones, and temporarily paused
disembarkation. Rachel's launch was neither unloading nor

leaving the steps. Monte kept *Capwood* out of the way of the troopships, but across the water he could see the couple halfway up the steps. Her right leg slightly lifted beneath her coat, she arched back and his hands held her head firmly through her long dark hair.

Eventually a less emotional lieutenant shouted out, to the boos of all around him, 'Come on, you two, we need to get off!'

Rachel and Tom separated again, smiled at each other and he whispered to her, 'That is the last time we will be apart.'

***

Six months later they were married in the Vale Church, close to L'Ancresse common and the Le Breton family cottage. They had barely any money at all, nowhere to live, and technically, Rachel was Jewish. But nothing was going to prevent them from sealing their love forever. It was the happiest day of their lives, in Rachel's case often a very unhappy life.

Whilst staying at the home of Apple's family - or the Appleyards as they were more properly known vigorous enquiries had been made about Rachel's mother. Her fate was finally established just a few months before the Liberation. English and American troops had entered a concentration camp on the outskirts of Belgium. Amongst the emaciated inmates was an old man who knew of her mother and confirmed that she had died early in 1943.

Rachel had been prepared for the worst as the brutality of Hitler's concentration camps became common knowledge. Nevertheless, confirmation of her mother's fate deeply hurt her.

With no family left, her relationship with Tom was everything. She saw no reason to return to Germany after the war, and concentrated on building her life in Guernsey.

Tom's parents adored Rachel, and the feeling was mutual. His father - John - had returned intact from the Navy and was offered the post of harbour master for the commercial port of St Sampson, a job which he loved. Daisy was delighted to have the company of another woman, and although she could never replace Rachel's own mother, her presence did help her to get through some of the times when she felt the loss most acutely.

With the grandparents now ageing, Tom and Rachel moved into their cottage at Rocquaine, in the remote south-west of the island, so that the grandparents could be looked after by Tom's parents. At least, that's what the young couple were told. In fact, the grandparents were in good health, but the family knew that Tom and Rachel would welcome a home of their own.

Tom sailed his trusty *Flying Fish* down the west coast of the island and took up a mooring opposite their cottage.

The post-war years were idyllic for the couple living at Rocquaine. Tom would supply fresh fish and worked a small tomato vinery to eke out a living. This income was augmented by taking supplies out to the Hanois lighthouse that dominated the rocky horizon off the south-west of Guernsey. Rachel found work doing translations for the island government - the States - and later, in the Information Bureau, helping visitors.

On most summer evenings the couple would join a small number of neighbours sitting on the sea wall and they would talk about their day. These balmy evenings would often end with a glorious sunset as the neighbours parted and found their way home.

In this romantic setting Rachel and Tom's children were conceived. Nine months later, when their two healthy children were born, their joy was complete.

CHAPTER TEN

In the closing months before Germany surrendered, Levi Industries ceased production. Helmut Stein had approached the general manager, who was seconded to run the factory from the military throughout the war. This small, dour man had maintained the accounts and run the factory like clockwork from the day he walked in and told Joshua Levi that he was now in charge.

With the same detachment, the manager had handed the factory over to Helmut when the fighting ended. Helmut had engaged a lawyer to make the necessary adjustments to the legal register, proving that he was effectively the new owner, since he held forty-nine per cent of the shares and the other fifty-one per cent had been owned by a deceased Jew. It was not clear if any of the Jew's family had survived to claim their inheritance, but the manager thought it unlikely, so was untroubled about handing over complete control to Helmut.

As the war ground to a halt and the German military machine went into meltdown, Helmut had sought to keep his head below the parapets and did everything he could to avoid having himself or his sons sent to the front line. All three had survived, and the two sons also worked in the factory when hostilities ended and they were finally demobbed.

Levi Industries was renamed Stein Pharmaceuticals and in the post-war years the family undertook a root and branch review of every aspect of the business. A small workforce was employed, and by 1946 production had started again.

Although clothing dyes were the main income stream for the business, Helmut believed they could diversify, and spent some time looking into the pre-war activities of the research and development department. Soon realising he was out of his depth, he employed an experienced chemist to review previous research and possible new products for the factory.

This chemist, a young woman called Ingrid Hoffman, became

fascinated with the late Joshua's work. She found that not only had Joshua synthesized a permanent dye that was completely stable but he had been working on technologies that would exploit polymers in a wide range of chemical applications. Excited by what she found, she reported the news to Helmut and his sons.

'Hr Stein, the man Joshua was something of a genius. Not only had he invented a dye so stable that we could have avoided the many reapplications that have been needed for the military uniforms, but he also did some ground-breaking work on polymers that was frankly years ahead of the field.

'There is just one thing I don't understand. From his notes, Joshua had obviously made the key breakthrough back in 1937. From then onwards he seems to have gone completely astray with all sorts of investigations down blind alleys. A man as clever as him must have known this, so why didn't he announce his breakthrough earlier?'

The three men looked at each other as if to say, will you tell her? Hans spoke up, whilst Helmut turned to gaze out of the window and Freddy looked unemotionally at his brother.

'Ingrid, Joshua once owned the factory but he was a Jew and you know how these people were treated. He was allowed to keep his job because it was considered useful to the Reich if he could find a stable uniform dye. He would have known that as soon as this was achieved, the Reich would have no further use for him. So he must have created these false trails on purpose.'

It took a moment for this to sink in before she asked what became of him. Freddy, unrepentant, cut in.

'It has become unfashionable for us to say these things with the occupying forces everywhere, but we had to purge our nation of ...'

Helmut turned back towards them and interrupted his son.

'We only know that Hr Levi was killed in 1940 after he attacked a group of young men near his home. That is now history and we will speak of it no more. What I want from you, Ingrid, is a list of the products that this factory could make on the back of his research. I want to know how much investment would be needed, if any, in plant and machinery; and when you have done this, Hans, you and Freddy will work out the market potential. Lose no time - if he had worked all this out nearly a decade ago, others will also have done the same, or be close behind him.'

Together Ingrid and Hans produced a plan to introduce a whole new range of products based upon Joshua's work. Freddy tried to help, but was neither intellectually nor emotionally up to the demanding workload and quickly got left behind. There were regular update meetings during which Freddy's lack of understanding was plainly apparent as he tried to impress his father by chipping in at the wrong time with statements that displayed his ignorance.

Nevertheless, the plan came together, and Helmut found a new rôle for Freddy. This time he was put in charge of the operation of the factory. Fortunately, an experienced production manager was also employed to report to Freddy. He kept the plant running and managed all of the logistics of the business, despite Freddy's interference and ineptitude.

Within five years, Stein Pharmaceuticals had grown to a substantial business employing hundreds of people and shipping products all over Germany. Within ten years they employed over a thousand people and shipped products all over the world.

The Stein family fortunes grew steadily as the business went from strength to strength. Helmut maintained a tight grip on the business, with Hans and Freddy his seconds in command. Logically, it would have made more sense for Hans to be his only number two, but Helmut had always been closer to Freddy emotionally. They were similar, and both considered Hans to be too liberal. However, Helmut was far from stupid, and he begrudgingly accepted that his favourite son was also a fool in business.

He ensured that Freddy never suspected he felt this by constantly belittling Hans in front of him. Anything that Freddy suggested was received enthusiastically but rarely adopted, unless the idea had come from his able production manager.

With the increased growth, Stein Pharmaceuticals quickly outgrew its modest office accommodation on the outskirts of Munich. The first major move was to a brand new industrial park financed by Allied redevelopment funds. Helmut had been able to secure a long lease at virtually no rent in return for a promise of hundreds of local jobs. Production moved to the new site along with all the administration, leaving only research and development at Munich.

By the mid-sixties, the booming German economy funded the expansion of Stein's overseas facilities. Optimism was at an all-time high.

Helmut was a shrewd businessman and he knew that his empire could now shift into a new gear with the right management, but he was already in his sixties and needed to start handing over power. He also wanted to reap the considerable benefits of his work. He didn't wish to invest his own funds into the next phase of the business's growth, and very significant investment would be needed to fund it. Although Stein Pharmaceuticals was an international business, most of the production was still in Germany. This resulted in high costs to move their products to overseas customers.

He knew the answer was to set up factories closer to these customers, especially in America and Japan. In order to raise the money and bring in the expertise to execute his plans, Stein Pharmaceuticals must go public. Shares in this highly successful company would be prized by investors and millions could be raised. The sale of his own shares would make him the wealthiest man in southern Germany.

This would also neatly sidestep the problem of handing over power to his sons. They would both inherit his wealth eventually and, as a public company, Stein would of course be expected to introduce a new executive management team.

This plan seemed perfect and it was, except for one small problem. Joshua Levi's shares had never been finally resolved. On paper, a controlling fifty-one per cent did not belong to

Helmut.

The Stein family 'problem' was the subject of many a heated debate at family get-togethers. Freddy could not understand nor accept that they were anything less than the outright owners of the business. They employed the best legal advisors in Germany to try to unravel the situation, but there was no legal remedy. When the company was originally formed many years earlier as a family business, it was always assumed it would stay in the Levi family. If one shareholder died, their shares automatically transferred to the deceased's estate and were inherited by their family. By what they did and did not state, the formation documents allowed this situation to arise, and German law did not permit the shares to be cancelled or transferred other than with the written permission of a family member or a signed transfer document.

Without a majority shareholding, the Stein family could not execute their plan to place the company on the German Stock Exchange, the Boerse.

Disappointed, Helmut announced his plans to retire and reluctantly pass control over to his two sons in March 1972, at the age of seventy.

Helmut's wife had passed away some years earlier, but it had always been one of her desires to go on a cruise, and he decided this would be a fitting way to start his retirement. The cruise liner left Southampton in the spring en route for the Caribbean by way of the Canary Islands, but first it would anchor off Guernsey in the Channel Islands for a day.

Helmut was intrigued to see the islands where the Jewish girl had been sent all that time ago and where she must have met her death. Ironic, he thought, that so much had been achieved in his working life, but his crowning glory had been denied by the girl's family. There would not be time to take a boat to Alderney, but he decided to take the cruise liner's launch to see the beautiful town of St Peter Port in Guernsey.

At first, he followed the group of other day trippers from the cruise as they meandered through the cobbled High Street and

Arcade. But he soon tired of their window-shopping and went in search of more familiar interests. Guernsey still had the German fortifications left behind from the occupation, as well as what remained of a German underground hospital constructed by slaves, and an occupation museum. He found his way to the quayside office of the Tourist Information Bureau.

On the windows outside, amongst the cluttered notices and advertisements, was a sign written in French, German and Spanish, indicating that those languages were spoken by the staff. His English being truly appalling, Helmut was relieved to see German amongst them.

He entered and approached a young blonde woman behind the counter, sure that she looked characteristically Aryan. Presumptuously he asked, 'Sprechen Sie Deutsch?'

To his surprise the reply came not from her but from a dark-haired woman sitting behind her and facing away from him.

'Ich spreche...'

Rachel turned to look directly into his face.

He was taken aback. This woman, she looked... surely not... no, it can't be...

His mind raced back to the shabby office all those years ago in Munich. The Jewish woman had been attractive; she too had long curly dark hair. Then there was the child. He remembered how the woman had pleaded with him to allow time to say her farewells. The child had been on a chair just outside the door. As the Jew had looked back into his office, the child had turned her head in as well. Those eyes... tears had started to roll from them... these were those same eyes.

Rachel looked inquisitively at the man who seemed to be staring at her. What was wrong with him? Why was he staring? Forcing a smile, she asked in fluent German how she could help.

He stuttered, then regained his composure and, looking up at one of the advertisements for inspiration, asked if there was somewhere he could hire a rowing boat. The occupation museum had disappeared from his mind.

Rachel obliged by directing him along the harbour to a slipway where rowing boats were available by the hour. They politely said goodbye and were both turning away when he stopped and spoke again, this time in broken English.

'I must to speak English more often. You German is excellent - where did you learn it?'

Rachel replied that she was born in Germany and, although she had left when she was very young, had retained her fluency by working in the Information Bureau and sometimes doing translation work. He probed just a little further to be sure.

'Where.... um.. whereabouts in Germany were you lived?' he asked amicably.

'My family lived just outside Munich. Do you know the area?'

'No, sorry ...' he lied, 'I from another part of Germany. I never been around there I think.'

A polite smile, and he left the Bureau - his head now spinning. What did this mean?

As he walked along the harbour he saw a group of distinctive yellow telephone boxes close to the large town church. Checking his pocket for change, he found an empty box and telephoned a long distance number.

'Fraülein, this is Hr Stein Senior. Put me through to my son, Friedrich... Hello, Freddy. Listen .. No, don't talk, listen. I am fine... Freddy, she is alive. The girl - she is alive. All those years ago, she didn't drown after all. I've just seen her.'

The other end went silent for a moment as Freddy took in what he was being told.

'She can't be. It's a mistake. Remember? I went there. I asked questions, met people and spoke with the police as well as our own people. She can't be alive, Father. After so long, what makes you think you have seen her? How would you even recognise her?'

'Freddy, listen to me, she is alive. I recognised her by her eyes and spoke with her. As a child she lived near Munich. Freddy, she had her mother's eyes. Even her hair was the same. It's no mistake; it's her. But I don't know what we should do about it. You need to speak with Hans and the lawyers. She obviously has no idea about the firm.'

Helmut heard the pips intervene to signal that more money was needed, but frantically searching for change, he realised there were only deutschmarks in his hand.

'Listen, Freddy, I have to go. I am out of change. Speak with Hans and I will phone again when I can.' He just got this out before the continuous tone ended his call.

Making his way back to the launch, Helmut's pulse was racing. He stared across at the Information Bureau as the launch pulled away to make for the liner. Back on board, he made straight for the bar and ordered a large whisky, then another. Just an hour later, having consumed several whiskies, Helmut made his way to the deck.

The last launches were returning from St Peter Port now, and the liner was making ready to up anchor and set a course for the Canaries. He stared across at St Peter Port, his mind still racing. Could he trust the boys to sort this out? What would the lawyers say?

Before long the ship was underway and the moon was replacing the sun to guide it. Guernsey and Herm had slipped away and Sark was disappearing as Helmut leaned on the rail and looked out to sea.

Lost in thoughts about the future of the firm, he hardly noticed the pressure on his temples, the slight dizziness. He did take note of the indigestion - or was it heartburn?

- squeezing on his chest. The ship seemed to be moving erratically. He hung on to the rail. Some people stopped and asked if he was all right. He looked pale, they said.

When Helmut collapsed onto the deck, concerned passengers had already summoned the ship's doctor. He was there in minutes and did everything he could, everything anyone could. But it was too late. Helmut Stein was dead.

CHAPTER ELEVEN

For some years Hans and Ingrid had been lovers, and she regularly stayed at his farmhouse in the country. She was there enjoying an intimate dinner when the phone rang. Hans took the call and she watched as he went pale and sat down, still holding the phone.

'What is it?' she asked. 'What's happened?'

'It's Father, he... he's dead. That was the chaplain on the cruise ship. It seems he suffered a fatal heart attack just half an hour ago. I can't believe it.'

The two held each other whilst Hans took in what had happened. Helmut had suffered from a mild heart condition, but nobody imagined it was that serious. A few minutes later Hans remembered that he must inform Freddy. As Helmut's favourite, he was sure to be devastated.

The phone call was not what Hans would have expected at all. At first, Freddy was shocked, or perhaps surprised would have been more accurate. He was surprised because he had spoken with his father only a few hours earlier. Although Hans asked, Freddy had decided not to discuss the subject of this call, except to say he had sounded all right then and hadn't mentioned feeling poorly. The initial surprise transformed into a strange mixture of annoyance and apparent amusement. Freddy was almost crowing about the irony of his father dying as soon as he retired, and in the Channel Islands of all places. Before long these emotions gave way to thinly veiled greed. Of course, their father's shares and control of the business would now fall to them, not to mention the substantial estate.

Freddy was not sad to lose his father at all; he was too distracted with how it affected him to be sad.

The funeral was not a grand affair. A few of Helmut's wartime cronies turned up and several people from the business, who mistakenly thought Freddy would be impressed with a show of grief. In fact, the only person who seemed genuinely to care was the son who had always been treated so badly - Hans. Even Ingrid, usually a warm person, could not find it in herself to be hypocritical and pretend she would miss Helmut. She only cared that Hans was saddened.

It was a cold, wet day, darkened by storm clouds gathering in the sky overhead. After the formal service, with a short diplomatic eulogy from Hans and an even shorter, almost curt reading from Freddy, the small crowd assembled around the grave to witness Helmut's burial.

The wake lasted a barely respectful hour before people started to make their apologies and leave. Just Hans, Ingrid and Freddy remained in the Munich apartment to drink the final toast to the men's father.

'He was quite an act to follow.' Freddy offered this silence breaker. He had been looking out of the window and now turned in to the lavish room.

'Yes, Freddy. You're right. He was a born leader, and as well as being our father, he also was a great business partner. It's such a shame that after all his work, he should be denied a peaceful retirement.'

Ingrid put her hand on his shoulder to comfort him. 'Maybe he wouldn't have wanted that. I mean, maybe he was not the kind of man to have enjoyed retirement. I think sometimes he was lonely since your mother passed away.'

Freddy tried to look interested but soon became impatient with the direction of this conversation. Hans had always been too soft, and now he had found a soul mate in Ingrid, who was just as bad. What are they talking about? Of course the old man wanted to live; he had made all that money. Anyway, what did it matter? He was dead now. They should get on with thinking about their lives. He muttered a kind of agreement with Ingrid and turned back towards the window as if to conceal his emotion. Ingrid started to go over, but Hans took her arm and signalled her to leave him. He would deal with his loss in his own way.

As Freddy stared into the gloomy, wet Munich night, he

thought about how much money he would have inherited if the Jewish girl's family hadn't prevented the stock market listing of Stein Pharmaceuticals. Of course he was still extremely wealthy, as his father had paid them well over the years and had still left them a small fortune. But it wasn't enough. Freddy was still furious about the listing.

Now that half of Helmut's shares went to each son, the potential for friction increased. Although the split was almost fifty-fifty, Helmut had left 4,999 shares and the odd number meant that one son would effectively have control. Despite his affection for Freddy, Helmut had been astute enough to realise that he should not have overall control of the family fortune, so Hans had one extra share. This frustrated Freddy and worsened the already fragile relationship between the brothers. At work, Freddy and Hans disagreed about almost everything. Freddy decided he could wait no more and contacted one of his seedier ex-colleagues from the Hitler Youth.

Over a drink in one of their regular downtown haunts, Freddy explained his problem. His friend was tall and thin with characteristically blonde hair smoothed back with hair cream, and blue eyes. His pale face was speckled with acne and the scars of previous outbursts which belied his forty-six years of age.

'Günter, I always thought we should just forge the share certificates and the business would be ours, but the old man wouldn't agree. Now we have this situation where the girl is still alive and stands to inherit her father's controlling shares in our business if she ever finds out. In the meantime, we can't list the business which would bring in millions for our shares. We could just sell, but that would get us a fraction of the money we could get with a listing, and I'm not sure Hans would cooperate.'

Günter was quieter than Freddy and although his friend, he indulged Freddy and often allowed himself to be manipulated. Freddy was much wealthier than him and got him into places he could never have afforded on his own, so he put up with

Freddy's domineering, bombastic personality. But here was a chance for him to increase his own capital. Freddy had never opened up to him about this problem, and apart from family and legal advisors, nobody had been told. Günter calculated that if he could help, it may make him a rich man in his own right.

'So let me get this right. The old man's shares would go to his daughter and she would control your business. But she doesn't know she has got them?'

Freddy nodded, and Günter went on. 'So if the daughter hadn't survived, what would have happened to the shares?'

'Our legal people tell us that if she had been killed in the camp, the whole lot would have been lost because of the conditions on the transfer. But if she had just died in an accident or through illness, there would have been nobody to inherit the old man's shares and the Government would have allowed them to be dissolved. Our shares would then be the only ones left, so we would have control.' He paused. 'We thought the bitch had died in an accident. I even went over to check it out, but we never found a body, and now it turns out she survived after all.'

'How do you know she doesn't already have the shares but just hasn't bothered yet, or maybe doesn't know the value?' He thought and then went on, '..and what would happen if... if she had an accident now, a fatal accident?' Freddy looked at his friend. He could see where this was leading and liked it, but needed a moment to reflect.

'Let me get us another beer, Günter.'

As he made his way to the bar, he thought about their conversation. What would happen if they got rid of her? But... maybe she has got the share certificates by now. Maybe she has got family? If they get rid of her and she has both, the shares would just go to her family and they might even start looking into them to see what they are worth. What about Günter, could he be trusted? Yes, he's an old friend and he knows what I would do if he crossed me. Yes, Günter might be the key.

'Here you are, my friend.' He handed Günter a bottle of lager. 'Look, you might be able to help. Your job is not exactly going to make you rich. Why don't you come and work for me? Not at Stein, more in a private capacity.'

They grinned at each other knowing full well what Freddy was really asking, and raised their bottles in agreement.

'Freddy, you need to be a bit more specific than that.' Günter was still grinning, seizing this chance to get some of his friend's fortune. 'You want me to get rid of her? That will be expensive, you know.'

'Of course not, Günter. I am a respectable businessman. No, all I would want from you is to do some digging around. There is too much we don't know about this woman. I need you to go to Guernsey and find out as much about her affairs as you can. I want to know if she has family, but most of all I want to know if she knows anything about any shares or Stein Pharmaceuticals.' His eyes then turned cold and he reached across the table to grip Günter's hand tightly, preventing him from taking another sip of beer. 'But you know, Günter, accidents can sometimes happen.'

Günter felt a chill down his spine. Was Freddy referring to him or the woman?

With a nervous laugh the two moved on to discuss the details of the arrangement. Günter was to act as an agent and would receive all his expenses plus a daily fee. He would also receive a large commission if the controlling shares passed to Freddy. These shares would remove power from Hans and so Günter's activities were to remain a secret between the two of them. Freddy reflected on his good judgement in not passing on the message to Hans when Helmut rang to say he'd seen Rachel in Guernsey. The commission would make Günter rich, but there was a condition that Stein Pharmaceuticals had to go public before he earned this, and the more money the listing brought in, the more Günter could earn. If all went well it could be over a million deutschmarks.

CHAPTER TWELVE

The twin engine Dakota taxied into position on Guernsey's austere airstrip. A few minutes later steps were in place and the door opened to reveal the passengers and stewardess on this *Intra Airways* charter flight from Frankfurt via Jersey. Although a tourist flight, the first passenger to disembark appeared in a suit with folded overcoat on his arm. Günter looked completely out of place, but seemed oblivious to this as he strolled across the apron towards the single storey arrivals hall. On the roof of this building a small wall and rail enclosed a lookout point where a group of children now watched the line of passengers snaking their way towards the baggage area.

Günter waited patiently amongst the chattering crowd for his suitcase to be passed through the window onto some crude rollers that ended on a table. His height enabled Günter to avoid eye contact with the rabble surrounding him. Cringing with disdain, he shuffled from side to side as clutching arms reached past him to grab the bags that were descending the rollers. Two children attached to the leg of an overweight tourist stared up at him without speaking, as if he were one of the tourist attractions laid on for their holiday. Unsmiling, he moved closer to the rollers. For God's sake, where is it? he thought.

Having taken the initiative to be first off the aircraft, Günter was not amused that his case was among the last to appear. Angrily, he snatched the brown leather valise and marched towards Customs. As Guernsey was a duty-free destination, Customs on the way in was a bit of a formality, and Günter was allowed to pass through without hindrance.

Outside the building a line of ageing but tidy taxis waited for fares. Günter found a large Peugeot driven by a middle-aged woman taxi driver and gave his instructions to find the hotel he had booked.

En route to the hotel, the woman tried to make conversation. Was he here on business? She realised this was no tourist. What line of business was he in? But Günter's abrupt replies soon made it apparent that conversation was not going to yield a tip. So she turned up the radio volume in protest against his ambivalence, and 'All Right Now' by Free played loudly, much to his irritation but to her apparent delight.

The taxi raced along the island's narrow roads, missing oncoming traffic and the roadside granite walls by what seemed no more than millimetres. Günter found himself involuntarily breathing in through some of the closer encounters. As the taxi approached the outskirts of St Peter Port, the houses became grander. Some were set behind large gardens whilst others fringed the road more closely, with drives that arced past large-fronted Georgian homes.

Brightly-coloured yellow telephone boxes and blue pillar boxes periodically adorned the road as it twisted and turned on its way into the town. Even the road junctions were peculiar as yellow - not white - lines were used for markings, and a bizarre system of filtering in turn replaced the usual roundabouts and most traffic lights. Günter could not fathom how people could operate such a system; surely everyone would just barge through? This was characteristically stupid British politeness.

He pondered on the fact that despite this politeness and the grand Georgian buildings, in other ways the island did not seem British at all. In fact, the road signs were all in French and the climate was decidedly more continental than British.

Another turn in the road and the taxi was descending a final hill into St Peter Port. The road widened towards the foot to reveal a panoramic view of the sea and neighbouring islands. Even the insensitive Günter could not fail to be impressed by the sight of the bright sunlight reflecting off a glassy smooth sea. In the background, lush green vegetation on the island of Herm blended into a long white sandy beach with small outcrops of rocks slightly offshore.

The taxi turned left at the foot of the hill and pulled over almost immediately, outside the Royal Hotel.

'Here you are, my dear.' She was out of the taxi and opening his door before he had gathered his totally superfluous overcoat.

Once open, she collected Günter's case from the boot and was about to take it into the hotel when he interjected. 'That won't be necessary; I'll take it from here. How much do I owe you?'

With the fare settled, the woman thanked Günter, bid him farewell with a 'Cheerie' and was on her way again.

Just a road and low wall separated the hotel from the sea, and Günter decided he would take a stroll along the sea front once he had checked in.

The reception area of the hotel was a little tired, but still held the atmosphere of days when in its previous glory, the Queen of England had, among other dignitaries, graced the guest list.

Günter checked in without really noticing the receptionist and porter who assisted and took his bag to his room. They tried to be pleasant - after all, this guest had not given a leaving date - but he was hard work.

His room on the second floor overlooked the sea front and was furnished with old-world comfort. This suited Günter, who felt like a man of substance for the first time in his life. This was a hotel he could never have afforded, but what the hell? Freddy was paying.

His first day on Guernsey almost managed to please Günter. True, he was not usually given to relaxing in scenic locations. Still single and in his mid-forties, he lived at home with his ageing mother and rarely travelled outside Germany. He had grown accustomed to his own company and largely ignored his mother's conversation. But the chemistry of this island and his new found status penetrated his dense emotions, to the extent he almost felt like making conversation with strangers. Almost, but not quite, except for a chef he passed on his way down a side road as he returned to the hotel after a walk.

He heard some local youths bad-mouthing the chef, who scurried towards the kitchen entrance, distractedly uttering expletives and waving his arms. Expletives Günter understood clearly as they were in German.

He approached the man with a kindred spirit.

130

'Youths today, they have no respect. Your accent - you must be from the south, yes?'

Taken somewhat aback, the man looked suspiciously at Günter. He was of medium build, with black greased-back hair and a smart but dated dress sense that gave away his middle age.

'Yobs, this lot are yobs. They can't get over the war, and they aren't even old enough to have fought in it. Munich, I come from Munich - and you sound like you do as well. Are you staying here?'

'Yes, I am here for a while. Hopefully you can get me some decent sauerkraut. And is there a decent beer cellar here?'

'You will be lucky, my friend. This lot drink warm ditchwater and listen to hippy music. You can get some decent lager in most bars, though. If you are in the hotel bar tonight, I'll buy you a couple.'

They parted company, agreeing to meet up later, and Günter returned to his room.

A local contact from the Fatherland - quite a good find on my first day, he thought, as he returned to his room to change for dinner.

Günter enjoyed his meal in the hotel restaurant, complemented by an excellent bottle of wine which he consumed on his own. His metabolism allowed him to eat and drink without gaining any weight; a mixed blessing, he often thought. He was glad he didn't get fat like so many middle-aged men, but would have liked to have filled out more, as he often thought himself to be scrawny. This drove him to build what muscle he could through exercise and, although he liked to eat, he also worked out regularly.

But tonight was his first night in the rôle of a well-todo businessman, and exercise was a long way from his thoughts. He left the restaurant and found his way to the hotel bar.

He was perched on a bar stool with a glass of brandy in his hand when the chef, now in casual clothes, entered the bar. The chef began to make his way towards Günter when two men in their early twenties stepped in front of him, blocking his way.

With a look of resigned exasperation he tried to sidestep around them. They moved in his way again. This went on two or three times before the barman intervened and the young men moved away quietly and left the bar.

'What was all that about?' Günter asked when the chef finally joined him.

'The same as earlier. These kids won't leave me alone.' He signalled to the barman who brought him a bottle of lager and a glass. 'Will you join me, Herr..Herr..'

'Just call me Günter, and yes, I will. Let me knock this back.' Günter downed his brandy in one and poured himself a lager when the barman brought him a bottle and glass.

The chef was a good ten years older than Günter and judging by his appearance, life had not been kind to him. He was slightly overweight, and although his dark hair was slicked back - much like Günter's blonde hair - the two looked very different.

'So, do all Germans have to put up with this?'

'No, not all - although the resentment is never far from the surface. They have a particular problem with my wartime service, if you know what I mean.'

'I see. I think perhaps we may have similar political leanings. I was too young to join up, but the Hitler Youth did what they could.'

As the evening went on and the lager flowed, the chef became more open about his rôle in the Gestapo. He was clearly hated by his fellow kitchen workers, some of whom were French and had lost friends and family to the Gestapo. He told of the attacks made against him, and of one occasion when broken glass was left in a washing up bowl before he used it.

Günter said nothing of his true rôle on the island, preferring to describe himself as a wealthy traveller who was considering investments here. But he did ask about other German nationals in Guernsey.

Chef could not help. He was aware that there was a German working in the Information Bureau and another managing a hotel locally, but they had nothing in common and had never met.

So the evening ended amiably enough, but Günter hadn't learned anything of value.

The next morning he decided to get a look at Rachel. Wearing sunglasses and some very tourist-like clothes, he went up to the Bureau window and pretended to scrutinise the advertisements in the window. The door was open and visitors were wandering in and out. Looking around at the staff, he noticed a woman who fitted the description he had been given. She was speaking to a visitor and...yes she was speaking in German. This was her, the Jewess.

Günter fixed her impression on his mind and walked away, having first noted the opening hours displayed on the door. He didn't want to be seen.

Just before five thirty, he returned to take up a position a few yards from the Bureau, reading a newspaper for cover. Rachel emerged a few minutes later chatting to another woman who locked the Bureau doors. They were immersed in conversation as they crossed the road to a double bus stop on the other side. Rachel bid farewell to the other woman, who walked on to the second stop for the north of the island whilst she waited at the first.

Before long a grey single-decked bus had arrived at the first stop and a green one at the second. Günter slipped onto the end of the queue for the grey.

He found a seat a few rows behind Rachel, diverting his face as he walked past her. The bus pulled away.

Stopping every few minutes to let passengers on and off, the bus meandered its way across the island until it emerged on the southern corner of the west coast. By now most of the passengers had left and apart from an old man sitting close to the driver, only Rachel and Günter remained. The old man was chatting to the driver as they travelled and occasionally turned to face down the bus as if to invite the other two into their conversation. Rachel just smiled politely without responding, and Günter quickly pulled up his newspaper to hide behind. He had no intention of entering into a conversation that included Rachel.

Finally, she rose and walked down the aisle to get off at the next stop. Günter watched from behind, admiring her figure. Not bad for early forties, he thought. Rachel possessed a spring in her step that was more like a girl than a woman. She looked happy as she sauntered away along the coastal path towards home. As soon as Rachel descended the steps to leave the bus, Günter got up quickly and followed several paces behind. On the right of the road a Napoleonic fort, known locally as the Cup and Saucer, was connected to the island by a granite slipway. The slipway secured a number of small boats through ropes and iron rings, and close to one such boat a man was tending to his nets. As Rachel approached the man rose, walked towards her and as they met, he kissed her cheek and placed his arm around her waist. They were soon deep in conversation and paying no attention whatsoever to the man now seated on the sea wall, watching their every move.

After a while, Günter heard Rachel mention something about dinner, and she left to walk a short distance across the road to a cottage. As the door opened, Günter heard more voices, and a loud greeting, 'Hi, Mum.'

So Rachel had family, but a family living in such a small cottage would not have much room. Would they live like this if they had access to the wealth that the family inheritance could bring?

Günter returned to his hotel, satisfied that the omens were good.

Inside, Rachel was soon joined by her husband Tom and their daughter Rebecca who sometimes came to them for dinner. The conversation was about Rebecca's new job working for a bank in St Peter Port. Rebecca was a beautiful young woman who shared her mother's features. At just twenty-one, this was her first 'proper' job since leaving university, and she was learning the ropes. They talked about the people in her office, her boss and then her twin brother David who also worked in the finance sector, but for an investment company.

Apparently, David had just succeeded in attracting a wealthy new client to his company. The conversation was easy and after dinner, the three of them strolled out to the sea wall to catch the sunset.

Back in the hotel bar, Günter once again was in deep conversation with the chef Reiner, as he now revealed to be his name. They sat until the early hours, putting the world to rights. What a disaster for the world that the Führer had been prevented from purifying the species. How stupid these people were to fail to realise the importance of the political agenda – even some of their own people could not grasp the significance of the work carried out by the SS. As Reiner progressively became drunker and drunker, he became more and more self-pitying. Eventually, he revealed that this pathetic island would not be his home for much longer; he planned to get away to South America as soon as he could raise the money.

Günter kept pace with the late-night drinking but remained more sober than Reiner. So much so that he realised an opportunity might be arising. Determined to test his idea, he needed Reiner to sober up.

'My friend, I may be able to help you, but let's not talk about it here. Grab your jacket and we can take a stroll along the harbour.'

Reiner looked puzzled. Why should they go outside when they could continue to drink in the bar? He wanted to protest but was already feeling a bit drowsy and there was something about Günter's tone that intrigued him.

They left the bar and staggered across the road towards the main streets of St Peter Port. There was a large taxi rank and groups of young people were heading towards it from a nearby club. It was one in the morning and the Cellar Club had just closed, with many of its regulars the worse for wear with drink. The two middle-aged men tried to avoid eye contact and walked purposely through the taxi rank. They would have made it to the other side, but two swaggering men rounded the corner and immediately spotted Reiner. One of them made straight for him.

'You bastard! What are you doing out and about? You get back to the hole where you came from. We don't want to see your Nazi face on our streets.'

Günter's attack was instinctive. His fist entered below the ribcage on an upward trajectory that immediately winded the man who fell forwards as Günter raised his arm again to complete his assault with a blow to the back of his neck. A crowd gathered as the other man launched into Reiner, who was neither as fit or as well prepared as Günter. Reiner was soon lying on the street and not just his single attacker but a group of young men were now laying into him with their boots.

Günter turned to the crowd with a fearsome look on his face and seeing what he had done to the man lying in pain at his feet, they backed off. Günter confronted them. 'You want some of this, you stupid shits? Come on then, let's see what you are made of!'

One of the youths ventured forward. Günter's move was lightning fast; he grabbed his throat and, with no sign of exertion, lifted the young man off the ground before thrusting him backwards into the crowd. He collapsed in a heap. Shiftily looking around at each other to see if anyone else would have a go, the crowd could see that Günter was too much for them. They slowly dispersed, each mumbling as if this was not really anything to do with them.

Günter looked down at his friend. His face was bleeding and he was trying, painfully, to get up off the street. As he reached down to help him, a police siren could be heard approaching.

'Quickly! I know you are in pain, but let's get you back to the hotel. We don't want the police involved.'

Reiner was in too much pain to argue, and put an arm around Günter's shoulder. The two hobbled back across the road to the hotel, disappearing into the doorway as a police car sped into the taxi rank.

Günter helped Reiner to his small room at the top of the hotel. There was barely enough space for two of them and apart from a few clothes hanging on a rail behind a curtain, little evidence that anyone lived there. A small window looked out onto the back of the hotel, but there was only blackness reflecting from the glass.

Reiner lay on the single bed that occupied most of the floor space. He explained to Günter where a towel could be found and some hot water so he could clean himself up. He had sobered up now and winced when he tried to sit up.

As Günter tended to his wounds, he told Reiner how he could earn some money to help him get away from the island.

'I have some work to do here that may suit you, my friend. It seems that one of the Jews that escaped our clutches has got her hands on some information about our colleagues in the Reich and is hell-bent on passing it to that Weisenthal cretin - the Nazi hunter. We must stop her, but first we must find out what she has got. Your help will be well rewarded.'

'Simon Weisenthal and his cronies tried to indict me for so-called war crimes, but they didn't have enough evidence to make it stick. It would be a pleasure to help our friends keep safe from him. What do you want me to do?'

'First, I just want you to keep an eye open while I look around the bitch's house. I don't want anyone turning up while I'm there. If you are up to it, tomorrow would be good, when they are all at work.'

Günter had decided the Weisenthal story would allow him to disappear without trace afterwards. The last thing he needed would be this old man turning up at Stein Pharmaceuticals begging for money. He arranged to meet Reiner the next morning at the back of the hotel. Reiner would explain to his manager that he needed to visit the hospital for treatment as he had suffered an unprovoked attack.

The hotel manager was aware of the hostility towards his chef locally and although he felt no warmth towards him, he knew that Reiner kept his head down and did not initiate the abuse. He also needed a good chef, so put up with the inconvenience.

CHAPTER THIRTEEN

As Rachel arrived at the bureau, she pondered what Tom and she had been discussing that morning. Tom had risen early to catch the tide and would be out all day, so they couldn't meet at lunchtime to continue their talk. Their silver wedding anniversary was approaching and they knew that the children and grandparents would want to arrange something special for them, but they would struggle to afford it. How could they arrange a get-together on a shoestring that would make the family feel happy?

Greeting the others in the bureau, her friend Jeanette told her a call had come in from a German-sounding visitor who said he would ring back later. He sounded very proper and wanted to know the full name of the German translator so he could ask for her. Jeanette had given Rachel's name.

Further along the harbour Günter was collecting a small red hire car.

At ten o'clock, as arranged, Günter pulled up in the side road at the back of the hotel. Reiner moved awkwardly to get in, his bruises hurting badly. As the car moved away, Günter went over his plan. They would drive past the cottage to see if there was any sign of life. Then they would find a phone box and ring, and if nobody answered they would assume the coast was clear. Günter now knew Rachel's married name and the telephone number was in the directory.

Half an hour later, at an isolated phone box on the western coast, Günter emerged and climbing into the small hire car, confirmed that the cottage was empty.

Günter drove to the bend in the road where a slipway to the Cup and Saucer opened out, giving enough space for a car to wait. They could see Rachel and Tom's cottage, and Reiner agreed that if anyone approached he would give two long blasts on the car horn. Günter got out and walked to the back of the car. Opening the boot, he took a wheel brace from the toolkit and placed it inside his jacket then walked briskly towards the cottage.

There was a low wall with a gate and tiny front garden comprising a few hardy plants that could survive exposure to the westerly winds and salt air. Gravel lay between them, and a couple of Tom's lobster pots that had seen better days were discarded near the door. The front door was inside a small porch that housed a tomato plant and two pairs of Wellington boots, stashed beneath a shelf. He entered the porch. Still nobody was around; he felt inside his jacket for the wheel brace with his left hand whilst his right tested the door handle. To his amazement it opened. No need for the brace, then, he thought; this island was unique!

Once inside, he closed the door behind him and dropped the brace onto the floor. He took his bearings. This was the hall; one room to the left, one to the right and another at the end of the hall where light flooded in. Probably the kitchen down there, he thought.

First the room on the left; this was a bedroom but looked more like a teenage girl's room so he lost interest and moved to the room on the right of the hall. Another bedroom - or was it? There was also a desk and a bookcase. Maybe this was now used as a study.

He darted out to the back of the house where he found a long conservatory with easy chairs at one end and kitchen at the other. In the middle was a wooden table with chairs left distractedly, as if in a hurry. Turning back to face down the hall, he saw another door off the kitchen. This led on one side to a bathroom and the other to a small staircase. He climbed the stairs and at the top was Rachel and Tom's bedroom. This was in the roof of the cottage, and so there was full standing headroom only in the centre, or in the two dormer windows that looked out over the coast. The Cup and Saucer was there on the right with a nervous-looking Reiner in the car below. In front and to the left, the bay swept round to be protected by a large hill in the south. Out at sea a large lighthouse was visible in the distance.

Looking around, Günter saw no signs of paperwork. There was a double bed, made up but with a dressing gown thrown casually across it. A fitted wardrobe with louvred doors contained all of their clothes and shoes. Not many, he thought. This was no good. He charged down the stairs and along the hall to the study at the front. The desk, what is in the desk?

First the right-hand side drawers; there were files, but these seemed to contain receipts for Tom's fishing supplies or lists of what he had sold to the fish merchants and hotels. The left-hand side drawers contained a mixture of old chequebooks, bank statements and letters, mainly from the bank. There was a tin in one deep drawer that contained about twenty pounds, mainly in Guernsey notes and odd coins. Nothing seemed interesting. He closed these drawers and looked around the room. There was nothing else. Finally, he went for the centre drawer that spanned the foot well between the two sides. More letters. What was this ?... His concentration was broken by the sound of two blasts on a horn. No, not now. What is this...?

The letter seemed to be from an investment company, a local firm of advisors. He grabbed the letter and as he turned, he saw a figure approaching the house through the window. He rushed down the hall and was leaving the conservatory through a back door when he heard the voice. 'Hello, anybody home?'

Now in the back garden, Günter made a beeline for the side where a corrugated shed stood with an old boat beside it. He could see inside - it was a tool shed. There was a path along the side of the cottage, and some bushes with a pungent smell. He slipped past them and found that just a few feet of gravel separated him from the road. He could see that Reiner had pulled the hire car up in the road at the end of this path. He ran to the car and as the door shut behind him, Reiner sped away down the coast road.

'That was close; did you see who it was?' Günter asked. 'It was an old man, perhaps one of their parents. Anyway, how did you get on? Anything on our friends?'

Günter lied that he had found a letter from Simon Weisenthal asking about the information they could give him.

'It proves our suspicions; the bitch is definitely up to something. I didn't take it because I don't want them knowing we are on to them. Not yet, anyway. Listen, I also found a letter from a local company - Castle Cornet Investments and Trusts - have you heard of them?'

'No, I haven't.'

'I didn't see anything that had names or details of our friends, but if they have some kind of bank vault somewhere, they might be keeping the list there for safety. This firm might be the key.'

They drove back towards St Peter Port but took a diversion to a pub that Reiner knew on top of the cliffs. Leaving the car in the car park above the L'Auberge Divette pub, they descended some steps into the beer garden and took a table overlooking the sea and islands to the east. The view was spectacular.

Günter ordered lagers and two ploughman's lunches from the bar. As they ate and talked, the next part of his plan began to take shape.

CHAPTER FOURTEEN

The morning had been quiet at the small but modern office of Castle Cornet Investments and Trusts. A couple of clients had come in to meet their relationship managers, and they had purchased one of the new IBM personal computers to store client details in a database, and maybe do word processing - if it turned out to be as easy as using the Golfball typewriter.

The office on the top floor of a modern building called The Albany in St Peter Port overlooked Castle Cornet, the most impressive landmark in the town. But the morning had one very interesting event. The office manager had taken a call from an inspector with the fraud squad in London. It appeared there was a money laundering investigation going on and they wanted some help with a particular client of Castle's. Someone was being sent, and could they please cooperate?

The manager was a young man called Phil who needed some excitement in his life. Being an office manager was not really in his life plan, so any opportunity to liven things up was welcome. When another man arrived later that day with an air of authority, following up on the earlier call, he was keen to be involved. The man said his help would be noted in the investigation and if a prosecution followed, he could be sure the owners of Castle Cornet Investments and Trusts would be given a glowing report from the fraud squad.

'Now, we just need to look at anything you have on deposit for this person or their family, in particular share certificates. The name is Le Breton, but it could also be under her maiden name, Levi.'

Phil's jaw dropped. 'Are you sure?'

'Of course I'm sure. What is it? Do you know something?'

'No, no - it's just that...never mind. We do look after the Le Bretons, but there is not really much to report. Tom has a very small pension he set up with us and a life insurance policy; they bank with a High Street branch and don't have anything else.

I'm pretty sure we would know if they did.'

'No other bank accounts or investments? What about trust companies? Are you sure that is it?'

'Look, I'll be open with you. I know their son, David. I went to school with him and he also works here. There is nothing else to know.'

Günter was shocked; he hadn't wanted to get this close, and bowed out as quickly as he could.

'Okay. You have been very helpful; someone in London may have got their wires crossed. We will eliminate them from our enquiries. Please keep this conversation to yourself.' With that, he left.

Phil felt uneasy about this visitor. Perhaps he should have asked for some ID; he didn't want to explain to David that he had discussed his family affairs without asking for it. When David returned to the office later in the day, he said nothing.

That night the phone rang at Freddy's apartment in Munich.

'Freddy, it's me, Günter. There has been some progress.'

'Go on,' said Freddy, dryly.

'The woman has family, but she has nothing that links her to the business - no shares, no funny accounts, nothing. I've been over her home - it's a tiny cottage. They have no money.'

Günter explained how he had been through their personal documents and he described the visit to Castle Cornet Investments and Trusts. Freddy seemed satisfied.

'So, only the woman is left. There will be one last task for you out there, Günter. You know what that is. It must look like an accident, you understand?'

'I understand, Freddy, an accident. But how will you get the rest of the shares?'

'Don't worry about that, Günter; just do what I ask.'

The conversation closed and Günter knew exactly what must be done, although he was intrigued about how Freddy would achieve the overall control he was so desperate to get, and he had certainly changed his tune from the 'I'm a respectable businessman' comment.

Another day - and Rachel kissed Tom goodbye as she left for the bus stop. She walked along by the sea wall distractedly, thinking about Tom's latest suggestion for their wedding anniversary. Ahead at the bus stop was the usual small group of shop assistants who travelled into St Peter Port each day. The higher paid office workers took their cars.

Out at sea a storm was developing, and sinister clouds could be seen speeding over the horizon. The high tide was sending the sea crashing over the wall and white foam wisped across the path in front of Rachel. She pulled up the collar of her coat and strode on towards the bus stop.

Leaving the path, Rachel joined the other would-be passengers congregating at the red and white striped pole with the small enamel square, announcing the bus stop. She chatted to the other regulars about the approaching storm and they hoped Tom wasn't out there today which, of course, he wasn't.

Before long a green single-decker bus arrived and consumed the waiting queue.

The rambling journey into St Peter Port saw a number of new passengers board and some leave, including Rachel's friend, who sat next to her for the first few miles. Sitting alone now, she reflected on something a little odd that had happened earlier. Tom had walked barefoot to the door with her to say goodbye, and in the narrow hallway next to the door had trodden on something. With an 'ouch' he crouched down and picked up – of all things – a wheel brace. How it got there they had no idea, but Rachel was uncomfortable that someone must have been in their house whilst they were out. It must have been Dad, she thought to herself, but why would he have brought a wheel brace inside?

She was still pondering as the bus arrived at St Peter Port, just a few yards from the Information Bureau.

Her morning was uneventful, the usual tourists coming in and out wanting accommodation, brochures or directions to the aquarium. At lunchtime Rachel often indulged herself in some window-shopping in Town. Today, she left at one o'clock and strolled across the road and up the Pier Steps opposite. The steps were steep, made of local Guernsey granite, and formed a narrow passage between the high-walled buildings on either side. About halfway up she crossed a shaded alleyway. It was usually deserted, leading on either side to just a few doorways, hidden around corners and out of sight. Rachel glanced to her left as she passed and noticed a figure in a long coat, stationary and looking directly at her. A chill ran up her neck. But the figure furtively turned away and disappeared around a bend in the alley.

Rachel took a deep breath to regain her composure and continued to where the top of the steps opened onto the busy town High Street. She looked back over her shoulder, but all she could see was the steps leading to the pavement below. There was nobody there, not even the usual midday shoppers, and the familiar steps now felt a little sinister to her.

In the High Street, Rachel was soon consumed with the shops on either side of the narrow, cobbled, traffic-free street, and with the sight of familiar faces that the small town regularly turned up. She turned left and meandered downhill through a usually mobile crowd, punctuated by small groups who stopped without warning to converse in the middle of the road.

So distracted was she that she failed to notice the figure several yards away, lurking in shop doorways, with one eye on her every movement.

Rachel had perused both sides of the High Street and now headed back up the hill, her shadow inconspicuously attached behind her. As she approached the top, she disappeared from view below an archway off the main street. Her shadow moved quickly to close the gap, and as he reached the archway, his hand thrust into the right-hand pocket of his coat.

Realising that she would no longer have time to buy a snack from the small supermarket under the archway, Rachel stopped in her tracks, turned and walked quickly back towards the High Street. What happened next both confused and horrified her. She emerged at the very moment her pursuer turned under the arch. He saw her first and thrust his hand forward; Rachel tried to sidestep this stranger and was concentrating on the cobbled street below, worried that her high heels would cause her to fall. She didn't see his face and the sharp pain in her side rapidly consumed all of her attention. Feeling faint, she started to fall, then everything around became dizzy, until finally the daylight left and with it, her consciousness.

CHAPTER FIFTEEN

Tom sat anxiously by the hospital bed where his wife lay unconscious, her skin cold and white.

The doctor had not been overly encouraging about her chances. Tom was distraught; the woman he adored was on the brink of death.

He could not fathom what had happened. Earlier that day she had been in perfect health, beautiful in fact. She was always so full of life.

Of course, the family had arrived at the hospital as soon as they heard. They had gathered around her bed and listened attentively as the doctor had tried to explain what had happened. Rachel had collapsed in the busy High Street for no apparent reason. She had been seen brushing past someone and just dropped to the street as they walked off without seeming to notice her fall. The rudeness of some people, they all thought. But then there was the needle; what was that all about?

Lodged in Rachel's belt was the end of a hypodermic needle, snapped off. The nurses had almost been injured by it. It seemed the needle had scratched Rachel's skin just above her waist. They didn't know if that was connected to her collapse; it was only a surface scratch, but it had been sent for analysis.

If it was that, why was she struggling for her life? Tom could not understand it.

It was around midnight when the white-coated doctor returned, accompanied by a nurse and man in a suit.

'Mr Le Breton, this is Inspector Ogier from the local CID. He would like a word with you. Would you mind stepping out of the ward for a few minutes? The nurse will keep an eye on your wife.'

Tom rose silently, his expression bewildered. The ward doors quietly swung closed behind them. What was all this about? Why were the police involved?

The doctor spoke first, slowly but deliberately. 'The lab tests show that an unusual substance was present on the needle we found in your wife's belt. It appears to be a rare but very deadly virus and had more of it entered her bloodstream directly, instead of the small scratch she received, I'm sorry to have to tell you she would certainly be dead by now.'

Inspector Ogier cut in, 'I know this must be hard for you to take in, but can you think of any reason why someone might want to harm your wife, Mr Le Breton?'

Tom was emotionally drained; he was tired, hadn't eaten all day or night, and his head began to spin with this news.

The inspector spoke again. 'I can see you might want to think for a minute. In the meantime, let me tell you what we think might have happened. We think perhaps a person pushed past your wife under the archway off the High Street and either deliberately or unknowingly stabbed her with a needle containing this virus. It is just possible, I suppose, that they were not aware they had caught the needle on her and carried on, oblivious to what they had done - but frankly, that is so unlikely we are not even considering it. For one thing, we can think of no legitimate reason why anyone would have such a substance in a syringe in the first place.'

Now Tom was starting to come to terms with what was being said. 'Some bastard has deliberately attacked Rachel and left her for dead? ... No, I can't believe it, who could possibly want to harm her? ... Listen, Inspector, we are ordinary people, we have no enemies. Rachel is popular... no, there is absolutely no one who could have a reason to hurt, let alone kill Rachel. Doctor, what does this mean? Can you save her?'

'The next few hours are crucial, Tom. Rachel's own immune system is fighting the virus. Fortunately, the dose was extremely low, but we don't have anything we can give her to help. If she is going to make it we will know by morning. I am really sorry, I can't be more definite than that.'

Tom started to fill with anger. 'What the hell is this thing? Where did it come from?'

The inspector looked around him before he replied. 'Mr Le

Breton, the only thing I can tell you is that this virus has been known about for sometime. Recently, a man thought to be working as an agent for the intelligence services on the mainland was injected with a lethal dose from the tip of an umbrella as he walked through London. That dose was thought to originate in East Germany.'

'So who the hell pushed into her? Do you know who it was?' Tom asked.

'No, unfortunately we have no description yet, as this afternoon we had no reason to suspect foul play, but tomorrow we will question everyone we can find who was in the town when Rachel was there. Mr Le Breton, believe me, we will do our best to find this person.'

Tom turned back to the ward, leaving the two men standing and whispering to each other.

'I know the way these things work, Inspector, and I can assure you there is no couple more devoted to each other.'

The night was long and uncomfortable in a hospital chair, wooden arms and a backrest too upright to get comfortable. Tom shuffled from side to side continuously through the night. He couldn't sleep at all, and didn't want to try. As the ambient daylight in the ward replaced the low-level artificial night lights, Rachel seemed to look less white, her skin colour and her temperature gradually started to change; she became warm, then hot, then she started to murmur. Tom called the nurse who in turn summoned the doctor. He was there in minutes.

'She is fighting, Tom. This is what we were waiting for.'

As the hours passed, Rachel's temperature increased dramatically; she rolled from side to side and occasionally thrashed out. Her mumbling turned into ranting, so much so she was moved to a private side ward for the benefit of the other patients. With her husband, son and daughter at her side and Tom's parents hovering in the corridor, Rachel's body fought the virus. The morning was the worst, but by early afternoon she seemed to calm, and her temperature stabilised.

As the afternoon passed by, Rachel began to recover. At

almost exactly five o'clock she opened her eyes and there was recognition of Tom's face; no words but a faint smile told him that Rachel was back, and she was going to survive. Tom was not given to showing his emotion, but as he looked into his wife's eyes tears poured down his cheeks.

His son and daughter hugged him and kissed their mother before heralding in the anxious in-laws.

It was several days before Rachel was fit enough even to walk. Her body was still weak but her mind had returned to its full vigour. She wanted to know what had happened, who this person was who had attacked her, and why.

The police returned several times to talk with her and report on their progress interviewing local shoppers and shopkeepers. The full story was not given and the local paper simply ran a few lines saying a woman had collapsed in the High Street. Inspector Ogier didn't think a high-profile story would help with his investigations.

Unfortunately, progress was slow. Several people had seen a man in a long coat in the High Street, but none could give a decent description. Rachel's brief glimpse of the man in the alley was about the best they had to work with, but he had turned away so quickly that even her account could have described half the male population in the island.

One thing the inspector was sure of was that this was no random crime.

His belief was confirmed a week later when Rachel left hospital and returned home to Rocquaine. Tom had arranged a small welcome party with the family to greet Rachel as she came in, and stopped his car in the road outside the cottage front door. She was much stronger now, but Tom still insisted on holding her arm as he led her to the door.

As the door opened everyone inside called out 'Welcome home' in unison, to Rachel's delight. Instinctively, she placed her handbag on the small table in the hall and then stopped suddenly. She looked at her husband. 'Tom, you don't think that....remember that wheel brace you stood on? You don't think that could have had anything to do with what happened to me?'

Tom looked at her intently. He didn't want to spoil her homecoming with thoughts of the attack, but she had a point. Of course, there may have been a connection. Why hadn't he thought of that before?

He smiled at Rachel and assured her he would speak to the police when she was settled in.

Half an hour later, with the family fussing over her as she relaxed with her feet up on the long settee, Tom slipped back along the hall and dialled the local police.

Inspector Ogier was keen to know exactly what had happened and, more importantly, if they still had the brace. When Tom explained it was in the shed, a car was dispatched immediately to pick it up for forensic analysis.

Tom returned to the family gathering. As he entered the room his wife looked across at him and sensing he had something on his mind, asked if he had called them. Daisy wanted to know what they were referring to but rather than raise the painful subject of the attack again, Rachel just said it was nothing, just a call Tom needed to make. Although not entirely satisfied with this answer, Daisy was happy to let it pass if that's what Rachel wanted.

Inspector Ogier called a few days later to confirm they had identified the make of car that used such a brace but, sadly, the fingerprints matched none on record and it would take a few days to trace every Fiat car on the island.

***

The atmosphere at Castle Cornet Investments and Trusts had been a little strange since Rachel's attack. In particular, the manager Phil seemed very edgy around David Le Breton. David was aware of this, but had too much on his mind worrying about

151

his mother to broach the subject. But now that she was recovering and some kind of normality was returning to his life, he decided it was time to sort out Phil. A pint after work should do the trick, he thought.

Sure enough, Phil accepted and they found their way to The Yacht Inn further along the Esplanade. With a pint each, they sat at a table near the window and made small talk about the English football team and the antics of George Best. Eventually, an embarrassing silence fell and Phil could stand it no longer.

'Listen, mate, there's something I need to tell you and frankly, I've been putting it off.'

'That sounds ominous!'

'I hope you won't hate me for this, but a few weeks ago I took a call from some big shot in the serious crime squad and he wanted information about one of our clients.'

'So, what's that got to do with me?'

'Well, you see, I didn't know it until he turned up, but the client was your parents, in particular your mother.'

David's jaw dropped. 'What? You spoke about my family affairs without telling me!'

'I know it sounds bad but as I said, I didn't know who they wanted to speak about until the guy got here and when I found out I told him there was nothing to know. The thing is, I didn't ask for any ID. I know that is dumb but I didn't, and in view of what happened to your mum… well I don't know, do you think it could be important?'

David thought how gullible Phil had been, but he also knew he wouldn't have deliberately done anything to harm them. He was more interested in who the person was.

'Well yes, I do. This may well be the person who attacked Mum; you should have mentioned this earlier. Tell me exactly what he wanted to know.'

Phil explained that the man was interested in any bank accounts or investments Rachel or the family may have had, especially shares. He sheepishly told how he had quickly withdrawn when Phil had mentioned the fact that David worked

152

there.

David mulled over what he had been told, then rose quickly. 'Let's go, Phil.'

'Where are we going? What about our drinks?'

'Phil, you're not getting this, are you. We need to go to the police.'

The two men marched purposefully through the streets of St Peter Port, to the main police station. David went up to the desk and asked for Inspector Ogier. Minutes later he appeared and the two were led into an interview room.

The meeting took much longer than either had anticipated and when they emerged, a police artist was first to exit, thanking Phil for his help. 'This photofit will help us greatly; we'll start by running it past the witnesses in Town, just in case it jogs any memories.'

The description and photofit was distributed to the police officers who were checking all Fiat owners for a car with a missing wheel brace. They had almost exhausted the list supplied by the motor tax office and to their amazement, so far all of them when asked could show their wheel brace still intact with the tools.

The officers could not match any of the faces seen so far to the description.

Inspector Ogier was frustrated by the lack of progress and the following morning a meeting was called with all the officers on the case.

He stood at the front of the room with a large whiteboard beside him. On it were the known facts about Rachel's case. Arrows linked a rough drawing of the Le Breton cottage with another 'building' labelled Castle Cornet Investments and Trusts. A Fiat car and oversized wheel brace were just about discernible on one side and in the centre, as if the most crucial, an A4 paper was taped with the photofit copied onto it. This was their prime suspect. Several other images and words adorned the Rich Picture diagram on the whiteboard. Inspector Ogier addressed his troops.

'Okay, everyone, listen up. This is a serious assault, an attempted murder with no obvious motive. All the worse because the method has decidedly sinister overtones: it smacks of a professional hit, perhaps a contract killing. If that is the case we must assume the worst: whoever did this will probably try again. If that isn't the case, we must assume we are dealing with a psycho, maybe a serial killer starting a spree. Either way we must find and stop this person before anyone else gets hurt. The facts so far, if you please.' Various officers reported on the progress of their investigations, concluding with the search for a Fiat without a wheel brace. The young policeman began.

'Sir, we have almost completed the list of owners, and the only ones left are either away on holiday or in one case, in hospital recovering from a hip replacement. We still have Forest Road garage, the main dealers, to ask, otherwise it's down to hire cars.'

The inspector signalled thanks to his team and continued, 'Yesterday new evidence came to light that suggests the assailant was of German or Dutch origin. Someone posing as a serious crime squad officer visited Castle Cornet Investments and Trusts asking about the victim's affairs. This ..,' he pointed to the photofit, ' …. is what he looked like, and his accent was German or possibly Dutch. So, before checking on anyone else, I want a visit to each hire car company first thing today; our man could well be a visitor. Take your Photo-Fit and report back immediately. If he is still here I don't want any heroics. Just find out where he is staying and if any Fiats are still out on hire, I want to know. Oh and, Constable Le Noury, get a copy of the photofit up to the airport and docks.'

Four police constables were given the job of investigating the island's hire car companies.

***

Günter was furious; he paced around his hotel room repeating the same questions to himself. What was the stupid bitch doing? She had just walked through the archway; why did she turn back? Did she get the full dose? Did I get rid of her? That damned needle snapped as well; did anybody find it?

He was interrupted by a knock on his door; Reiner entered holding a tray with a glass of whisky. As the door opened, he spoke loudly for the benefit of anyone who might see him, 'Good afternoon, sir. You ordered a drink from the bar.' Günter waved him in.

'What happened? Did you get rid of her?'

'I don't know. I followed her through an archway in Town, but she turned back and walked straight into me as I was preparing to get the needle to her. She got it in the side and went down, but the needle broke off in my hand and most of the stuff was left in the barrel of the syringe. I had to leg it, as the do-gooders were all over her straightaway. I just don't know, but she did drop pretty suddenly.'

'I told you the stuff was good; we used to use it to get rid of the French when we ran Lyon. Some of them were in the way, but we couldn't always remove them without our own military command getting in a huff. So we gave them a sudden illness that nobody could trace. It worked a treat; in fact the East Germans still use it. I kept a small supply in case someone recognised me.'

'Why haven't you used it here on some of these louts who pester you?' Günter was curious.

'Two reasons. First, these people have no idea what I really got up to. They just know I was Gestapo and that's enough. Second, there are now too many of them to hit without suspicion falling on me. No, I will keep the rest of my supply for a rainy day. But what do we do about her?'

'Not *we*, my friend, *you*. It's time I got out of here, before someone puts two and two together. She may have seen me and if she didn't, someone else will. I can't risk it if she survives. I need to leave as soon as possible. This is what we need from you...'

Günter told Reiner that he would need to check the papers and the hospital. If she survived he must let him know. Most important of all, he needed to watch her every move. He gave him enough cash to support himself but he was to keep his job for cover as long as was possible. More cash and a ticket to Brazil would follow as soon as the job was done. There he would be welcomed by the old guard and honoured for his part in keeping them out of harm's way. 'You know our friends did not leave empty-handed... ,' he went on, '... there are great riches out there ready to finance the next Reich, and you will be well rewarded.'

Günter packed hurriedly and left, paying the hotel in cash and leaving a false address. He drove the hire car to the airport and left on the next available flight out of the island. He had been careful to cover his tracks; only Reiner had any way to reach him, through a telephone number in Munich.

Reiner did as he was told and scanned the local paper. Within a few days the incident was reported. It just said the woman had 'collapsed' with no further details. He decided to visit the hospital and check. It was not difficult to find out all he wanted to know. He just turned up with a bunch of flowers for the 'poor woman who collapsed in Town' and was warmly thanked by the nurse and told, 'She is much better now and should be back at home very soon.'

So there was still work to do, and he had no idea if Rachel's sudden illness was being treated as anything suspicious.

That night Reiner called the number in Munich. A cold and defensive voice answered without giving a name.

'Who is that?'

Reiner replied and the two discussed Rachel's apparent recovery. It was clear what had to be done, and the urgency in Günter's tone left no doubt that it needed to happen quickly.

Günter replaced the phone and looked around the office that had been converted into a temporary apartment. It was in the old Levi factory in Munich, now unrecognisable from the early days. As the firm had taken off, Helmut had created a suite with bedrooms and showers for late-night meetings. Freddy still kept an office that led onto one of these, and he had allowed Günter to stay there until they were sure there would be no ramifications from the attack in Guernsey.

Standing in the corner, Freddy spoke quietly. 'I assume from what you said that there is unfinished business in Guernsey. Is he up to it?'

'Yes, with his background it should be over soon.'

'Okay. We will worry about how we deal with him later. For now, we have another job to do. Are you ready?'

Günter acknowledged and left the room.

Five minutes later, Freddy checked his watch and grabbed an overcoat hanging on the back of a panelled door. His expression was intent as he left and marched along the corridor to another doorway from which a light spilled onto the plush carpet in his path.

'Are you ready yet, Hans?' he called.

His brother smiled as he emerged from the doorway.

'What is your hurry? If it has been as bad as you say for so long, a few more minutes won't hurt.'

Freddy made small talk as they continued through the research centre, now empty as the workers had left for the day.

'Okay, we need to go this way up through the old fire stairwell to get there.'

At the end of the corridor, a white-painted door confronted them. Freddy felt in his pocket for the key and they were soon climbing up an austere concrete stairwell with wrought-iron railings towards the roof.

The door that led out onto the flat roof was sheltered behind a large water tank, otherwise a cold wind would have circulated around them. It was dark, but some moonlight found its way through the cloudy sky sufficiently to guide them.

'It's over here.' Freddy pointed to the edge of the roof where a small brick buttress was clearly in a state of decay. 'This building is falling apart. If we want to stay on here, the whole roof will need sorting out. I got a builder to look into the costs and we are talking about a lot of money.'

Hans peered down at the buttress and asked if it was safe.

'Well, it's not that bad, but if you look at what's below us here you can see the danger from falling brickwork. I wouldn't like to have something drop on me from this height.'

Hans edged closer and looked down into the darkness below. He was tentatively trying to achieve a balance between seeing what was down there and not falling when the figure approached from behind.

There was nothing to grab, no way to save himself as he pitched headfirst over the edge and into the night below. The fear mixed with panic on his face beseeched Freddy to help him somehow. They made eye contact, but Freddy just looked coldly into his brother's desperation. Freddy felt just a twinge of guilt when the thud from below confirmed he had reached the pavement.

Moments later, although it seemed much longer to the two on the roof, a scream from below penetrated the night. Freddy let rip with a howl.

'No! Oh no! Hans! My BROTHER!'

Günter looked into his face. This man has just had his own brother killed, and he hardly flinched. I must be very careful of Freddy. Freddy smiled. 'That just leaves the woman.'

The police suspected nothing - a tragic accident, of course. Günter and Freddy had witnessed Hans slip, lose his footing and fall. Freddy had warned him to be careful, not to go too close to the edge. Even Ingrid, who suspected that Freddy resented Hans and was capable of being extremely unpleasant, had no doubts that this was simply a tragic accident.

Over the next few days a great deal happened at Stein Pharmaceuticals. Ingrid was shocked that before her dear Hans was even buried, Freddy had started the process to take Stein to a stock market listing. Of course he feigned sadness whenever they met, and used the excuse that it helped him to keep busy. But Ingrid knew his brother's death had not touched him deeply, and this knowledge troubled her.

Everyone knew that Freddy was an unemotional individual; however, there was one occasion when he totally lost his cool reserve.

He was involved in a meeting with the firm's legal advisors when a call came in from Günter. Günter had bad news; it seemed Reiner had messed up another attempt to get rid of Rachel.

Günter explained that Reiner had been watching her carefully and decided the time to strike was when she crossed a busy road in the middle of St Peter Port. Appearing to be alone, but amidst a small group of other pedestrians, Rachel had half crossed the road to the old harbour. She was waiting for a break in the traffic before continuing to the other side. A single-decker bus sped along the road in their direction and the group of pedestrians ensured they were not too far into the road. A mother with a pushchair pulled her child back slightly to be sure the little boy was safely out of its path. Rachel smiled down at the boy and he beamed back up at her.

As the bus approached, Reiner had crept in just behind Rachel. The bus drew closer and Reiner looked around. Everyone was looking in the direction of the vehicle speeding towards them. Behind them traffic was flowing, preventing the next group from crossing to the centre. The bus was about to career past them when he struck. He pushed forward and Rachel stumbled into the path of the bus. As she fell forward the driver instantly swerved away from the centre of the road and braked hard, but Rachel was still falling. Her left arm instinctively went out to break her fall and she twisted slightly, flaying her right arm out behind her. Out of the blue, a hand thrust forward and grabbed this arm. From amongst the group a figure had pushed to the front and with an immense effort, Rachel was pulled back to safety. Now behind this figure, Reiner gasped and blurted out, 'I am so sorry. I stumbled. Are you all right?' The figure turned to face him and to his surprise it was Tom, who now looked back, holding Rachel tightly, his eyes studying Reiner's face.

'You fool; she could have been killed.'

All traffic had now stopped, and Tom hurried Rachel to the other side of the road where some seats overlooked the harbour. The bus driver came over and Tom thanked him for his instinctive reaction. Rachel was shaken but otherwise unharmed. Tom had seen his wife heading across the road and decided to catch up with her. He was about to greet her from behind when the bus passed.

The bus driver looked around for Reiner, determined to give him a piece of his mind, but Reiner was nowhere to be seen. He had moved away whilst everyone fussed over Rachel.

Freddy had listened impassively until Günter relayed the fact that Reiner had been seen by Rachel's husband. Not only had he failed but now he had been seen as well.

He exploded, 'Don't bring me any more excuses! The shareholders' meeting is in two weeks' time. Get that idiot to complete the job - or you will both have me to answer to.'

Around the room, the lawyers looked at each other, then, as Freddy turned his attention back to the meeting, they diverted their gaze - to some papers, to their laps anything but look Freddy in the eye.

That night in Guernsey, Tom called a family get-together and invited Inspector Ogier.

'I don't know what is going on here, but I've been thinking about what happened today. Rachel...' he looked at David and Rebecca '...your mum nearly had a bad accident in Town. A man fell against her, pushing her in the path of an oncoming bus. Inspector, the man had a German accent.'

Inspector Ogier asked if they knew the man. Did they get a good look at him? Could they describe him? Only Tom had really got a decent look at Reiner, and his description was not immediately helpful, other than establishing he was not the same person who had attacked Rachel before. Even if they had identified Reiner, he could not have been arrested; it was just too plausible to argue he had slipped and it was all an unfortunate accident. As Rachel had not been harmed, nothing would be gained.

The big question was, why was she being targeted?

Nobody could understand why, but she was clearly in danger. Rachel tried to joke. 'Maybe I upset someone?' But it wasn't funny and nobody felt like laughing. Inspector Ogier offered to put an officer on duty to watch her, but Tom had other ideas.

Early the next morning, Tom's latest fishing boat *Flying Fish 2* left its mooring next to the much smaller *Flying Fish*, and motored across the bay. Dawn was breaking as the front door to the Le Breton cottage opened and the family tiptoed out into the half-light and found their way to the slipway, just across the road. They carried a suitcase and two smaller bags, which they left on the slipway. David helped his mother and sister into a dinghy and, pushing off, jumped in himself. He rowed the few yards to where Tom was waiting and the two women climbed aboard *Flying Fish 2*. David returned to the slipway to collect the bags, rowed back once again and boarded himself.

Moments later, *Flying Fish 2* motored away and out of the bay. Reiner awoke suddenly from his uncomfortable position in the back of his hired car. He watched helplessly as the trawler disappeared over the horizon.

CHAPTER SIXTEEN

As Rachel took in the familiar faces around the oak kitchen table, the warmth that radiated towards her was tangible. Tom, Rebecca, David, Harold and Olive waited for her to speak.

Although Harold's brother Monte was not with them that day, over the years they had met quite frequently with the 'Hermits', as they were jokingly known, and now they were all like extended family. The couple had aged well, as had Monte, but Olive's cooking had added substantially to their waistlines. Rotund and rosy cheeked, Olive prompted her, 'You take your time, my love.'

'I don't know why anyone would want to kill me. You all know that I have no enemies and I have never done anything to hurt anyone. All I can imagine... and this seems too bizarre to even contemplate... all I can imagine is that it is something to do with my background. There is all this in the news about the Middle East conflict; could it be because I am Jewish?'

The radio news that day had been bad; apparently there had been an attack by terrorists at the Munich Olympics. A group of Israeli athletes had been taken hostage by 'Black September'.

Tom reached out instinctively and placed his hand on hers. There was a pause whilst everyone took in what Rachel was saying and Olive fussed around pouring more tea. Rebecca spoke first.

'Why is there so much hatred in the world? It is sickening; all these people who kill and maim and all in the name of religion. What on earth is going to happen to those poor athletes? It's bad enough that the IRA keep trying to blow everyone up, but now wherever you go there is violence. Mum, surely that can't be what this is all about?'

Rachel smiled at her daughter. They were all at the farm in Herm, her sanctuary. There was nowhere on earth that Rachel felt more safe. This was the place where her hero, Tom, had delivered her from the clutches of the soldiers. It was here that she fell deeply in love with him and spent those idyllic months during the occupation.

'I never really bothered about my religion. I know that may sound terrible, but when I was little I asked God to look after my mama and bring her back to me. I thought God let me down and I saw what they did to my father, all because of what he believed. But worst of all was when I learned about what had happened to Mama and the fate of all those people in the camps. I had always been told that God was all-powerful - omnipotent, they said. I thought, if he is so powerful, how could he let such things happen? How could he have made human beings with so much evil in them? I decided he was either not so powerful after all, or rather horrible and not worth worshipping.

'Then you only have to look at the fanatics on all sides and see the glare in their eyes. They are brainwashed. They all believe in the same God, just different prophets. They all believe that their God supposedly put love, kindness and decency at the heart of their faith. Yet they have all, at some time or other, waged war and mutilated innocent people in his name.

'So I don't care much for religion, and being Jewish to me is just about keeping some kind of link with my past, with my family. If I am being targeted because of that, there really is no hope for the world.'

Tom looked at his wife and was once again reminded about what she had been through as a child. She was so strong, but she was also enlightened. He learned from her. In all this time, however, they had never really spoken of her religion. Even when they married, the subject had been cast aside quickly as Rachel had been happy to go with Tom's 'beliefs'. Now he realised why: Rachel did have profound beliefs, but they could not embrace the many interpretations placed upon the words of so-called prophets. They certainly did not include a kind old man in the sky watching over the human race. Rachel saw religion as the problem, not the solution to many of the problems in the world.

She spoke again. 'Look, I'm sorry. I shouldn't attack religion.

Certainly not here in your home.' She looked at Olive and Harold. 'In any case, we are clutching at straws; it might be nothing to do with that. The news stories about Arabs and Jews are probably giving me an over-active imagination. It's just that I really can't think why anyone would be trying to get rid of me.'

Olive replied, 'Don't you apologise, my love. You are right, the world has gone mad and you have more reasons than anyone I know to feel let down by this whole religious mumbo-jumbo.'

Harold looked at his wife; he was amazed. In all their years she had never been so outspoken. 'Mumbojumbo!' He laughed. 'Mumbo-jumbo, you mean all these years we have been going to church and you think it's mumbo-jumbo?'

'Well okay, maybe I'm not quite as deep as Rachel here, and I do need to believe in something. But let's face it, there have been more wars about religion than anything else. If the powers that be at the top of these religions can't get together and agree to preach tolerance, they don't deserve to be at the top!'

Tom had been listening attentively but decided the conversation was drifting.

'I find it hard to believe that this is about you being a Jew. Let's not forget that the main suspects are German not Arab, and although they could be still on a mission for the Reich, I don't think you would be their main target. There are other Jews, even in Guernsey.

'No, let's think about what we know. There was the person asking questions at Castle Cornet Investments, the attack in Town and then the so-called accident crossing the road. Let's not forget the tyre lever as well; someone had been in our house.'

The room went quiet as they concentrated on what Tom was saying. David broke the silence. 'Mum, this looks like they think you have some kind of investment. At least something of value; they were searching for something of value. That would explain why they are prepared to kill for it. It's nothing to do with your religion!'

'But what? I don't have anything of value. Do they think we are millionaires or something – do we look like millionaires?'

'Unless there is something you don't know about.'

Everyone looked at Rebecca. 'Mum, perhaps there is something in your name that you don't know anything about. What about an inheritance? You did say your family was wealthy before the war?'

'Well yes, they were, but I thought all that would have gone when the Nazis took over our possessions. When Mama and I left we had nothing, nothing but the clothes we stood up in.'

A tear was forming in Rachel's eye. 'Mama was taken away. She didn't have anything.'

The memory flooded back of their last moments together.

'Mama was so upset. She could hardly speak. The nasty soldier in the room only gave her moments to say goodbye.' A questioning look started to form on Rachel's face. She thought for a moment, and then she said, 'There was something I thought was a bit strange at the time. Mama was concerned about my shoes. We were both so sad; I didn't expect Mama to think about my shoes at a time like that. I didn't expect Mama to say I must look after them; I always looked after my things.'

Tom jumped up. 'Your shoe, I remember. Your shoe, when we first met you insisted on taking your shoes, even though we needed to leave a false trail. You insisted on taking one shoe!'

'That's right; Mama said to look after them, especially the right one. What a thing to say at a time like that, why would she care about the right one?'

It took a moment to sink in and then Olive got up slowly. She had a purposeful look on her face as she left the room.

'Why would my mother have cared about my right shoe? Anyway, that was all a long time ago and has nothing to do with my problem now. No, we had nothing when we left Munich, but I suppose it is possible that my parents may have set something up before it all went wrong. Maybe they had some money somewhere. I don't know how we could find out.'

David was the investment expert. 'We should check this out,

even if it is only to eliminate this as a reason why you are in danger now. Try to think, Mum, is there anyone, any relation or family friend that might still be alive who we could ask?'

Rachel thought hard. 'No. I was too young to remember lots of people. The only people I really remember were my close family, and they all died. No, when I learned about Mama's fate, well - that ended my family. Wait a minute, there was someone. It was way back, but I learned what happened to Mama from someone that Apple found who survived the camp. He said he knew her. It's a bit of a long shot, he's almost certainly dead by now, but he's the only person I can think of who would be a link to my past.'

The door opened and Olive sauntered in with a distinct 'cat who's got the cream' expression on her face. 'Does this bring back any memories?' she said as she placed a small shoe in the centre of the table in front of them.

Everyone looked at Rachel as her expression riveted on the shoe.

'Oh, my... Oh, Olive, you kept it all these years! I had no idea.' She reached out and picked up the shoe. 'This brings back so many memories for me.'

As she examined the small shoe, she glanced occasionally at her husband who looked equally surprised. They laughed as he joked, 'You and that blasted shoe, it nearly ruined our escape plan! *I can't leave my shoes*, she says, with the Germans hot on our trail!'

It was Rebecca who first realised the significance.

'Mum, your mother must have had a good reason for saying that. She was so distressed; she wouldn't have bothered about something so unimportant at a time like that.'

Then Tom excitedly cut in, 'Wait a minute, let me see that. I remember Dad telling me about an airman they picked up in the Channel. He had been shot down and bailed out close to their ship. When they got him on board and sorted him out, they got talking and the airman made a joke about his shoe. Apparently there was a small saw concealed in the heel. The RAF used to

166

do this for their pilots in case they got caught behind enemy lines and it might help them.'

He fondled the shoe as he spoke.

'Maybe, just maybe, that's why the right one was so...'

He broke off as the now aging shoe yielded to the pressure he was placing on the heel. It almost crumbled apart and then, as they all watched intently, the edge of a small flat package became visible.

'What on earth...?' Tom very gently pulled on the corner of the package as it slowly emerged from the shoe. Brown greaseproof paper surrounded something that was around two inches long and half an inch wide. He unwrapped the package.

Inside was a small key and a metal plate with something inscribed on it. What did it mean?

There had been total silence as Tom revealed the package and they all leaned forward to get the best view of what was happening.

Now they could see it clearly, but they were no wiser.

2011856 2021940

'Before we left Munich, a kind old man took Mama and me in. We were homeless. The man was a cobbler. I remember it now, Mama asked him to do something with my shoes. This must have been it, but what on earth is it for? You are so clever, Rebecca. I never thought about why Mama was so insistent I looked after my shoes.'

But Rebecca wasn't finished. 'Mum, look at that second number, look at it!'

'20...2...1940, twentieth of February 1940; it's the date of one of my birthdays! Hang on...' She thought for a moment. '...my twelfth birthday. Why would she have that printed on a plate and put in my shoe?'

The family sat back and waded through various theories about the numbers on the small metal plate. Was it just a coincidence that part of it was Rachel's twelfth birthday? Was it some kind of serial number that the cobbler put in all his shoes, some early version of batch control?

David was convinced it was none of these. Working in Guernsey's finance sector, the first part of the number was a familiar format to him. It looked just like an account number, a bank account and the key to a deposit box.

'I have seen this so many times with clients, especially those with Swiss numbered bank accounts. They often have this number of digits, at least the number that is in the first part. They have numbered accounts and deposit boxes, but there seem to be too many numbers for any account I've seen, and they would never have a date like this.'

So the family began to come around to David's view that this just might be at the heart of the all of the threats to Rachel. It might just explain the enquiries at Castle Cornet Investments, the break-in at their cottage and, of course, the threats on her life.

But if this was the case, what was in the account that was so valuable that someone would kill to get it, and where could it be?

***

Early evening in Herm saw the last of the day trippers from Guernsey returning on the ferry.

Tom walked hand in hand with Rachel along the lane where so many years earlier they had been discovered by Harold. It was warm and the September sun was slowly descending in the sky.

It had been a long and emotional day and Rachel needed some air. They stopped at a gateway into one of Harold's fields.

'I know you could do with a rest from all of this, but there is one thing I have been meaning to ask you. When you came back after the liberation, you said that Apple had contacted someone who knew your mama in the camps. Someone who survived. Do you know who this was?'

'Well no, I don't know. I just imagined it was another inmate; but now you mention it perhaps he – it was definitely a *he* – perhaps he knew more. Do you think I should call Apple?'

Tom looked at his wife; he knew she was weary of this and needed to clear her head.

'No, darling, I don't think you should. I think you need a quiet evening ; perhaps a pre-dinner drink at the White House, and I will treat the family so that Olive doesn't have to cook.'

'Doesn't have to! You must be joking, Olive wants to cook; she likes nothing more than filling us all up with her wonderful food. But you are right, we should offer. It's lovely of them to put us all up out of the blue like this and she probably hasn't had time to shop for eight portions. Let's get back before she tries to start.'

Olive had been worrying about how she would cater from the moment Tom's boat had moored in Herm harbour as she and Harold were chatting on the quayside. After a few protestations about how Tom shouldn't squander his hard-earned money on restaurant meals, she accepted his invitation with quiet relief.

The group changed into fresh clothes, titivated themselves and walked along the path from the farm to the White House Hotel. In the small bar, pre-dinner drinks were arranged by Tom and David who took the orders and stood at the bar.

With the family engaged in conversation behind them, Tom whispered to David. 'Can you keep everyone distracted for a few minutes, son? I want to make a quick call and I don't want your mum to have to think about it.'

David agreed and ensured the conversation and pre-dinner drinks flowed as Tom slipped away into the hotel reception area.

He wasn't gone long before Rachel looked around and asked David what had happened to him. As David began to speak, Tom walked back into the room and smiled at her.

The evening was just about perfect for Rachel with her family and dear friends around her at a window table overlooking the stretch of water between Herm and Guernsey. The sun set over Guernsey as their dessert plates were pushed aside and Harold breathed a sigh of relief, having polished off all of his apple pie and most of Olive's, who was full halfway through her main course.

The food, as well as the company, had been excellent and the view, even with its familiarity, was breathtaking.

Conversation had flowed, and for most of the evening they had carefully steered it away from the events that had led them to escape from Guernsey. But now, with their guard down as they sat drinking coffee in the hotel lounge, Rachel returned to the subject.

'That horrible man must have been beside himself when we all piled into the boat and headed out to sea,' she joked.

Olive asked how they could be sure he hadn't worked out where they went.

'Well, Dad took us straight out over the horizon before turning in a big circle to head for Herm. He couldn't have seen us from the coast and we were halfway to Sark before we turned for our final leg back here. No, he must have assumed we were headed for the mainland from our direction. We will be safe here.' As David spoke confidently, a young waitress approached Tom and quietly informed him there was a telephone call. He excused himself and walked back to reception.

Rachel looked puzzled. 'Nobody knows we are here. Who could that be?'

David thought it best to quell her fears immediately and he explained that Tom had phoned someone earlier and perhaps they were now returning his call.

'Very curious...' Rachel joked. 'What is he up to now, I wonder!'

A few minutes later, Tom returned and could see from their expectant faces that an explanation was necessary. He looked at Rachel. 'Darling, does the name Weinstock mean anything to you?'

Silence fell on the small group who were now alone in the lounge in an atmosphere softened by warm yellow occasional lights and those of distant Guernsey twinkling through the windows.

All eyes again fell on Rachel, who had clearly recognised the name. Her expression moved from relaxed to slightly flushed, almost embarrassed, as she answered.

'Tom, it was him. How did you know? It was the old man I spoke of earlier. Hr Weinstock was the cobbler. I don't understand - how could you know? I had forgotten his name.'

Rachel began to cry uncontrollably; she was back there in the small shop with her dear mama. The tears rolled down her cheeks as the family rushed to comfort her. Tom was devastated.

'I am so sorry, love. I had no idea it would affect you like this. That was Apple on the phone; I called him earlier to ask who it was who knew your mama in the camp. He had to look through his old papers to find the name.'

They all rallied around to comfort Rachel and eventually she composed herself and asked Tom, 'Is he still alive, Tom? He seemed old, even then.'

'We don't know, but Apple gave me an address in Germany where we can check. Apparently, he was very ill when the Americans got to the camp. Like most of the inmates who survived, he was close to dying of starvation and was transferred to a hospital before being moved to a rest home. I have the number to ring in the morning.'

The drama of the evening had quite exhausted Rachel, and Olive had empathised so much with her that she also felt drained. The group walked quietly out of the hotel and back to the farm, where they said their goodnights and turned in.

CHAPTER SEVENTEEN

David knew as he approached the check-in desk at Guernsey airport; he just knew someone was watching him. He looked around, occasionally stopped suddenly and glanced behind, he even tracked his reflection in the glass of the windows, but there was no sign of anyone. Probably the police, he thought to himself. After all, Tom had called Inspector Ogier from Herm and explained the theory in great detail. That would be it; the police would be watching him for his own safety.

Of course, David had never actually seen Reiner, and the man with greased-back hair, engulfed in a newspaper and sitting amongst the tourists, drew no attention at all.

In fact, David barely noticed that he moved to be almost beside him when he checked in for the twelve o'clock flight to London Heathrow.

It turned out to be a busy flight, and Reiner only managed to get a seat due to a last-minute cancellation. Fortunate, he thought. Günter would not have been too happy if this one had escaped. Especially as he was convinced that David would lead him to Rachel's hiding place somewhere in the UK.

Reiner attempted to be inconspicuous and sat well away from David during the flight, but his sinister presence was felt by those around him as he whispered his request to the stewardess for a beer to accompany the in-flight lunch being served. His true purpose in whispering was not to reveal a giveaway German accent to David, but the effect was decidedly creepy to a little girl sitting across the aisle and watching him intently.

With no luggage, Reiner shuffled amongst the crowds to avoid any accidental eye contact with David. He knew it would be difficult from here on, as he would surely be noticed following David once they left the airport. He would need to act quickly. Could he really say, 'Follow that taxi!' if that was how David was planning to travel?

There was no choice; Reiner had to stick with him somehow.

David had only one small bag to claim and quickly passed through the green 'Nothing to Declare' channel. Younger and fitter than Reiner, he was striding purposefully through the airport as Reiner struggled to keep up from a discreet distance.

But to Reiner's surprise, David was no longer heading for the exit; instead he marched towards the departure hall. This was not what he expected; for some reason Reiner had just assumed Rachel was in England. He had seen the boat heading off towards the south-west of England, but of course they could easily have left the boat somewhere.

It soon became clear that David was heading for a Lufthansa check-in desk. Surprised as he was, Reiner felt a slight relief. If David was flying to Germany he could arrange for Günter to meet the flight and take over from him.

Reiner's luck was in; David didn't appear to notice him standing close by as he handed in his ticket for the 15:45 flight to Munich. As he disappeared towards the departure lounge, Reiner phoned Günter with the flight details.

Günter received the news with mixed emotions. True, it would be easier to deal with the bitch if she was on his home territory, but if she was in Munich, it was certain she now knew something.

***

The olive green Mercedes convertible sped towards Munich International Airport. Günter tried to visualise David's image. He had seen him in Guernsey and knew that David may also have glimpsed him. He was not a vain man, but Günter was aware that his tall, thin build was not indistinctive and he could be recognised, perhaps from a description given by David's mother. He considered what the Lufthansa desk had told him when he rang: the aircraft should touch down around 17:15 local time.

As the car cruised onto the pickup area outside Arrivals, there were just a few minutes to spare. By now David would be collecting his bag and heading towards the taxi rank. German airlines were always punctual.

As he waited for the Guernseyman to arrive, Günter's mind wandered to his current predicament. Here he was, working for a powerful but ruthless man he had once thought just a wealthy friend. Freddy had shown uncharacteristic trust in opening up to Günter about this 'situation', but he was now relying heavily upon Günter to deliver. Günter was under no illusions that he would quickly become disposable if he failed Freddy, and the omens were looking bad at the moment. She was here, here at the centre of Freddy's empire. How could she have suddenly found out? Even when David led him to her, as he had no doubt would happen, Günter would have to deal with all of them.

In Günter's reckoning, they had all left Guernsey that day on *Flying Fish 2*, heading for the south coast of England. Rachel, Tom, David and Rebecca must have moored the boat and flown to Munich. For some reason, David had returned and was now heading back out to join the others. Was it that the last attempt at removing Rachel had panicked the family, or had they learned something about Rachel's shares? He had no way of knowing, but there was no apparent reason for them to take refuge in Munich if they had been spooked.

Unless, unless of course there is still a relative here... he thought for a moment about the implications. If someone else had survived all this time living in Munich, they must surely know about Stein Pharmaceuticals. If there was someone ...

Günter's train of thought was interrupted by the sight of a half-familiar figure striding out of the arrivals hall towards a waiting taxi. It was him, no mistake: this was David. The taxi pulled away and moments later Günter was about to follow, when the horn of an approaching car warned him to pay attention to the road.

David's driver glanced in his mirror. 'Another fool who shouldn't be on the road,' he complained to his passenger. 'Nice car, but more money than sense!' They headed for the autobahn.

David's mind was on other things; he wondered how the old man would be. The rest home staff couldn't have been more helpful - they knew that Hr Weinstock had no family, and when they had spoken of Rachel, he had been delighted to hear of her. He remembered the young girl well and even more so, her charming mother. He had often wondered what became of Rachel in the dark days of his endurance. The episode had been locked into his memories about the last hours of freedom before the nightmare.

But since that call, he had moved to the general hospital, and David had been alarmed when the rest home had called back to him.

'You can come, but Hr Weinstock is quite poorly now and without wanting to sound brutal, it may be a wasted journey.'

The taxi sped on towards Munich General, unaware of the green Mercedes that followed a discreet three vehicles behind.

As the two cars pulled into the main car park, the idea was forming in Günter's mind that he may have been right about the long-lost relative. Why else would David be visiting a hospital? He parked quickly and ran across the car park, so that when David walked up to the main reception he was just a few paces behind.

David's German was poor, and there was a delay before an English-speaking receptionist confirmed that he could find Hr Weinstock on the third floor in Ward J, but he must report to the Ward Sister. He must also be as quiet as possible as this ward was for the old and terminally ill.

Günter was now confused; he found the nearest telephone kiosk and called Freddy.

As he explained events, Freddy listened attentively.

'...so he has flown here to Munich, and although we thought he would lead us to her, he is now visiting an old man – with a Jewish name – here at the hospital. Does it mean anything to you?'

There was a silence. Freddy reflected on everything he had

175

been told about Rachel and her mother from the moment they walked into his father's office all those years before. He could think of nothing. There was no mention of this man; he must have been part of her life before that or maybe connected through someone else. Eventually, he spoke.

'Günter, listen. I don't know from under what stone this man has crawled, but he is a danger to our plans. We cannot afford to have either of them leave the hospital or make any calls. As David has come all this way, it is just possible this man knows something. You know what to do.'

With that, the line cut off.

Günter was not happy. It was one thing to commit murder on some faraway island from which he could disappear, but to do it here in his own backyard, that was something else. Worse still - a double murder. Why must it be in the hospital, as long as David couldn't tell anyone ..? He knew as these thoughts went through his head that Freddy was right. The only way to stop this was to kill them both, and do it as soon as possible.

The lift was just across from where Günter stood. As the doors opened and a small crowd of patients and visitors moved in, Günter pushed his way unceremoniously to the front. Oblivious to the disapproving frowns of his fellow passengers, he pressed the illuminated 3 button for the third floor.

As the lift ascended, the passengers avoided looking at each other by finding an imaginary point of interest above their heads, studying the floor indicator, or staring down at their feet. Günter stared impassively at the doors, willing them to open. He fumbled in his coat pocket. Was it there?

His fingers wrapped around a small, slender box and he sighed inwardly with relief. The syringe inside may be needed. As he was still planning his next moves, the doors opened and he emerged on the third floor.

Ward J was clearly marked, and he approached with heightened senses. Scanning the beds he could not see David. Patients, visitors, nurses and the occasional doctor milled around. No clues.

His presence in the centre of the ward and his obvious confusion attracted the attention of a nurse who asked if she could help him. He mumbled, not appreciative of the intrusion into his thoughts.

'Er…, Hr Weinstock?'

The nurse explained softly that the old man had been moved to a private room and was being bathed. She pointed at a waiting room. They would tell him when he was ready. Who should she say was visiting?

Günter mumbled again and lied that he was from a firm of solicitors. He gave a false name, thanked her, and walked towards the waiting room. Approaching, he could see the outline of several figures through a half-glazed door. With just a few feet to go, the door opened and a woman stepped out. The other figures were now clearer and amongst them, half turning towards the door, was David.

Günter walked on past, he was not ready to face David in case he was recognised. He scrutinised the side rooms. A small kitchen, a store room, and then a room with a frail old man sitting up in bed, smiling as a nurse was folding a white towel next to a bowl of water by his side. He could hear her speaking through the door. A visitor, she was saying, a visitor had come all the way from England to see him, how special! Hr Weinstock continued to smile, but his eyes peered straight ahead. He explained that the visitor was not from England but the tiny Channel Islands; he was the grandson of someone very special.

The nurse moved the bowl and towel across the room but Hr Weinstock's gaze did not follow her. He was blind!

Back in the waiting room David was becoming impatient. He had travelled a long way to see the old man - the old man who knew his grandmother, who was in the death camp with her. Emotionally, he was wrung out. This whole business had taken its toll. He decided to stroll along the corridor.

The nurse now appeared to be leaving; Günter watched as she squeezed the old man's hand and whispered something in his ear. He reached his other hand across and grasped hers. 'Bless you,' Günter heard him say.

As the nurse walked towards the door, Günter turned around to see David emerging from the waiting room. For a moment he hesitated. David looked directly towards him, and for an instant their eyes met. In both, an emotion stirred - a quite different emotion.

David felt something, although he wasn't quite sure what. As his eyes met Günter's, there was recognition that this was a vaguely familiar face, but that was ridiculous - he didn't know a living soul in Germany, and yet...

Günter's emotion was altogether colder. He was angry. The chance eye contact with the man he was soon to kill was inconvenient. Why couldn't the idiot stay in the waiting room a bit longer? If he was recognised, that would be a real nuisance.

David was now walking in his direction, and Günter instinctively felt in his pocket as he diverted his gaze in the other direction. He did not leave his position outside the side room. As David approached, his expression seemed to out-race his thoughts, his face was saying 'Wait a minute, I do know you...?' and it studied Günter more carefully; his thoughts were catching up as his conscious mind began to connect with his unconscious mind. He was now just a few metres away, and Günter could see the growing recognition in his face. A few paces more and...

The door to the side room opened and a nurse emerged, brushing past Günter as she did so.

'Ah, there you are!' She saw David approaching. 'Let's have a little word.' Her English was perfect. As she directed David back towards the waiting room, he half-turned to look back at Günter and thought to himself, 'Do I know you?'

As they disappeared into the waiting room, Günter slid into Hr Weinstock's room. The old man was immediately aware of a presence and his head turned towards the door. 'David, is that you?'

Günter spoke softly. 'Yes, at long last I got here. How are you feeling?' Günter moved towards him and squeezed the old man's arm before returning to the centre of the room. His expression was unmoved throughout.

'I am just fine. No, more than that - I am delighted to see you.'

Günter froze.

'Of course, when I say *see you*, I don't exactly mean see,' he joked. 'Tell me, David, how is your mother? I want to hear all about her.'

'Of course. Yes, of course - all in good time. But first, can we just talk a little about you?'

Hr Weinstock's joy was slightly dampened; he desperately wanted to know about the fate of that young girl he helped so long ago. The girl whose mother he tried to see in the death camp whenever the guard's attention was diverted. He remembered so well how the beautiful woman had become ill in those appalling conditions, and how when he called to her from the men's compound she had waved back.

But that was a different time, and now her grandson was visiting him. He had so much he wanted to speak about. Did his mother ever find out about the shoe? He could hardly wait. Hardly, but something made him uneasy. Something about David's manner; he couldn't quite put his finger on it.

'About me, David? What do you want to know about me?'

'Well, my parents didn't have time to say much before I left, so I don't know exactly... I mean, it was my mother, was it? Who you knew?'

Hr Weinstock's senses started to heighten; he began to feel distinctly uneasy. He doesn't know who I am? The care home said Rachel's husband had called; they said David was coming. He must have been told about me.

Günter could see the old man's nervousness. He looked around. The semi-glazed door had a blind; he turned, looked briefly into the corridor, and closed the blind.

He felt in his pocket for the syringe, but then on a shelf at the side of the room another option presented itself - a large white pillow.

In the waiting room, the nurse was smiling at David as she gave him an update.

'Hr Weinstock has told us that he has no family and he doesn't mind us discussing his condition with you.

Basically, he is just very old now, and his time in the camps has not helped with his health. He lost his sight shortly after the war but otherwise he has been quite remarkable. The only real problem now is a lung infection, which is why he is here. But he is quite weak and to be honest, we can't be sure he can fight it.'

David sighed. 'Oh dear, the poor man. He has been through so much. He knew my grandmother before the war, but we never knew he existed until recently. Can I see him now?'

'Yes, of course. He is really looking forward to seeing you - but please don't tire him too much. As I say, he is quite weak.'

Back in the side ward Günter was getting impatient. 'So they didn't say much at all to me, in fact I don't even know what you spoke about before I left.'

Hr Weinstock became more suspicious. 'Tell me, David - I am getting old. Your mother, what was her name again?' 'Rachel. My mother is Rachel and my father is Tom and I have a sister, Rebecca.' Hr Weinstock felt slightly easier. What an old fool he had become - too suspicious by far.

'David, I didn't speak to your mother or father. My care home told them I was here and they said you would be coming to see me. I suppose they sent you to ask about the account details in the shoe?'

A snide smile grew across Günter's face. This was it: this was what it was all about.

'Shoe, Hr Weinstock? What shoe?'

'Oh dear, don't tell me she lost it. Inside your mother's shoe was a metal plate, with the account number and a clue to a password for a Swiss bank account.' Hr Weinstock now smiled. 'I know, because I put it there. I assumed she had found it and wanted to know what the numbers meant. I must admit, it has been so long I just assumed that either she had not survived the war or the shoe had been lost.'

Günter reflected. So, he hasn't yet told them anything about this and quite clearly, if they did have this shoe, they would have acted upon it by now. No, this old man is the only connection to the account and the account is most likely the only connection with Stein Pharmaceuticals.

Hr Weinstock became nervous again; it had gone quiet. He had just revealed the secret of the shoe and it had gone quiet. He spoke tentatively. 'Your mother is living in the Channel Islands, I believe. She was sent there to Alderney for her protection. You must have grown up there, but your accent is German?'

Günter reached for the pillow and without another word, coldly placed it over the old man's face. He leaned forward with arms fixed, and his body weight was enough. There was little struggle - Hr Weinstock was too frail to resist.

CHAPTER EIGHTEEN

As David and the nurse approached the side room, David caught a glimpse of Günter's back walking away down the corridor. The hairs on his neck bristled. Immediately the nurse entered, she knew. She rushed over to the old man's side and felt for a pulse whilst calling to him, 'Hr Weinstock, are you all right?'

David was completely taken aback. Oh no, surely not, the old man had died. Of course he was old but.... without thinking, he looked back towards the door. That man, who was that man?

It was always sad when someone passed away, but the nurse seemed particularly distressed about Hr Weinstock. 'He was such a kind old man, despite all he had been through; he was gentle and kind to everyone. He could hardly wait to see you. He kept chatting about how he had known your mother as a little girl, how he had helped her escape the death camps. He said you would be pleased when he told you about the bank account.'

'Bank account? I don't suppose he said where it was, did he?'

'Not exactly, but he did say it was a Swiss bank account and was just over the border from Munich, because there was a lawyer or someone who was going to take the contents over. He had discussed all this with your grandmother. I'm sure he would have wanted you to know. Oh wait, there was something else as well; there was a shoe, he said he had put the details in a shoe belonging to your mother.'

David thanked her and explained that his family would want to attend Hr Weinstock's funeral if they could be informed, and they wanted the best for him; they would cover any costs.

He walked slowly away, imagining the hard life Hr Weinstock had been through, then his thoughts turned again to the image of the other man. At first he just wanted to play down any suspicions. No, the nurse would have said if his death looked suspicious.... Then those nagging doubts crept back in.

Although, when Mum was attacked, they couldn't find any trace for days. Maybe, he thought, just maybe this isn't how it seems.

***

As Günter walked through the hospital he was pleased with himself. Not only had he disposed of the last link between Rachel and Stein, but he may not even have to risk another killing. David clearly hadn't been told anything.

When he called Freddy from the same kiosk near reception, the satisfaction in his voice was evident. 'That takes care of the loose ends here. Now all we need to think about is the woman, and Reiner will get rid of her if she shows up again on the island. I will keep tabs on David; he is more useful to us alive now as he might just lead us to her.'

Freddy was less complacent. 'Listen, Günter. You did well to get rid of the old man before he spoke, but we can't ease off. I have been given a firm date for the flotation launching now, and I want her dealt with before then. It will all go out to the media during the first few weeks of October and we go public on the 31st. You must find her.'

Günter was just a little crestfallen, but he knew how Freddy pushed him at every opportunity and his persistence was predictable. He took up a position behind a huge rubber plant where he could watch without being seen. As he skulked, he thought how these plants seemed to turn up everywhere these days. These and piped music and eastern-looking carpets; it all seemed to start when the Beatles visited Germany, he thought. He was drifting into flower power and long hair when David's figure emerged from the lift and walked distractedly towards the exit. As he approached the door he stopped, realising he had no transport, and turned back into the hospital. Günter had already moved from his position and was pacing towards David when he turned. The two men now faced each other just a few feet

183

apart. Their eyes met and David spoke.

'Do I know you?' he demanded.

Günter was totally wrong-footed.

'Ich spreche kein Englisch.' But his quick reaction was faultless.

David stared for a moment. Then without flinching, Günter ran with his luck. 'Kann ich Ihnen helfen?'

David was floored; he couldn't reply, and although Günter appeared familiar, he wasn't sure where from. The world is full of people who look alike, he said to himself.

He muttered that it must be his mistake and walked just a few paces back to the reception where he asked how he could get a taxi. Günter listened, before setting off for his car.

Outside the hospital some fifteen minutes later, David got into a taxi which sped back towards the airport, followed again by the olive green Mercedes.

This time Günter was careful to keep a safe distance as David got out at a hotel close to the airport, but he was concerned that if David saw him again, the penny would drop.

That night he called upon the services of a private investigator to keep track of David as he left the hotel the following morning. He was not going to risk another close encounter. The very ordinary-looking man in his middle age was able to report after just a few hours' work that David left at 9 a.m. for the airport, where he boarded a flight to London Heathrow with an onward connection to Guernsey in the Channel Islands. He would arrive in Guernsey at three o'clock in the afternoon. This was a short but well paid job for the investigator, and he enthusiastically offered his services for any future work Günter may have.

Twenty thousand feet over Europe, David closed his eyes and contemplated the events of his brief journey.

Hr Weinstock's death was sad, but he was an old man and given the condition of his health, it shouldn't have been a total surprise. But it was just a bit of a coincidence that he died moments before meeting him. Then there was the stranger, loitering around the ward before he died, walking away just after and right behind him when he was about to leave. The aircraft tannoy intruded with a muted 'bong' as if to alert that an announcement was coming, but nothing followed and he returned to his thoughts. The stranger didn't seem to understand English, so where would he have seen him before?

David contemplated the nurse's words; this was more promising. He had been right, it was a Swiss bank account, and she even mentioned the shoe. It may be a long shot, but when he got back he would study all the banks he could find near the border in Switzerland that would have been close to Munich. As the thoughts played through his mind, exhaustion began to overwhelm him. A mural of images including Günter, the nurse and poor Hr Weinstock lying lifeless in his bed pushed out his consciousness, to replace it with sleep. The duty-free trolley rumbled by, David oblivious to the disappointed expression on the stewardess's face. No sale here, then.

Many miles away on the ground, all it took was a phone call from Günter to ensure David's return to the island would be monitored by Reiner - his return to the island and hopefully, his return to his mother.

* * *

David stepped out of the Vickers Viscount, head crouched slightly forward. He straightened and looked out at the sunny, late September Guernsey afternoon. He was glad to be back; he always was when he had been travelling, usually on business.

After descending the steps and walking across the apron, he entered the arrivals area. His movements were closely watched by a figure on the rooftop observation area.

Before long he had cleared Customs and was walking towards the car park where his White Triumph Herald convertible awaited him. More fun than flash, David's car was a passion for him. It was in terrible condition when he had bought it, and he spent hours lovingly improving it to the point of it being immaculate. Still a death trap of course-with its unconstrained steering lock -but a fun death trap.

Once the roof was down and David was back behind the wheel, he allowed himself to forget the past twenty-four hours for a while as he motored off towards the coast road. On the radio, Chuck Berry was singing about his 'Ding-a-Ling', not a great favourite of David's, so he pushed in an 8-Track cartridge and turned the volume up to the 'Best of The Doobie Brothers'. Reiner's hire car maintained a discreet distance - more by its lack of performance than his design - but he managed to stay with David until he eventually turned in to a driveway a few paces from the west coast beach of Cobo. By now the sun was descending quite rapidly through the sky. David deferred the luxury of a shower in order to grab a large glass and half-full bottle of Merlot to carry to the sea wall. En route he passed the best fish and chip shop in the island; he could rarely pass it without calling in, and this evening was no exception.

Positioned a few minutes later on the sea wall, with the glassy water just below his dangling feet, David's meal was accompanied by the large orange orb of the setting sun dissolving into the horizon whilst lighting up the pink granite rocks for miles around. This sun's swan-song was impressive, to say the least. Fish and chips consumed, one final glass of wine relaxed him completely as he centred himself once more, at home in this familiar scene. Just the final few rays of sun now, the last fireworks of the display, and David made his way home, a figure in the shadows never far away.

Inside, he showered, and as the evening was now advancing, slipped on a dressing gown. Then, to the phone.

The report to Tom was factual, even a little matter-of fact, considering it was from son to father. But David still wanted to impress his dad with how professionally he had handled the trip. He was also keen to hear how the family was and whether there had been any more threats to his mother. Although he doubted any harm would come to her in Herm.

All was well, but on the advice of Inspector Ogier, David would not join them in Herm just in case he was being watched. In any case, another trip would unfortunately be needed quite soon, but all he was told was, 'More about that later.'

In the meantime, David promised to do some research on Swiss banks. 'Has Mum thought any more about the date?'

'Oh yes, son, she has, and she is almost sure she knows what it is about. These Swiss banks, would they need a password?'

'Some do. In fact that might help to narrow down my search. So you think the date is the password or a clue?'

'Your mum thinks it is a clue. There was a special birthday present - a doll, or rather a nest of Russian dolls. Listen, we won't go into that now but when we see you, all will be revealed!'

As the final week of September passed, David spent his days at work in St Peter Port. Castle Cornet Investments and Trusts was the ideal place to search for the Swiss bank and with the help of his manager, the bank was traced to the Swiss town of Lucerne.

An English-speaking assistant manager at the bank was most helpful. The rules were very clear - if they turned up at the bank with the number and password, they would be taken to the deposit room and a key would be needed to open the deposit box. The number was definitely one of theirs, but he could not give any more information.

David's excitement was palpable; he couldn't wait for them to go and examine the box.

That night he called his parents in Herm.

CHAPTER NINETEEN

Reiner's persistence had paid off. A pleasant lunch at the street-side café below David's office was interrupted when his prey left the building and walked to the old harbour. Here he waited, until a ferry could be seen pottering towards the slipway with *Herm Seaways* emblazoned on the captain's small upright wheelhouse.

Reiner watched as David first shifted his stance on seeing the ferry, and then waved enthusiastically towards the small vessel.

It was Rachel and her daughter; they were back. What a damned cheek - had they been in Herm all this time? Reiner anticipated their next move, and instead of waiting to watch the embrace as the family reunited, he rushed off to find his hire car nearby on the Albert Pier. He sat with the engine running as David helped to carry the bags to his car. What he hadn't noticed was *Flying Fish 2* moored on the other side of the pier with Tom watching him intently from the cockpit.

Reiner followed David's car back to the cottage at Rocquaine and took up position near the Cup and Saucer where he could monitor their movements whilst planning his next attack.

That night, or to be more accurate, early the next morning, he took the precaution of returning to his miserable room in the Royal Hotel and packing his few belongings into a rucksack. There was one wartime possession he was particularly pleased to feel in the outer pocket - a loaded Luger pistol.

He returned to Rocquaine before daylight and was amazed to find movement in the house. The lights were on and there was distinct milling around. The door partly opened and he heard a clear voice. 'Take care on the ferry, Mum!' A woman's figure emerged from the house with collar up to keep out the edge of an early October morning. Then the silhouettes of two men appeared in the light of the doorway. Certainly Tom and David, Reiner mused.

They quickly found their way to the car and moments later, the two red tail lights diminished before Reiner switched on his engine and followed.

So they are on a ferry again, but this is too early for Herm; it must be going to the mainland, Jersey or even France. Reiner knew he would need to stick close to them and he planned as he drove. Yes, he had passport, money, in fact all he needed apart from a ticket, but these ferries were never full. He would need to dispose of his car, get a ticket and get on board. He would need to see without being seen - he mustn't lose them on board. What would he do if they had a cabin?

He decided to risk it and put his foot to the floor. His hire car rattled as he raced up behind the family. Closer... closer still, and then a final acceleration and he swerved out to overtake. Foot still on the floor, Reiner drove like a madman to the docks.

As he descended the hill into St Peter Port he saw it. There at the quay was a large ferry.

Reiner abandoned his hire car and ran to the ticket office. By the time the family arrived, he had paced up the gangway.

He turned at the top and noticed David's car pull up. Two figures in long coats got out, and one of them grabbed a bag from the boot before they leaned down to say farewell to their driver. Reiner was relieved that David would not be joining them.

The pair already had tickets and walked straight through to board a few minutes later, collars still up. Rachel even seemed to be wearing a headscarf almost covering her face.

To protect her from the night, or from me? Either way it was not much of a disguise. Reiner laughed inwardly.

It was not difficult to track the pair from the cover of the milling masses searching for seats. Reiner kept them in view as they walked around the deck to a cabin marked with a brass number five on the door.

With them safely inside, he descended the gangway and went back into the departure area, where he found a telephone kiosk.

'Günter, at last it will soon be over. She is back, and now nicely trapped on board a ferry to Santander. God knows why she is heading there; I didn't even know there was a ferry to Spain. Anyway, you can now consider the job done. By tomorrow it will all be over. I will call when we dock tomorrow sometime, to arrange how to get away from here. South America is looking very appealing.'

Günter reassured him that all was in place and as soon as he arrived in Santander he would be whisked away to a well deserved life of luxury with like-minded friends. Just one thing, Reiner must call from the ship's radiophone to confirm it was over.

'You won't be free to talk, so just say "the contract is signed" and I will know what you mean.'

The call was obliterated by the ship's loud whistle blasting out, as if to remind him to get aboard. Moments later, Reiner watched the flurry of activity below from the deck of the ferry as the stevedores made ready to undock.

As the sun came up, *Spanish Queen* glided over the calm seas away from the Channel Islands. Passengers walked around the open decks or just peered over the rail as the bow wave cleared its way through the water.

Reiner had positioned himself on a deckchair near cabin number five, but nothing stirred from within. A couple of times during the day, crew arrived with trays containing food and drink, but the couple seemed intent upon their privacy.

So it was not until later that he could make his move. The ferry was scheduled to reach its destination the following day.

***

The board room at Stein Pharmaceuticals exuded wealth and power. A large room with three panelled walls and a fourth of glass that looked out over the Munich rooftops, it was a statement of success and just how far this business had come. At one time this room was a store where Levi industries kept

190

machine parts for the factory floor. Now a large French oak table dominated, with twelve comfortable executive chairs placed around it. At the head of the table sat Freddy.

'Thank you all for coming,' he began. 'Today is a momentous day for our business. As the major shareholder, I can only say that I am completely confident about the action we are about to take.'

Over the years, Freddy had distributed small numbers of shares to key executives, in return for lower remuneration packages. These, he promised, would one day be worth a fortune when the company floated. Now was the time to deliver on that promise. The small group listened attentively as their Chief Executive outlined the process over the next few days.

'Our flotation is being handled by Severs and Severs a firm of investment bankers with experience in this area. They will set the price at 9 a.m. on the 31st of October, just one week away, and it is likely to be in the range of seven to nine deutschmarks per share. That will make everyone in this room a deutschmark millionaire.'

The group lost their collective cool, and what followed was a combination of excited chatter, large intakes of breath and straightforward exclamations of delight.

A number of questions followed about the factors that would determine where in the range the price would be set - was there anything that could upset the float? One director even asked when he could sell and get at the cash.

Freddy introduced them to the businessman on his left.

'This is Hr Deiter from Severs. He is handling our business and can answer your questions. Please be succinct.'

Hr Deiter was a rotund, middle-aged man in a pinstriped suit with slicked back grey hair, every inch the merchant banker.

***

Several hundred miles away, darkness began to fall as the *Spanish Queen* continued its passage across the Bay of Biscay.

As the evening went on, fewer and fewer passengers meandered along the decks, and by midnight just a group of young men remained. They had drunk a fair amount and were animated by the prospect of a camping holiday in Spain. Several friendly attempts were made to get Reiner to join them. But they eventually gave in to his persistent refusals. How he wished they would go away.

A little after three they decided to call it a night, and wandered back inside to find a more comfortable place to sleep.

Reiner was now alone on the deck. He looked around and listened hard to detect anyone else who was still up. There was nothing, just the unremitting sound of the waves lashing down the side of *Spanish Queen* and the distant rumble of her engines. He looked at the door of cabin five. They were in there. No sounds emerged, no telltale light crept under the door, no diffuse glow through the thin curtains. They would be asleep. He reached for his rucksack, still poised on the deckchair nearby. The left pocket contained a screw-on nozzle, the silencer. The right pocket contained his Luger. He looked around again - nothing. The silencer was perfectly engineered and screwed smoothly onto the barrel of his Luger.

One more look around - no one.

First, he tested the doorknob to see if it was locked. No. The fools - they hadn't even locked it! In a single sweeping movement Reiner rushed through the door and into the dark cabin. There in the middle of the room was the bed with the shapes of two bodies underneath the bedclothes, his targets lying asleep. He quickly raised his Luger and fired, once into each body, then again to the position of the heads. He paused for a moment and thought, at last the job was done and Günter would finally reward him.

The unexpected light was blinding. Reiner turned, ready to fire at whoever was responsible, but he was too late. As he turned, the strong younger man locked his gun arm safely out of the way and immobilised him. His head wanted to explode with rage. 'No....!' he yelled. David's fist silenced the protest.

'Sorry about that, Inspector. I couldn't help thinking about what he just tried to do to my parents.'

Reiner struggled to turn his head towards the bed as his gun hand dropped the Luger on the floor. There were people all around him now. One of them was Rebecca, who walked over to the bed and pulled back the covers for him to see. There were just a couple of pillows and some blankets, torn apart by the bullets. Reiner's anger gave way to resignation at the futility of his situation. Yet again, his life had not worked out the way he planned. His thoughts summed up the trend - what did I expect, some luck for a change?

He was vaguely conscious of someone reading a caution to him as he was taken away to the brig in handcuffs.

Inspector Ogier had needed the cooperation of the French and Spanish authorities, as it was not clear which territorial waters *Spanish Queen* would be in at the moment of arrest. Officers from each were present just to make sure, in addition to the ship's own officers.

Reiner knew he would go down for at least one attempted murder and he had no hope of defence. The only option was to cooperate for a reduced term, and loyalty was not in his character. Inspector Ogier knew that he wasn't working alone and that the first priority was to get as much information as possible about his paymaster.

It didn't take long for Reiner to give up what he knew, including a briefing on the arranged call.

'Here is the deal, Reiner - you make the call to your man and tell him it's done. Cooperate fully with our enquiries and give us a statement, and we will see about a lesser charge. But you have no time to think about this. I want a decision now, or I will get you put away for a very long time. A man of your age might not come out again, and of course you might not be too popular in a French prison with your war record.'

Of course Reiner did not know all the facts, but he did have a contact number for Günter. It was decided the call would be made first thing in the morning.

Nobody slept much that night; David and Rebecca were joined by the police for a nightcap in cabin five, where they chatted over the successful operation, including the deception of David and Rebecca posing as their parents. This was not just to set a trap for Reiner, but also to lay a false trail so that Tom and Rachel could travel in safety to Lucerne. They had arrived by air earlier that day.

At 9 a.m. a tired-looking Reiner sat uncomfortably in the ship's radio communications room. The radio operator set up the VHF call to the shore-based telephone and with three policemen standing over Reiner, he responded to the voice at the other end.

'It's me. I am calling as arranged. The contract is signed.'

'Good work. Get in touch when you dock.'

With that, Günter, clearly suspecting nothing, ended the call.

That day, the police questioned Reiner and obtained a full description of Günter. When they approached David, he confirmed that the tall, thin man with the slicked-back blonde hair fitted exactly the description of the man at Munich hospital. This was the same man who, according to Reiner, had twice attempted to kill their mother.

***

Freddy's day was getting better by the minute; the analysts were talking up the flotation in three days' time and, with the Jewess finally disposed of, the path was clear for a huge windfall. He had dreamt of this moment for years.

CHAPTER TWENTY

Early on the morning of October 29th, Rachel and Tom stepped out of their small, tastefully decorated but inexpensive hotel and onto the pavement in Lucerne. This trip was costly and to save money they walked the half-mile to Devere Bank to arrive just after opening. They were greeted by the assistant manager, who took them to a small side office for their discreet conversation.

Tom handed him the key and a slip of paper with the account number on it.

'2011856. Yes, that is correct and your key looks fine, but you must keep this. There is of course one more detail before I can release the box to you.'

Rachel smiled at him and then at Tom before speaking. 'Anoushka. It's Anoushka, my Russian doll. It was my birthday present.'

The assistant manager was young, but conservatively dressed, perhaps too much so for his age. But he knew that box 2011856 had been in the bank since the war and that so far no one had come forward. He knew this moment was poignant for Rachel.

'That is correct, madam. I will fetch the box for you and leave it with you in this room. Can I get you anything? A coffee or soft drink, perhaps?'

They declined politely and waited in the small room.

Tom looked around at the old-fashioned printed wallpaper, a burgundy pattern embossed with green leaves. They sat at a wooden table on comfortable but utilitarian wooden chairs. He joked, 'You would think they could afford a bit better furniture than this!'

Rachel giggled; their eyes met and they both glanced at the painting on the wall. It was an oil, probably sixteenth century, in a gilt frame. It depicted a small village, typical of medieval Bavarian times. In the mountains behind was a castle. Rachel thought of her father's stories and her eyes saddened. As she started to dwell on her family, the door opened again and the young man presented a metal box. It was larger than they had expected and not at all dusty, or rusty, or in any way showing its age. About the size of two biscuit tins put together and coated in black enamel, in the middle of the top was a brass handle and there, in the centre of one side, was the keyhole.

So intent were they on the box that they barely noticed the young man departing or his whispering, 'Please just let me know when you are ready. I'll be outside.'

Rachel handed Tom the key and he placed it in the lock. A single turn, an immediate click and the top was released.

***

Freddy was sure everything was in place. He sat at the desk in his apartment going through the papers. It was ten in the morning. Just two days to go!

Amongst the papers were a pile of share certificates secured by a large jubilee clip. Most of them were the original certificates inherited by Freddy and his brother. Hans had kept his in the company safe and as he had never actually married Ingrid, they had passed to his closest living relative, Freddy. Then there was a further batch - very nearly identical. To all but an expert eye, these were as legitimate as the first batch, but Freddy had paid thousands of dollars to a Russian with Mafia connections to get them forged. There was no reason why anyone should look too closely; nobody knew the history and once the flotation was concluded, they could conveniently be destroyed.

The small number of shares given to loyal employees were taken from Hans's batch, so they were 'clean'.

He fingered these certificates for several minutes, staring down at them. How could these scrappy pieces of paper be worth so much? They had been worth killing for - even his own brother - and worth the risk of a life prison sentence.

Today he would hand them to the lawyers dealing with the flotation. Within a few days he would be worth millions.

***

Slowly raising the lid, they peered inside as if opening a time vault. The small package of papers looked innocuous at the bottom. But Rachel caught her breath.

Her mother had been one of the last people to touch these documents, in the last hours of her freedom.

The memories flooded back. Rachel paused as she relived the days of homelessness and the old cobbler's shop. Dear old Hr Weinstock, she thought, he risked everything to help us. All that time ago Mama planned for this moment. What could have been so valuable for her to go to all that trouble?

'Shall I?' Tom looked into her eyes and realised what she must have been thinking.

'No, it's okay. I feel I owe it to her to open them myself. I just can't imagine what could have been so important or valuable for Mama to lock this away for me at a time like that.'

Rachel did not have to wait long to find out. First, she opened a folded paper that appeared to be the deeds of a house. 'Of course, it was our house! I thought we had lost all rights to it. Perhaps we have. After all, this is just a piece of paper, and it's a very long time ago.'

There were details of a bank account; surely her parents' account, but she thought that like the house, this had been confiscated by the Nazis.

Finally, there was a single certificate for five thousand shares in Levi Industries.

They both stared at it. At first the surprise left them silent. They looked at each other and both gestured as if to say, 'I don't know what to make of this.'

'Dear Mother, she hoped she would help me somehow,

197

perhaps provide for me. She couldn't have known I would meet you.' She looked into Tom's eyes. 'She couldn't have known I would have all I could possibly need.'

Tom reached out and squeezed her hand.

'I sometimes think that we are the wealthiest people on the planet when I look at you.'

'Maybe we should just take these away and go back to Guernsey. After all, we've managed well enough without lots of money all these years.'

Tom looked through the papers again.

'You know, I'm not sure about this. After all, your mama went to a lot of trouble to set this up. Maybe we owe it to her. Maybe we should see if these things are valuable. What do you think?'

Rachel considered for a moment.

'I need to think what she would have wanted, and you are right. Mama did this for me, she would want me to benefit as much as possible. We are Jewish, don't forget!' They both laughed and Tom collected the papers together.

Leaving the bank, they walked arm in arm back towards the hotel, passing various shops along the way. Amongst them, an estate agent's window advertised a number of houses in the area. They paused to look.

'Most of these are to rent,' Rachel commented.

'That's right. I heard that lots of Europeans rent their homes - they don't often buy them. Too expensive, I imagine.'

Tom found one house that was for sale.

'Here's one. It doesn't look all that grand. Not much bigger than our little cottage - three bedrooms. Crikey! Look at that price!'

He quickly did a mental conversion from deutschmarks to sterling. 'Sixty thousand pounds - you could get a mansion for that in Guernsey! No wonder nobody buys.'

Rachel thought for a moment.

'Our house in Munich was a mansion! At least it seemed huge to me, although I was only a child. If it was expensive in the nineteen forties and prices have gone up, what must it be worth in the nineteen seventies? Especially if this one is worth so much?'

Was it possible that this was the key? Was this why someone was trying to get rid of Rachel? Perhaps someone else now owned it and wanted to sell it.

They decided to ring David and Rebecca from the hotel, to see how they were after the excitement on the high seas, and to give them their news. They knew the call would be expensive but were starting to feel mildly affluent.

Sitting alongside Tom on their hotel bed, Rachel explained. '...so you see, we have these papers, but we don't know if they are worth anything. What do you think?'

Sharing the earpiece of the telephone receiver, David and Rebecca turned to each other and raised their eyebrows. Rebecca spoke first.

'Mum, I don't know about what happened when the few Jewish people who survived returned home, but I suspect they either got their properties back or a lot of compensation. The German government is still ridden with guilt over the Nazis. I would say you will do very well. I don't know how this is linked to all the trouble you've had, though.'

David chipped in. 'Neither do I, but I do know that you shouldn't overlook those shares either. One of our wealthy clients at work got rich because his family had owned shares in Rolls Royce. He had no idea, but found out the shares were worth a fortune. You should... no, let me... I can do it for you from here. Let me check it out. Levi Industries it said on the certificate, didn't it? I will ask some colleagues with international experience if they know anything. I'll call you back later, or you call me.'

Rachel and Tom decided they would cross the border and go to Munich to see if the old house was still there.

This was not an easy decision despite their curiosity; it had been just weeks since Munich had hosted the summer Olympic Games. Just weeks since Black September had murdered Jewish hostages in a notorious terrorist attack.

The world was shocked as images of brutality and murder appeared on the television. There was the inevitable debate on whether or not the games should be halted, and the inevitable mixture of opinions on the resulting short suspension.

When the tragedy unfolded, Rachel and Tom had been in the sleepy backwater of Herm. She was many miles from the horror, but like most people, Rachel felt pain for the athletes and all those involved. Being Jewish, the pain would always have an extra edge to it. She still found it hard to fathom the contradiction between religious fanaticism and acts of callous violence. That it happened in Munich - the place where her own family was destroyed and Nazism fermented - was all the more atrocious.

The journey by rail would take just a few hours, depending upon stops, so Rachel and Tom checked out of their hotel and made their way to the station.

With some trepidation, they boarded the carriage and settled in the clean and comfortable seats. Before long they were rolling through the spectacular scenery of the alpine landscape. Lunch was served on board, so when they arrived, they were refreshed and rested. There was no reason for Rachel to have felt her knees tremble as she went to disembark, no reason except the emotional turmoil she was now going through.

Recent events served to reinforce her anxiety about returning to the place where her young life had been shattered.

Tom held her arm; she took a deep breath, and stepped bravely onto the platform.

'I won't let this thing defeat me,' she whispered to Tom.

He smiled back. 'That's my girl! Come on, let's get out of this place and find a taxi. Have you got a note of the address?'

'Yes, it's in my handbag, but shouldn't we call David and Rebecca first?'

They wandered off to find a telephone kiosk and rang David's office. Just a quick update, to let him know where they were, they thought. So David's reaction was somewhat surprising.

'Thank goodness you've called; I have been going mad here

waiting to speak to you! Listen, Levi Industries no longer exists...' In the usual family way, Rachel and Tom were both sharing the handset, and their eyes met with indifference to the news. 'What we expected, I think.'

'No, let me finish. Levi doesn't exist, but Stein Pharmaceuticals does!'

Tom commented that he was none the wiser, but good for them, and why should they be interested?

'Dad, everyone knows of Stein; at least everyone other than you, it seems! They are huge, a worldwide organization, and the reason why you should be interested is that Levi Industries became Stein Pharmaceuticals.'

The phone went quiet for a while whilst David allowed them take in what he had just said.

'Are you saying what I think you are saying, David? Have we really got shares in a worldwide organisation?' Rachel was stunned by the information. 'Could these be worth a lot of money?'

'Mum, it gets better. Whilst you have been enjoying yourselves...'

Not quite, Rachel thought.

'... I have been speaking to our business investment guru. It appears that Stein is just about to go public and when I say just about, I mean tomorrow! Not only that, but Ian here has got the prospectus because he fully planned to buy some of their shares for funds we manage. Mum, you need to prepare yourself for a shock...'

***

As the Press gathered outside the huge glass monument that was Bavaria International Bank, VIPs were escorted in through the main entrance. Access for normal banking business was temporarily moved out to a side entrance.

It was eight thirty on the morning of the last day in October.

Inside the meeting room a large area had been set aside to accommodate around two hundred invited guests and the media. These were the big institutional investors, pension scheme fund managers and the like, who had committed to buy large numbers of the soon to be issued shares. Rows of chairs were filling and a buzz of excitement filled the air.

Over the heads of the crowd, a high vaulted ceiling was draped with chandeliers. Ornate, gilt-edged archways ran through to its far end. Here on a platform was a long table, set up to face the crowd, with a cluster of microphones in the middle. Behind the table, on a row of chairs, a group of twelve businessmen and one woman watched the hall fill. In the middle, Freddy looked confidently out whilst nodding at the comments being whispered in his ear by the grey-haired businessman on his left.

Hr Deiter was optimistic about the interest in the flotation and pleased with the final value of the share price being offered. The investment community was bullish it seemed, eleven deutschmarks a share was more than they could have hoped for.

At precisely 9 a.m., the large double doors were closed, and the meeting commenced.

Hr Deiter commenced proceedings by thanking the audience for attending and waxing lyrically about the prospects of Stein Pharmaceuticals PLC. After several minutes, he announced the offer price and there was an uproar of excitement. The top table team smiled at each other and everyone tried to catch Freddy's eye to congratulate him. But Freddy was looking directly at a skinny, blonde-haired man in the front row. Günter coldly looked back and an acknowledging but barely perceptible nod followed.

Freddy was in his element; he felt as if his whole life had been about this moment. As he stared around the room, a frenzy of flash photography dazzled him. Rubbing his eyes, he imagined the huge double doors were moving. He refocused and yes, they were. Someone was late arriving - typical.

The doors opened wider and not just one person but a small

group appeared through the entrance. Four, no five of them; four men, one of whom he recognised from his lawyer's firm. There was a woman. At first he thought she was vaguely familiar, perhaps also from the law firm. The group walked around the side of the room and towards the platform. He followed their movements as they advanced. Scrutinising their faces, he turned to look at Hr Deiter, but he was now engaged with a question from the floor. Freddy realized his mind had now filtered out the entire noise of the room. His attention was locked on this small group, now almost at the right-hand end of the platform.

Who were they, what did they want? He stared intently; there was something about the woman. Her clothes...and the man next to her - they weren't business types.

Freddy's blood turned cold. The recognition overwhelmed him; blind panic set in. He remembered a photograph of Rachel from one of Günter's reports. His attention quickly turned to him. Günter had been watching Freddy, but couldn't understand what seemed to have come over him. Now he was communicating directly with his eyes. Look, you fool, look... He turned back to Rachel.

Günter leaned forward to see, but still couldn't make out what the fuss was about. He did, however, realise that it was serious, and he stood to get a better view.

Immediately, he saw the group slowly walking towards the platform. One of them was now climbing the four steps up onto it. What was he doing?

When Rachel came into view, Günter almost fell backwards. No, it can't be. That's not possible. He recalled the phone message from Reiner. She is dead. She can't be here. He turned again to Freddy and saw him mouth the words, 'You will pay for this.'

Günter turned and ran through the hall towards the doors. The whole room paused as he darted to get away. 'Most probably wants to sell quickly and take a profit,' one guest said to his neighbour. 'The man's a fool; he should wait at least a month or two.'

Günter made it to the doors, which had been closed again after the small group had entered. He grasped the handles and pulled them both towards him. The doors yielded and as the outside hall unfolded, Günter looked straight into the eyes of Inspector Ogier. Flanked by six armed local policeman, the Inspector coolly stared at Günter and could not resist saying, 'Going somewhere?'

Freddy and half the audience watched through the open doors as they led Günter away in handcuffs.

By now, the lawyer who led the group had walked across the platform, much to the confusion of the team at the table, and was whispering to Freddy, 'There appears to be an irregularity with the share certificates. This woman is now the majority shareholder in Stein PLC.'

Freddy looked coldly across at Rachel. She was a warm, relaxed-looking woman, still attractive and shapely. More intent upon chatting to her husband than the catastrophe she had unleashed. Hatred filled his cold heart.

'What are you talking about? I have the majority, and anyway, we have now issued another twenty million shares to the public. She can't be the majority holder.'

The lawyer was confident and clear. 'The stock exchange was notified early this morning before any shares were traded, but we needed to check the authenticity, and I can confirm that this has created a highly unusual situation. There is no precedent anywhere, but you must come with me now for a brief word in private.'

Reluctantly, and totally crestfallen, Freddy rose and followed the lawyer to the side of the room.

Tom looked at him with disdain.

'I don't know yet how much you have been involved, but we will find out. You will pay, you slimy ...'

Rachel interrupted, 'Don't, darling. Let's not enter his world of greed and malice.'

Freddy could contain himself no longer. 'Don't give me your

sanctimonious attitude, Jew. It is my family that has ...'

Tom's blow was lightning fast, and accurate. It left Freddy gasping on the floor and clutching his face. He crawled, then staggered towards the front row. Guests got out of his way as he stumbled, then turned to run across the room. By now, the police were fast approaching, but Freddy was in full flight and heading for a side door.

As he disappeared from sight, the lawyer spoke to Rachel.

'Don't worry, they will find him and until then he can't go home, to the bank or any of his so-called friends. Hr Stein is now homeless and penniless, and he will not find Munich any more hospitable than it was for a young Jewish mother and child in the 1940s.

'You are now a very wealthy woman, Rachel, but, looking at you and Tom, somehow I don't think that will change very much. '

Inspector Ogier had organised a discreet exit for Rachel and Tom with the local police, to avoid the media interest.

He bid them a fond farewell and they thanked him sincerely, before a driver whisked them away to the airport and home.

On the way, Rachel looked at Tom, and he knew there was one last thing to do before they left. He instructed the driver.

The car pulled up outside a splendid-looking house with steps onto the street in what was once a suburban area of Munich. Rachel tapped Tom on the knee and got out.

This was where it had begun. The buildings were much bigger then, and the road much wider, or so it seemed. But the house was grand.

The curtains were open and, inside, the lights blazed on this dull October day. Children were laughing in the house, their mother and the family were milling around.

Rachel wanted to remember it this way, without looking at the street where her father had been slain. She turned, got back into the car and smiled mischievously at Tom.

'Do you know what I want more than anything else in the world right now?'

Tom cast a suspicious look at his wife.

'I want you to take me out in *Fish*. I want you to take me to Shell Beach the moment we get home.'

Part 3: The Causeway

CHAPTER TWENTY-ONE

Munich 1972

Panic-stricken, Freddy burst through the door into a long corridor. He glanced left and right to quickly assess the fastest escape route. Already the footsteps from behind were getting louder.

By no means obese he was however, overweight and being quite tall this gave him a bulky, ungainly appearance. He was now also sweating profusely. The few passers-by were clearly bank employees, dressed as they were in smart, conventional attire. They stared at this intrusion into their ordered world.

To the right and opposite, a stairwell broke the long expanse of plain wall and Freddy pushed his way to it. Here he found a large marble stairway with an ornate iron banister around the centre spiral shaft that created a mirror-like effect up and down the height of the building. From this he could see just a few floors below but many more above. Leaping three steps at a time, he made for the first landing below, hearing a burst of sound from behind as he landed. They would soon be on him.

Emerging moments later into the corridor, three uniformed police officers were in hot pursuit, themselves followed by three more detectives in plain clothes. They looked quickly for their prey but he was out of sight. Seeing the uniforms, the 'corridor workers' were keen to assist and two pointed frantically at the stairwell, shouting, 'Down there; he just went down there.'

Freddy was alone on the stairs but could hear the commotion clearly behind him. In seconds they would see him descending, but going up would be worse as he would need to backtrack.

He felt like a trapped animal. 'It's impossible... wait, there's another door on the landing.'

The pale colours ensured the door blended inconspicuously into the wall around it. If there hadn't been a small plaque with the figure of a man, it would have been easy to miss. He almost dived through the door and pulled it closed behind him but was cool enough to prevent a final slamming noise. 'Thank God it wasn't fitted with a slow auto-closing device.'

The large marble-walled room contained a neat line of sinks on the left and toilet doors on the right. Above the sinks, a row of full-length mullioned windows rose with semi-frosted glass allowing the light from outside to beam in. A horizontal shadow crossed his face. As Freddy could hear loud steps again on the stairs outside, it dawned on him: the shadow was cast by scaffolding. Sprightlier than his forty seven years would suggest, he leapt onto a sink and within seconds had opened the window above and mounted the scaffold outside.

The detectives and two of the fittest uniformed policemen had run straight past the doorway and were striding down the stairs beyond. The third clutched the banister and deftly tap-danced down the stairs, peering up and down the shaft as he descended to the landing. He was the first to notice the door. He strode directly for it and entered at the precise moment Freddy reached back to close the window behind him. The officer walked slowly into the room, breath abated to hear more closely the giveaway sounds of his prey. One by one, he checked the stall doors.

Outside, Freddy dared to look back through the window. He could just make out the figure inside, attention diverted as he checked each of the doors. There were just moments before he would focus his attention onto the windows.

Freddy looked around. He was balancing on the iron scaffolding pole that had cast the shadow into the room and holding a vertical pole to his left. Below, a few feet down, planks formed a walkway along the side of the building. Just a few metres further was the street and the hustle and bustle of the busy city. He could see no workers on the walkway and so climbed carefully down.

Taking his bearings, he realised the main entrance to the building was to his right onto the busy Fraunhoferstrasse. The road below was one-way leading on to it, so he decided to make his way against the flow and headed along the walkway to his left. Above him, he could now hear the sound of workers shouting and a radio blaring. Soon, a ladder came to hand, and he scrambled to make his way to the street. As he did so, a penetrating yell came back from along the walkway.

Head peering through the opened window, the police officer was now shouting instructions to Freddy to stop or he would shoot to kill. Momentarily, he froze, and the hairs on his neck bristled with fear.

Then a siren split the air as two police cars skidded to a halt in Fraunhoferstrasse at the end of the side road. More police emerged from these cars seemingly frustrated by their inability to drive against the one-way flow in pursuit.

This distraction broke the spell and ignoring the armed officer, Freddy jumped to the street and began to run in the opposite direction until to his horror, yet another police car sped into the street, this time from the other end. A chef appeared carrying boxes on the opposite pavement through an open fire door. Freddy ran between the traffic to the sound of blasting horns and, shoving the man aside, rushed through the door.

Leaving the shouts of abuse behind, he pushed his way through the busy kitchen and out into the restaurant. Diners froze as this frantic figure charged bull-like through the tables. As he emerged onto the street he could see the commotion to his right where the police cars still blocked the side road, but the officers had now left their cars and were out of sight. He ran to his left, taking cover amongst the crowd of pedestrians on this wide Munich boulevard. 'Walk,' he told himself. 'Don't run, and blend into the crowd.'

So Freddy made his escape through the busy streets, leaving his pursuers standing in confusion and desperately trying to pick up the now cold trail.

Within an hour, the serious crime team had assembled in the third-floor briefing room of Munich Central Office. Chief Inspector Muller was quick to gain order, and unflinching in his criticism.

'I gave the victims a personal reassurance that this man would not find refuge in our city. I still can't believe he got away from the building. How the hell can you lose someone running free in a bank?'

Three members of the team in particular avoided Muller's piercing eye contact. Muller was a large man at over six feet tall, heavily built and for someone in his late forties, looked remarkably fit. But any sense of gravitas this physique may have given him was sadly undermined by what can only be described as a "quirky" dress sense. As if the checked red trousers with a blue striped shirt and somewhat dated sports jacket weren't enough, his long, jet-black, bushy hair was the finishing touch. Certainly he still had presence, but this was a consequence of his command of language and the gold-plated reputation that left everyone in the room in awe of him.

'We will revisit this cock-up later when you have all shown me what you can do to redeem yourselves. In the meantime, I have a story to tell you about our fugitive, and maybe you will then understand why I want him caught.

'First, let me introduce a colleague from the police force of Guernsey in the Channel Islands, Inspector Ogier has been involved with this case for some time, and I would ask him to please correct me if any details that I give are inaccurate.' Muller nodded to a stranger standing discreetly at the side of the room who acknowledged him with a polite smile.

'To give the headline first: Freddy Stein is the top dog of Stein Pharmaceuticals, or was until today when we discovered he forged, deceived and, quite possibly, murdered his way into that position. Two of his accomplices are in police custody and are singing like birds. Stein is in the frame for attempting to murder the rightful heiress to the business, a gentle old man who survived the Holocaust, and quite possibly his own brother. Needless to say, he left most of the dirty work to others, like the two now helping us with our enquiries. But, as for the death of his brother, he is now the prime suspect.

'Of course you all know about the company. It is one of

211

Germany's most successful private businesses with exports and factories around the world. Earlier today, it was due to go public and, owning most of the shares, our friend Freddy would have raked in a fortune. Not that he was exactly hard up before. Greed is a dangerous thing, my friends.'

Around the room, Muller's team looked to each other for a reaction. There was a slim, blond woman named Ida; Ali, a shortish, very dapper man of Middle-Eastern appearance; and the three detectives from the bank. The first of these, Raj, looked like a larger, scruffier version of Ali, and the two others, Pieter and Kirk, both had typically German blond hair, wore smart suits and were well built. Smart suits, that is, with loosened ties since the somewhat energetic chase an hour earlier. All eyes landed on Ali who had a reputation for collecting fast cars and smart clothes. The reference to greed seemed to amuse them.

'First thing this morning, I was contacted by the financial regulator who told me that a woman had come to see him with evidence that she was the heiress to the Stein business. She held share certificates in her father's name and proof of her identity as the sole survivor after the death of both her parents. The certificates amounted to fifty-one percent, a controlling interest. So how, you might ask, did Freddy produce evidence that he held the majority of shares? Yes, my bright-eyed friends, that is where the forgery comes in. Although it was his response to being confronted that really gave him away.

'Clearly, the forgeries must have been expertly done, so we will be very interested in understanding how this came about.

'Inspector Ogier has a file on this case with considerably more detail, and I would ask you all to read it, but for now those are the main points. Any questions?'

Raj was the first to respond. 'Presumably Stein has no form. What about the other two?'

'Good question, but negative. An old school fascist called Reiner and slightly younger controller, Gunter Smitt. Both are unknown to us and claim to have been recruited by our man,

Stein. Yes, Ida.'

'What do we know about other contacts or associates Stein may try to get to. Has he family?'

'No family left as far as we know but so far we haven't had time to investigate further. This line of enquiry will now be a priority.'

Whilst the team thought about this answer, Muller continued. 'Look, there is much we don't know yet, and time is slipping away rapidly, so whilst you may have lots more to ask me, I'm going to ask you to hold any more questions until later and get back out onto the streets to find this man. First of all, Ali, there is an "APB" out for Stein, but I want you to sit on control to make sure you are at hand when anything comes in. Find out what car he drives and get that circulated asap. Get officers to his home, his office and anywhere else he might turn up.

'Raj, get over to the offices of Stein straightaway and flash your badge to get access to the company records. I want that place totally pinned down, nothing and nobody goes in or comes out without you knowing. Correction: nothing goes out, full stop. Ida, do the same with his house and check for any boltholes he might have: holiday homes, apartments, that kind of thing. Also, get onto his bank. I want his accounts frozen and any attempt to withdraw cash reported immediately. Kirk, close the borders to this man, I don't want him leaving the country so contact Border Control and get his details to every German airport and crossing point. OK, finally, Pieter, go with Raj and find Stein's appointment diary and address book. He'll have a PA and secretary so I want you to find out who he is close to, where he has been recently; get inside his head and tell me his next move. Now, everybody, go to it. We'll meet again first thing tomorrow and, in the meantime, you can reach me through control. I'll be interrogating his accomplices but first I need to speak with the lady at the centre of all this before she leaves the country.' He paused; then, 'Go, get to it!'

With that, the room emptied and Muller turned to Inspector Ogier.

'How much of a threat do you think this man is now he has been flushed out?'

Inspector Ogier thought for a few moments before answering. 'Of course, we have little first-hand information about the man himself; only his manipulation of others and, of course, our suspicions about his brother's death. But, it seems most likely he is ruthless and dangerous because he may think he now has nothing to lose. He knows he will be in the frame for a life sentence, and I would expect him to stop at nothing to prevent capture. As for other ambitions, he may try to access his wealth, and he may want revenge, but this is highly speculative.'

It was Muller's turn to reflect before replying. 'From what you told me about Gunter, he was not exactly a sensitive soul but he was clearly terrified of Stein. We'd better play safe and treat him with extreme caution. I don't want any more casualties. What are your plans now?'

'I have no jurisdiction in your country, and it was good of you to allow me to sit in on the "collar" at the bank, but now I need to return to Guernsey with the couple I came here to protect. Rachel and Tom Le Breton are good, straightforward people. The last thing they ever wanted was to be caught up in a deadly intrigue or power struggle for an international corporation. But, like it or not, Rachel is now the majority shareholder of a huge company, and there is a lot they will both have to consider. For my part, I want to be sure they get back safely. I don't know what, if any, tricks Stein has up his sleeve, and I think he would be mad to go anywhere near them, but rather than second-guess, I want to be there keeping an eye on them. They're waiting at the airport in a private lounge with some of your officers, I believe. Shall we join them?'

With that, the two men left Munich Central and headed for the airport.

A short drive later, they met with Rachel and Tom and broke the news that Stein had so far eluded capture. A middle-aged couple they might be, but both were still alert and attractive: Rachel with an hour glass figure and long black hair, and Tom

214

with the kind of rugged good looks that come from a life at sea. Tom was forthright. 'This man has been a blight on our lives, and I want him caught but, failing that, I want him and any of his playmates kept well away from Rachel. You understand, don't you, that I won't be held responsible for my actions if he turns up within a country mile of my wife or family? Other than that, we are still a little shell-shocked, and we're trying to take everything in. We discussed a few things on the way to the airport, and Rachel doesn't want to upset the family now living in her parents' old house. It is their home now, and we want them to keep it. We'll look into the legal side later. As for the business, we need to learn about it before we decide anything. Our son is in the investment business at home, and he can guide us, but it would be helpful if we could take some information back with us for him to make a start. Can you help us with this?'

Muller reached for the radio microphone attached to his collar. 'Munich Control, this is Muller. You read me?'

A response crackled that they did.

'Patch me through to Raj, would you?' Then a few seconds later, 'Raj, listen, I want you to find the finance guy at Stein. Tell him to assemble the last few years' accounts and senior management reports, as well as any brochures they may have that describe what Stein do and where they do it. Also, go into Freddy's office and see if you can find anything else that looks relevant. The new owners need to get up to speed quickly on any decisions that need making. Let's not forget there are thousands of jobs depending on them as well as suppliers, shareholders and customers.'

Rachel looked apprehensively at her husband as Muller went on. 'Take copies of everything and get them to us at the airport within...'

He turned to Tom. 'How long before your flight leaves?'

Tom signalled two hours.

'Get them here within the hour; understand? OK, have you anything for me?'

The conversation closed abruptly a few seconds later, and

Muller signalled that they should all sit down in more comfortable chairs to continue their conversation whilst they waited. Although Rachel and Tom would much rather have been left alone to wait for their flight, they understood the importance of helping Muller as much as they could.

Meanwhile, a few miles away in the city centre, Freddy Stein waited impatiently by a public telephone booth. A dark Mercedes with smoked windows pulled up at the kerb a few metres away and a back door opened. Freddy peered in for just a moment, and responding to the invitation from within, he looked around and slid into the car.

As the limo sped its way through the city, the two passengers in the back seat made little eye contact as arrangements were discussed.

'We are taking you to Max like you asked, but he isn't happy.'

'You think I am? Like it or not, we both have a problem now and, if you want to keep the game in play, you are going to have to help me.'

'Save it for Max, Freddy. You know he makes his own mind up so there's no point in appealing to me. Just sit back and enjoy the ride. At least you are still free at the moment.'

With that, they turned away from each other and peered out of the window. The houses were less frequent now with long lines of trees bordering both sides of the road. Before long, the car slowed and the indicator signalled it was about to turn off into a discreet driveway breaking the treeline. Just off the road, a pair of large iron gates barred the entrance, and the driver spoke into a small entry system to announce their arrival. The gates immediately swung open, allowing the Mercedes to follow a meandering gravel driveway for a further half a mile until it pulled up outside a substantial baroque, manor house.

Freddy was escorted inside and told to wait in the hallway. A vaulted ceiling thirty feet above gave proportion to the impressive staircase that spilled onto a highly polished marble floor at his feet. The first flight culminated on a landing with two galleries leading away on either side. Above this division, a huge oil painting by Rembrandt dominated the wall. The Night Watch depicted a company of civic militia guards being led by a small group believed to include the captain who originally commissioned the painting. What was especially brazen was the fact that this painting was supposed to be hanging safely in a museum in Amsterdam. No stranger himself to the trappings of wealth, Freddy was nonetheless impressed with the splendour of Max's home.

As Freddy gazed up at the painting, he was surprised by a quiet cough uncomfortably close behind him.

'I see you appreciate fine art. Of course, some might say I should hide this away, but most callers who have any knowledge of art assume it to be a copy. I'll leave you to draw your own conclusions.'

Freddy spun around to face the diminutive figure of a man in his late fifties dressed immaculately in a pale linen suit and sporting a red polka dot tie with matching handkerchief in his breast pocket.

'Max, it is good to see you. I am grateful for you allowing me to come here. I know how you value your privacy.'

'Enough of the pleasantries, Freddy, we both know you are only here because you have lost your grip on the business, and I need to understand how that affects our little arrangement. Come through to the drawing room and tell me what has happened.'

Max led the way to an oak-panelled room surrounded by shelves containing antiquarian books, and more familiar oils adorning the walls. In the centre, two leather Chesterfields faced each other over a low wooden coffee table. They sat, one on each sofa, Max leaning back relaxed, Freddy leaning forward eagerly. He was rambling and this was uncharacteristic of Freddy, Max guessed the situation was as serious as he had first thought.

'So, Freddy, you are telling me that papers showing the accounts of the Bogota plant were left in your office? That isn't good, but I'm guessing they only contain creative accounting, yes?'

'Naturally, the books don't give anything away, but it wouldn't take a genius to work out that the business is just a front. Lots of suppliers paid in cash, and international customers who aren't exactly recognisable on the established pharmaceutical scene. I had no idea I wouldn't be back in the office later to file it all away in time for our tame and somewhat stupid auditors but now I can't risk going back there.'

The expression on Max's face was enough to silence Freddy. Agitated, he was still perched on the edge of the Chesterfield looking across into Max's expressionless face. He knew this man was now deciding if his crime empire was compromised and, if it was, what he should do about it. Perhaps he was deciding whether to call in a couple of the large minders waiting outside; maybe suggest they take him somewhere for safety and then dispose of him. Max had not got to his position without a large measure of blood on his hands, or at least those of his thugs.

'Is there anything that connects Bogota with my supply chain into Europe or the US? Anything at all? Think hard now. Any other documents they might find; names; meeting places; anything?'

'I don't keep anything like that written down. I only need the accounts because we have to show the Colombians the business is legitimate or they would simply shop us to the FBI. As it is a Stein business, they think it is all OK, but the board here also need fobbing off with numbers. No, nothing connects you but we have a good business and, if I can just get these bloody papers, we can fake a disposal of the business by Stein and tell them locally it's a management buy-out. There is just one loose end we need to take care of; my PA has dealt with all my travel arrangements and she might give them enough to work it out. Otherwise, nobody questioned what I did with the business. It was hardly high-profile. We just need to get rid of Stella.'

Neither man flinched at the prospect of stubbing out the life of Freddy's PA. Max simply moved onto more practical matters.

'If it is as you say, and we can keep going with just a couple of "adjustments" and perhaps a new owner in Bogota, we might as well. After all, the profits on this powder are still strong and growing rapidly. But you know, Freddy, if it isn't as you say, I will feel you have let me down very badly. You won't let me down, will you, Freddy?'

The eye contact was penetrating. Freddy sat back to draw in a breath and loosen his tie. He was sweating again and in no doubt what Max meant by this.

'I can't let you down; you know that. You have me in the perfect grasp. With your help, I can still get my fortune back. If I fail, we both know there is no hiding place.'

'Just so long as we both understand that.'

CHAPTER TWENTY-TWO

The family of four sat together around Rachel's kitchen table in the small coastal cottage on the south-west of Guernsey. The atmosphere was electric.

Momentary silence had descended upon them as they took stock of their situation. The twins, Rebecca and David, now in their twenties had imagined their lives would be much the same as all their other local friends, working in the island's finance industry, slowly trying to climb the career ladder.

Both quite tall, from their father's side, but with dark features clearly echoing their mother, the two had a distinctive blend of local and European features. Rachel was Jewish with thick black hair; deep ebony eyes and a figure that confirmed her life had by no means been one of excess. Tom and her had always been short of cash and had always worked hard; consequently they both looked great for their forty-plus years although materially they had little to show for it.

Tom glanced at the pile of files on the kitchen dresser,

'We will have to get around to that lot sometime you know.'

His wife just smiled at him knowing how he abhorred anything to do with paperwork. In any case she wasn't quite ready for such a pragmatic approach.

'You know what I think Rebecca?' There was a mischievous smile on her lips.

'I think we should go shopping today. I think we should just go out and buy that little black dress you wanted and absolutely anything else you fancy.'

Hardly containing her excitement, Rebecca's reply was unconvincing.

'But shouldn't we wait until there is actually some money in our bank account, after all we have just committed to buying another house?'

They all turned to David, although everyone deferred to Tom for most things as the head of the family, David was the financial wizard.

'Well I should probably advise caution until we actually have all the cash, but I've called the bank to explain everything and they said we could assume, and I quote... 'A considerable amount of leeway'...unquote, until the money transfers come through.

The family erupted in laughter. The usually stuffy, no personality, bank manager suddenly seemed to be warming to the Le Breton family now that they were probably the wealthiest family on the island.

It wasn't really that funny, but a release was needed for the emotions they were all trying to keep a cap on.

David had explained to the bank manager that Rachel now effectively owned a substantial shareholding in one of the world's largest pharmaceutical companies. The business had floated on the German stock exchange so most shares were now traded publically but as the largest single shareholder, Rachel was clearly in control. The money from the floatation ran into many millions of pounds and was almost all Rachel's since the discovery that she was the rightful heiress to the business. This once poor family was now fabulously rich. The new house they were buying, with commanding views over the north coast of Guernsey, wouldn't even make a small dent in their finances.

David had been working as an investment advisor so when the decision needed to be made about how many Stein Pharmaceutical shares they should keep and how many they should sell, he was able to call in some favours from his connections in the industry. They had all been unanimous in their advice; the share price would rise so they should keep a sizable holding. Rachel had been pleased with this approach, as she hadn't quite worked out how she felt about selling what had been her family's business before the war.

One thing she did know was that she had no intention of becoming a businesswoman. In any case, there really was no need, as her newfound wealth would provide for all her family's needs for the rest of their lives.

It was now ten-thirty in the morning and they had been at the table for over an hour since finishing their uncharacteristically late breakfast. It was time to make a start and Tom led the way saying to Rachel.

'You say my love if you don't agree, it's your money, but how about we all have a really good think about our futures. David and Rebecca, you chose your careers partly because it was what you wanted to do but partly for the money and prospects. You don't need to think like that anymore, you just need to think about what you would really like to do. There's no way I'm going to stop fishing but I don't want to have to do it for a living anymore. I would like us to spend more time together. There's no rush, we probably all need a bit of time to let it sink in.'

Rachel considered his words and then with a 'cats got the cream' grin, she responded.

'I know, why don't we take a holiday to think it all over?'

To a unanimous 'Yeah...' she continued.

'You know Tom, I've always loved coming out with you on your boats but dear old 'Fish' is too small for a holiday and I don't really fancy a couple of weeks on your fishing boat, so...' she paused for effect...

'.... And I'm assuming here that you all feel like I do that a holiday with airports and suit-cases might be a bit wearisome, why don't we buy a new yacht?'

A few days ago this suggestion would have led them to believe Rachel had been at the sherry, but now, well why not?

It was just a matter of weeks later that Tom piloted his new 'Seadog' ketch into 'the pool' at St Peter Port harbour. At thirty feet she was just the right size for the family of four to navigate around the Channel Islands and the northern coast of France. Tom had been lucky that another customer had dropped out at the last minute so he avoided the waiting list and his new ketch had all the modern gadgets he wanted. She was built to the highest specification and with three keels, could even take to the ground on a sandy beach without keeling over.

The family soon joined him on board and it was a clear sunny morning when they let go of the mooring buoy to head out into the waters of 'Little Russel' off St Peter Port.

On board, Rachel and Tom claimed the aft cabin and settled in whilst David took the helm in the protected central cockpit. He and Rebecca shared the main cabin with berths either side of a central folding table. Painted proudly on the ketch's transom was the name 'Anoushka', after the Matryoshka dolls that Rachel's parents bought her as a child. Her mother had used 'Anoushka' as the password to unlock the Swiss accounts that eventually yielded her newfound wealth.

As Rachel sat back in the cabin she eyed a pile of documents placed on one of the cabin shelves. 'What's this Tom, don't tell me you're planning to work whilst we're cruising?'

Tom gave a broad grin before responding that he felt he ought to have them on board and maybe he would glance at them, but then again maybe he wouldn't.

Their course first took them north to the island of Alderney where many years ago Rachel and Tom first met on a beach at night during the German occupation of the islands. She had been a young Jewish girl working in the labour camp, he a teenage boy evading soldiers on a fishing trip. The island they were returning to now could not have been more different. Of course, it retained the rugged unspoilt beauty that made it unique and the sand was just as golden, but now it was free. Alderney had been almost completely evacuated of locals during the war so unlike the other Channel Islanders who celebrated the 'liberation', each year the residents here celebrated the homecoming of their families to the island.

Anoushka's snowy white sails filled with the southwesterly breeze and she slipped through the clear water towards Alderney.

Their cruise was planned to take them to each island in turn spending a few days, or if the fancy took them, weeks at each before returning to Guernsey. It was just a few hours before

Anoushka edged around the long harbour wall of St Anne's 'Braye Harbour' and took her place at anchor in the bay. Her short trip had been flawless and the family now appreciated why Tom had been so keen on this particular type of yacht. Within minutes the wooden cockpit table was up, food was being prepared in the galley and a bottle of wine un-corked ready for supper.

The family sat together around the table and toasted their successful first trip together amidst the splendid scenery of one of Alderney's prettiest bays.

'Is this our new life do you think then?' Tom mused as the wine and conversation flowed in equal measures.

'I could get used to it.' Rachel leaned against her husband to the ribbing of son David.

'OK you two love birds, we know this is a bit of a romantic setting for you but try to remember you're supposed to be our parents. Put her down Dad!'

'When I first met your mum, romance was the last thing on my mind; she was a bit young you know. In any case, I was in a bit of a quandary, what with the Germans and all. I wasn't too sure how we would get away but I knew one thing. There was no way I was leaving her here.'

'My hero...' Rachel grinned at him, 'you were actually; you absolutely saved me from that scary group of Nazis and the storeroom floor where I slept. God knows what would have become of me after Hans left.'

Rebecca looked at her mother solemnly, 'What became of him Mum? We know all about the nasty Freddy, and the old man apparently snuffed it, but what about Hans?'

Tom explained that the young German soldier who had protected Rachel had later joined the family firm where he worked until mysteriously 'falling' from the roof of the Stein building. Inspector Muller had confided in him that Freddy was thought to have been involved and one of his henchmen had even claimed he pushed his own brother off the roof.

Rebecca looked horrified. 'Jesus, we knew he was ruthless but this bloke was in a league of his own. How could anyone do that to their own flesh and blood?'

David's attempt to lighten the mood by strangling his sister had the desired effect. So they settled down to another helping of Rachel's lasagne before starting on the strawberries and cream.

As the evening wore on the light began to go and Tom lit a small oil lamp swinging from the boom above them. It was a balmy evening like many an Indian summer in the Channel Islands, although now well into October, this one was exceptional.

The banter ricocheted between them until the early hours of the morning punctuated by laughter and giggles at frequent intervals. This was a family very much at ease without a care in the world and as they bid each other 'good night' and made their way sleepily to their cabins, the last thing they imagined was that danger would continue to stalk them.

The family of four sat together around Rachel's kitchen table in the small coastal cottage on the south-west of Guernsey. The atmosphere was electric.

Momentary silence had descended upon them as they took stock of their situation. The twins, Rebecca and David, now in their twenties had imagined their lives would be much the same as all their other local friends, working in the island's finance industry, slowly trying to climb the career ladder.

Both quite tall, from their father's side, but with dark features clearly echoing their mother, the two had a distinctive blend of local and European features. Rachel was Jewish, thick black hair; deep ebony eyes and a figure that confirmed her life had by no means been one of excess. Tom and her had always been short of cash and had always worked hard, consequently they both looked great for their forty-plus years although materially they had little to show for it.

Tom glanced at the pile of files on the kitchen dresser,

'We will have to get around to that lot sometime you know.'

His wife just smiled at him knowing how he abhorred

anything to do with paperwork. In any case she wasn't quite ready for such a pragmatic approach.

'You know what I think Rebecca?' There was a mischievous smile on her lips.

'I think we should go shopping today, I think we should just go out and buy that little black dress you wanted and absolutely anything else you fancy.'

Hardly containing her excitement, Rebecca's reply was unconvincing.

'But shouldn't we wait until there is some money actually in our bank account, after all we have just committed to buying another house?'

They all turned to David, although everyone deferred to Tom for most things as the head of the family, David was the financial wizard.

'Well I probably should advise caution until we actually have all the cash, but I've called the bank to explain everything and they said we could assume, and I quote... 'A considerable amount of leeway'...unquote, until the money transfers come through.

The family erupted in laughter, the usually stuffy; no personality bank manager suddenly seemed to be warming to the Le Breton family now that they were probably the wealthiest family in the island.

It wasn't really that funny but a release was needed for the emotions they were all trying to keep a cap on.

David had explained to the bank manager that Rachel now effectively owned a substantial shareholding in one of the world's largest pharmaceutical companies. The business had floated on the German stock exchange so most shares were now traded publicly but as the largest single shareholder, Rachel was clearly in control. The money from the floatation ran into many millions of pounds and was almost all Rachel's since the discovery that she was the rightful heiress to the business. This once poor family was now fabulously rich. The new house they were buying, with commanding views over the north coast of

Guernsey, wouldn't even make a small dent in their finances.

David had been working as an investment advisor so when the decision needed to be made about how many Stein Pharmaceutical shares they should keep and how many they should sell; he was able to call in some favours from his connections in the industry. They had all been unanimous in their advice; the share price would rise so they should keep a sizeable holding. Rachel had been pleased with this approach, as she hadn't quite worked out how she felt about selling what had been her family's business before the war.

One thing she did know was that she had no intention of becoming a businesswoman. In any case, there really was no need, as her newfound wealth would provide for all her family's needs for the rest of their lives.

It was now ten thirty in the morning and they had been at the table for over an hour since finishing their uncharacteristically late breakfast. It was time to make a start and Tom led the way saying to Rachel.

'You say my love if you don't agree, it's your money, but how about we all have a really good think about our futures. David and Rebecca, you chose your careers partly because it was what you wanted to do but partly for the money and prospects. You don't need to think like that anymore, you just need to think what you really would like to do. There's no way I'm going to stop fishing but I don't want to have to do it for a living anymore, I would like us to spend more time together. There's no rush, we probably all need a bit of time to let it sink in.'

Rachel considered his words and then with a 'cats got the cream' grin, she responded.

'I know, why don't we take a holiday to think it all over?'

To a unanimous 'Yeah…' she continued;

'You know Tom, I've always loved coming out with you on your boats but dear old '*Fish*' is too small for a holiday and I don't really fancy a couple of weeks on your fishing boat, so……' she paused for effect…

'…. And I'm assuming here that you all feel like I do that a

227

holiday with airports and suit-cases might be a bit wearisome, why don't we buy a new yacht?'

A few days ago this suggestion would have led them to believe Rachel had been at the sherry, but now, well why not?

It was just a matter of weeks later that Tom piloted his new 'Seadog' ketch into 'the pool' at St Peter Port harbour. At thirty feet she was just the right size for the family of four to navigate around the Channel Islands and the northern coast of France. Tom had been lucky that another customer had dropped out at the last minute so he avoided the waiting list and his new ketch had all the modern gadgets he wanted. She was built to the highest specification and with three keels, could even take to the ground on a sandy beach without keeling over.

The family soon joined him on board and it was a clear sunny morning when they let go of the mooring buoy to head out into the waters of 'Little Russel' off St Peter Port.

On board, Rachel and Tom claimed the aft cabin and settled in whilst David took the helm in the protected central cockpit. He and Rebecca shared the main cabin with berths either side of a central folding table. Painted proudly on the Ketch's transom was the name '*Anoushka*', after the Matryoshka dolls that Rachel's parents bought her as a child. Her mother had used '*Anoushka*' as the password to unlock the Swiss accounts that eventually yielded her newfound wealth.

As Rachel sat back in the cabin she eyed a pile of documents placed on one of the cabin shelves. 'What's this Tom, don't tell me you're planning to work whilst we're cruising?'

Tom gave a broad grin before responding that he felt he ought to have them on board and maybe he would glance at them, but then again maybe he wouldn't.

Their course first took them north to the island of Alderney where many years ago Rachel and Tom first met on a beach at night during the German occupation of the islands. She had been a young Jewish girl working in the labour camp, he a teenage boy evading soldiers on a fishing trip. The island they were returning to now could not have been more different. Of course, it retained the rugged unspoilt beauty that made it unique and the sand was just as golden, but now it was free. Alderney had been almost completely evacuated of locals during the war so unlike the other Channel Islanders who celebrated the 'liberation', each year the residents here celebrated the homecoming of their families to the island.

Anoushka's snowy white sails filled with the southwesterly breeze and she slipped through the clear water towards Alderney.

Their cruise was planned to take them to each island in turn spending a few days, or if the fancy took them, weeks at each before returning to Guernsey. It was just a few hours before *Anoushka* edged around the long harbour wall of St Anne's 'Braye Harbour' and took her place at anchor in the bay. Her short trip had been flawless and the family now appreciated why Tom had been so keen on this particular type of yacht. Within minutes the wooden cockpit table was up, food was being prepared in the galley and a bottle of wine un-corked ready for supper.

The family sat together around the table and toasted their successful first trip together amidst the splendid scenery of one of Alderney's prettiest bays.

'Is this our new life do you think then?' Tom mused as the wine and conversation flowed in equal measures.

'I could get used to it.' Rachel leaned against her husband to the ribbing of son David.

'OK you two love birds, we know this is a bit of a romantic setting for you but try to remember you're supposed to be our parents. Put her down Dad!'

'When I first met your mum, romance was the last thing on my mind; she was a bit young you know. In any case, I was in a bit of a quandary, what with the Germans and all. I wasn't too sure how we would get away but I knew one thing. There was no way I was leaving her here.'

'My hero...' Rachel grinned at him, 'you were actually; you absolutely saved me from that scary group of Nazis and the storeroom floor where I slept. God knows what would have become of me after Hans left.'

Rebecca looked at her mother solemnly, 'What became of him Mum? We know all about the nasty Freddy, and the old man apparently snuffed it, but what about Hans?'

Tom explained that the young German soldier who had protected Rachel had later joined the family firm where he worked until mysteriously 'falling' from the roof of the Stein building. Inspector Muller had confided in him that Freddy was thought to have been involved and one of his henchmen had even claimed he pushed his own brother off the roof.

Rebecca looked horrified. 'Jesus, we knew he was ruthless but this bloke was in a league of his own. How could anyone do that to their own flesh and blood?'

David's attempt to lighten the mood by strangling his sister had the desired effect. So they settled down to another helping of Rachel's lasagne before starting on the strawberries and cream.

As the evening wore on the light began to go and Tom lit a small oil lamp swinging from the boom above them. It was a balmy evening like many an Indian summer in the Channel Islands, although now well into October, this one was exceptional.

The banter ricocheted between them until the early hours of the morning punctuated by laughter and giggles at frequent intervals. This was a family very much at ease without a care in the world and as they bid each other 'good night' and made their way sleepily to their cabins, the last thing they imagined was that danger would continue to stalk them.

CHAPTER TWENTY-THREE

'So Stella, are you going to report your old boss?'

She turned around to face him, and then froze on the spot. This was her apartment, how did he get in?

'No need to worry Stella, we go back a long time I wouldn't harm you. Anyway you've probably been fed a load of crap to get you to open up to them.'

She loosened just enough to reply unconvincingly that she wasn't worried. His dramatic escape and the police chase were only the previous day and the revelations about Freddy were still sinking in.

'Look all I need from you are some papers I left in my office. You will go in first thing before anyone else arrives and slip them in your bag. Are they watching what gets taken out?'

Stella knew he wouldn't like what had been happening at the office but struggled to decide if she should just tell him and risk his fury or lead him on to get rid of him. This was not what she had signed up for as a professional PA, she had dedicated her life to her career and now alone in her forties she felt she had even sacrificed the prospect of a relationship to be at the top of her profession. She should not be scared by a criminal ex-employer who clearly needed her to help cover up his dubious activities. But then, some of the things she had been told about him...

'I don't know if I can help Herr Stein, they have officers all around and we aren't supposed to take anything out.'

Freddy moved closer towards her and his eyes hardened.

'Stella you wouldn't lie to me would you? You know I always get what I want, you remember that don't you Stella?'

'OK, what papers do you want? I can try, but they have copied the papers in your office.'

Freddy felt his blood surge in anger.

'What do you mean they have copied them, all the papers in my office; they have copied all of them?'

231

'It's not my fault Herr Stein. The police just took a pile of loose papers and copied them to give to the new owners and then put them back.'

'Stella, do as I say and you will come out of this alive but cross me and...'

He didn't need to continue.

'OK look it's just a job for Christ's sake. I'll do what you want but that's it yes, then you'll leave me alone?'

Stella rose early the next morning and made her way to the office. The security guard was used to her early starts but didn't think to work out that in the past these had been because her boss had insisted and now, well now the notorious Freddy Stein wasn't supposed to be around anymore. He doffed his cap and wished her a good morning.

Outside the director's suite Raj was still engrossed in the diaries Stella had given him. He didn't think to question the need for her early start either. She breezed into Freddy's office.

As instructed by Freddy she looked around his desk and the Bogota file was exactly where he had left it. It took no more than a few seconds to scoop it into her cavernous handbag and Stella was pleased, pleased this would get her off the hook and she had performed as a loyal professional to the last. She didn't need to, or want to, know what dubious practice he was attempting to cover up.

That lunchtime she left the building as planned and made her way to the underground car park two blocks away.

Moving from the bright light outside down the car park ramp and into the concrete cavern below made her squint as her eyes adjusted. As they refocused she could see the car park was full of vehicles but despite the busy pavement outside it seemed deserted. She took a few steps down the first lane, starting to feel anxious, starting to wonder what she might be getting herself into. Then two bright lights dead ahead blinded her temporarily. Was this him? The dark limo advanced slowly towards her and instinctively she looked around, still no one else to be seen. She could now see that the windows were smoked and totally concealing the occupant. With a sudden surge the car accelerated towards her, the blur of a descending window and then the familiar face of Freddy looking out at her.

'Did you get it?'

There was no small talk and this did not faze Stella as her boss of a few days ago rarely indulged in conversation. She held her bag up to the window.

'Get in.'

As the limo glided out onto Corneliusstrasse amid the museums and theatres of Munich's cultural centre Stella asked where they were headed.

'Not far. I want to check you have the correct file and then you can go, I'll...I'll drop you off.'

They circled the grass and floral roundabout of the Gartnerplatz where same sex couples walked hand in hand around the shops and before long they were surrounded by trees on the embankment of the Isar River. Freddy turned into a small lane through the trees and stopped at a concrete floodwall.

She didn't notice his eyes flick quickly around to ensure they were alone; Freddy had used this place before.

As she removed the file Stella looked coolly into his eyes.

'This is it; I'm quite sure it's what you wanted and as far I could see the file is still complete.' He took the manila folder and started to browse through the papers within. 'Remember I told you that this was copied so don't blame me if the new owners find whatever it is you are looking for.'

Freddy continued to leaf through the pages without looking up. 'So it's just them that have a copy, not the police?'

'No. All I was asked to do was copy a bunch of papers, put the originals back and give the copy to one of the police who had to rush it to the airport before they left. There are no other copies now that you have this.' She paused... 'Don't tell me any details but surely there is other Bogota information. What about the Accounts department?'

Freddy grinned, he had what he wanted and he knew there was no longer any reason to be secretive with Stella. 'The only references to my little side-line in Bogota are here in this file and in the accounts of a bogus Swiss holding company that owns another company then another and so on, all of which appears to be squeaky clean Stella.' He pressed the button that opened her side window. Puzzled, she looked around then turned again to face him as he went on. 'No, I think we can safely say it ends here. At least, it does for you.'

Stella hadn't noticed as Freddy's hand slid to his driver's door pocket and curled around the familiar shape of his Colt handgun. The silencer stifled the sound so there was just a thud as the hammer struck the bullet and Stella's final shocked expression was carved onto her face, a two-centimetre hole in the middle of her brow.

He wasted no time. Time meant blood and that was messy. Within minutes her lifeless body was unceremoniously man handled over the wall and into the fast flowing waters of the Isar. Freddy returned to the car and releasing a catch, opened the boot. Inside there were sufficient cleaning fluids and rags to remove any trace of his passenger. When he and the car were spotless this evidence too joined Stella in the river.

As the rear window of his Mercedes showed Munich receding into the background, Freddy took stock.

He was pleased that at least this had gone well. Execution seemed to come naturally to him, perhaps he might consider a career change, and he mused at the prospect. Then came the focus on reality, so the local police would struggle to ever make a connection with Bogota but these bloody interfering nobodies from the sticks... maybe the Jewess and her flock might realise the significance of that file.

There was no choice, he would let Max know it was so far so good but a loose end needed tidying up in the Channel Island of Guernsey.

Back at Munich Central Police HQ a few hours later Raj was addressing Inspector Muller.

'Look it could be nothing but Stein's PA didn't show up after lunch and I'm sure something's missing from his office.'

Muller wasn't impressed, his instructions had been emphatic – nothing was to leave the building. There were just the two of them in his private office and Raj felt the pressure. 'I know, I know what you said about keeping everything there but she must have concealed it and I think we must assume she's helping him. Before you ask, I've no idea what the contents were about I just know there was a manila file there in his office and now it's gone.'

There was little to be gained by labouring the point but a note would go into Raj's performance record. 'You have let me down Raj, but we must move on. Have you checked Stella's home? Are you sure she wasn't due an afternoon off? There might be another explanation for the file going missing.' He knew as he spoke that he was clutching at straws but no one had suspected a relationship between Stein and his PA, she appeared too plain for the extroverted Freddy. Then, after all it wouldn't be the first time a boss had seduced his personal assistant.

Muller ordered Raj back to the office with instructions to question anyone from the admin team or other directors who might conceivably know about a file in Freddy's private office. Then he pondered the significance of this latest development. Why would Freddy want paperwork from the office? At least he must still be nearby - or then again maybe not – Stella was taking it to him, he could be anywhere. Muller buzzed through to Kirk who was in charge of checking the borders for Stein. 'Listen Kirk we also need an APB out on Stella DeVere, Stein's PA. She may have flown the nest to be with him. Get borders onto it straight away with a description, and try to get hold of Raj when he arrives at the office. Maybe their personnel department or security will have a photo of her. Failing that Ida can check out her home for one. Get onto to it straightaway Kirk!' he slammed the phone down and his thoughts returned to the file. 'Wait a minute; we copied all the files in his office to give to the English couple.'

235

When the call came in to Guernsey Police, Inspector Ogier was about to leave for the day. The front desk caught him just in time and he leaned on the wall against a wanted poster for 'Bible John' whilst a young PC dealt with a couple of locals who had spent their day in the Helmsman Public House and emerged three sheets to the wind and causing a ruckus. 'George, give me a minute will you?'

George purposely manoeuvred the duo into an interview room along the corridor as the Inspector took his call.

'Sounds intriguing... OK, we'll contact the Le Bretons but how do we know what we are looking for? ... Sure, we'll borrow the files and my officer will call you to discuss the contents... OK see you.'

Ending the call, Inspector Ogier gave instructions to his young constable to recover the files and telephone Munich to see if they could work out which one had been taken from Freddy's office. He needed to make radio contact as the family were cruising in their new yacht but George knew the Le Breton family and quickly concluded his task with the help of a local ambulance vessel, the 'Flying Christine' making a routine call to Braye harbour. By the middle of the next morning both police Inspectors were fully aware of the contents of the Bogota file and had deduced that if Freddy had gone to the trouble of getting the file he would also know that a copy existed which he would want to retrieve. Freddy might be heading for Guernsey and Rachel may once again be in danger.

CHAPTER TWENTY-FOUR

Max was tentative about the situation Freddy had described over the phone but conceded it was probably best for him to go to the island, as he knew what the woman looked like. Knowing there would be problems for Freddy accessing cash, he arranged for a bag containing various currencies to be taken to him along with instructions on how to get out of Germany and into Guernsey.

Freddy was not used to travelling rough and took great exception at being forced to hide in the back of a truck whilst the driver passed through border control at the German/French border. Whilst the driver ensured a smooth transition by discretely handing over a bulky envelope to a nervous officer, they took no chances and kept Freddy well out of sight. Inside the roadside building, a photograph of Freddy adorned the wall along with a description of the missing Stella.

The truck rumbled on, and after a few kilometres Freddy was allowed to rejoin the driver in his comfortable cab. Indignant, he demanded more information about the travel arrangements.

Freddy was not a good sailor and didn't react well to the news that they would be taking to the sea from a cove close to the French port of St Malo, albeit in a powerful cabin cruiser. But he was no fool and could see this was the best way to avoid detection; there would be lots of other boats around the port and, as the cruiser would appear to be from Guernsey, nobody would question its course back to the island. Weather permitting, once at St Malo, he would be just hours away from the island.

For the remainder of the journey Freddy dozed, partly because he knew he might not rest well on his sea voyage later but mainly to avoid conversation with his driver. When the truck pulled up in the port of St Malo, he was deep in an agitated sleep with troubled dreams. The driver unceremoniously prodded Freddy to wake him and instantly regretted his action.

Freddy's return to consciousness was like that of a high-speed elevator soaring up a lift shaft. As he hit floor twenty his eyes bulging and state of mind still confused, he reacted instinctively. Before the driver could move, Freddy's hands were around his neck squeezing the life out of him. He wasn't thinking, just reacting and deep inside his bulging eyes the driver saw no trace of awareness or worse still, compassion; he was about to die.

The rage mist cleared and with saliva almost dripping from his mouth Freddy realised where he was. As he released his grip, the driver slumped forward gasping for air but riveted by the pain of every breath.

He wanted to curse his ungrateful passenger. He expected remorse to follow, perhaps a heart-felt apology. Instead it was Freddy who cursed him.

'What the fuck are you doing prodding me like that, you stupid bastard? Where are we?'

The driver thought better than to antagonise Freddy; he was still smarting from the pain and taken aback by the surprising show of strength. He could only wheeze.

'We are here, this is St Malo.'

'What... good; what's the name of the boat again, where do we find it?'

'I'll get your bag; we need to go down to the slipway. You see over there? The man standing by the Dory, he is Francois. He will take you to the cruiser on the Dory.'

With that, the driver reached behind for Freddy's bag and jumped down from the lorry cab. Freddy eased himself out after him. As the two walked towards the slipway, Francois recognised the driver and nodded an acknowledgment.

A few minutes later the Dory sped out of the harbour and Freddy without a backwards glance or word of gratitude to the driver held tight to the sides as the outboard engine ramped up the Dory to full speed. As the wind rushed noisily across their faces, Francois attempted pleasantries.

'Well monsieur, we are at anchor in a cove not far from here and as the tide is good we can leave immediately. We should be in Sark by evening.'

'What do you mean Sark? We are supposed to be going to Guernsey!'

'First we stop in Sark, which is just nine miles from Guernsey. It's much smaller and nobody will bother us dropping anchor off the island. Then tomorrow morning we cross the 'Russel' to Guernsey aiming to arrive just before the mail boat puts in. It goes via Jersey in the morning so when we see it passing Sark, we will edge just ahead. That way customs won't bother too much when we put in to St Peter Port.'

At that point a wave hit them and the Dory bounced over, causing Freddy to tighten his grip. He said nothing more until they rounded the headland and approached a luxurious cabin cruiser lying at anchor in a picturesque cove. He looked back at the fortress town of St Malo behind them and the countless boats dotted around the harbour. Another day, in another life, this place might just have impressed him. But this was Freddy, in this life, and he had always disliked all things French. Although capable of good taste, he would never allow this to interfere with deep-felt prejudices.

The Dory bumped alongside Guernsey Lilly and Francois manoeuvred to the boarding steps.

Ten minutes later as Freddy relaxed in a sumptuous cabin below, the grinding noise of anchor chain on winch resounded through the vessel and the twin engines sprang to life.

As St Malo diminished between the twin davits holding the Dory securely over the transom, the engines let forth a further roar and Guernsey Lilly reached planing speed. Through the cabin porthole, Freddy could see the spray as occasionally the boat bumped over the slight sea. It was just four in the afternoon and the diffused light from the weakening sun glinted across the blue sea surrounding them.

Although well out to sea, before long they were amongst a crowd of tiny islets known locally as 'The Minkies', the southernmost part of Britain. White sand linked the low-lying isles with seabirds diving and landing all around. A crop of

239

colourful houses adorned the largest isle, and Lilly slowed to a cautious speed as she passed between outlying rocks and isles.

Further out the expanding coast of Jersey could now be seen on the horizon and Lilly's engines once again returned to full power. Francois called below to Freddy:

'Hey mister, do you want a drink?'

Freddy decided to brave the cool autumn air and, holding tightly on the handrails, emerged from below.

'You have a beer?'

'Sure. You're German so I suppose a lager, yes?'

Freddy nodded as Francois left the helm on autopilot and reached into a nearby fridge. He handed Freddy a cold tin of lager and took one for himself.

'How fast does this thing go?' Freddy asked

'She can reach up to thirty knots on a flat, calm day, and even with a slight swell like today we are in the mid-twenties. Not bad eh?'

Freddy was impressed; he liked the idea of a vessel that could probably outrun the older displacement designs mostly used by the official services.

'It will do. I take it your instructions are to have the vessel at my disposal for as long as I need it... and you?'

'You got it. My Lilly and I are yours for as long as needed. All expenses are taken care of and we will keep you away from the authorities. Also you don't need to be concerned about our papers, Lilly has been registered in Guernsey officially so she shouldn't attract too much attention. It's just you we need to keep out of sight.'

Despite his uneasiness at being out at sea, Freddy was starting to relax. The beer was helping, and he was soon on a second can. As the island of Sark came into sight, Freddy watched from a comfortable seat in the cockpit; they powered closer and closer to its granite cliffs.

Francois explained they would drop anchor in Dixcart Bay off the southern coast where they could take the Dory ashore and get a meal a short walk up from the beach.

It was just half an hour later at six in the evening that Lilly silenced her engines and the anchor chain rolled off the winch.

The conversation that night between Francois and Freddy was stilted and Freddy construed the easy way of his fellow traveller as stupidity. Once Lilly was safely at anchor they took the dinghy ashore to a deserted beach, and followed a footpath to an equally remote hotel that provided the sustenance of a lavish meal. They declined the convenience of a room for the night and made their way back to Lilly.

After a troubled sleep, Freddy awoke to the smell of bacon cooking in the galley. Francois had risen early and was already fully alert and playing the perfect host, despite his indifference towards his paying guest.

The mail boat would be on its way from Jersey to Guernsey by now, but they would easily catch up en route and follow a safe distance behind. As Freddy enjoyed a hearty breakfast, Francois made ready to up anchor.

It was early in the day when the Flying Christine ambulance launch brushed up against the fenders of Anoushka in Braye Harbour. Having called to alert the family, a helping hand was offered as George stepped aboard, climbing over the guardrail.

'Thanks Tom, and it's good of you to delay your departure. I won't hold you up for long.'

'You've got us worried George; it must be pretty serious for you to hitch a ride on the Christine to get over to us?'

'No, don't worry; it's not that serious at all. It's just the way we like to do things. Shall we go below?'

George manoeuvred his tall frame down the companionway and into the main cabin where the rest of the family were waiting. They sat around the saloon table, and Rebecca offered tea or coffee to their guest.

'No thanks Rebecca, I can't stop. The launch is taking me back in a few minutes when they've dropped off some medical equipment. I'd better be as brief as I can. When we made radio contact you said you had the Stein papers with you on board, and I need to borrow them for a while, if that's OK?'

'Of course George, I've got them here ready, but what's all this about?'

George explained that they needed to compare what had been copied with the originals for their enquiries into Freddy's whereabouts. He was deliberately vague and moved off the topic at the first opportunity.

'Well here you are. To be honest I haven't really studied them yet, and I can't say I've been that motivated but I know I need to, so let me have them back when you can.'

The familiar low-pitched drone of the Flying Christine's engines could be heard approaching, so they made their way back on deck and bid George farewell.

As the launch sped away from Anoushka, the family prepared for their own departure.

CHAPTER TWENTY-FIVE

'I want a tight watch at the airport and keep harbours on top alert. Oh, and don't neglect the coastline either; it wouldn't surprise me at all if this guy tried to get in on a private boat. Are any of our more colourful locals out at the moment?'

George knew exactly what Inspector Ogier meant, and had already been down to the harbour office to check the movements of any local vessels owned by the more "maverick" members of the island's community.

'Guernsey Lilly is out and has been for a few days. He never bothers to radio in a course so he could be anywhere. Ormer is also out but was seen potting off the west coast so he's out of the way. The other usual suspects are safely tucked up in the harbour.'

'Good work George, do some digging and if necessary spend a bit of time on binocular watch around the coast. Put the word out to anyone who might let us know if they see her or any other suspicious looking vessel.'

As Anoushka weighed anchor smoothly from the sandy seabed of Braye Harbour and motored out into the "Swinge", a stretch of sea between Alderney and the much smaller Burhou Island, hundreds of puffins took to the air around them. The tiny, yellow-beaked birds made for the sanctuary of their burrows on Burhou Island as Tom hoisted the large white mainsail that filled instantly in the cool north westerly breeze behind them.

With plenty of wind, Anoushka's engine could soon be silenced, and she glided peacefully down the west coast of Alderney, infamous for its choppy seas at other states of the tide. Returning to the cockpit, Tom put his arm around Rachel and kissed her cheek where a tear was gently rolling down her face. She was looking eastward to Clonque Bay. Everyone knew; Rebecca squeezed her mother's hand as the family shared the poignancy of the moment. All those years ago, Clonque Bay was where Tom had first rescued Rachel from the clutches of

243

the occupying German army.

But Rachel's tears were not of sadness; on the contrary, she was overjoyed to be here with her family and as Tom eased out the mainsheet and pointed to the exact spot they had met, she grabbed her husband and passionately kissed him on the lips. David and Rebecca couldn't bring themselves to interrupt the moment with their usual joking quips; they disappeared quietly below.

The years of love in their eyes, Tom and Rachel held each other tight for the few moments an unattended sailing yacht would allow.

'I better bear away a little.' Tom whispered, as if divulging a guilty secret.

'How different things might have been.' Rachel mused. 'That night... that night was more special than any one person deserves.'

She relived the moment the teenage boy had announced himself on the rocky shore they were now surveying. Certain her young life was about to end or result in cruel enslavement, with the memory of her dead father and missing mother still haunting her, hers had been the most terrible of despair.

Then Tom had arrived and quite literally swept her off her feet. Not only was he young and handsome, but also his strength as he effortlessly lifted her petite frame to the waiting boat gave her the sense of security only known in the arms of her father. He rescued her, saved her life, while risking everything in the face of incredible danger.

Their journey in Tom's small fishing boat was intended to return to his home island of Guernsey, but a German patrol boat put paid to that and they instead made for the tiny island of Herm, three miles to the east of Guernsey. Here Rachel found refuge in the house of a local farmer, and her love for Tom grew.

It was however; too dangerous for a teenage Jewish girl to hide in the midst of a tiny occupied island, and when the opportunity presented itself she was whisked away to the safety of England in a British submarine. Their years apart did nothing to dampen Tom's affection for Rachel and when, at the liberation of the island, Rachel, now a mature and beautiful young woman had returned, their love found its freedom. They married and lived an uncomplicated life with their two young children until the legacy of Rachel's inheritance was exposed years later.

So here they were again, sailing away from Alderney but this time making purposely for the island of Herm.

Just a few miles south the mail boat ploughed through the sea towards Guernsey and between its two wakes, a cabin cruiser followed at a discreet distance.

Alone in Anoushka's main cabin and preparing hot drinks for the family, David and Rebecca reflected on the surprise visit by Guernsey police earlier that morning. David spoke in a hushed voice to ensure Rachel didn't hear.

'I don't know what all that was about earlier but if the police have an interest in our copies of the Stein files, we can only assume they don't have all the same files any longer in Munich. How could that be? In fact, what would make them think there was anything missing?'

Rebecca had her mother's eyes and could easily have doubled as a young Rachel; she looked quizzically at her brother before replying.

'You're not saying you think Freddy has something to do with this, are you?'

'I don't know sis, but after everything that happened, I won't feel truly relaxed until he's behind bars.'

Freddy was far from being locked up as he sat alone on the flying bridge of the cabin cruiser now speeding away from the mail boat's wake and heading for the east coast of Guernsey.

Francois called up to him.

'You'd better get down from there now; I'll be dropping you off any minute. Take anything you need from the cabin and I'll look after the rest.'

Freddy climbed down and indicated he had all he needed for the time being.

'I've an address, a map and this.' He pointed to a holdall bag. 'That's all I need just now.'

The cruiser slowed down and once the autopilot took over, Francois lowered the dinghy once more.

'OK, this will be safer than St Peter Port; you see those steps ahead? They are the Ozanne Steps and you can beach the dinghy in a small cove on the right. Don't forget to pull it high up and tie it securely or you'll be stuck there. Climb the steps and you'll reach a cliff path that goes left and right. Right is towards town but don't go that way. Head left until you get to another path that leads you to Fermain Bay. On the beach at Fermain, you'll see a boat that will take you into town with a bunch of tourists. It's safer than the direct path, you'll be less conspicuous and you will be dropped almost opposite the bus station. And before you say anything, the bus is also safer than taking a taxi. Take a grey bus marked Pleinmont and get off at the stop near Fort Grey. Just ask the driver for The Cup and Saucer, he'll know what you mean. I hope you are right about their address. Where did you get it?'

Freddy gave a look that told Francois to mind his own business, so he continued.

'When you've done whatever you came here to do, I'll be waiting in the same place here. I'll stop by every day for a week as agreed, and then you're on your own. If you need help on the island, get to Fermain Bay again and ask for Jerry. He helps with the tourist boat and is on a 'bung'. That's about it. Any questions?'

Francois depowered Guernsey Lilly's engines, the bows lowered, and before long she was rocking gently in the water just twenty yards from the steps, with the dinghy alongside. Freddy stepped down into it carefully maintaining a grip on his holdall. No further words were exchanged between them.

Clumsily, Freddy wobbled until he found his seat and then began awkwardly to row the dinghy ashore. Looking back at the cruiser as he rowed, he watched Francois nervously peering at the cliffs above and then out to sea, until the dinghy crunched onto the tiny beach, and Guernsey Lilly made her departure at full speed.

Freddy stumbled as he tried to step out onto the beach, the waves sucking at his feet. But he maintained his grip on the "painter", a small rope connected to the bows of the dinghy. A few minutes later, having retrieved his holdall and secured the dinghy above the high-water mark, he scrambled up the slippery granite to the base of the Ozanne steps. He checked the contents of his bag; fumbling inside there was a parcel wrapped in brown greaseproof paper, and beneath it, his Colt pistol.

He took a moment to familiarise himself; this was where he must return. Further down the coast the brown trunks and greenery of a pine forest surrounded by ferns contrasted with the shades of blue sea and sky. In the other direction, a castle set away at the end of a granite pier, guarded the approach to the harbour of St Peter Port. He turned and looked up at the ornate but solid steps that rose above him. They might have been designed by Maurits Escher, resembling as they did his famous architectural drawings; a vertical rise boxed in by a low wall of yet more granite.

Freddy strode forward and mounted the steps, at first climbing two at a time then adopting a more leisurely pace as he ascended through a series of small landings.

In the clifftop car park at Jerbourg on the southeast coast of Guernsey, PC Le Page replaced his binoculars and radioed the station.

'Guernsey Lilly dropped off a suspect matching the description at the Ozanne Steps, Sergeant. Time: 14:30 hours, but I can't see which way he's heading, over.'

'Good work George. I'll send a car to the bottom of the "Cow's Horn" in case he makes for town and you hold your position. He could emerge on the Fort road, Les Varclins, or a couple of places on Jerbourg Road, so I'll send you some support. Keep your eyes peeled, over.'

'OK Sarge, will do; out.'

The cliff path from the Ozanne Steps led to a myriad of other trails which did indeed emerge at a variety of locations, ensuring the local police force were fully occupied for the next few hours. What they didn't anticipate was that Freddy would take the boat from Fermain; after all, if he was heading for town, the cliff path could take him straight there.

His march from the steps snaked along a narrow path mostly covered by overhanging trees with undergrowth on both sides and just beyond a rocky drop to sea on his left. The sun cast a flicker of shadows across his face as he moved confidently forwards. But a family of tourists cheerfully pacing in the other direction interrupted his progress. Freddy stepped away from the path to make room for them to pass, diverting his attention to conceal his face he looked out to sea. There, to his horror, he saw Guernsey Lilly slowly making way for St Peter Port Harbour, accompanied by a customs patrol launch.

PC Le Page scanned the path to the best of his ability from his vantage point, now located in the beer garden of a tavern called the L'auberge Divette. Using pedestal mounted tourist binoculars, he watched as Guernsey Lilly was intercepted following the precise location he had given to his fellow officers in customs and immigration. Francois would have some interesting questions to answer. But the real problem was how to track Freddy down, and time was running out if he was to go to ground in the island.

Freddy continued his march towards Fermain now very much concerned that the local police were onto him. Narrowly missing an enthusiastic PC who could be seen running towards the pine forest beneath him, he approached a fork in the path that led toward the bay.

By now, the entire Guernsey police force, in addition to customs and immigration, were on the lookout for Freddy, and his description had been widely circulated.

Approaching a headland and descending, the path he was on turned to the right and below him Fermain Bay was revealed.

The bay was sheltered on both sides by high cliffs and a large granite wall rose above the pebbly beach against which the sea was gently stroking. Behind the wall, a Martello tower could be seen that once guarded this sheltered bay. He could also see a large wooden gangway with spoke wheels being manoeuvred into place by a small group of sun-tanned young men. Then above him he heard shouting.

'Check the Pepper Pot, Simon.'

Just yards above on another path, a PC looked inside the former watchtower.

'Nothing Sarge; shall we go down to the bay?'

'No, let's get back to the car and check Les Varclins, the others will be watching the road up from the bay.'

Freddy quickly moved on and within a few minutes broke from the cover of the cliff path for the open grassy platform above the wall at the bay. He could now see the long, wooden tourist boat having rounded the headland, making its way towards the gangway. Two men in bathers perched on either side of the gangway ready to receive the launch's bow rope, and assist the queue of tourists now winding down the beach. Freddy briskly made his way across the grass until, at the base of the Martello Tower, he found a metal ladder that descended to a slipway leading to the beach between two high, granite walls. On one side, children played in a rapidly flowing stream, placing rocks to dam the flow and racing 'pooh sticks'. Freddy strode down the slip way and onto the beach. He staggered across the uneven bay towards the gangway where a bronzed young man stood at the front of the queue.

'I'm looking for Jerry?'

The man nodded towards the business direction of the gangway where the other two had now caught the bow rope and were bracing themselves for the launch to make contact. As it did so the whole gangway was pushed back up the pebbly beach almost three feet.

'Steady Percy!' one of the men shouted to the skipper.

'You'll have us in, you old bugger, eh!'

Moments later, the bows were secure and passengers embarked onto the launch with the help of the two young men. Freddy made sure he was last on the gangplank, and when he reached the embarkation point, he spoke quietly to one of the long-haired men reaching out to assist him.

'Is one of you Jerry?'

'Who wants to know?' The one on the left with "John Lennon" style, circular spectacles looked quizzically at him. His friend looked the other way.

'Francois gave me your name. I may need some assistance.'

A broad smile lit across Jerry's face. 'What's up then?'

'It seems my arrival has been less discreet than we hoped. The law is everywhere and they've pulled Francois in.'

'Come on, Jerry, pull your finger out, we can't hang on here forever!' The skipper of Fermain V was getting impatient.

'OK man; stay cool. Go back up the beach. If they got Francois, they'll be waiting.'

With that Jerry threw the bow rope back on board Fermain V and waved to the skipper to pull away. As the launch manoeuvred backwards then turned and motored out of the bay, he meandered back up the beach stopping for a while to joke with three bikini-clad sun worshippers on the way.

Freddy sat uncomfortably amongst the group of girls and young men with Jerry. There was a sweet, but suspicious, aroma emanating from the "roll ups" they were smoking.

'Listen man, a mate of mine is bringing his van down here sometime this afternoon to drop off some gear. Hold tight with us for a while and we'll get you out of here. That's cool, eh?'

Despite Freddy's impatience and intense dislike of this longhaired hippy, he knew it was his best option. So with as much disdain and sarcasm as he could muster, he agreed.'

'That's cool.'

A mile away in St Peter Port, several plain-clothed policemen watched as Fermain V touched against the slipway in the old harbour. Further away on the Albert pier, several uniformed colleagues stood by, just in case there was a chase.

But the tourists disembarking failed to match Freddy's description, and when only the skipper and engineer were left onboard, one of the officers decided to question them.

'Percy, got a minute?'

At Fermain Bay a new face joined the group and much to Freddy's relief, Jerry brought him straight over to him.

'This is Keith, man, where do you want him to take you?'

Keith was an even larger version of Jerry, with long, frizzy, brown hair. Beneath his "Grateful Dead" sleeveless T-shirt and Levis jeans, he was clearly muscle-bound. Freddy gave the address on the other side of the island, where he hoped Rachel's family still lived. With a deep inhalation from the joint Jerry was holding, Keith beckoned to his passenger to join him and they left the beach.

Smiling at the girl serving in the beach cafe, Keith walked to the side of his Bedford van and slid the door open.

'Listen man, you'd better not sit in the front if the fuzz are after you. Get in here and pull this sheet over you until we're out of the valley. If I stop, keep quiet and keep still, got that?'

Only one road serviced the beach cafe at the foot of the steep valley that led to Fermain Bay and having recently descended to the cafe, the delivery van with "Ringwood Eggs" inscribed on each side failed to excite the two policemen when it returned up the hill a few minutes later. Nevertheless, they stopped Keith and insisted on sliding back the door to look in the back. It was full of supply boxes and the old sheet on the far side crammed between them looked harmless enough, so considering their job done, the door was slammed shut.

Keith put his foot down and they were on their way.

Three miles out across the sea, Anoushka dropped anchor on the beach at Herm's harbour and Tom waited for the tide to recede. The family were in great spirits and looking forward to a few days on their favourite island. Rachel emerged from the cabin below with a chilled bottle of Chardonnay and four glasses.

'Something's not quite right', she said.

Tom and David were relaxing in the cockpit whilst Rebecca lazed on the deck, soaking up the afternoon sun. Rachel poured them all a glass of wine.

'If our documents from the Stein office are just copies, why did the police need them? Surely they had the originals back in Munich?'

The totally relaxed expressions left their faces; David was the first to reply.

'Rebecca and I thought the same thing. It smells suspiciously like Freddy doesn't it?'

Tom looked exasperated as he reached out for Rachel's hand. 'For god's sake, I thought we were rid of him. What are you suggesting? '

Rebecca now joined the others in the cockpit as David explained. 'Suppose Freddy had some assets squirreled away somewhere he thinks he can still get access to, I don't know, maybe a bank account, or shares. Let's not forget he was sitting on a fortune.

Now, if he was able to retrieve the details from his office, but the police found out and knew something was missing, maybe they needed our copies to work out what it was?'

The theory sounded plausible and Rachel and Tom knew it. With a worried glance towards her husband, Rachel embellished the theory.

'If that was true then he might well also know about the copies. After all, he must have had inside help to get the originals out of his office. And if he knows about them, he might want them out of the way. It's all speculation, but I'm quite pleased the police have got them now.'

A few sips of wine and several theories later, Rebecca went quiet. At first nobody noticed but with a mother's instinct and some gentle probing, the reason was tentatively given. 'What if

Freddy doesn't know the police here have got those papers? What if he thinks you have them? After all, the copies were taken for you to read through.'

When the engineer from the Fermain Ferry confirmed that he had seen a man fitting Freddy's description on the boarding gangway at Fermain, it did not take the police long to radio the nearest patrol and get them down to the beach. Not long, but long enough to miss their man. They settled for a robust interrogation of Jerry but he simply grinned and told them nothing about Freddy's whereabouts. He was released two hours later by which time Freddy was the other side of the island.

CHAPTER TWENTY-SIX

Anoushka had now settled her triple hulls on the harbour beach in Herm, which meant she remained upright at low tide and having made his phone call ashore, Tom climbed the boarding ladder to rejoin the others in the cockpit.

'Listen everyone, I don't want you to panic but Inspector Ogier just confirmed that Freddy has arrived in Guernsey and, yes, it does seem as if he's after those papers. On close inspection, it seems they implicate a high profile villain back in Germany. But there's no reason to suspect he's after anything else and the police are searching high and low for him.

'Our cottage has a contingent of officers discreetly keeping an eye on things and they've even sent a constable to check out the new house. But they think he's on to them as he disappeared not long after landing on the island.'

The family settled into an animated discussion about how they should react to the news but a consensus was quickly agreed. With the police on high alert, they could just continue their holiday at sea on board Anoushka, even if Freddy was to come looking for them. Rachel seemed untroubled about their situation, at least outwardly.

Freddy watched the Bedford van as it disappeared along the coast road and then he turned his attention to the cottage opposite.

He was at Rocquaine Bay on the western shore of Guernsey with the sea wall behind him and the small fisherman's cottage on the other side of the narrow coast road.

He was about to cross when the cottage door opened and out stepped a uniformed policeman directly opposite him. Freddy froze.

What happened next sent his adrenalin racing. Police constable Le Prevost looked straight at Freddy, who watched helplessly as the recognition clicked into place. At the precise moment his eyes widened, the side of the Grey bus that stopped in front of Freddy, obscured the constable's view.

Still clutching his holdall, Freddy jumped on board and, as he was the only person boarding, the bus pulled away immediately. By the time Freddy got to his seat, Le Prevost had raced out of the cottage garden, dodged oncoming traffic, and was running for his car. But in the few minutes it took for him to radio the base and get under way, the bus had pulled over again, at another stop, and Freddy disembarked hastily into a small crowd of waiting tourists.

Weaving through the crowd to the cover of a parked van, Freddy heard Le Prevost's car slide to halt in the car park next to the bus, and whilst the constable's attention was on the vehicle, he darted for the slip way and the cover of the grey concrete sea wall.

Le Prevost emerged from the bus moments later, and looked around the area. The radio in his car crackled, and he responded to base with the latest news.

Heart pumping, Freddy looked around. To the south lay a long sandy beach, punctuated by rocky outcrops that led to what looked like a small hotel, to his north was the rise of a promontory, with the welcoming structure of a German watchtower dominating its summit. He swung his holdall onto his shoulder and made for the north.

On reaching higher ground, his vantage point gave an uninterrupted view of the activity all around. Another officer had now joined Le Prevost, and a car could be seen speeding towards the car park from the northern coast road. The only clear route was to the west, so he pushed on further to see what cover could be found. Passing another car park, Freddy reached a small slipway with a sign that told him he was about to cross the tidal causeway to Lihou Island. Although still exposed, the tide was rising and parts of the causeway were already flooding.

The winding, and somewhat rocky causeway seemed to cover about a half kilometre and was highly exposed, but there appeared to be no other choice. He picked his way down to the slippery trail and started to cross to the island.

Inspector Ogier had now joined the group of police officers who, after a quick briefing, were now panning out in all directions. Le Prevost headed west towards the headland.

His leather shoes and the bottom of his trousers now soaked from misplaced footings on the increasingly watery path, Freddy scrambled towards the island. It seemed to take forever. He cursed each time his path was blocked by deposits of slippery, wet seaweed. Before long he could no longer see his feet, as the sea reclaimed its territory. Constantly peering over his shoulder, Freddy saw the uniformed figure entering the car park behind just as he neared the tiny island. The sea advanced more rapidly across the causeway, much more rapidly than he had anticipated, and the water was deepening all the time. He felt as if it, too, was pursuing him. A lapse of concentration whilst looking back caused him to misplace his footing, and he slipped beneath the rising waves.

Instinctively, he held on to his bag but with his face now submerged, he panicked and thrashed out at the dense brown seaweed that entwined him. His mouth opened to curse, and he spluttered as the salt water filled his airway. He tried again and again to pull his weary legs free, but he was trapped, and as time took on the illusion of slowing down, he became increasingly convinced he would not survive the powerful hold of the sea. What surprised him most, was his apparent resignation to his fate.

With eyes now open, Freddy surveyed his watery grave. Down here the colours were more vivid than he had imagined from the surface, and the weeds no longer seemed to cling and entwine, but rather they enticed him and invited him to stay. A swirl of water below, and a crab scurried away, its alien form startling him and signalling to his subconscious, the mortal peril of his situation. He kicked down his legs and forced a bracing position against the powerful current. With a surge of will more primeval than conscious, Freddy forced his head upwards towards the sky. Breaking the surface, he coughed and spluttered then, slowly regaining his senses, he looked once more to the shore of Guernsey. With eyes still blurred by salty water, the figures on shore seemed not to have noticed his clumsy, drenched body and were ambivalent to the trauma he had just experienced.

Above the high water mark, a rowing boat named Lihou was beached and upturned. He dived behind it, exhausted, and his legs heavy from the weight of soaked clothing.

The sun was setting as Le Prevost checked out the headland, carefully probing any bushes, undergrowth, or other potential hiding places. He made his way to the German watchtower, and after checking the padlock on the outside of the door, headed for the car park. It seemed clear, and he made for the slipway. With no sign of Freddy on the beach, he looked in the direction of Lihou, now once again an island.

For a few hours, the activity on mainland Guernsey was frenetic. The area around Tom and Rachel's old cottage became the centre of attention, and every guesthouse and hotel was contacted. Door to door enquiries commenced but, as light began to fade, the police effort was suspended, apart from a few strategically placed vehicles, with officers placed on watch through the night shift.

Cold, tired and still overwhelmed by the experience on the causeway, Freddy lay uncomfortably on the rough ground next to the boat. Guernsey now seemed quite distant, as darkness added to the bleak isolation of Lihou Island. It was, he judged, now safe to move.

Sitting upright, Freddy's leg muscles ached. He took stock of his surroundings, which wasn't easy in the fading light, then struggled to his feet and stiffly made his way to the west, and further inland on the small island. Before long, a path led him to a solitary house, the darkened windows of which suggested nobody was at home.

In the peace of Herm harbour, Tom was undertaking a final

check of his anchors before returning to the aft cabin, where Rachel was waiting for him. David and Rebecca had already gone below, and the soft murmur of their banter was all that Tom could hear, apart from waves gently lapping against Anoushka's hull. It was high water and they had the mooring to themselves; even the Mermaid Pub was quiet, a few yards away on shore. 'A mixed blessing,' he thought. If Freddy were to come now, there would be few to raise a warning, or help, if somehow he was taken by surprise; but Tom consoled himself with the thought that surprise was all the more unlikely in the solitude of this quiet anchorage.

Guernsey too, had settled in for the night, and as PC Le Prevost finished his shift, on watch at the Cup & Saucer, he exchanged a few words with his relief constable.

'There's been nothing, George. He's well and truly gone to ground, and if you ask me, he won't turn up here again.'

'Depends how much he wants those papers I suppose. But he knows we're watching the place.'

George looked around at the coastline, lit partially by filtered moonlight.

'Yeah, he'd be mad to risk it, probably the other side of the island by now. You get off home.'

As George positioned his vehicle for the optimum view of the cottage, he watched his colleague drive away, knowing he would be disappointed not to have apprehended Freddy when he had been so close. That was police work though; sometimes they are just within reach and sometimes just beyond it.

The reality was that Freddy was not far beyond reach at that moment in time. The dark outline of Lihou Island was still visible on the horizon behind George's car. But Freddy was out of sight. He found his way to the rear of the house and was busy working on the kitchen window. Within minutes, he had prized it open and gained access to the kitchen. Exhausted, and beyond hunger, he ensured his entry point into the house was closed and gave nothing away to suggest an uninvited guest; then he made for the bedrooms.

Discarding his wet clothes on a banister to dry, he found a made up bed and quickly surrendered to the fatigue now overwhelming him.

Freddy awoke to the sound of chickens in the yard outside. Sunlight pierced the bedroom window as he blinked to life. What a racket those chickens made, but they probably wouldn't have penetrated his deep sleep, had it not been for the hunger pangs now acutely besetting him. He found a bathroom, dressed and made his way to the kitchen.

Nothing fresh came to hand, but some black coffee and biscuits proved close enough for his continental taste.

He was starting to relax, when the squawking of the chickens reached a crescendo, and amongst them he detected something that sounded altogether more human. A female voice was talking to them.

Freddy ducked beneath the kitchen window and, remaining on all fours, he found a vantage point upstairs from which he could see what was going on. A woman was feeding the chickens and seemed completely unaware of his presence. He watched as closely as he was able without risking discovery, but she was already moving out of sight, and all he could really make out was a scruffy rain coat tied with a belt of string, and wellington boots. 'Not fashion conscious then,' was the thought that crossed his mind. But her movements suggested someone who was still relatively young; they seemed too easy for an old person, the kind of person who would dress like that.

Chickens now quiet and contented to be fed, the figure moved away from the house. Freddy could make out the causeway from his vantage point, and the realisation hit him that it was uncovered. Of course! It had to be for this intruder to cross to the island. And if she could, so could the police.

He scanned the coastline for activity and decided now was the best time to check this place out, and maybe even get back to the main island.

Freddy left the house by a rear window, leaving it partially open in case he was forced to return. The path leading off to the west was exposed, with no tree or undergrowth cover to hide him, so he crouched forwards in an apelike gait as he strode along it. Before long, he came to the ruins of an ancient priory and rested for a while.

"What was this place?" Freddy pondered, as he took stock of his predicament.

His options were quickly diminishing, and he knew it. Resting amongst the ancient ruins, Freddy thought about his mission to recover the papers. The police clearly knew about him and had anticipated or stumbled upon his arrival on Guernsey's eastern coast; that meant they probably knew about the papers as well and if they knew about them, then maybe they had even found Stella's body.

He thought about Max's possible reaction; it wouldn't be good. The papers were now centre stage and that meant the Cocaine operation was compromised. Returning to Munich was obviously out of the question; both sides would hunt him. Laying low for a while seemed like the only option, but he needed to get off this god-forsaken island to find the anonymity of a city before this could happen. With Francois taken in by the police and the certainty that the airport would be watched, this seemed like an impossible dream. He resolved to press on and deal with the more immediate questions about the island upon which he was temporarily stranded. He needed to know his immediate terrain.

At the most westerly point of the island, the path turned north. To his left, large rocks formed the only barricade from the pounding sea; a pounding sea that spread uninterrupted for thousands of miles before washing the shores of America. He wished he were the other side of that sea. Then he saw her.

At first the flash of dark hair almost escaped him, but looking for danger sharpened his eyesight, and he moved onto the rocks to improve his view. Her naked shapely body took his breath away, and he almost lost his footing. Her back was towards him, and the long dark hair that had caught his attention flowed down it to her hips. Below her, a narrow but deep rock pool reflected suggestions of what he might enjoy if she were to face him. Her knees bent and she thrust forwards into the pool, creating a splash that broke the spell Freddy was under.

She was rising to the surface, now facing towards him, and he dropped to his knees to conceal himself behind a rock.

Thoughts of his predicament left him, as Freddy became a voyeur behind a rock on the west coast of Lihou Island. As she swam and dived in and out of the Venus Pool, Freddy became increasingly aroused. He wanted her and felt no compulsion to wait, win her over or risk her refusal. Freddy got what he wanted by taking it and instinctively he felt for the means to secure his desire; his gun. But his lust was replaced by panic as it dawned upon him that his gun and his holdall were still at the house.

She dived again and Freddy rose quickly to make his way back along the path. He started to run and, passing the ruined Priory, reflected on what he had just intended to do. He had been stupid. A brief pleasure could have risked everything; she might have screamed and been heard on Guernsey. Even if he had subdued her, what would have happened next, if he'd killed her? It had been uncharacteristic of him to lose control like this and he vowed not to let it happen again. But she had been astonishingly beautiful.

As he approached the house, Freddy looked across the causeway to Guernsey; something was happening.

In the car park, three police vehicles had assembled and a group of officers were standing nearby, deep in discussion. Crouching slightly, Freddy reached the side of the house and found his window entrance. Once inside, he made his way to the bedroom and quickly retrieved his bag before looking again at the group of police officers. There was movement, and then to his horror, a tall officer pointed directly at Lihou Island.

Freddy was exasperated and his knees felt like buckling as he sat on the bed behind him.

They were approaching the causeway, two of them. Did they know he was there or was this just a routine check? The other officers now seemed to be dispersing in different directions, two of the police cars were pulling away. This was good news; it must mean they didn't know where he was, but they would be certain to check the house.

He could feel his heart pounding in his chest and his senses were on high alert. So when he heard the door down stairs open, the hairs on the back of his neck bristled; they couldn't have reached the house that quickly. He grabbed the pistol from his bag and hid behind the door, just keeping within sight of the window. There were noises below; someone was looking around. The police were now on the causeway.

He could hear footsteps outside on the landing, and then someone came into the room. Freddy lunged forward and grabbed the figure from behind, wielding the gun in his hand.

'Call out and you're dead.'

The young woman stuttered, 'Ok. Ok, I won't do a thing.'

He had his left arm around her neck and held the pistol to her head with his free hand. He pushed her towards the window.

'When they come in, you tell them there's nobody here. You've been all over the house and nobody is here, got that?'

She nodded.

'Don't get clever or you and those two nice policemen will get a bullet each. I'll be watching your every move and how they respond.'

'I won't do anything.'

'Good girl, do as I say and you will be just fine.'

They stepped back from the window, and he released his hold.

'Go down and open the front door wide, then come back up here and wait on the landing where they can see you. When they call, stay up here to speak to them.'

She walked slowly down to the door and did as he instructed and then for the first time turned to face him and returned to the landing. 'Who was he, what did he want?'

'Why are you hiding from them, what've you done?'

'Too many questions, all you need to know is I have used this before and won't think twice about using it again, but only if you make me. What's your name?'

'Emmaline... Emmaline Le Page.'

'OK, Emmaline, they're nearly here now so take off that coat and remember what I said.'

Freddy watched as she removed her old mackintosh, placed her hands on the ornate banister and looked down towards the front. Her clothes were old and made her look much older than the beauty he had watched at the Venus Pool. He thought for a moment about removing those clothes but steeled himself to concentrate on the danger ahead.

The sound of talking and footsteps drifted up from outside, then they appeared in the doorway, looking around the downstairs hall. One of them knocked on the open door.

'Is anyone here? Hello?'

Emmaline called down, 'Up here, what do you want?'

'Oh hello, Emmaline, it's Bob Taylor. How you doing?'

'I'm alright, Bob, just cleaning the house as usual.'

'Listen, my dear, have you seen anybody on the island, a man? It's important; since the last tide.'

She hesitated, 'No, nobody, why?'

'We're after a bloke of about fifty, a bit overweight, with a German accent but if you come across him keep well away and let us know; urgently, dear, OK? Your sure there's nobody in here? Have you looked around the entire house? Maybe, we'd better take a quick look? 'They started into the hall and Emmaline glanced briefly in Freddy's direction. His eyes said it all.

'No! No, there's really no need I've just cleaned everywhere. I'm sure there's nobody here or anywhere else on the island.'

'How can you be so sure about the rest of it?'

'I went out to the west as soon as I got here after the causeway cleared, to the Venus pool.'

The two policemen looked at each other and shrugged their shoulders before Bob called up again.

'Ok thanks, that saves us a trip, but you remember what I said, if you see him, give us a call.'

263

Emmaline confirmed she would and they left. She turned slowly towards Freddy and the barrel of his pistol.

'What happens now?'

'For the time being nothing; we'll just watch those two trundle away, wait for the tide to come back in and then we'll see.'

'I'll be missed if I don't go back.' Emmaline didn't sound too convincing and so he pressed her.

'By who?'

She tried to look convincing but had never been an accomplished liar. 'My parents.'

Freddy's gaze drilled into her and decided to call her bluff.

'You're a big girl. They won't worry for a few hours. Let's just relax, shall we?'

He knew what he wanted but thought better of it as lowering his defences, even for as long as it would take to fulfil his desires, wouldn't be a smart move. He motioned with the pistol for her to lead the way downstairs and they found armchairs, opposite each other, in the sitting room.

'You know you needn't look so worried, I'm not going to harm you, not if you do as I say.'

CHAPTER TWENTY-SEVEN

The sun reached the apex of its arc as the causeway flooded; Emmaline, still captive on the island, had no idea how to behave in the situation cast upon her. There were no clues from any part of her experience, so she trusted to her intuition, and tried to make conversation in the hope that familiarity might protect her.

'What will you do? You can't stay here forever.'

Freddy surveyed his prisoner. Obviously she was right but her words were just noise. There was no point in answering, yet he felt an inexplicable compulsion to do so.

She sat upright, with head high, revealing her long neck; she had held this position for hours, since they first sat down after the police left. For someone so dishevelled, she had stature. Her poor clothing contradicted this proud posture.

'Perhaps not for ever; but for a while until the attention out there abates.'

The response seemed a notch or two less hostile and she felt she could risk a more detailed appraisal of the man who had so menacingly taken control of her day.

Imperceptibly she hoped, her eyes turned in his direction. He was looking down now, apparently deep in thought. He was a large man, she thought, typical of the domineering male stereotype she abhorred. His clothes looked expensive, despite fitting him badly, as if he had been sleeping rough, or they had been washed and just scrunched up to dry. He wore a days stubble, she assumed, longer would have been more like a beard. Then, remembering her lack of experience in the matter, 'what did she know about male shaving?'

Freddy sensed her eyes on him and ensured his gun was well within reach. However, he allowed her curiosity; enjoyed her curiosity. He imagined her hands, her eyes, on his body. Then he rose abruptly, grabbed the pistol and strode to the window. He became uncomfortable with the feelings developing for his captive.

'The tide is in, now. We're cut off. Go and rustle up some food'.

She rose demurely, tentatively, and backed away to the kitchen her eyes still watching him suspiciously. Freddy ignored her discomfort and stared out at the causeway. He remembered the sea enveloping his entire body, and his helplessness in that moment when he was under. He pictured himself emerging from the swirling water, his eyes bulging. Hans, his brother, had eyes just like that when Freddy had pushed him to his death from the roof of their factory in Munich. For the first time in his life, he felt the slightest twinge of sorrow for his cruelty.

But the moment soon passed, and Freddy pushed the picture of Hans from his mind and closed his heart to the rising flicker of emotion. 'That bloody causeway', the dowsing was making him soft.

Emmaline was used to catering to herself on the island, as the owners had left the house in her care whilst they were abroad travelling, and she often missed a tide and stayed over.

She used to sit on the upturned Lihou rowing boat, behind which Freddy had hidden, staring across the causeway between Lihou and Guernsey. Patiently waiting for any last visitors to cross, and the tide to once more wrap its powerful arms around the island, she would ponder the activity on Guernsey's west coast.

Emmaline's life was very different to that of the people rushing about on the coast road. To her, they all seemed so busy, so self-important.

One day on her way up the lane towards the causeway, a young car driver had looked disdainfully at her as she tried to move her bicycle out of his way. He sat revving the whole time, didn't offer to help her, even when she slipped and her bike had emptied the contents of its front wheel basket all over the road. He just sat in his cocoon staring impatiently, and as soon as she moved, accelerated past her, destroying half her vegetables still scattered across the road. But that look on his face, as if she was some lower life form. That look had hurt her; why so

266

disdainful? Why so impatient?

Her unease lasted only for as long as it took her to recover the remaining contents of her basket, but it reminded her of the acute differences between herself and most of her peers.

She knew deep down inside she was OK; she was the one who had it all worked out. She may look quirky in her old raincoat, tied at the waist with some hay bale twine, her wellingtons may not have designer labels, and her beret may not be the height of fashion, but she knew 'which way was up', as her father used to say. Unfortunately this never sounded much like a compliment and she preferred her uncle's description from her childhood, that 'his little Emmaline was sassy'; but that all seemed a long time ago.

Even when there was no real prospect of rain Emmaline rarely considered taking off her mackintosh. In truth, she was a bit scruffy and never did anything to improve her appearance. Her dark hair was left un-groomed, except for a wash once or twice a week, in soapy water, and it was then tied back into a ponytail. It was easier that way, and with her beret perched on top, her hair rarely bothered her. After all that was the point wasn't it – to keep it out of the way? She had no idea that 'scrubbed up' she would turn many an eligible male head walking down the High Street. But then why would she care, and anyway she never went down the High Street; never had a reason. Most of her twenty-two years had been spent here on the west coast of Guernsey, running errands to Lihou. She once calculated the exact spot where, on average, most of her life had been spent and it was half way across the causeway.

Etienne had been a strict father to his only child and when old enough to consider why, Emmaline wondered if that had been because her mother had died giving birth. He seemed to blame her and when he took up the family tradition of becoming a Lay Methodist preacher, things got worse, not better. He had never really shown much emotion about anything. That part had been switched off when her mother died, but what little he displayed, after gaining his new position in the community, was directed at

God. God filled the hole left by Emmaline's mother and restored a vestige of vitality to Etienne's dreary life.

Unfortunately for Emmaline, this vitality focused primarily on ensuring her virginity remained intact at all costs. Long before any sexual interest in boys would have emerged, Etienne restricted her every movement and attempted to brainwash his young daughter, about the evil intentions of all men and boys. 'You might think you are safe to go about your daily routine without fear, but danger lurks around every corner. Men will trick and tempt you with their evil ways. Even here, in this pocket of paradise on Earth, a man lived nearby who kidnapped and raped young girls before tossing their lifeless bodies into the sea.'

Etienne had a fixation about 'The Hermit'.

As the coast road wound its last remaining miles around the south west of Guernsey, it passed a small German Bunker on which an inscription 'ONMEOWN' was written. For about a decade, the bunker was the home of Steve Picquet, known locally as 'the Hermit'. Although Steve had never really done anything to harm Etienne, he was everything Etienne wasn't.

As a young man Steve was keen on boxing, which Etienne believed to be sinful, and a pursuit of would be gangsters.

During the German occupation, Steve reinforced this reputation by stealing from the Germans, who eventually sent him away to prison. Of course, this made Steve a folk hero for many locals, a status that Etienne resented and when his attempts to discredit Steve fell upon deaf ears, he raised his game by embellishing the wrong doings to a demonic status. When Steve eventually returned to the island, homeless, and settled in the bunker around the corner along the coast, Etienne became incandescent with rage.

Over the years, 'the Hermit' became a rich vein for Etienne's hell fire sermons and the incontrovertible proof that his young daughter should eschew the modern trappings of short skirts and fashionable friends; this despite the fact that the unique and largely innocent life of Guernsey's Hermit was over by the time

Emmaline was thirteen.

Ironically, Emmaline had never really cared much about the fashionable set anyway. She resented her father's attempts to destroy any friendship that might show signs of life, but she was in any case a self-contained child. Living a few hundred yards along the coast, she had long been fascinated by Lihou island and when her friends were encouraged to join youth clubs or play badminton, Emmaline had been left to her own devices in that small corner of the west coast of Guernsey, away from the vices and dangers of modern life. The fact that this small child's play ground included a tidal causeway capable of washing her small body far out to sea, seemed to elude Etienne.

Emmaline had studied the history of Lihou Island and knew every inch of it. Apart from the early Benedictine Monks, few people had lived on the island but for Emmaline; the most interesting by far was the current tenant, 'the colonel', a larger than life character with a handlebar moustache. The colonel had brought chickens to the island and given Emmaline the job of looking after them, as well as various jobs around the house.

When Emmaline was just eighteen, Etienne died suddenly from heart failure. The loss didn't devastate her, he had been a hard man to love, but she was alone at home, and that took a while to get used to.

The years after her father died had been frugal for Emmaline, she had very little to live on. Fortunately her small garden afforded some space to grow food and her uncle had let her use a single span, three hundred foot greenhouse, adjacent to her cottage. She used this to grow tomatoes that were then sold from a box on her garden wall as 'hedge veg', along with potatoes, leeks and a variety of other vegetables, cultivated with the colonel's permission on Lihou. Her father had left her a modest amount of money and she had, of course, a plentiful supply of fresh eggs to eat and sell. Most young women would have wished for more, at least enough for fashionable clothes and a social life, but Emmaline was content with her lot and valued what she had greatly.

She felt Freddy's presence behind her, several heartbeats before he spoke.

'Well what have you got? All I could find was a few biscuits.'

'There's a well stocked larder, you needn't worry. At least not about that.'

He bristled, but then stepped closer and looked over her shoulder at the omelette being prepared. It looked delicious, but his hostility was instinctive. 'Just get on with it.'

Emmaline hadn't prepared a meal for anyone other than herself since her father died and the experience felt slightly alien to her. The pine table was large enough for eight, so at first she laid knives and forks at the end of one side and near the head of the table. That was how she would have laid it for her father, but this man was a different matter. The closeness was far too familiar so she moved them to opposite sides.

He had left her to the cooking and preparation and she was grateful for the opportunity to think without him around. His presence only allowed room in her thoughts for the immediate threat he represented and reactions to his unpredictable behaviour. She could now think about her escape, for escape was the only logical course of action. But how? And when? This was the first time she had been out of his sight.

She glanced sideways at the kitchen door and beyond, through the window to the west coast of Guernsey. Never before had it looked so inviting. The door would be unlocked, she could be out of it in a moment, but he had a gun and the causeway was flooded. She would have to bide her time a little while longer.

'Good, Emmaline, you've done well. Now sit and let's eat.'

She hadn't noticed his return and, somewhat startled out of her thoughts, she gasped and then turned in his direction, wiping her hands on a tea towel as she did so. He had cleaned himself up, shaved and even found some clean clothes. They must have been the colonel's and it was surprising how well they fitted.

'You see, I can be appreciative when you cooperate. Just keep in line and you will come out of this in one piece.' Freddy continued his rough theme, even though he now felt it slightly embarrassing in her presence. Despite her obviously humble background, Emmaline was dignified and that undermined his attempts at superiority, a superiority that had always been necessary, to justify the callous disregard he felt for his victims. He abhorred weakness; weakness was to be dominated, subjugated or eliminated. But this woman was proud and strong and it was he who was the fugitive in hiding, unable to face up to his pursuers. It was he who was weak.

As Emmaline placed his meal before him their glances met. He was close now and the eye contact electrified her. He, too, was taken aback, her beauty so near, so tempting, but so untouchable.

Nothing was spoken but much passed between them in those fleeting seconds.

He shuffled his chair; some movement was required to replace the silence. Then, grasping the cutlery, he ate heartily whilst Emmaline tentatively played with her meal. She chose not to decipher her feelings.

Throughout the meal he devoured, and she picked. Neither sought the other's eyes. Emmaline forced her thoughts back to escape. It must be when the causeway was uncovered, when the ebb was low enough to make a complete crossing. She knew the island and its waters intimately; for her the movements of the tide were as predictable as her period.

She knew, without reference to the moon, or any tide table what time she could cross the causeway, and by what time she must leave or be stranded. The daily cycle of ebb and flood, high and low, cross or wait, were ingrained in her DNA.

But the cycle wasn't a simple 'in or out' of the same volume of water, and Emmaline knew the depth over the causeway varied with the positions of the moon and sun. On this late October day, they were approaching right angle positions in the sky above Earth; they were approaching Neap tides, tides that would leave the causeway fully submerged for almost a week.

She must get away that afternoon.

CHAPTER TWENTY-EIGHT

The morning in Herm had been tranquil, with few visitors to disturb their peaceful anchorage. Tom and Rachel had walked all around the island they knew so well, and stopped off at their beloved Belvoir and Shell Beaches. This was a pilgrimage they had repeated many times during their life together, as it brought home how lucky they were to have found each other, the dreamlike days of that summer in 1941, and just how fragile their liberty had been, when Tom had first rescued Rachel.

David and Rebecca had visited family friends at the Farm, who had hidden Rachel as a child and then returned to the harbour.

It was over a lunchtime drink at the Mermaid Tavern, that they discussed their next destination.

'The plan was to go on to Sark next and drop anchor off Havre Gosselin, what do you think?'

Tom addressed the question to all of his family, with more than a slight emphasis towards Rachel. He was still concerned about how she might be dealing with the fact her attempted murderer was at large nearby.

'Splendid idea!' Rachel replied.

She seemed to have put Freddy out of her mind; perhaps it was the isolation on board Anoushka, with only her immediate family and the sea around her that helped her to feel secure. The family chatted on for a while before strolling back to the dinghy, tied up against the harbour wall. Tom and David rowed out to the yacht, raised the anchor and motored alongside the harbour wall, ready for the ladies to come onboard and begin a leisurely cruise to the next island. With only a light southerly wind, it was nearly two hours before they rounded the isle of Brecqhou and nudged into Havre Gosselin bay. Other than a large cabin cruiser, again they once again had the anchorage to themselves.

Tom guided Anoushka into a position on the north side of the bay, far enough away from what he referred to as 'the Gin palace', to ensure their privacy. On its deck, there appeared to be just the solitary figure of a man, seated and wearing a straw boater and dapper yachting clothes that would look more in place at Henley Regatta than the rugged, cliff bound bays of Sark.

Once the anchor was tested, Tom silenced Anoushka's engine, and it was then that they noticed the sound of an outboard motor, a little way off. A dinghy with two men on board had pulled away from the narrow Gouliot passage and was now heading for the cruiser.

'No doubt investigating the caves,' David observed.

Rebecca emerged from the cabin below and watched the two men speed across the bay towards the cruiser.

'They'll be disappointed if they hoped to get into Jewel Cave; the tide is all wrong.'

Gouliot Caves were something of a treat for wildlife enthusiasts, with an array of multi-coloured sea anemones and sponges adorning the walls. But the most impressive cave could only be accessed on foot at very low tides, and today that wasn't going to happen.

'Shall we go ashore for a while?' Rachel suggested.

She and Tom elected to go exploring whilst David and Rebecca remained on board and found comfortable positions to laze and read their books.

As Tom rowed past the cruiser and waved a greeting, one of the men on board responded with feigned interest until something clearly caught his attention. He shouted, 'Ahoy there, Anoushka isn't it?'

Tom replied that it was, and asked if he knew them.

'No, just seen you in the pool. Couldn't help noticing your nice new yacht!'

Tom grinned with pride and pulled towards the shore. He was now too far away and too pleased with himself to notice the frantic conversation, taking place on board the cabin cruiser.

Sark was a quiet, rural island unspoiled by the trappings of the modern world, with no cars or motorcycles to disturb its tranquillity. Fortunately, Tom had relations who lived on the island, with a ready supply of bicycles for him and his family to use on visits. So he and Rachel sped off through the lanes like a couple of teenagers, weaving and racing until they reached a favourite resting place, high on the cliffs overlooking the isthmus that connected the main island to Little Sark. From here they could see Anoushka and the cruiser down in the bay of Havre Gosselin, and straight over Little Sark to Guernsey in the north-west. They also had a spectacular view of the largest Channel Island, Jersey, to the south and east, to the coast of France.

Below them, the narrow isthmus known as La Coupee straddled the three hundred foot precipice to Little Sark with only a meagre railing to protect those who crossed.

With their cycles discarded in the lane, they sat behind a hedgerow and Tom explained to Rachel how before the war, this razor edged cliff top had to be traversed by the inhabitants, with nothing to protect them from the abyss below. One child even used to lead a horse and cart across at night when the farmer had over-indulged at the local pub. It was inconceivable to imagine how, when a wrong footing or strong wind could dispatch the child three hundred feet to certain death.

The afternoon sun was still strong for October, and they decided to return to Anoushka for refreshment. But not before the closest thing to a roller coaster thrill on the islands. The lane that led to La Coupee was steep and Tom liked nothing more than tearing down it and across the isthmus, on a bike. Rachel, not to be outdone, would be right behind him.

He set off first, and was half way across before his wife pushed down on her pedals and began the descent. Almost immediately she felt something was wrong. The steering suddenly seemed loose and the bike was wandering sideways. By now Tom had reached the other side, and had turned to watch his wife. The look on her face mortified him; he yelled to her but Rachel could only focus on stopping the bike. She squeezed both brakes. Nothing. The bike gained speed and headed ever closer to the edge. Intent on regaining control, she looked up briefly to see the chasm rapidly unfolding below.

By now Tom was running towards her, but he was too far away to reach her, before the inevitable collision with the railings that would catapult his beautiful wife to her death on the rocks below.

He screamed uncontrollably, 'No!'

Moments away from the edge, Rachel shifted her weight and flung herself off the cycle, which hit the railing and continued over the precipice. She was shaken and quite badly grazed, when Tom reached her and lifted her up into his arms. As he carried her back off La Coupee, two figures ran towards them.

'Is she alright?' One was shouting.

'We saw her bike go out of control and, oh my god, I thought that was it for her.'

It was the men they had seen in the dinghy, who boarded the cabin cruiser. They looked genuinely shocked at what they had seen.

Rachel was more composed now and still clinging to Tom. As he put her down gently on the grassy verge, she replied. 'I'm OK thanks. My own stupid fault, messing around up here. But I can't think what happened to my bike, it was fine on the way here, it must have worked loose or something.'

One of the men had rushed across to fetch Tom's bike and now returned. He was powerfully built, with short dark hair and he spoke with a Spanish accent. 'The lady is alright?'

Rachel smiled, 'Yes the lady is alright thank you, but' looking at Tom 'I fear your uncle's bike won't be.'

Tom dismissed her concerns, and although something was nagging him about the whole incident, he just wanted to get her leg cleaned up and see her safely back on board Anoushka. 'I don't suppose I could ask a favour of you?'

The Spaniard nodded, 'Of course, my friend.'

'I wondered if you could take my bike and go for a carriage to take Rachel to La Maseline Harbour? I don't think she should risk that steep descent back down to Havre Gosselin.'

Before long, Rachel and Tom rattled their way between the hedgerows on a horse drawn carriage that delivered them to the harbour, despite Rachel's protests that she could easily have managed the steps.

Their new found friends had rushed back to their dinghy and were now speeding around the headland to collect Tom and Rachel, having offered them a lift from La Maseline to Anoushka.

The powerful outboard made short work of the trip to the harbour and minutes later, as the engine noise subsided and the dinghy dropped from its plane to a more sedate speed, they retuned to Havre Gosselin bay.

Tom assumed they would be delivered back to his yacht and the sight of David and Rebecca waving to them from the deck of the cruiser, took him by surprise.

'When we told the boss about your scare, he insisted on inviting you all on board. Said you must be shaken up; I hope you don't mind? By the way I'm Raphael and this is, well we call him Gusto.'

'Pleased to meet you both and thanks again for your help, but really there was no need...' Tom was interrupted by Gusto who, so far, had said very little. Gusto was tall and also well built, with cropped brown hair that gave him a slightly intimidating appearance, but he spoke softly with a German accent. 'The boss is what you call a philanthropist; he's a very kind man. It's just a little gesture but he won't be offended, if you'd rather not?'

Rachel assured him they would be pleased to come on board for a little while and moments later they bumped alongside 'Follie'.

As David helped his mother onto the deck and saw that her injuries were only minor, his concern gave way to enthusiasm for the plush cruiser and its flamboyant owner.

'Come and meet Max, mother he's a real gent.'

Several canapés and cocktails later, and after much pampering to ensure Rachel's grazes were properly cleaned and dressed, the conversation turned to where Max was from and whether he was he living locally.

'No my dear, I'm not from around here and despite this little break, my mission here is not a happy one.'

His calculation that the intrigue would arouse curiosity in his guests was, of course, accurate and Rachel posed the question.

'Oh dear, that sounds unpleasant. Of course, if it's private…?'

'No, it's not especially private my dear. You see I'm in pursuit of somebody. At home in Munich, I run a children's charity and somewhat stupidly we put our trust in a local businessman we thought to be of good standing. He managed our bank accounts, and said he would ensure we received the same high interest rate he had secured for his business, a very large pharmaceutical company.'

Tom and Rachel exchanged worried expressions.

'What is it, have I said something to upset you?'

'No, not at all, please go on.' Tom insisted.

'Well, unfortunately this man turned out to be a crook and once the police were on to him, he fled the country taking our funds with him.' Max paused for effect and stared disconsolately into his glass, before adding the final touch. 'We had hoped to build a new children's home with the funds.

'The police said they would do what they could, but he was wanted for even more serious crimes so our money might be difficult to recover. So, along with my young friends here, I decided to try and track him down myself. A friendly policeman told me he had been spotted in your beautiful islands, so here I am.

'But please don't let my worries spoil your day.

'Gusto, our guests have empty glasses.'

Rachel was about to speak but Tom cut in quickly. 'That is terrible Max; I can only hope you find this villain and recover the funds. I'm sorry your reason for being here is so tarnished. We do need to get back to Anoushka, as the tide is on the move and we haven't checked our anchor for sometime but I would like to thank you, Gusto and Raphael for your kindness today.'

David, slightly merry from the champagne tried, but failed to constrain himself.

'Dad, surely this must be, you know who?'

Max feigned a slight interest but let it go when Tom reasserted his authority.

'We don't know that David. In any case, it's time we got back. We'll have a think and if there is anything we can do to assist Max, we'll drop by in the morning.'

With that, the family took their leave and boarded the dinghy once again.

As the family moved away from 'Follie', powered by Tom's powerful rowing, Max turned to the younger men. 'That was very clumsy of you; whatever our friend Freddy thinks, we don't want her dead. That's a complication we can do without.

'We'll sit tight until the morning and keep a close watch on our new friends. If Freddy is still around here, they may lead us to him. Just as I feared, he's now become an embarrassment to the organisation. We can't afford to allow him to fall into custody. Did you manage to hide the guns in that cave earlier?'

Their guilty expressions answered his question.

'This isn't good. You over-stepped the mark today with that woman and if we're boarded by Customs, we'll have to ditch the pieces over the side. You'd better find a way to redeem yourselves before we get back, hadn't you?'

CHAPTER TWENTY-NINE

Emmaline scrutinised the causeway from the kitchen window, time was running out.

'I'd better fetch some eggs if you want to eat in the morning.'

Freddy nodded an approval.

'Stay close to the house and don't try to signal anyone. Remember, I have this.'

He drew out just enough of the pistol from his pocket to reinforce the point.

She took a basket and made her way to the chicken run, her eyes constantly scanning the encroaching sea. The tide was already dangerously high and close to covering her only means of escape other than the Lihou rowing boat.

The boat was too heavy for her to drag all the way to the sea now; it was beached safely over the high water mark and even if she could manage the weight, Freddy would get to her well before she reached the sea. No, the only way out was to risk the swirling waters of the causeway.

Emmaline glanced quickly behind her then discarded the basket and ran across the pebbles towards the causeway. Although the first twenty yards were already under water, she knew of a narrow ridge where it would still be shallow, and further along the watery path would still be uncovered.

Her heart was pounding as she hitched up the long folds of her heavy skirt and waded into the cool water.

Freddy became suspicious within a few minutes when Emmaline hadn't returned and scanned the area outside. The fool, she was making a run for it.

With a firm hand on his pistol, he rushed out of the house and towards the causeway. She was within range and an easy target stumbling through the surf in the diminishing evening light. He paused to find a secure footing on the pebbles and took aim at the centre of her back.

'A pity, I would like to have run my fingers down that back.

You stupid girl.'

Emmaline struggled against the increasing currents that washed her first one way and then the other so she could barely make progress across the narrow ridge of shallower water. The depth was also rapidly increasing and further along; the crude granite pathway was also now submerged. She felt distraught but it was too late now to go back, she must risk a crossing.

The muscles in his trigger finger began their deathly squeeze but a fraction of a moment before the mechanism compelled Emmaline to certain death, he froze. Lights flashed across his face, breaking his concentration and he remembered how close the main island still was. The car headlights also lit up his prey, still struggling on the causeway. They continued their sweep as the vehicle turned in the far car park on Guernsey but people would be there, and they would hear the gunshot. They may have even seen her.

Emmaline was elated, the car headlights however fleetingly must have alerted the driver to her plight. She waved frantically and mustered what little energy she could to shout to the car.

'Over here, help me. HELP ME PLEASE!'

Then she turned and saw her assailant aiming directly at her.

'NO...!'

Turning rapidly to continue her flight, she was overcome by the waves and pitched into the foaming sea.

Freddy pocketed his gun and raced in after her. His lack of knowledge made it hard for him to reach her but he was a powerful man and was on her before she could get to her feet. He grabbed her hair and pulled her towards him as she coughed and spluttered to remove the water from her lungs.

'I told you not to try anything, you stupid bitch.'

Emmaline grabbed his wrist and sunk her teeth into his hand with such ferocity he screamed like an animal. Her hair now released, she fought for her life amongst the powerful currents surrounding them. Freddy was taken aback by her strength and determination. He clawed out in vain to grasp her clothing but he too now fell into the violent flood of the tide. For a second time he was beneath the waves but this time Emmaline pushed him further under and, as he floundered, she made her way towards Guernsey.

She shouted again to the car, but loud music just wafted over the causeway on the breeze. It was useless. They would never hear her and, by their indifference, could not have seen her either. As if to confirm her fears, the headlights flashed on again and the car moved off, away from the car park.

In the mottled moonlight Emmaline could see the extent of the flood. She was exhausted and knew she lacked the power to swim the remaining distance, but she had to try. She looked back towards Freddy. There was no sign of him. Where was he? She looked harder, balancing to keep upright in the water.

'On no, I've killed him!'

As evil as her attacker was, Emmaline was horrified at the thought of drowning him. She waded back towards Lihou, arms out-stretched to aid her balance. Her skirt now weighed heavily and her boots, full of seawater, were like lead weights on her tired legs. With all her strength she shuffled forwards, the causeway now completely inundated. Her right leg stumbled on something submerged in the water and she fell once more, pushing her arms out to stop herself. Expecting her hand to find a sharp rock, she was astounded to feel something soft beneath her. At first she assumed it was seaweed, but as her weight pressed down, Freddy's head rolled to one side and she reeled back with the shock.

She reached down into the water and grabbed whatever she could get hold of to pull him upwards. Heavy and weighed down further by his wet clothes, Emmaline struggled against the tide and her fatigue, desperately trying to rescue the man who would have callously ended her life only minutes earlier.

Bright, pulsating lights shattered the void then slipped into images that almost resonated with memory, but not quite. They evoked disturbing feelings; feelings that prodded and gibed.

The eyes again, the bulging eyes of Freddy's brother Hans, panic stricken and unbelieving. They were falling away now. Hans was falling away, outstretching his arms and pleading for help.

Now Freddy was falling too. It made no sense but they fell away from each other into the blankness broken only by the ripples of water. They were drowning.

Freddy watched a succession of images float before him on the black water like discarded photographs of his life, each one encapsulating an emotion, hitherto suppressed.

His mother at the school gate, waving him off on his first day at school, he was terrified but more than that; he was deeply hurt that she could abandon him. An image of his father floated by, sitting at the family dinner table, Freddy must have been ten or eleven at the time. His father was cold and indifferent to him. Then there was Hans, his brother Hans who succeeded in every challenge that school and life laid before him. How he had hated Hans for being everything he wasn't. But as the pictures flowed, interspersed with the unrequited passions of his youth, humiliations and failures, the images of Hans stirred a different emotion. Hans at the sports day encouraging Freddy before he ran; Hans patiently explaining Freddy's homework; Hans lying to their parents to protect the young Freddy, taking the blame himself for the destruction of their mother's best china dinner plates, and taking the harsh punishment from their father, the beating until he cried, but he never told on Freddy. The feeling wasn't hate, it was love; he loved Hans. Now Hans was back on that rooftop in Munich and again the falling haunted him, the bulging, pleading eyes, the disbelief, betrayal.

'NO…!'

Freddy's chest heaved as he gulped in the air saturated with the saltiness of seawater and his own vomit. His eyes blinked open frantically and he grabbed the arms in front of him, believing he could undo his crime and save his brother from plummeting to his death. But as his eyes, and his consciousness focussed, he saw not Hans but a woman holding him. She was dressed only in a white towelling dressing gown, her hair wrapped in a towel, and she was reassuring him.

'It's all right, you're safe now; back in the house. You were unconscious, it was just a dream.'

Emmaline leaned over him, and with undeserved compassion, she held his hand and told him again he was going to be all right now.

In the hours that followed, she explained how he had gone under for long enough to black out and swallow a great deal of seawater. She had reached him just in time and managed to drag him to the beach where, on being turned onto his side, he spontaneously vomited.

He had been slipping in and out of consciousness for sometime but she managed to drag him back up the beach to the house. He was far too heavy for her to carry.

Now, wrapped in just blankets and lying on the settee in the sitting room he took stock. 'Where were his clothes, his gun? What about the police, had she turned him in?'

Emmaline guessed what he was thinking, at least the first question.

'Yes, I took off your clothes and dried you. You were shivering and I thought you might die from the cold. Your stuff is all drying. Don't worry, I can cope with seeing your naked body.'

Freddy was still in shock and this was the last of his worries, he wasn't used to playing the victim and found it difficult to find the words.

'I don't understand. Why did you help me? You know I would have killed you without a second thought. Why on earth would you...?'

To his own surprise as much as Emmaline's he choked slightly on his words. The distress was short-lived but they were both taken aback when he continued.

'You saved me. Why would you do that?'

The question went unanswered, but their eyes met and he

found her beauty mesmerising.

'No doubt you've reported me by now. I take it you got across? No wait, if you're here; I'm not thinking straight.'

'I haven't, I couldn't report you because there is no working phone here and obviously I didn't cross to Guernsey. I saved you instead.'

She was nervous now, she expected his violence to return at any moment and capitalise on her selflessness.

There was silence for what seemed like an age, but in reality was just a few moments. The towel on Emmaline's head was slipping and she discarded it, allowing her ruffled, dark hair to fall onto her shoulders. He watched as a few locks settled around her neck, below her pretty chin. His eyes followed the opening in her gown down towards her cleavage.

'Thank you. I'm so sorry for the way I've treated you. You've done nothing but defend yourself.'

She blushed at the tenderness of his words. But when he reached out she was startled and pulled away sharply.

'I won't harm you again, I promise. Don't be frightened of me.'

She relaxed and let him rest his hand on hers.

'I saw some things you know. They say your life flashes before you. I saw some things.'

'What sort of things? Is that what you were calling out about?'

'Was I calling out? I didn't know, but yes, I suppose it was. You see I've done a lot of very bad things. I've been full of rage, maybe I still am, but right now I don't feel it. I feel different.'

Freddy was talking in a way he had never done before in his life. It was as if his near-death experience on the causeway had resulted in some kind of epiphany. This forceful, usually brutal, always callous, man had spent his entire life thinking of himself, his only concern for others being how they could satisfy his own needs. But as he lay there, still traumatised by his ordeal, the wind had been knocked out of his sails. His emotions, for the first time since his childhood, were raw and exposed. At this moment, with the wrongdoings of his past still reverberating in his senses, he wanted to purge his soul, to equal Emmaline's virtue and courage. The young woman he would gladly have taken against her will, abused and discarded, he now revered. She was everything he wasn't; strong, virtuous, unselfish and astonishingly beautiful. He felt inadequate by comparison and wanted more than anything to impress upon her his desire for atonement. If he could convince her, then maybe he could find the strength to ensure this transformation would be permanent. He seemed more concerned about his behaviour towards Emmaline than his own liberty, but inevitably, the subject returned.

'What the hell Emmaline, turn me in. The stuff I've done, I don't deserve my freedom. I don't even deserve to live.'

He rested his head back on the pillow Emmaline had positioned on the arm of the settee. Suddenly he was smaller, more vulnerable than before, and tears were even forming in his eyes.

She gripped his arm and he smiled plaintively.

'Tomorrow, when the tide goes out, I'll turn myself in.'

Emmaline was stunned. It had been an exhausting day and she no longer trusted her emotions, but this Freddy was extremely attractive to her. She could hardly believe the words she muttered next.

'Maybe you just need to sleep on it. Maybe in the morning, things will look different. If...'

She hesitated, not wishing to reveal too much of her feelings.

'If you can change and, you know, stop the bad things; maybe there's no need to turn yourself in. What good would come of it now anyway?'

Freddy smiled gratefully at her.

'Maybe I could just stay here with you Emmaline, maybe I could stay out of trouble that way?'

She thought how the Colonel would react when he returned to Lihou, but decided not to break the spell of this moment. Thanks to her over-protective father, Emmaline had never had a real man in her life, and if the feelings that were overwhelming her now might continue, she saw no reason to stop them. So what if he had a past? They were both outsiders and alone; two people the rest of the world would never embrace.

'You should rest now. You need your strength and I need to clear my head. This is a bit of a sudden change of heart. Let's see how you feel in the morning.'

'I don't blame you for doubting me, after the way I've treated you, but what happened tonight really hit me. If you want me to go in the morning, I'll leave you in peace.'

Outside the tide was once again ebbing from the causeway but Emmaline knew that, with the moon and sun at quarters, for several days they would remain isolated together on the island.

CHAPTER THIRTY

A full-scale search was still underway on Guernsey and Inspector Muller's team from Munich had joined the local police. The harbour and airport were as tight as a drum with everyone who entered or left the island being scrutinized before boarding all the commercial aircraft or ferries.

Anoushka weighed anchored off Sark and made way for the next leg of the cruise, this time to Jersey.

Tom took the helm whilst Rebecca navigated a course to Gorey on the east coast of the island. David and Rachel were below preparing lunch when the radio sprang to life.

'Anoushka, Anoushka, St Peter Port radio, over.'

David picked up the microphone and replied.

'St Peter Port, this is Anoushka, over.'

'Anoushka go to channel 8, over'

'St Peter Port, moving now to channel 8, over.'

David selected channel 8 on the VHF dial and waited.

'Anoushka, Anoushka, St Peter Port, over.'

'St Peter Port, this is Anoushka, what seems to be the trouble?'

'Tom is that you?'

'No, it's David, do you want me to get him? He can hear you in the cockpit.'

'That's OK David. I have Inspector Ogier for you, he wants a few words.'

'Hello Tom, everyone, I thought you should be aware that so far we've had no luck in locating Freddy Stein. All our best people are still on the case and we've even got inspector Muller's team over from Munich.

'I don't want to worry you or Rachel but I thought you should be aware of the situation. Please keep your guard up but, for the time being, you are best out there at sea enjoying yourselves. Over.'

David handed Tom the microphone.

'Message understood Inspector. It's disappointing you haven't got him yet but I appreciate the update. If that's all..? Over.'

'Yes, Tom we'll keep you informed of any developments. Enjoy the rest of your cruise. Out.'

As Tom replaced the microphone and took a bearing on the nearby town of Carteret on the French coast, a cabin cruiser edged behind the long breakwater at St Catherine's bay, a short distance from Anoushka's position.

Max spoke quietly to Gusto as he reduced the radio volume.

'So Muller is here too now. That puts a different spin on things. Raphael should be OK, but you and I might just alert him to a connection. We had better remain well out of sight.

'Raphael, pack a bag, you're going to Guernsey. Make a shore to ship phone call when you've located him and we'll bring the piece over to finish the job. But do it quickly. The longer we're around here, the more the chance Muller or his cronies might stumble across us. We'll keep an eye on Anoushka.'

Raphael was dispatched ashore at St Catherine's and Gusto motored back out to Les Ecrehou, a remote group of tiny islands connected by sandy beaches in the bay of Saint Michel. From here, using powerful binoculars, Max could keep watch on Anoushka without being seen and listen to any radio messages which, by nautical tradition, always began on the "calling" channel sixteen.

The slower yacht, Anoushka, picked up a vacant mooring underneath the impressive and ancient Gorey Castle, or Mont Orgueil as the French called it.

The mooring was on the open sea side of the harbour wall which, although still sheltered from the prevailing westerly winds, afforded more privacy than the harbour itself. The family made Anoushka ready for a long stay and after lunch took the dinghy into the harbour where they spent the rest of the day browsing and relaxing in the friendly pseudo-French community.

By evening, Raphael had crossed the short distance between Jersey and Guernsey in a bright yellow "Islander" aircraft, a flight that took just fifteen minutes, and taken a taxi to the south-west coast of Guernsey, where he booked into the Imperial Hotel. The view from his room overlooked picturesque Rocquaine Bay with its sandy shore and the distinctive 'Cup and Saucer' Fort, all the way to the headland at L'Eree and the small island beyond that meant absolutely nothing to him – Lihou island.

CHAPTER THIRTY-ONE

That night, Emmaline slept in the room above Freddy. He listened as she stepped on each squeaky stair and creaking floorboard above him. He heard her dressing gown fall to the bare floorboards and knew she would now be naked as she climbed into the bed just a few feet over him. Just thin floorboards separated them.

She lay face down on top of the sheets, exhausted on every level, but too tired, or excited, to sleep. The moonlight seeping through the window illuminated the room and she stared over the edge of the mattress at the floor, her thoughts on what lay below.

Freddy was restless too and only the floorboards now separated both of their gazes. He lay on his back, regaining mental strength, acutely conscious of the desire that reached every sinew of his body.

When the morning came Freddy awoke first, surprised to find himself on the settee, and in the few moments it took for him to remember what had happened the night before, he was his old self; agitated and demanding. But the memory soon returned, and with it a tranquillity he was not used to feeling. Where was she?

He jumped quickly off the settee and found his clothes on an airer in the kitchen, dry and warm from the range. Outside he could see the causeway was submerged, but he had no idea which way the tide was running. He was safe and that still mattered, he could defer the decision about turning himself in a little longer. He made two cups of black coffee and went upstairs.

He knocked and spoke quietly.

'Are you awake yet?'

A drowsy voice answered.

'Yes, just a minute, OK you can come in now.'

Emmaline sat up in bed with a sheet draped over her. He asked how she had slept and placed a cup on the bedside table. She pretended to be grateful for the strong black coffee.

The conversation danced around what had happened and what was said the night before. Although few words had passed between them, those that had were so charged with emotion they were still reeling.

Both of their lives had changed because of those words. As totally different as those lives had been, they were both turned upside down by the impact. Emmaline, a young woman in her twenties whose entire life had been spent in the innocence of this tiny coastal peninsula; Freddy a middle-aged, overweight, businessman-cum-gangster who had travelled widely and always lived on the seedier side of life.

His worldliness aroused her and the hairs on her neck whispered suggestions that she found hard to ignore. Her purity enticed him; he wanted to protect but at the same time devour her. She wanted to reform him but be carried away in his strong arms.

His body had never embarrassed Freddy, but it did now. He had never cared enough about a woman seeing it, but he now cared very much that Emmaline had seen it.

'Do you want me to go?' Eventually the topic had to be raised.

Both their eyes widened in the brief pause before she answered.

'No, I don't want that.'

Her body was no longer whispering to her, it was shouting. She tentatively pulled down the sheet.

Freddy could hardly restrain himself; he wasn't used to restraining himself, but he took his time and slowly removed his clothes without looking away for a moment from her naked body.

Slowly, he lay on the bed next to her and, with a touch that electrified her, gently followed the contours of her body. His passion was clear to see and she began to explore the first man her twenty-two years had brought to her. She followed his lead and when his index finger reached the moistness between her legs, she instinctively ran hers along his erection. They kissed passionately and he held her head as their bodies manoeuvred closer together. The lovemaking began slowly and he was more considerate than he had been to any of the countless women in his life. Emmaline felt transported to another physical level, her body in ecstasy and yet the pleasure did not abate. Involuntarily, she began to articulate without words the overwhelming sensation that engulfed her until, at the pinnacle of her rapture, she wept uncontrollably.

Freddy felt her joy and with every confirmation of the pleasure she transmitted, his arousal intensified. He was no longer Freddy, she was no longer Emmaline, they were a single pulsating organism accelerating towards sensual infinity.

They reached their destination together amongst a cacophony of exclamations and tears.

It was a full minute before they could speak and only the sound of their breathing and the sea against the shoreline broke the silence.

'Did I hurt you? Only you wept.'

'Not those kind of tears. You're shaking.'

Now Freddy's eyes began to well up.

'I have never in my life experienced anything that comes remotely close to what we just did.'

They hugged each other tightly, neither wanting to release the other. But Emmaline needed to know where she stood.

'Does this mean we are together?'

'My God Emmaline, if you think I'm going to let anything part us now, you must be crazy.'

'I think I am, crazy I mean. What kind of a girl makes love with a man who kidnaps her and tries to kill her...?' Although her comments where intended to tease, not rebuke him, Freddy broke in immediately.

'You didn't, I'm not that man. I never want to see him or be him again. You must believe me Emmaline, all I want is for us to be together.'

Emmaline did believe him but, out of the fear of losing him, needed to know how they could possibly be together.

'You know we can't stay here don't you? I mean, we're OK for a while, but long term we can't stay here, the house belongs to someone else.'

'I figured as much and whilst we're airing our problems, I doubt if it's just the police who are after me now.'

Freddy explained about the events that had brought him to Guernsey and the support Max had given him financially. He had also taken a chance by not simply eliminating him when Freddy's situation endangered his own criminal empire, a lost opportunity he would now surely be regretting.

'The horrible man, why can't he just leave you alone? Isn't it enough to have the police hunting you?' She sensed that somewhere in there was a logic that didn't really stand scrutiny, but this moment was for feeling, not thinking.

'In the world I was in, he should have despatched me to the fishes as soon as I went to him. But now we're connected by events and if I don't get away or get killed, he could be exposed. It wouldn't surprise me if his henchmen were already on Guernsey.'

For now at least they were safe. The sea provided a natural barrier that few would attempt to breach. High water was becoming synonymous with safety and low with the risk of discovery. They spent the day exploring each other's worlds and returning frequently to the physical manifestation of their attraction. After one such occasion, as Freddy held her in his arms, they talked about Rachel.

'I grew up to believe that Jews were not really people like you and I. They were more akin to a virus or a plague that had beset the Fatherland. All our social and economic problems were a direct result of the influence they had gained in our society. In truth, of course, we envied their commercial success. Our race had lost the first war and the economy was failing again, our national pride was in pieces and we needed a scapegoat.

'Then Hitler came along and promised a return to prosperity. He welded the Aryan race into an organised, well running machine, with an army to match. We thought it was our time to regain our lost pride and the territories conquered by our ancestors. But the Jews had to be cleared from our lands.

'It's hard to imagine now but we thought we were in the right. The religious, not that I was ever one of them, thought God was on their side, a revenge for killing his son.

'For most of us it wasn't even hatred that allowed us to ignore their plight, it was indifference. Rachel was a Jewess. Her parents were victims of the time and she would have been too if her young hero hadn't intervened. His bravery, or ignorance, saved her life and we all thought she had perished in the sea off Alderney.

'We felt nothing for what that young girl might have suffered, only the impact on our business, only the profit.'

Emmaline spoke softly.

'I know her you know, Rachel that is. I know her and Tom and their children. They lived less than a mile along the coast from me for years.'

'Tell me about them.'

'There's not much to tell really. They seemed decent enough. Never had much money or anything but the kids were always kind to me, unlike most in our neighbourhood. Despite our age difference, Rachel always treated me like an equal, never talked down to me. If we met at the bus stop, she always had something to say or asked how I was. I like her.'

'You know I paid people to kill her?'

Emmaline flinched.

'Not you Freddy; I don't want to talk about the old you, not yet.'

'I don't want to pretend I'm any better than I am, not to you. I want you know I have been a terrible person, have believed in the worst you can imagine. I see it now, but that doesn't change what I've done.'

As Freddy's guilt was exorcised in the remote house on Lihou, officers from Guernsey and Munich gathered around a map of the west coast in the St Peter Port police station.

Raj asked about the search immediately after Freddy's escape, he followed the track explained by the local sergeant. Pointing at L'eree car park he began.

'So if he was lost about here, and running roughly north, what about this headland and this place? What exactly is it, an island or what?

'That's Lihou, connected by a causeway at low water and cut off at high. Of course we checked it out at the time, didn't we Bob?'

Bob replied confidently.

'Oh yes, we got there as soon as the next tide permitted and saw young Emmaline Le Page at the house. She'd been cleaning all morning and swore there was no sign of anybody on the island.'

'So you didn't actually look yourselves?' Muller questioned.

Inspector Ogier wasn't pleased and the expression on his face chilled Bob. Ogier turned to PC Le Prevost and instructed him to get down to the causeway immediately with a couple of cars and collect firearms on the way.

'Would you like to join us?' He directed at Muller.

'Thank you, yes very much. Raj, you and Ida go with PC Le Prevost and, if we may, Ali and I will accompany you Inspector Ogier?

En route across the island, Ogier was checking a tide table.

'Damn, as I thought, it's neap tides at the moment. We can't get across on foot. I'll radio for a dory to take us across.

The cars sped across the island, sirens blaring until they were within a mile of the west coast. But Ogier's calculation that the last mile would be unannounced proved misjudged.

As Freddy embraced his newfound love in the upstairs bedroom on Lihou and the breeze through an open window cooled their warm bodies, it carried fleetingly on it the faint tones of approaching sirens.

CHAPTER THIRTY-TWO

Less than a mile away, in the public bar of the Imperial Hotel, Raphael was mixing with the locals.

'I thought I had picked a quiet spot for a fishing holiday, but from what I hear, all sorts have been going on around here lately.'

The barman continued drying a pint glass, but grinned as he replied.

'The most excitement we've had in years! Some escaped murderer, by all accounts. They never did get him, but he'll be long gone by now.'

'Where did it all happen then?'

The barman took Raphael to the window and pointed out across the bay.

'You see that grey and white fort in the middle? That's the 'cup and saucer'. Apparently, he was in one of those cottages on the right just by it, Tom Le Breton's place. Anyhow, the local police came across him and gave chase, but lost him on that headland.' He was pointing to the far end of the bay.

Not wanting to arouse suspicion, Raphael changed the subject.

'All too racy for me. Where's the best place to drop a line around here?'

They continued the conversation back at the bar and Raphael was about to finish his drink and leave when another local man rushed in excitedly and addressed an elderly man sitting on his own at a nearby table.

'What's your sassy little Emmaline been up to then, Mick?'

'What do you mean?' Came the surprised reply.

'Well, assuming the colonel is still away, them police over by Lihou is all after your niece. A couple of cars parked up in the car park, coppers everywhere, and they've even got the dory to get across to the island! She been up to her old tricks, arms smuggling?' He joked.

'Funny, she don't usually stay over more than a night, and she

296

knows her tides. She must have known it was neaps this week. I'd better get along and make sure she's alright.'

Raphael supped the remaining beer in his glass and asked for the nearest phone. Minutes later, the telephone operator confirmed the radio connection and on board Follie Max answered; he listened to Raphael's news.

'That was quick Raphael, you're sure of your facts, over?'

'I can't be sure, but it looks very likely. If I'm right, there won't be much time to conclude our business here, over.'

'Keep your eyes open for us. We'll get to you as soon as we can, out.'

Raphael walked towards the headland, following the granite sea wall that described the arc of the bay. As he approached the headland, he could make out a small crowd gathering where the police were barring the way. There were a number of officers crouched in the undergrowth of the headland and three more were launching a Dory on the slipway.

Freddy had ignored the sirens and imagined Emmaline hadn't heard the wafting menace of their tones. He was resigned to his fate and waiting for the door to burst open at any moment. She had heard, but the moment was so special, she couldn't bring herself to acknowledge what was happening. Now the immediacy of the situation was sinking in and she jumped out of bed, pulling his arm.

'Come on, we can't give up yet. How can they be sure you're here?'

'Maybe that car, perhaps they saw everything last night and they've been waiting for the right moment. Look my love, I'm ready.'

'Well I'm not! You're not going anywhere, at least not away from me, not yet. Put these on.'

She threw his clothes to him and quickly dressed herself.

They cautiously approached the window and peered through. Dazzling reflections signalled the presence of policemen with binoculars on the headland and they could see others struggling to launch the dory without making a noise. The powerful outboard on it's stern would have been a complete giveaway, so perhaps it was just there as a precaution, the causeway had a reputation.

'They'll soon let us know they're coming if they start that monster.' Emmaline joked. 'It's not like they need it in this weather and neap tides. What do they think we'll do, run across the water?'

'It's not us they think will do anything. It's me - you mustn't get involved. Quickly, if I tie you up, you can be my hostage again.'

'No, listen to me. They trust me. Keep away from the window and follow me. Freddy if you care for me at all, do this. I need you.'

Although he was resigned to his own fate, he couldn't bear the thought of Emmaline being unhappy.

She led him down to the kitchen and stopped at the larder door.

'Hardly anybody knows about this.'

She opened the larder door and knelt to move some boxes on the floor. Below them a wooden hatch door was uncovered.

'It's a well. Been here for years but only the family know about it, as the house is supplied from a bore hole now.'

Freddy opened the hatch to reveal a deep and dark shaft with a thick iron bar placed across the top on which there was a pulley.

He climbed in supporting his weight on the bar whilst he found footholds.

'It's about eighty feet to the bottom, I believe, but I've no idea how far down the water is. Take care and I'll come and get you as soon as they've gone.'

She blew him a kiss, closed the hatch and moved the boxes back over it.

Rushing to the window she checked on the progress of her intruders. They were only a few minutes away.

Emmaline darted from room to room checking for any trace of Freddy, his clothes, the telltale sign of two glasses or plates, a pair of his shoes. When all evidence was safely hidden away in the colonel's wardrobe, she returned to the kitchen and started preparing a lunch for one.

Inspector Ogier whispered final instructions to his men.

'Avoid any gravel, there's plenty of grass to walk on and if you see him, remember he may be armed, no heroics just signal to me. When we're all in position around the house, I'll go in and find Emmaline.'

The team heeded his instructions and a few minutes later all the windows and exits were covered by armed police. Ogier cautiously approached the house until he could see Emmaline through the part glazed door. She seemed to be alone. He made his move and seconds later stood behind her with his hand over her mouth.

'Don't worry Emmaline; I'm with the police. Please don't be alarmed. Are you alone here?'

She nodded and he released his grip.

Instinctively still whispering, he asked her again.

'You're definitely alone?'

Understandably, he thought, she looked shocked. He looked around.

'Would you please just come with me?' Again she nodded, and he led her out of the house and towards his men, who immediately broke cover and pointed their weapons at the house.

Convincingly she whimpered.

'What's going on? What I have I done wrong? I don't understand.'

'We just need to be sure Emmaline. If there was someone in the house with you he may have been pointing a weapon at your back.'

'No, it's just me, I was making lunch.'

'Ok, I'm really sorry we startled you. If you don't mind we'll take a look around whilst we're here?'

Freddy stared into the abyss below him and his head began

swirl. The drop into the well reminded him again of the night in Munich on the roof of the factory. His foot slipped and a stone worked loose. He heard it drop, bouncing off the sides until a load 'plop' confirmed the depth to the water. He tried to shake his head to stop himself feeling dizzy and his arms were now aching from his uncomfortable position on the bar.

Just as the stone hit the water, PC Le Prevost was entering the kitchen. He stopped dead in his tracks and cocked his head to one side, as if this would improve his hearing. Inspector Ogier was right behind him.

'What's up Phil?'

'I heard something. At least I thought I did.'

'What sort of something?'

'Well odd, I know, but it sounded like a splash.'

The two of them looked outside at the waves crashing against the rocks. Ogier grinned.

'Well there's a surprise!'

'No, it was different. Probably just the plumbing.'

After searching the house thoroughly, including a glance in the larder, the team left to check the rest of the island. It was nearly two hours before they returned, declaring Lihou safe from the clutches of Freddy.

'Sorry to disturb you, Emmaline, but we had to check.'

Disappointed, they made their way back to the awaiting dory and across the causeway. Emmaline could hardly contain herself, but waited tolerantly for them to leave and tried not to reveal her impatience to get back to the house, to Freddy.

As the dory beached, Raphael watched from a nearby vantage point. Their dejected expressions and lack of a prisoner confirmed to him the police were unsuccessful. He pondered whether or not to cancel his rendezvous, but decided Max should still come. After all, he would need the gun eventually.

When her uninvited guests had departed Lihou, Emmaline walked back to the house. Every inch of her wanted to run, but she maintained her cool. Once back in the house however, it was another matter. She dashed to the larder, calling as she did.

'It's alright they've gone, your safe now, my love.'

Hurling the boxes to one side, she yanked open the hatch and reached down to help a somewhat awkwardly positioned Freddy. His face red from the exertion, he took her hand.

'I thought they were never going to go. It's been hours.'

Grappling to free himself, vulnerable and undignified, the once ruthless businessman climbed back into the larder. He was panting and slightly claustrophobic.

'I need air.' Before she could stop him, Freddy was at the door gulping in fresh sea air.

She pulled at his arm.

'No, come back inside, somebody might see you.'

He returned to Emmaline's waiting arms.

Raphael had been on the point of turning his attention to the walk back when he took one last look at Lihou. It was too far to see clearly, but the figure that appeared fleetingly in the doorway certainly didn't look like that of a young woman.

Darkness was falling and a sea mist setting in as the cabin cruiser inched between the treacherous reefs on Guernsey's west coast. The Hanois lighthouse towered above, projecting a beam of light far into the distance to warn ships of the very rocks Follie was now attempting to navigate. Fortunately, it was calm and Follie was equipped with radar as well as a depth sounder which, when used in conjunction with a nautical chart, allowed Gusto to pin point their position, and that of the reefs, with surprising accuracy. But better sailors than him had come to grief many times on the west coast and he was taking no chances. Despite protestations, Max was required to sit up in the flying bridge and keep a close look out for rocks or crab pots in the water.

Raphael had found a point on the headland nearest to their approach and was now signalling with a torch towards the tiny

Portelet harbour. They spotted him immediately and were soon dropping anchor amongst the local fishing boats. He made his way onto the pier, where Gusto collected him in the dinghy. Back on board Follie, Max quizzed him.

'So all you have to go on is a fleeting glimpse of someone on this, what do they call it, Leehow island?'

Raphael tried to explain, but Max continued making the point.

'This girl could have had anyone there, a lover, a friend, anyone. Why on earth do you assume it's him?'

Raphael was getting irritated but he knew better than to let this show.

'Of course, you are right, Max. It could be anyone and I almost called you when the police drew a blank.'

'Yes, that's another thing, if the police didn't find him, what makes you think he's still there? That Muller is sharp enough, was he there looking as well?'

'Max, I thought there was a chance, however remote, that it could be Freddy and that he could have eluded the police. I also thought that if I were going to finish the job, I'd need that shooter anyway. So the sooner I'm tooled up the better, in case the opportunity arises.'

Begrudgingly, Max could see the point and let it go.

'OK, so what do you have in mind?'

They were anchored directly across the bay from Lihou and, although it was now too dark and misty to see, Raphael indicated the direction and assured them that by morning, if the fog lifted, they could move to a position where the island could be watched through binoculars. If Freddy moved past a window or appeared at a door, they would see him. But they had to be vigilant. It was agreed Gusto and Raphael would share the surveillance as soon as they could see the island again.

CHAPTER THIRTY-THREE

Muller replaced the phone and looked across the desk at his colleague from Guernsey.

'That was my chief in Munich. There have been some developments. Following up on the missing documents, we discovered a subsidiary of Stein in Bogota. As you can imagine, this aroused interest, so our financial crimes' team have been poring over the corporation's accounts and our narcotics division, looking into the supply chain.

Our friends in the FBI picked up these investigations and called my chief. They have been monitoring the Bogota operation for some time and have our friend Freddy in the frame. But they're after a bigger fish. There's no suggestion that anyone else at Stein is involved other than Freddy's PA, who has mysteriously gone missing. In any case, he was just one supplier to a European and North American distribution network controlled by one of our most evasive local villains, Max Bauer.

HQ also reported that Max and two of his cronies have disappeared from our radar and our informants tell us he may well be pursuing Freddy.'

Inspector Ogier pondered this latest development.

'So when you say 'pursuing', to what end?'

'The financial crimes team say that Freddy used a honeycomb of subsidiaries to hide the Bogota factory from the others at Stein. Even their auditors had no idea what was going on. But there are tenuous links to Max's operation that I'm sure Max would be keen to erase. The trouble is that we picked up the documents immediately after we confronted Freddy, and his PA knew this. Max must be wondering how much information about his end has been revealed and how much more would be if they collared Freddy and cut a deal. He isn't the kind to risk Freddy talking.'

'So if this Max and his henchmen know about the documents,

they may also know that Rachel and Tom were given the copies, and that places them at risk as well.'

'Exactly. Where did you say they are now?'

'They're cruising the islands on their yacht. We all thought it safest if they were at sea with Freddy on the loose. But your Max won't be restricted in where he goes and if he is here...'

Ogier left the sentence open ended as the two of them got to their feet. Muller spoke with urgency.

'I'll get photos of Max and his men wired over here immediately. What will you do about Rachel and her family?'

'Only one thing we can do, get them back where we can look after them. This is all getting very messy. What about the FBI?'

'They would rather we let Max roam free for the time being so they can gather more evidence, but we need to think about that. I'll keep them posted through HQ. For now, let's just try to locate him, then we can decide.'

The two men sprang into action, but despite their efforts, no sighting had been made of Freddy, and the radio aboard Anoushka was not responding to their calls. The only progress reported was that Max's suspected hit man, Raphael, had been recognised by a customs officer at the airport, arriving from Jersey on an inter-island flight. There was no record of how he got into Jersey. This news suggested Raphael might have entered Jersey by sea, a worrying development, as Tom's last known position was that he was sailing Anoushka in that direction.

As the sun rose behind Guernsey, the first rays splintered through the curtains of Lihou House. Emmaline rose and walked towards the shaded, south-facing window. Her nudity, in the presence of a man, aroused her, knowing that he was watching the curves of her body with only partially restrained desire.

The foghorn of the Hanois lighthouse bleated its repetitive

warning that seemed to contradict the light now engulfing their bedroom.

She drew back the curtains and looked out over the bay.

'Hmm, still a sea mist further out, but the bay is clearing. There's just a shroud-like low cloud... wait a minute, what's that? Freddy, come here a minute.'

Emmaline directed his attention to the flying bridge of a large cabin cruiser that protruded above the low mist in the bay.

'That wasn't there yesterday and I don't recognise it.' She observed.

Freddy shivered and stood back from the window.

'Could be anybody, couldn't it?'

'This part of the island doesn't usually get visiting cruisers of that size; the rocks are too treacherous. It might have put in last night as a safe haven in the mist, in which case it'll be gone as soon as the visibility improves.'

Freddy was distracted by the softness of her skin as it brushed against his body. He reached for her hand and, both wearing only a smile, he led her back to bed.

The first to get up was, as usual, Gusto and all was quiet on board Follie, so he put the kettle on and stepped into the morning air. A quick visual check confirmed the anchor was holding and the mist appeared to be slowly clearing. From the flying bridge, he could now see Lihou quite clearly.

Below, the kettle whistled, so Gusto returned to the galley and made three coffees. Max and Raphael emerged from their cabins on hearing the noises above.

'Get some food on the go, Raphael.' Max's blunt instruction was typical of his pre-caffeine mood exhibited every morning.

'When is this bloody mist going to go?'

Gusto replied optimistically.

'It's lifting quite quickly now, Max. You can see Lihou from the flying bridge, perhaps an hour or two and the sun will burn it off.'

'Good, then we'll get closer yes? See if we can see this fool and get the job done. I'm getting tired of camping.'

Follie was a luxurious cruiser with a polished cherry interior, deep pile carpets, and en-suite cabins that could hardly be described as camping, but it wouldn't do to express disagreement with Max.

Whilst the three of them prepared breakfast, a mile away Freddy carefully shifted his weight off Emmaline and lay on his back breathing rapidly.

'I meant to check if the tide was still on the causeway. Did you look?' He asked her.

'There's no need; it will be covered until tomorrow afternoon. Then walkers and the few remaining tourists at this time of year may interrupt our peace. I wish it would stay up for ever.' She turned to look into his eyes, as she spoke.

'When I first came here, the tide felt like a trap. Now it's our only defence against the outside world. A world that offers only hostility and an end to this amazing thing that's happened to me.'

'To us,' she corrected.

They kissed.

'To us,' he confirmed, placing his arm around her. He could feel her heart beating. Seemingly out of the blue, he asked.

'Are there any binoculars here?'

'Not binoculars, but the colonel keeps a brass telescope that I must regularly polish whenever he's travelling. It's in that wooden box on the cabinet.'

'Good. That cruiser in the bay, it's probably nothing, but I just want to take a look at it.'

'Are you expecting someone?'

'Not necessarily, but you remember what I told you about Max?' She nodded, a worried expression now replacing the contentedness of a moment earlier.

'Among his many toys, there is a large cruiser.'

Gusto's prediction proved accurate and by midday, Follie was underway across Rocquaine bay in search of another safe anchorage, this time closer to Lihou Island. The bay was riddled with rocks, making it hard to find a suitable location, especially as the only clear passages between them would be used by all the local fishing craft to enter or exit the bay. They settled for a spot a little further out, but consequently more private, and still commanding an excellent view through the powerful binoculars on board.

Their manoeuvrings hadn't gone un-noticed on Lihou, and Freddy could now confirm his fears as he picked out Max on deck, using the colonel's telescope.

'They'll be watching every move on the island, hoping to establish if the police missed me in their search. What have I done to you? How could I place you at such risk?'

'It's not your fault, my darling....' She corrected herself. 'Well ok, it is,' She said grinning mischievously. 'But that doesn't matter now. The only thing that matters is that we are together and I want it to stay that way. You must keep away from the windows and doors, and I must make sure if ever I can be seen, I'm not talking to you or carrying two mugs or plates, or anything.'

Freddy paused and considered hard how to phrase his next question.

'The gun, Emmaline, what happened to my gun?'

She bristled and looked him straight in the eyes.

'That was the old you; you don't need it.'

'I need to protect you.'

'We'll find another way.'

'Darling, you don't understand, these men are killers. They aren't a threat like the police; they don't want to lock me up and they won't just finish me off. If they think you can identify them, they'll kill you without a second thought.'

'I don't know where your gun is. All I know is that you had it on the causeway but you fell into the sea and I haven't seen it since. It must be still out there somewhere. Thank God the police didn't stumble upon it.'

'They used a dory so if the tide was up, they would have gone right over it. We've got to get it, and from what you said earlier, we've got to get it before the tide goes all the way out on the causeway and somebody else stumbles across it.'

CHAPTER THIRTY-FOUR

Rachel was awoken by Anoushka's radio calling out urgently. They had returned late the previous night from the hospitality of a local couple they met in one of the bars at Gorey harbour. Far from being the type of people who would usually go back for a nightcap with complete strangers, they made an exception after meeting and immediately hitting it off with these regulars in the harbour community.

The family hadn't returned until just before two in the morning and the rude awakening was most unwelcome.

'Anoushka, Anoushka, this is St Peter Port Radio, over'

The call relayed from Inspector Ogier welded the sleepy crew into action. He had strongly advised the family to return to Guernsey with all haste and be met en-route by a police launch that would accompany them to St Peter Port, where they should be taken into protective custody.

Tom had railed against this, explaining they would be more of a target if these people knew where they were. It was only when the descriptions were passed on and the family realised it was Max they had met off Sark, that he changed his opinion.

'Listen everyone, if they got that close and let us go, the chances are they aren't really interested in us but were hoping we might lead them to Freddy. Rather, by watching us, Freddy would be bound to show up and they could get rid of him.'

'And maybe us at the same time,' David added.

Tom continued, 'That's a distinct possibility.'

Rebecca suddenly gasped and grabbed her mother's arm. 'My God, that accident on La Coupee, wasn't an accident at all; they were trying to kill you! Oh Mum, what are we going to do?'

Trying, with great difficulty, to remain calm, Tom continued, 'So we'll sort of take Inspector Ogier's advice. We'll agree to an armed escort and we'll go into protective custody but I want this on our terms. Let's not forget that nobody really knows what they might do next or even where they are now, not even the police. We can't assume they have all the answers, but we do need some protection.'

'What are you saying Tom?' Rachel had been silent through all this and uncharacteristically meek but now she wanted to know exactly what her husband had in mind.

'Guernsey is a small enough island for word of our whereabouts to leak out but large enough for these guys to stay undetected. I don't want to rely upon some police 'safe house' and I think Inspector Ogier will go along with my alternative suggestion; there is really only one place I know I can protect you.'

They looked into each other's eyes and spoke in unison.

'Herm!'

Within the hour arrangements were made and Anoushka was on course once again for Herm. Given the advancing years of their old friends at the farm, they decided to stay at the Whitehouse Hotel along with several armed officers who were delighted with this assignment. Once again, the police used the fast ambulance launch, 'The Flying Christine' to accompany Anoushka, this time with officers well out of sight below decks to minimise local interest.

It was mid afternoon when Anoushka's keels bumped slowly onto the beach at Herm Harbour and they picked up the chain, fore and aft, mooring. She would be safe at any state of the tide and protected from all but the most northwesterly winds. As Anoushka was prepared, plain clothed policemen discretely checked in at the hotel, taking up rooms on the first floor. The family disembarked shortly after and whilst David and Rebecca shared a twin room on the first floor, Rachel and Tom moved into the only second floor bedroom. This room, called The Crow's Nest, not only ensured their privacy but also gave stunning views across to Guernsey. Tom was determined their forced seclusion would be a comfortable one.

This late in the year, the hotel had few other guests, all of whom were quickly screened and declared to be no threat to the family. Herm itself was relatively easy to defend. It could be circumnavigated in less than an hour and being long and narrow, all that was needed were officers placed at a few strategic locations to watch the entire coastline. A fast 'RIB' launch was also on hand in case any suspicious craft approached too closely.

It was therefore considered safe to allow the family some freedom of movement and Rachel wasted no time in returning to the place she loved most on the planet. She and Tom wandered barefoot along Shell Beach paddling in the cool sea as they remembered the first time she had seen the myriad of bright shell fragments washed up by the Gulf Stream.

She pulled his arm around her waist and looked up lovingly at him.

'Remember, I was just a scrawny girl barely even a teenager when you scooped me up in your arms and rescued me from Alderney? By the time we reached this place, I had faked my own death, been taken out to sea at night in a small boat, avoided a mine, evaded a German patrol boat and then watched it be obliterated thinking you too had been blown to smithereens. Then, with the sirens screaming and the searchlights probing all around us, we slipped around the coast and between all those rocks.' She inclined her head towards a huge reef known locally as 'The Humps' and continued:

'Then Fish glided gently past this beach. I looked at you on that balmy night, my handsome rescuer, as the moonlight illuminated millions of these tiny shell fragments and felt transported to heaven on earth. Every time we come here and the aroma of warm sea and fern from the common permeate my senses, I want to cry with joy.'

'I know, I struggle to find words that adequately convey the emotions of that night. We were both so young and you so vulnerable. Half starved with only the torn frock you were wearing to your name, apart from that shoe of course!

It was like a huge bonfire night when that patrol boat went up in flames, I've never seen anything like it. Those poor soldiers, I know they were the enemy but I just remember how they let off steam that night at the Casquets with their terrible singing. Anyway, it doesn't pay to dwell on that. Who knows what would have happened to you if they'd taken you. Even then, that Freddy was a threat. I just hope they catch him soon and we can get on with our lives.'

'I don't want to tarnish my thoughts about this place by thinking about Freddy or what might   have happened. This place will always be my sanctuary and the only thoughts permitted are happy ones.'

She bent down to collect a small but perfectly intact Strombus shell from the beach.

'This little chap travelled half way across the world to get here and whilst nearly every other shell has been snapped and crushed by the waves, it's still in one piece. I'm still in one piece too, love. You don't need to worry about me, let's just savour today and tomorrow can look after itself.'

The couple strolled along the entire length of Shell Beach and along the cliff path to Belvoir. Sitting on the rocks next to the tiny inlet where Fish was beached and where they had slept that first night, they remembered the mackerel breakfast Tom had prepared which they had feasted upon with just their bare hands. It was the most delicious food Rachel had ever eaten, her appetite exaggerated by months in the labour camp and her taste buds suppressed by a diet of mainly bread and water with the occasional leftovers brought to her by Freddy's brother Hans whenever he could.

They looked out across the bay that looked the same today as it had all those years ago.

'Just a few things in life never change.' Tom went on.

'Remember that time we were swimming here and that soldier turned up in a boat?'

'How could I forget, he embarrassed me completely with his innuendos about us being girlfriend and boyfriend. Still he didn't turn me in.'

'No and when Freddy came snooping, he knew all about you. He turned a blind eye when we got you away as well.'

'That was a day I don't want to remember. That smelly old barrel and spending the night in Brehon Tower, yuck! Then our final boat trip together as you took me to meet the submarine. I could have burst; I was so upset to leave you. I hardly remember anything about the trip back to England or the first couple of days at Apple's house.'

'I don't remember sailing back to Guernsey either. I didn't want you to go, but you had to.'

Tom and Rachel continued their reminiscences and wandered around Herm for the rest of the day under the discrete but careful eyes of two burly police officers who maintained an appropriate distance.

When they returned to the hotel, Inspector Ogier met them at Reception.

'There is someone here I think you should meet.' He gestured for them to enter the bar where a couple a few years more senior were sitting.

'Our checks on the other hotel residents brought to our attention another German national and his wife. So as you might expect, we were keen to interview them. May I introduce you to Herr and Frau Bachmeier?'

They rose and turned to face Tom and Rachel, Herr Bachmeier smiling broadly.

'You may remember me as 'Spike.''

Tom grabbed his hand and shook it enthusiastically, his other hand affectionately holding Spike's arm as he did so.   They turned to Rachel as Spike joked.

'You see, I was right about your secret. There was something going on between you two!

Allow me to introduce my wife, Beth.'

Rachel was speechless, just a few hours ago she and Tom had been remembering the day a German soldier found them messing about in the sea at Belvoir and now here he was in front of her. She was delighted and as soon as she could speak, told Beth what a hero her husband had been to allow her to escape.

'He would have been shot if they had found out you know, but thanks to him I made it back to England. Your husband probably saved my life.'

Spike's chest expanded with pride and he explained how he had long been promising his wife a holiday in Herm and had chosen this week to fulfil his promise.

'What a happy coincidence!' He was positively gleeful.

Inspector Ogier left them to their memories and returned to Guernsey where the search for Max, as well as Freddy, was seriously stretching his resources. It was late in the day when the report came that at last they had a lead.

PC Le Page had been checking the local hotels and guesthouses for the man they knew as Raphael and had come up trumps.

'He checked in at the Imperial two days ago but left his room yesterday afternoon and hasn't been seen since. His bed wasn't slept in last night either. Oh, and the bag he brought is still in the room, but there's nothing in it of any interest, we checked. Only a few clothes, his passport, some money and an ID card.'

Ogier considered this news.

'So, either he struck it lucky with a local girl, or he's out there somewhere roughing it. Assuming of course, there's nowhere else he could have stayed. But why would he rough it?'

PC Le Page chipped in.

'Inspector, what if he is watching Freddy? Knows where he is and is waiting for his moment to get to him?'

'Yes George, you may have something there. I doubt he has a firearm as he flew in. The airport metal detectors would have picked that up and anyway it would be too much of a risk to try to bring one through. So if your theory is right, Raphael hasn't got to Freddy yet but has managed to find him before us.'

'Or thinks he has found him.'

'What do you mean?'

'Well, if he has found him, why wouldn't he just do what he came here to do and get away? If he hasn't, why sleep rough? So maybe, he's closing in on where he thinks Freddy might be, but so far hasn't got to him.'

The partially open door widened and Muller stepped in.

'Your logic is sound PC Le Page. But what if he's simply focusing on where he believes Freddy will go? Didn't you say Freddy was first seen leaving the Le Breton cottage at Rocquaine? What if Raphael is now watching the cottage, presumably it wouldn't be that hard to figure out where Tom and Rachel lived?'

Ogier continued this line of reasoning.

'Of course the Le Bretons now have another house so he could be at either, but I'm sure it's no coincidence he booked in at the Imperial which just happens to be a few hundred yards from the old cottage.

It all seems to point to that part of the island. We'll keep a man on the L'Ancresse house but let's tighten our net around Rocquaine.'

CHAPTER THIRTY-FIVE

It was first light when Emmaline made her way towards the causeway, carrying a long stick from the yard. She had but a few hours to find the gun before Lihou was once again connected to Guernsey.

Out in the bay a large cabin cruiser hovered menacingly amongst the waves whilst Raphael and Gusto shared a binocular watch of the house on Lihou. Freddy remained out of sight and the previous evening Emmaline had made a point of sitting alone on the steps outside the kitchen with her supper to convince them she was on her own. Now her every move was being scrutinised as she approached the slowly ebbing tide-line.

The familiar arc of stones that described a safe crossing was slowly revealing itself to her. She tried to remember exactly where Freddy had stood when he fell. She looked across to the car park, already there was some activity and a number of vehicles were assembling. She hoped it wasn't a tedious organised walking party about to intrude on 'her' island. As she looked up, she was taken back to that fateful day when her bungled escape had nearly cost her life. Her panic in the rising water and the terror she had felt when the gun was pointed directly at her still sent shivers down her spine. She had thought her short life was over before it had really started to begin.

She now focused upon the task at hand, probing every rock and pool with her stick.

On board Follie, Max was now surveying her pursuit on the causeway.

'What on earth is she doing? She looks as if she's searching for something. Completely mad!

'Last night there was no sign of him, you say?'

His henchmen confirmed that Freddy hadn't been sighted and she had eaten alone.

'So, either she is alone and you have wasted my time Raphael, or they're on to us and he's laying low. In which case I wonder if this little excursion is for our benefit.'

As they continued to analyse, Emmaline pushed aside the seaweed covering most of the rocks and meticulously continued her search.

Meanwhile, Freddy found a position on the far side of the house away from the prying eyes on board Follie and watched his lover as she worked tirelessly on his behalf. It was from this position that he first noticed the increasing commotion around the bay. Police sirens had again pierced the morning air, but had again fallen silent before the police cars came into view. However, this time they seemed to approach from every angle. All along the west coast people seemed to be rushing around, several were even running. But not long after, the activity subsided and now there was barely any vehicular movement on the coast road at all or even anyone on foot. Something was happening, but what exactly, he had no idea.

Max was getting restless.

'We could be here for days without knowing for sure. Raphael, get the dinghy, you're going ashore, but not via the causeway. Head off to the west of the island and land out of sight. If he is there, you need to take him by surprise. Take the pistol and get this job over with.'

Inspector Ogier drove through his own police cordon and into the car park at L'Eree where several of his officers were waiting.

'What have you got for me George?'

'Sir, we've effectively closed off the bay from the outside world with officers on every minor lane and road that leads here including the coast road. Residents have been asked to leave the area temporarily or stay indoors. If anything moves, we should now see it.

But there's something else.' He pointed out to sea close to Lihou.

'That cruiser isn't local and the position it's taken up is far from being a sensible one. We've got the name from her transom plate and her registered port and we're running a check.'

'Good work.' Ogier looked through his binoculars at the cruiser.

'She's a big one, we're looking at a lot of money there. Let me know as soon as you hear who she belongs to.'

Although Freddy was no longer in view from Follie, he couldn't see as Raphael boarded the dinghy and powered up the outboard motor.

Emmaline was getting frustrated at her lack of success, when a flash of light caught her eye and made her look up. She saw Raphael opening the throttle and powering out to sea, off the coast of Lihou. Her heart sunk, this was it. If she went back now she and Freddy would be defenceless against the assassin. If she stayed longer, Freddy would have no warning of the approaching danger. Her head span as more and more of the causeway became exposed. 'Where was that gun?'

The granite pathway was now uncovering and before long anyone would be able to cross.

'Where was it?' She knew the dinghy could reach a safe rock to land quickly as the tide was falling and he could be there before her unless she ran back now. But she knew they needed the gun for protection. Chastising herself at her inability to find it she lashed out with her stick at a clump of weed. Beneath it the shining barrel of the pistol pointed ominously towards her. As she reached down, she heard the outboard engine cut off and she knew her lover was just minutes away from death.

At L'Eree the radio crackled into life and PC Le Prevost took the message across to Inspector Ogier who was in deep conversation with Muller.

'Sorry to interrupt you sir, but the cruiser out there, Follie, is registered to a company in Monaco. 'Enterprise Holdings' is the name, seems innocuous enough.'

Muller cut in.

'Let me check this out with the Feds, they seem to have quite a portfolio on Max.'

Ogier walked over to a gap in the sea wall and looked out over the bay. He snapped a command at a passing officer.

'Terry, I want the fast inflatable patrol boat over here immediately, see to it will you? Oh and find out where the Christine is, ask St John's Ambulance Station if we might use her again.'

A few minutes later the PC returned.

'Our inflatable is on its way sir, should be here within half an hour, but the Christine is in use on a rescue between Alderney and Cherbourg, she won't be available for several hours.'

'Hmm, ok thanks Terry.' Ogier looked worried as he continued to watch Follie out in the bay.

Emmaline scrambled across the rocky causeway and ran awkwardly across the uneven surface of the beach. Clutching the gun, she pushed her body as hard as it could stand in a frantic dash towards the house. As soon as she reached the grassy final approach, she saw Raphael enter the house and instinctively looked up at the window.

There was Freddy smiling down at her, pleased that she had reclaimed their protection but puzzled by her frenzied dash and completely ignorant of the imminent danger downstairs in the kitchen.

From his vantage point, Ogier was distracted by the figure running from the causeway on Lihou towards the house. He watched intently as she dashed into the doorway and he was puzzled by Emmaline's unusual behaviour. Moments later a single gunshot rang out across the bay.

CHAPTER THIRTY-SIX

Tom was delighted to be reunited with Spike after all this time, and the two had been deep in conversation for the past hour, leaving their wives to become acquainted.

In common with many German soldiers, Spike had suffered terribly in the closing months of the war. After the Liberation of the islands, he was despatched without delay to the Russian front where the harsh winter killed many of his comrades. He held out a prosthetic hand.

'I was lucky.' He joked. 'I got frostbite and lost this. Without my trigger fingers, I was no use on the front line so they sent me back. It brought a new meaning to that expression of yours, "throwing your hand in"!' His black humour masked a bold spirit, but the poignancy wasn't lost when he explained that loosing his hand had certainly saved his life.

Eventually their attention turned to happier times and Tom and Rachel's recent good fortune, at least financially.

'So that beautiful yacht in the harbour is yours is she?' Spike had seen and admired Anoushka from the harbour wall.

'Yes, I'm pleased to say she's all mine; at least - ours!' he added promptly.

'I would love to look her over if it isn't an intrusion?'

'No, of course not, in fact we can do better than that. Why don't you come out for a sail in her this evening? It'll be quite late, I'm afraid, as the tide is still low, but it's such a beautiful moonlit night and it seems a shame to waste a force five southeasterly and flat, calm sea.'

'But won't the police object?'

'I'm sure I can persuade our minders to turn a blind eye for a couple of hours. In any case, we had a call from the police earlier and it seems all the action is currently on the west coast of Guernsey.'

Munich HQ had reported back to Muller within minutes of

speaking with the FBI. They had immediately confirmed that Enterprise Holdings was one of Max's offshore havens, and the boat was almost certainly his personal cabin cruiser. The news came in moments after a shot had been fired on Lihou Island, followed by the sound of Follie's engines starting and the whine of an outboard motor. Riveted into action, the police team at Rocquaine raced for the causeway and a squad launched the police inflatable seconds later when it arrived at the slipway. They prepared for a rapid pursuit.

The ladies declined Tom's invitation to join them for a moonlight sail, so it was only Spike, David and Tom who slipped away from the hotel and down to the quay. Fortunately, Anoushka had settled far enough out for the slowly flooding tide to lift her within the hour. They boarded and gave Spike a tour of the ship whilst they waited.

It was eight in the evening when her hull bounced to life and she was ready to drop her mooring and manoeuvre out of the tiny harbour. Ten minutes later and safe amongst marks ingrained in Tom's psyche, they prepared sail and headed out between Herm and Jethou.

'She doesn't point too close with her triple keels, I'm afraid Spike, so what say we take a reach across to the Lower Heads buoy and maybe even St Martins Point if this breeze holds?'

Spike barely remembered theses places but happily agreed, and as soon as they were clear of the reefs south of Jethou, David hauled in the mainsail and Anoushka responded by heeling over and gaining several knots through the water.

This pleasant evening contrasted sharply with events a few hours earlier on the other side of Guernsey.

Emmaline had entered the house on Lihou moments after Raphael but already he was through the kitchen and checking the sitting room. She grabbed an apron from the door and quickly concealed the gun in its pocket. Freddy was already approaching the landing and about to greet her when she addressed Raphael loudly for his benefit.

'Can I help you? What are you doing in my house?'

Freddy stopped in his tracks as Raphael turned to face this unexpected interruption.

'I... I'm with the police. Are you on your own here?'

'I've already told inspector Ogier I'm on my own here. How many more times do I have to tell you lot?'

'It's routine, I'm afraid I'll have to check the house again, miss.'

'You'll have to do no such thing.' She spoke boldly. 'I'd like you to leave please.'

Raphael's initial feeling of intimidation now subsided and he returned to his more assertive self.

'Madam, this is police business. I advise you to stay out of my way.' With that he pushed past her and made for the stairs hotly pursued by Emmaline. Freddy backed into their bedroom and hid at the side of a wardrobe as Raphael began to check the bathroom. Emmaline hurried to their bedroom, quickly found, and passed the gun to Freddy. Returning again to harass Raphael she pushed her luck.

'I'd like to see your warrant card or ID please.'

Raphael was now tiring with this game and turned to face her, this time with a gun in his hand.

'Will this do? Just back off girl, get back in there.' He motioned for her to go into the bedroom as he continued.

'I don't know if you're in on this or not, but right now I'm more tempted to blow you away than let you go, so keep your mouth shut.' He raised the gun towards Emmaline's face and released the safety catch.

'In fact, why bother risking it; you're too smart for your own good. You see, I prefer not to have any witnesses.'

He reached into his pocket for a silencer and screwed it onto the barrel.

'Goodbye.'

Freddy stepped forward and squeezed the trigger of his pistol. Raphael collapsed backwards with the force, a glazed expression etched upon his face as the bedroom was pebble-dashed with his blood.

For a moment he and Emmaline faced each other in shock. This could only mean one thing, and neither cared about the man lying dead on the bedroom floor.

They rushed together and held each other tightly as Freddy whispered in her ear, still ringing from the gunshot, 'I'm so sorry darling, I've brought all this on you and now it has to end.'

Emmaline said nothing; she clung to him knowing they would soon be parted.

'I have to go now, but I need to know you will be all right. Promise me you will say I held you captive, will you do that for me?'

She nodded tearfully.

Freddy kissed her forehead and turned to walk away. At the door, he stopped and looked back, then ran out of the house.

Already the police were headed for the causeway. Still gripping his pistol, Freddy looked around him. Out there in the bay, Follie was waiting and he could see the dinghy on Lihou's shore. He rushed towards it and as he did so Follie's powerful engines started. Max had watched intently as his henchman had entered the house, followed shortly by Emmaline. When he heard the gunshot he was sure the job was done, and Raphael would quickly emerge leaving Freddy's corpse behind on the island. He ordered Gusto to raise the anchor and prepare for a rapid departure. When instead, it was Freddy who ran from the house, the shock stunned him momentarily. Gusto brought him to his senses.

'The police are launching a Rib, I don't think we should hang around.'

Max was taking this in as he realised that, far from making a dash for safety, Freddy seemed to be heading in their direction.

'What's the madman doing? Does he seriously think we will help him get away? Run him down Gusto, quickly before that Rib gets to us!'

Within a few seconds Follie was bearing down on the small dinghy and Freddy was under no illusions about their intention. As the two vessels sped towards each other like a nautical jousting tournament, he raised his pistol and fired.

'OK Max, it's your turn to be the target. Let's finish this now,' Freddy shouted defiantly.

Follie swerved sending a huge wave in Freddy's direction that nearly flung him out of the dinghy, but he held his course in pursuit as Gusto tried once more to run him down. This time Freddy held his fire until the boats were just a few yards away from each other then he opened the throttle seconds before a collision. Now safely out of her path, he aimed over the broadside of Follie and Gusto took the fatal bullet squarely in his chest. As Gusto fell to one side Max struggled to gain control of the helm, but Follie powered on and glanced off a reef in the narrow confines of the bay.

Freddy saw his chance and again sped after the cruiser. The police Rib was now gaining ground rapidly on both vessels.

Follie had come to a standstill amongst the rocks and Max was clearly panicking; he had little idea how to control the vessel on his own. Freddy came alongside and scrambled aboard.

'Get out of my way!' He shoved Max aside and pulled both throttles hard astern. The bows lifted and Follie was freed. Max fell backwards heavily and moaned in distress. Freddy turned the helm to port and gently nudged both throttles forward. She responded and Follie eased her way through the maze of rocks scattered all over the bay. As low water was now approaching, the main reefs could be seen and Freddy pushed the cruiser throttles forward again, leaving the small police inflatable boat well astern and loosing ground by the second.

As they headed out of the bay to open sea, Freddy turned to Max.

'The only reason you're still alive is that you've kept quiet and not tried anything stupid. Keep it that way and you may just survive another day. But know one thing, Max, I've got absolutely nothing to lose anymore.'

Max wasn't used to keeping quiet but he also wasn't used to being without his thugs for protection. He sat and nursed his bruises as the cruiser circumnavigated Les Hanois Lighthouse and made its way along the south coast of Guernsey.

CHAPTER THIRTY-SEVEN

Inspector Ogier was livid. The absence of Flying Christine left his men powerless to pursue the fast cruiser for more than a mile before it disappeared from sight. To add to his frustration, the air search that followed was unable to locate Follie and it seemed his prey had once again eluded him. Knowing that Follie would be visible from the cliffs, Freddy had made an exaggerated course change due south as if heading for Brittany, and then as Follie sped over the horizon, Gusto was unceremoniously dumped over the side and the helm was swung hard over again in the direction of Sark.

On the plus side for Ogier, the girl on Lihou, Emmaline, had come through relatively unscathed, at least physically. Her lack of a nervous reaction, usual when death or mortal danger come close, led him to speculate she may have the so called "Stockholm Syndrome". But she would recover and at least she could soon be questioned about her period in captivity. In the meantime, his thoughts returned once more to Rachel and Tom and he called the hotel from a nearby call-box.

'Rachel, hello again, I'm sorry to disturb you but I've some news. Listen, I don't want you to worry but Freddy and Max are still on the loose so you should all sit tight a while longer. Is Tom with you?'

Her reply worried Ogier gravely, but he made light of it for her benefit.

'Ok, well when they get back it's probably best if they leave Anoushka in the harbour for the time being. Just until we know it's safe.'

They exchanged pleasantries and he hung up.

'Shit!' He turned to Muller.

'They've only gone for a moonlight sail; tonight of all nights!'

Muller asked if Tom could be contacted by radio but the answer wasn't helpful; if they did there was every chance Freddy and Max would also hear the message. Reluctantly, the police left Rocquaine and headed back to the station in St Peter Port leaving a solitary female officer on Lihou with Emmaline. She was steadfastly refusing to leave the island.

A few miles away, oblivious to the events that evening, Tom, David and Spike were enjoying a beer and each other's company on board Anoushka as she sailed across a smooth sea that twinkled with the reflections of moonlight. Her white sails billowed in the fresh breeze and powered the yacht on its course around the Lower Heads Buoy off the south coast of Guernsey. Despite their relaxed mood, normal maritime discipline was maintained and it was David's turn on watch when at first the noise, then the sight of a powerful cruiser caught his attention.

Instinctively, he reached for a compass and took a bearing on the vessel.

'Dad, there's a fast cruiser out there on a course just south of Sark at high speed. It looks like it'll miss us by a safe margin but I'll keep an eye on it.'

'OK David, and just make a quick log entry would you? Time and bearing should do, along with our position.'

David duly updated the ship's log and almost as an afterthought reached for the binoculars to take a quick look.

'My God, it's Max!'

Tom jumped up leaving Spike looking confused in the cockpit.

'Let me take a look.' David handed him the binoculars.

'What is it?' Spike asked.

Tom confirmed David's identification of Follie, and explained the significance to Spike. He then made a quick decision.

'Keep the glasses on her as long as you can David, I'll see how long we can track her. Oh, and turn the radar on would you? That should give us another twenty-five miles!'

But they hadn't reckoned on Sark getting in the way, and ten minutes later the radar images merged as Follie rounded the southernmost promontory of Little Sark and quickly disappeared into the larger shadow.

They reflected on this predicament and Spike seemed to state the obvious.

'Why don't we just use the ship's radio to call the police?'

Of course, this had crossed both Tom and David's minds but they knew that if they did so, Freddy or Max would probably hear the call and it would certainly reveal their own position. Tom explained this to Spike but admitted they hadn't ruled out the idea.

Options were running out too on board Follie as she powered past La Coupee and Freddy turned to his captive.

'Ok, so far so good. But we're now in this together and you'd better start to earn your keep. I picked up the driving bit coming from St Malo but I don't have a clue about anchoring this thing or even where to do it.'

Throughout the journey, Max had been in a state of shock embellished with a large helping of fear, but he was now slowly regaining both confidence and courage. He relaxed his grip on the bulwarks, slowly rose to his feet and began to approach Freddy.

'I've been here before; just ease off the power and there's a good anchorage in that bay.' He pointed towards Dixcart Bay.

Freddy barked at him to keep his distance, holding up his pistol to reinforce the point.

'I'm just trying to help.' Max spoke meekly; deliberately meekly. 'That large red button above the throttles is the anchor release. I've seen it done countless times; just pick the right spot with enough space around us to let the boat swing and press that button.'

Freddy guessed there would be more to it than that but for the time being didn't care and a short time later, Follie floated peacefully, completely alone and surrounded by cliffs on three sides, in the seclusion of Dixcart Bay.

During their frantic escape, so much adrenaline had pumped through Freddy's veins his hands were shaking. He was also sweating profusely but Max could see that his current state of mind was dangerously unpredictable. He trod carefully in his attempt to regain a vestige of authority.

'So Freddy, a lot has happened since you came to see me in Munich, no?' Freddy ignored him and rummaged in the fridge for a beer.

'Some might say it was bold, perhaps even foolish of you to repay my generosity this way. I don't need to remind you that I'm a powerful man, do I Freddy?'

Freddy snapped.

Discarding the beer can he leapt at Max and pinned him to the side of the boat, his hands firmly around Max's scrawny throat.

'You couldn't just leave it could you? You interfering, malicious old fool.' He squeezed Max's throat more tightly. Max's eyes began to bulge, panic emanating from them.

'I told you I would sort it out but you just had to interfere and now... Well look what you've got us both into. Don't pretend Max, that you are still the big man. The police saw your prank out there off Guernsey and they know we're connected; they'll have worked that out a long time ago. So right now...' He began to grin demonically. 'We're in the same boat.... so to speak.' With that he thrust Max to one side and began to laugh hysterically.

Max gasped to breathe in and massaged the muscles on his throat as Freddy regained his composure.

'There is only one way you will leave this place alive, Max, and that entirely depends upon you. I need to be convinced that no harm will come to any of these people, that's all. I don't want anything else you have to offer, I just need to know that if I let you live, Emmaline, Rachel, Tom, all of them can get on with their lives in peace. Is that a price worth paying for your miserable life Max?'

Max was taken aback; what had become of the hard man he knew as much by reputation as personal experience? The man who threw his own brother off a roof, who himself had done his level best to murder the Jewish woman, and who was this Emmaline?

Of course, the woman on Lihou, the fool had fallen for her! So he was still vulnerable after all.

Tom decided the only way to alert Inspector Ogier was to follow the course Follie had taken and if she had continued past Sark towards the coast of France, they could stop off at Creux Harbour and make a phone call from the top of the hill. With the southeasterly wind right on their nose, they were forced to use the engine and so Anoushka's sails were furled. This had the added advantage of making them slightly less visible as they rounded Little Sark, binoculars at the ready.

Tom and David had pretty much decided it would be stupid of Freddy to hang around, so their attention was very much focused on the dark expanse of sea to the east when Spike, spotted her.

'That's her in there isn't it?'

They span around in surprise to see Follie nestled into Dixcart Bay. Tom immediately grabbed the wheel and turned Anoushka to starboard, away from the bay.

'Let's hope they haven't recognized us.' He called just loud enough to defeat the engine noise. 'They're bound to have heard us coming. We just need to get to harbour.'

The reliable Perkins engine powered on as she motored past Derrible Bay and closed in on a course to Creux Harbour.

Max homed in on Freddy's weak spot.

'So this girl, who seems to have transformed your personality, you really like her yes?'

'Not that it's any of your business Max but yes, I like her.'

'So why don't you take her away and disappear from all this chaos?'

Freddy thought for a moment, the sudden interest in his love life took him completely by surprise. Strange he thought, he hadn't actually considered asking Emmaline to run away with him. But maybe the reason was that his running days were over, it was time to face the music. The new Freddy just needed to be

330

sure she was safe, that Max would leave her, and the others, alone.

Freddy knew how Max hated loose ends. He tried to see the situation through Max's eyes, through the old Freddy's eyes, and although Max may have risked blowing his cover when Follie very publicly tried to mow Freddy down, Max hadn't actually been at the wheel, he never allowed himself to be seen doing the dirty work. As for the rest, Max would have avoided any personal association with the Bogota operation. He would be livid if the business dried up but others would carry the can. No, the main threat to Max's liberty would be Freddy himself. He alone had all the pieces to the jigsaw that was this part of Max's criminal empire.

He felt stupid for admitting his feelings for Emmaline; this had put her in danger and given Max a bargaining position. If Freddy let him live, Max may just be callous enough to punish Freddy by sending his apes back for Emmaline when he returned to Munich. He was getting tired; the beer had gone to his head and he fumbled to find a way out.

'Shit, I don't care that much about her! She was just a lay.' He knew Max would see through this but rather than keep digging the hole he was in, he muttered that he needed another beer and headed for the fridge.

Max smiled sardonically.

'So if you don't care for her, you'll understand why it's better she and the other two are got rid of, yes?'

'Let me follow your reasoning, Max. You've no reason to believe Emmaline or the others can harm you but you're willing to risk a life sentence to get rid of them?'

Max was now starting to enjoy Freddy's discomfort.

'Don't be silly Freddy; you know I never get my hands dirty. My associates will take of these people once I'm safely back at home with a cast iron alibi. You know how it works. Anyway the Le Bretons had the papers from your desk at Stein, and they may well have worked out the Bogota connection. As for the girl, if your defences were down I can only imagine what pillow

331

talk went on.'

The discussion was about to get heated when the sound of an engine pierced the otherwise silent night in the bay. They both listened intently, as if that alone would reveal who was out there and simultaneously shroud them in a cloak of invisibility. Max pointed to where the binoculars were hanging.

'May I?'

'Be my guest.' Freddy handed them to him and waited for Max to proclaim who was out there. His wait was short.

'Well now, that's interesting. It seems your little friends are out there stalking us. And you think we should leave them be?'

'What do you mean, who is it?' Freddy blurted.

'I can't see who exactly is on board but it's definitely the yacht we saw here in Sark with the Le Breton family on board. But what really interests me is that the whole time you've been aboard, our radio has been on monitoring Channel Sixteen and there's been no communication between the yacht and anyone else. If there had been we would have heard.'

'So, what's so significant about that?' Freddy quizzed.

'Well if this yacht has followed our course, or even just stumbled across us, they've kept it to themselves and my guess is they know full well we would hear them if they radioed our position.'

'That's good isn't it?'

'My dear Freddy, there can be no doubt they've seen our rather lavish vessel sitting here and if, as we must surmise, they want to tell our friends in the police, they will do so as soon as they reach harbour and an ordinary telephone. The only rational thing to do, Freddy, is ensure they never make that call.'

Suddenly all Freddy's attempts to protect Emmaline and the Le Bretons seemed futile. He felt exasperated and in the brief moment he took to massage the bridge of his nose and the split second he closed his eyes, Max struck.

Gusto may have been unceremoniously dumped over the side, but his gun was still lightly wedged under the life raft close to where Max had been sitting. In a single sweeping movement,

Max had grabbed the gun and as the butt made contact with Freddy's temple, he keeled over instantly losing consciousness.

When he came to, the engines were running and Max was glaring into his eyes. He struggled but soon realised that the taut feeling around his arms, chest and legs were due to the stout rope Max had used to bind him.

'I'm glad you decided to join me before I bid you farewell Freddy. It seemed wrong not to say goodbye after all these years.'

Freddy was balanced precariously on the bathing platform at Follie's rear, just above the water. As Max tightened the shackle that connected a heavy kedge anchor to the rope around Freddy, he continued to goad him.

'It's a little too quiet around here for a gunshot so I hope you don't mind spending the last few seconds of your life with the fishes. You see Freddy, I told you not to let me down – remember, when you came to see me in Munich - and that's precisely what you've done.'

He leaned down and pressed his face close to Freddy's.

'It's bad enough you went soft and failed to get those papers, but then you have the effrontery to hold me at gunpoint. It just won't do Freddy, and to add insult to injury I now have to complete the job myself. And much as I would love to spend more time with you, those interfering morons on the yacht have to be stopped before they get a chance to call up Muller's cavalry. Time to go Freddy.'

Max thrust his arms forwards sending Freddy into the sea below, as he plummeted into the depths, a short length of rope whipped down behind him followed by the kedge anchor tumbling off the platform, but seeming to catch on something, before the splash that confirmed it would soon join Freddy amongst the sea weed.

CHAPTER THIRTY-EIGHT

The powerful beam of the helicopter search lamp focused on the body in the sea below. The Guernsey lifeboat was heading full speed towards it and a small light aircraft circled higher above. The air search Cessna pilot had spotted something in the sea and on taking a closer look, discovered the body.

It took just a few minutes to recover the body and confirm the man had been dead in the sea for some time.

When the information was radioed back to Inspector Ogier, he and Muller left the police station without delay to head for the harbour and to rendezvous with the lifeboat as the body was brought back to St Peter Port. They couldn't stop themselves speculating about who it might be.

As the vessel decreased speed on entering the harbour, it made for a mooring against the huge wooden uprights of the Cambridge Wharf. It was approaching midnight and low spring tides were again the order for a few days. Anxious to identify the body, Inspectors Ogier and Muller had descended the slippery granite steps into the myriad of timber latticework that supported the huge quay. As this area was underwater much of the time, it was dripping wet and dark on this otherwise moonlit night.

With the lines secure and a few words exchanged with the crew, they boarded and went straight for the figure below. It was covered from head to toe by a blanket. Ogier reached down to expose the face beneath it.

A little off Sark's Creux harbour, Tom made light work of anchoring Anoushka and launching the dinghy to take them ashore. The three men bumped alongside the harbour wall a few minutes later as the shadow of a large cruiser ominously inched through the darkness on its own final approach.

Max was less expert at handling his own vessel and wasted valuable minutes as he struggled to find a suitable mooring. With the main dinghy left behind off Guernsey there was the added ignominy of having to row ashore in the small inflatable; not something Max was accustomed to. Although this delay made it harder for him to track his prey, a tunnel through the cliff face and a long walk up the harbour hill at least ensured his arrival was unseen.

The face meant nothing to Ogier and so he beckoned his colleague from Munich to take a look.

'Not what I was expecting.' Muller said with only the slightest hint of surprise.

'This was one of Max's thugs, Gusto. Either he did something to upset Max, or Freddy has the upper hand. What with Raphael also out of the way, I can't help wondering if Max has any protection left with him over here. Not that I'd want to put that to the test.'

Earlier that evening, a few miles away, another individual had been washed up onto the shore of Sark's Dixcart Bay. Freddy had been luckier than he deserved. Not only had the rope that attached his deadly anchor snagged on the propellers and been severed by Follie's rope cutter, usually a device to ensure stray ropes don't foul the propellers, but Max had completely overlooked the return of shallow Spring tides. Freddy spluttered like a beached whale as he wriggled free of the remaining rope and gasped in precious oxygen to replace the seawater in his lungs. First the causeway and now this, it was beginning to feel like a recurrent dream, or nightmare, perhaps even some kind of violent baptism to mark his departure from past sinful ways. But there was no time to contemplate the metaphysical or to feel sorry for himself. Max would be well on his way after the others by now.

Without a plan or even directions, Freddy stumbled up the beach and made for the tiny pathway that marked its only exit. The moonlight soon failed him as the path entered dense woodland. It was uphill all the way and Freddy's throat was now rasping from the exertion. His legs felt like lead weights but he pounded on, frequently stumbling but determined to find the others before Max got to them. The dark woodland continued through most of the valley until he emerged near a small hotel. Outside, there were tables and he remembered having visited this place only a few weeks ago with Francois on their way to Guernsey. It was hard to avoid thinking how much had changed in his life since then; the transformation Emmaline had inspired.

As he emerged before the al fresco diners sitting in the otherwise peaceful valley, they looked around in unison, startled by the sight of this large man, soaking wet and with the look of panic on his face.

A stout looking man sitting at a table with three others, immediately rose to his feet and approached him.

'Are you alright mate? What's happened?'

Freddy tried to regain his breath and, not wanting to put anyone else at risk, blurted out the first plausible explanation that sprang to mind.

'Thank you, it's just that my dinghy capsized and I'm late to meet someone at the harbour hill.'

'Oh dear, well just you hang on a minute and I'll see what I can do.' The man disappeared into the hotel and returned a few moments later with a younger man wearing jeans and a checked shirt.

'Harry here will take you.' Much to Freddy's delight, Harry nodded towards a tractor parked nearby.

'Come on then my friend, can't have you keeping the little woman waiting can we?'

Freddy smiled at the assumption and thought how good it would be if his life were that simple; if he were just meeting Emmaline.

The tractor engine sprang to life, engulfing the tiny valley in a mechanical noise, although somehow a tractor engine, unlike any other motor vehicle, didn't seem at all incongruous. Other than bicycles, horses and carts, these were the only form of mechanised transport permitted on the island.

The young man tried in vain to strike up a conversation with Freddy who could just about hear him over the engine noise as he hung on to the sides of the small trailer that was his carriage. There were few people around the dusty tracks until they reached the main cluster of shops in The Avenue. Freddy asked; shouted; to be dropped at the top of Harbour Hill and warmly thanked the young man who parked his tractor and made for a nearby pub.

'No problem my friend, you go and dry yourself off and have a good night. Maybe I'll see you in the Bel Air later for a pint!'

When the pub door closed behind him, Freddy made his way down towards the harbour. Clouds had now gathered and were diluting what moonlight filtered between the branches of overhanging trees. He was now alone on the wide track that served as Sark's only conduit for the daily influx of tourists and goods that needed transporting between the harbours and the main village. As he progressed downwards, toward the harbour and away from the few noises of civilisation behind him, the hill took on a slightly menacing characteristic. Somewhere in the darkness ahead, his enemy would be approaching, armed with a gun and intent on killing Tom, the man who had only a short time earlier sent Freddy to what he believed was certain death.

Freddy's resolve began to weaken and he started to question what he was doing there. Why couldn't he just leave well alone? Max was certain he was dead so why risk disillusioning him? Why not just disappear into the night and lie low for a few days?

It was the re-born Freddy who gained ascendency in his troubled mind; the Freddy who knew he must attempt to balance the books of his life. The Freddy who could only think how Emmaline would judge his actions; how she would say he was wise to run from here and stay safe; but he couldn't bear to think about how this would diminish him in her eyes. There was only one real choice; he must ensure the safety of Tom and the others. He took a deep breath and paced forward more stridently but began to consider what he would do when the time came to

337

face Max, as it surely would.

But first there was the matter of how Tom would react to seeing him. Everything Tom knew about Freddy should persuade him to strike him down and summon the nearest policeman without waiting for an explanation. After all, Tom wouldn't even know who Max was, so why would he listen to Freddy?

These thoughts turned over and over again in Freddy's mind but he could see no clear answer. The only possibility he could think of was of somehow getting to Max first; if he could just do that, but it was surely impossible. Max had followed the others onto the hill and would still be behind them. That was assuming they were all still on this dusty trail. Freddy's heart sank as he began to worry that he was already too late. Perhaps Max had caught up with them down at the harbour and it was all over; or maybe he'd just find the bodies somewhere on the hill. As if to confirm this fear, a dark mass seemed to be lying ahead on the side of the trail. He began to convince himself this was Tom and next he would find…

'Wait! I have something for you!' Ahead in the darkness, Max's voice rang out. Freddy awoke from his conjecture, about what turned out to be the fallen trunk of a tree, and rushed forwards into the darkness of a bend in the trail. They were just a few yards ahead, three men who stopped in their tracks, and looked back in the direction of the harbour.

'Who is it?' He heard Tom shout.

'Just hang on!' The voice came back.

Freddy charged towards the three of them.

'No! Get clear, quickly, he's got a gun!' he shouted.

The three now span around to face Freddy and a look of horror spread over Tom's face. David squared up instinctively, but too late to stop Freddy barging through the middle of them, arms flaying to push them aside. A shot rang out.

Max was trying to line up his next shot when he saw Freddy bearing down on him. The look of horror on his face was the last thing Freddy remembered as the two fell backwards and the loud crack of a second bullet being discharged ripped through the silence of the valley.

CHAPTER THIRTY-NINE

Eventually, the policewoman left Emmaline to herself and she tried to come to terms with the loss of her one love. There was no doubt in her mind that Freddy would either be killed or captured when he left her, if he didn't just give himself up. Now all she could do was to wait.

The officer had been kind to her but she had no idea what was really going on in Emmaline's mind. She wasn't a victim; she was in mourning for the death of her relationship. The constant references to Freddy as "an animal" and reassurances that he would "get what was coming to him", left her cold, but she played her part just as Freddy had wished.

Now, alone once more with only memories for company, she stared out at the causeway and silently thanked it for the time it had given them. That it had also ended their isolation, didn't measure in her gratitude. She never expected it to last; that was always the way for her. Now it all seemed as short as a brief cycle of the tide in her life. With the flood she was bestowed with happiness; then the ebb stole every drop away.

Where was he now? She wondered, Was he safe?

As Emmaline pondered these thoughts, less than a dozen miles away, her beloved Freddy lay with a pool of blood soaking through his shirt.

Astonished by what had happened in front of them, Tom, David and Spike stirred into action. Tom's immediate reaction was to get his son and friend out of harm's way. He began to usher them frantically up the trail and away from the two figures whilst keeping a watchful eye on what might happen next. Was that it, was the gunfire over?

Suddenly, Freddy rolled away from the motionless body beneath him and staggered to his feet.

'It's alright, he can't harm you now.' Freddy kicked the gun away from Max's open hand as if to emphasise the point. Tom's reply was guarded; he needed to make sense of what had taken

340

place in front of him.

'So you're going to leave that are you? The gun, I mean.' Freddy looked pitiful, he simply nodded and raised his hands as if in surrender.

'Do what you will Tom, you've every right. Look, I'll back away and you can pick it up.' He gestured towards the gun. Spike didn't hesitate; the old soldier in him wasn't taking any chances. Tom continued.

'What is this Freddy, a change of heart? You've tried so hard to get rid of us and now, well now you seem to have risked your own neck to save ours.'

Spike maintained a safe distance as he kept Freddy in line with the gun barrel. The strained conversation seemed to last for several minutes but it was, in fact, only around thirty seconds before the commotion started. First, a tractor raced down the hill, lights blazing to investigate the gunshots. Then a crowd from the pub emerged from the shadows and from amongst them a doctor rushed forward in a futile attempt to attend to Max. As he passed Freddy and saw the blood still dripping from his shirt, he asked almost casually if he was hurt. Freddy ignored him; it was obvious from his stance that he wasn't the priority and the doctor knelt beside Max. A few short tests later, he pronounced him dead and a voice from the crowd shouted the question on everyone's mind.

'What's going on? What's happened?'

Freddy began to walk down the hill in a daze, as if oblivious to the crowd, with the gun still pointed menacingly at him. Nobody dared, not even Spike, to question him. He paused and turned again briefly towards Tom.

'I'm so deeply sorry.'

His figure began to disappear into the darkness when Spike snapped out of the momentary trance that beset him.

'What should we do Tom? We can't just let him go?'

'Somehow I don't think he's going anywhere,' Tom replied with a compassionate look on his face.

'You know I actually feel sorry for him and, after all he did just save our bacon. Leave him to Inspector Ogier and his team.'

After a short phone call, the nearby helicopter was summoned to the scene. The police once again utilised the lifeboat to bring them swiftly to Creux and as the powerful vessel approached, Inspector Ogier studied the solitary figure at the end of the breakwater.

Freddy made no effort to evade capture, he was resigned, almost relieved, to face his fate. In handcuffs and under the watchful eyes of two officers, Freddy sat in the medical emergency area of the lifeboat opposite the body bag containing his former business colleague and, more recently, deadly enemy. On deck, he could see Tom, David and Spike explaining what had happened on Harbour Hill. Despite the bleak outlook ahead, Freddy took some comfort from the fact that he had removed the potential peril from Emmaline and the others. With Max and his thugs now dead, there would be nobody to seek revenge and no reason for his former criminal fraternity to inflict themselves on these peaceful islands. His own punishment would seem light by comparison.

CHAPTER FORTY

Emmaline had never forgotten the sinking feeling in her heart when she had heard that Freddy had been taken into custody. But the feeling had been bittersweet, as despite her sensation of loss, she couldn't help being relieved that he hadn't been killed. In the years that followed, she had often wondered what might have been if Max hadn't turned up on the scene.

Would they, could they have led a normal life somewhere? Perhaps even had children? Those few days together had been short and precious; more so than any other time in her life. But despite the pain of losing him, she hadn't regretted a moment. He had made her feel alive, made her feel like a woman.

She was approaching fifty years of age and it was now the final day of the millennium in 1999. As the rest of Guernsey prepared for a loud and characteristically brash celebration, she sat alone on the upturned Lihou boat watching the causeway as she had almost every day since he had left and the rhythm of her life had returned to its former pace.

Much had changed in the intervening years. the colonel had returned from his trip and then left the island for good; a new "Lihou Trust" had been set up to care for the island and she had been allowed to stay on as a caretaker. She had never heard from Freddy but in her heart, she hadn't expected to. Emmaline knew she had meant too much to him for him to allow her to waste her own life waiting for him. She also knew there could never be another love in her life. Nothing could match that overwhelming passion and she didn't want to look for it. Somehow it would seem to diminish the experience to find love with another.

But the biggest change in her life had been her deepening friendship with Rachel. After the chaos and recriminations of that fateful day, Rachel had sought her out to comfort her. Rachel still believed that Emmaline had been held captive and felt responsible for Freddy returning to the island. She would

343

often return to look for Emmaline at her home, only to discover her once again on Lihou or sitting by the causeway.

Their lives couldn't have been more different, Rachel was now a wealthy woman with a large and happy family, while Emmaline had little more than enough to sustain her and was alone in the world. She declined Rachel's frequent offers to bolster her finances but appreciated this one friendship in her life. For Rachel, it was when Tom passed away that the true depth of that friendship became significant. She and Emmaline would walk together along the coastal path or around Lihou and talk for hours about their lives. On one such occasion, Emmaline explained what had really happened between her and Freddy. Rachel put her arm around her and squeezed her tightly.

'I often wondered about the emotions you were showing when it was all over. You spoke as if you missed him.'

Emmaline, relieved to have shared her secret, told how Freddy had transformed after nearly drowning on the causeway. He had been profoundly shocked by the near-death experience and the vision of his brother. After a lifetime of suppression, a chink had been opened in his armour and his love had been allowed to surface, with Emmaline as the focus of his release. Freddy allowed his guilt and regret to surface as well. Emmaline told how he would wake in the middle of the night, screaming his brother's name. The recurrent dream of Hans' death haunted him, but with renewed strength he had taken responsibility for his murderous past and had been determined to be open to the pain of his remorse.

So it had been for him in the days they spent together, oscillating between despair and bliss, reflecting the cycle of the tides that in their flood provided the sanctuary of isolation but in their ebb an easy passage for his pursuers across the causeway.

For Emmaline, their time together had been the happiest in her life. Here was a man who adored her, not just for her natural beauty but also her "sassy" mind. He had been a wild man but she had tamed him; an evil man who she had redeemed. They both had wished the floods would last forever.

Rachel spoke of the attempts on her life and the time in hospital when everyone believed her life would surely end.

But in spite of the gravity of Freddy's crimes, and the unique relationship Emmaline had found, they could still laugh at his demise when publically denounced at the Shareholder's meeting, just when he thought he was king of all he surveyed.

In a moment of frankness, Freddy had confided to Emmaline his begrudging admiration for Tom and Rachel. 'They seemed so pure, so devoid of the greed that besets the business world. They were alien and I hated them for their superiority. The Jewish woman who walked casually into that meeting and took my world apart represented everything my father had taught me to despise in my youth, yet even in my darkest hour, her dignity astounded me.'

Rachel explained how Tom's response had been more down to earth when he struck Freddy. She often spoke of her love for Tom and how much she missed him. Their life had been dreamlike from the moment Tom had sailed in and rescued her from the nightmare of her captivity. They too had been in hiding and their love had also grown under the shadow of would be assassins. But they had had many years together and Rachel could understand how Emmaline might feel cheated for the sudden end to her romance.

So here they were on the last night of the millennium and Rachel got up to leave her friend and make her way back across the causeway to return to her family. It would have been dark but a clear sky allowed the moon to light her passage across the slippery path. Just a few occasional clouds would temporarily cast a shadow but she was sure-footed, she had made this crossing many times before.

Emmaline watched her with affection and prepared herself for the inevitable explosion of noise and light soon to announce the New Year. This was Guernsey after all and the biggest, loudest fireworks display was a badge of honour.

At first Rachel didn't see the shadow of a figure approaching through a momentary darkness and when she did, she assumed

David had come out to meet her from the parked car where he was waiting. But this shadow wasn't David's build at all. It was someone a good deal older and slightly ungainly on the smooth rocks underfoot. She wondered who else could possibly be visiting Lihou at this time of night, on this of all nights.

They moved slowly towards one another and as they did so, a vague recognition began to form in Rachel's consciousness. She whispered to herself.

'No, it couldn't be.'

As their paths met, Freddy spoke first.

'It's been a long time. Not long enough I fear for you to forgive me.'

Rachel had long since lost her fear of this man and there was even a twinge of sadness that he was no longer a murderer who could dispatch her to her beloved Tom.

A million memories flashed before her, some containing images of the loved ones in her past; her dear mother who Freddy's father had sent to certain death in the camps and the killers Freddy had paid to end her own life with her dear husband as collateral damage. She thought about this man's overbearing opulence at the shareholders' meeting and his apparent contempt for her. Other memories were less visual but no less powerful. She could still smell the stale beer in the barrel they had used to smuggle her away from Herm under the rifles of the soldiers, and Freddy's eagle eyes.

But emotions and sensations in every nerve cascaded over her as she recalled her first sight of Shell Beach in the moonlight, the smell of her mackerel breakfast on the beach, and the day she returned to Tom on the liberation of Guernsey. It was true she had suffered hardship that no child should ever have had to bear but she had also experienced happiness beyond her wildest dreams. When the man she loved was finally taken from her, all she could think about was the precious time they'd spent together. That would sustain her until she joined him.

She knew why Freddy had returned.

The words almost came out, They let you out then? You're

right; it has been a long time. But somehow words were no longer adequate, certainly not small talk.

She watched his expression; uncomfortable and penitent but distracted as his eyes continuously flickered over her shoulder towards Lihou. Rachel just smiled and stepped quietly aside, touching his arm as she did so.

'You should go to her; she's been waiting a long time.'

THE END

Also available from Acclaimed Books Limited

Book by Peter Lihou

Book 2 by Peter Lihou

Book 3 by Peter Lihou

Rachel's Shoe by Peter Lihou

The Causeway by Peter Lihou

Passage to Redemption by The Crew

A Covert War by Michael Parker

North Slope by Michael Parker

Roselli's Gold by Michael Parker

Stretch by Brian Black

Last Mission by Everett Coles

1/1 Jihad Britain by Everett Coles

Merlin's Kin by Everett Coles

The Faces of Immortality by Everett Coles

The Last Free Men by Everett Coles

Venturer by Everett Coles

To Rule the Universe by Everett Coles

The Tourist by Jack Everett & David Coles

Druid's Bane by Phillip Henderson

Maig's Hand by Phillip Henderson

The Arkaelyon Trilogy by Phillip Henderson

Rising Tides a Channel Islands Anthology

Coming soon...

The Guernsey Donkey (working title) by Peter Lihou

Larnius' Revenge by Phillip Henderson

Available internationally in paperback and Kindle formats from Amazon and all good book stores.

See the entire catalogue, reviews, author interviews and much more at www.acclaimedbooks.com